CW00501721

Here Be Dragons

David P. Macpherson

Copyright © 2018 David P. Macpherson

All rights reserved.

Cover design by Rachel Lawston: www.lawstondesign.com

ISBN-13: 978-1-9831-4076-1

To Dad and other everyday heroes.

PROLOGUE

Drift is a place both old and new. Old in that the primary method of transport has four legs, a tail and is likely to kick you if you sneak up on it from behind; new in that explorers keep finding bits of it no-one had noticed before. Only last week the Grand High Navigator of Olop, ruler of that great merchant city, sent his bravest captain on a mission to chart the four corners of the world. [1] He was given the finest maps the Guild of Cartographers had in their vaults and told not to return until he had filled them in all the way to the edges.

Drift is also a place of magic. This is useful for some, interesting to others, and generally a bit of a nuisance to everybody else. When the level of nuisance begins to slip towards full-on magically assured destruction (as happens on a fairly regular basis, usually on a Tuesday) Drift needs heroes.

*

---

[1] The idea that there might be more or less than four, or in fact no corners at all, has yet to be considered.

Huggle was not a hero. You could tell from the way his thighs chafed as he ran. He was, however, hoping to find one.

He'd left his horse at the edge of the forest. After two days of solid riding it had refused to go any further. Stupid animal, he thought. Didn't it know what an opportunity this was? This was no tavern tale or fisherman's legend. This was his shot at the big time. This was saga material, and he would be the one to capture it.

It had everything. A young maiden – no, better than that, a virgin – stolen away in the dead of night by the evil sorcerer Garvock. The girl's dear old mum had watched helplessly as the full might of the Town Watch were effortlessly thrown aside. Then, a rugged barbarian appears through the smoke and destruction. He swears by his honour that he will bring the girl back, unharmed, before four suns have set. With only his courage to protect him he will enter Garvock's underground lair and challenge the fiend to single combat. A battle that will echo in eternity. Good vs. evil, light vs. dark, sword vs. sorcery. And if all goes well there could even be a bit of romance at the end. Perfect.

Yes, thought Huggle, a tale fit for the courts of noblemen across the kingdom. He would make a fortune.

The hem of his cloak caught on a branch and he toppled into the mud.

Get up, keep going.

He scrambled to his feet and was off again. The squelch of his moccasins and his panting breaths were the only sounds to break the silence of the dark wood.

Ahead, the path forked. Stone totems topped with gurning busts of trolls flanked one side of the path. This was the way to Garvock's barrow. And there, through the trees, yes, he was sure.

A lone warrior on a horse, long flowing hair, sword by his side, muscles so well defined they had their own page in the dictionary: he had found him.

Huggle took his quill and parchment from his satchel and rushed down the path to get a better look. He knew the first image was all important. He had to get it right, had to get down every detail.

He concentrated hard, scribbling furiously on the parchment. In fact, so focused was Huggle on capturing this first image of his great hero, he failed to notice that the mighty warrior was riding in the wrong direction. Likewise, and given the barbarian's eclipsing physique this is understandable, the young scribe did not see the scantily clad maiden perched on the rear of the warrior's horse.

Such minor details were pushed aside by Huggle's eager mind. He waved and called out to the approaching warrior. 'Hello there, brave sir! Are you the mighty barbarian who has sworn to kill Garvock the Sorcerer and rescue his virgin captive?'

'Err, yes. That's me,' said the warrior, rather unsure what to make of the bouncing ball of energy in front of him. 'Who are you?'

Huggle sucked in his belly and pushed out his chest. 'Allow me to introduce myself. My name is Huggle Hobswaine, recorder of great deeds, teller of heroic tales. I heard of your quest, your oath, sir, and travelled far across the land, braving many dangers, to record your daring deeds. I shall travel with you to the darkest depths of Garvock's lair and witness your mighty victory over that most evil spawn of the Devil's under-croft. It will make us both rich. Rich and famous and rich.'

'Ah,' the warrior paused. 'I don't quite know how to put this but... I've sort of... already done it.'

'You've already...' Huggle's hands fell to his sides, barely keeping hold of parchment and quill. 'Oh... Damn.'

At this point, the no longer distressed damsel poked her head round the hero's bulky form. 'What did he say?'

'He wanted to watch me rescue you.'

'Why?'

'To make a story out of it, I think.'

'Good idea that. He's a bit late though.'

'Perhaps not, my fair lady,' said Huggle, rushing round to the side of the horse. 'I may have missed the action but if you could tell me what happened I am sure I can still weave a tale the like of which is rarely heard. Tell me, how did you escape? Did this noble warrior free you first or did he do battle with that black fiend while you could only watch on helpless?'

'Hmm, I don't know really. I was unconscious for most of it, and it was pretty dark down there.'

'Ah. Not even… Damn,' said Huggle. Not one to give up easily, he turned his attention back to the maiden's rescuer. 'But you, brave hero, you must remember it all?'

The barbarian scratched his head. 'Ehhh, it's all a bit of a blur really. I was caught up in the moment, you know. Sorry.'

This time Huggle really sank. He sat down in the cold mud and his voice dropped to a low mumble. 'Nothing at all? What about the final duel? The escape?'

'Sorry,' they replied together.

'Are you going to be okay?' asked the hero. 'Only we're in a bit of a hurry. I swore I'd be back before tomorrow night. You could come with us if you like?'

'No, it's alright,' said Huggle, twiddling his quill between his fingers. 'I think I'll go and have a look round the barrow. Maybe I can piece together what happened.'

'Fair enough, it was good to meet you all the same.' The hero struck the horse's flanks with his heels. 'Hope you have more luck in the future.'

And with that, Huggle was left alone in the forest.

Damn, damn, damn. It was all his stupid horse's fault. If it hadn't given up he would have made it in time to see the final showdown.

Still, he might get something out of it. If he could find Garvock's body he would be able to work out how the hero dispatched him. And he could see the lair – he'd be able to tell a lot from that. Yes, all wasn't lost. Maybe he would get a saga out of this after all. The great hero's deeds wouldn't pass unnoticed. In fact, when Huggle was done with him, that barbarian would be the most famous warrior in all of Drift. Everyone would know the name of . . .

Bugger, what was his name?

*

Orus poked at the dying fire, sending a flare of embers into the night. Mavis huddled by his side, wrapped in his cloak. The ragged remains of her clothes protected her modesty but little else.

Next time, bring clothes for the maiden, thought Orus. He was fast finding out that there was a lot more to this hero business than meets the eye.

It had been a full three months since he'd set out from the Cromalot School for Heroes, sword in hand and fire in heart. There hadn't been much action in those months. Certainly nothing worth writing home about, not that he knew how to write anyway.

But now, now he had sworn an oath, explored a dark dungeon, fought an evil wizard and rescued a damsel in distress. And not just any damsel: a virgin. A proper virgin too, like the ones in the great sagas. Not like the one his friend Baradun had got when he went up against the Witches of Blort: a forty-eight-year-old accountant with an extensive and expertly catalogued butterfly collection was hardly going to get a cheer at the Axe and Gullet.

But this girl – she was the real deal.

'You okay? Not too cold?'

'No, I'm fine. Thanks for the cloak,' said Mavis. 'And for the rescue. For a while there I thought I might not make it out of this one.'

'This one?' asked Orus. 'Does this happen to you a lot then?'

'Oh yes, every month or so. Once word gets out that there's a virgin going about – well it's like moths to a flame. We're always in demand. This is my third kidnapping this year. It's all a bit of a nuisance really.'

Orus sat startled. Was this the way it was meant to go?

'But I'm never that scared.' Mavis stretched her arms out towards the fire. 'Someone like you always turns up before anything really bad happens. I mean, have you ever heard about a beautiful virgin actually being sacrificed? Statistically it must happen, but it's like all these things. The actual risk on a day-to-day basis is pretty small.'

'Suppose,' said Orus.

'Do you know, you're more likely to be killed by your own horse than by an orc? Sounds weird, but it's true.'

Orus gave a quick glance over his shoulder at his steed. Suddenly its deep brown eyes seemed to carry a hidden menace, like it was plotting to throw him into a ravine or off a bridge. He batted the thought away. What reason would his horse have for hating him? He'd even lost weight recently.

'Still, I do wish they would show a little more care. Look at these shackle burns.' Mavis grabbed Orus's hand and held it to her reddened ankle. A strange feeling rushed through his body as the snow white skin of her soft hands guided his tired arms. 'Feel it. It'll take weeks to heal properly. You aren't going to catch the attention of any passing princes with ankles like that.'

'I guess not.'

'Actually,' said Mavis, still holding Orus's hands against her legs, 'I'm getting pretty tired of the whole thing now.'

'Yeah?' Orus did not have much experience with women, and certainly not with women looking to have an experience with him. Being an all-boys school, the birds and the bees didn't have a place in the Cromalot curriculum. As such, his mind meandered towards Mavis's drift with all the speed of an asthmatic continent.

'Yes. In fact,' Mavis pulled his hands up to her knees and shot him a smile of pure improper suggestion, 'I was wondering, if you wanted to, you know, help me out?

'You mean?'

'Yes.'

'Like a bodyguard?'

'No, not really. Although, you would have to stay very, very close to me.' Mavis leaned in. Her lips hovered less than an inch from Orus's, setting the tiny hairs on his skin tingling. 'At least for tonight.'

'Oh . . . You mean . . . Oh.' Orus felt the blood rush to his face, amongst other places. Diabolical sorcerers he could handle. Rampaging centaurs: no problem. Girls though: that was a different matter. 'Well I'm very flattered and all. It's just, well, they don't really teach you about this kind of stuff at Cromalot.' Good going Orus, he thought, way to impress a girl.

'Don't worry. I'm sure you'll be great. And you'd be doing me a *huge* favour.'

'Well...' Orus was starting to sweat. This definitely wasn't the way it was supposed to go. But in this battle, he was powerless to resist. 'As a favour, as long as it's, you know, safe.'

'Oh yes,' replied Mavis, moving in for the kiss. 'It can't happen the first time. Everyone knows that.'

Unbeknown to him at that magical moment, Orus was about to learn one of life's most valuable lessons: virgins should not take safe sex advice from other virgins.

Nine months later he would also learn that being a wandering adventurer didn't bring in the steady income required for supporting a new family.

*****

CHAPTER ONE

All was not well in the town of Ditch.[2]

The flags above the Prince's castle were still flying proudly. The great gate stood wide open and the townsfolk went about their lives, unaware of the bitter struggle that had been raging at the foot of the castle wall for the last three days.

It was a secret battle that could very well change the whole future of life in Ditch, and Orus was right in the middle of it. The days of continual combat had taken their toll on him. His arms ached and his body was covered in scars, cuts and bruises. Perspiration filled his boots and the stench, that foul putrid wind, filled his every breath. This morning he had thrown away his blade, so notched and blunted it was useless now. But still he fought on with nothing but his brawn, his will and his purple pruning gloves.

---

[2] All is rarely well in most towns. Even in the most well-ordered of cities, someone is always burning the toast or losing their keys or being burgled or getting caught doing some burgling. But this is beside the point.

The Shadow-wart bush had dug deep into the stonework of the chute that disposed of the Prince's private burdens. An unsightly creeping menace of a plant, Shadow-wart's tangled arms were covered in suspicious berries and serrated thorns that oozed a sickly black resin. The resin was poisonous and caused almost immediate evacuation of the bowels. It was said by scientific types to be a defence mechanism to stop animals eating it. Given the smell the plant gave off, Orus thought this was rather wishful thinking: no animal would be stupid enough to try to eat a Shadow-wart bush.

This view was un-tempered even when Orus discovered how the sub-tropical plant had wound up in the Prince's privy chute in the first place. While no animal would be stupid enough to eat it, the levels of unexplainable thickness in the nobility are on a whole different evolutionary scale.

Apparently, Shadow-wart seeds were part of the latest diet the Prince had read about in *High and Mighty* (the premier magazine for monarchs of majestic size). The constant supply of water and fertilizer had allowed the bush to grow quickly and now it blocked the whole chute.

Orus's feet dangled out the end of the sewer outlet. His round belly made an almost perfect seal around the circumference of the pipe. Any fatter and Orus wouldn't fit. In light of this, his own diet was officially cancelled. The next time the Prince insisted on eating jungle vines, one of the stable boys could sort it out. Orus had given up on taking a candle with him after the first day. The resulting explosion of noxious gases had launched him into the open drain like a wobbly cannonball, burning a hole through the determined ring of hair that had yet to desert him. So he worked in the dark, feeling the structure of the bush with his hands. The first two days had been spent very carefully removing the barbs and thorns with his knife. When that was done he had started attacking the roots.

Now, finally, he had pulled all the vines from their anchor points in the stonework. He wrapped a length of rope around the thickest branch, before carefully backing down the tunnel, all the while expecting Fate to choose that moment to give him a familiar kick and send the whole foul tide chasing after him.

But, in defiance of all normality (or at least normality for Orus), it did not. He made it out safe.

Standing in front of the shallow moat into which the privy chute drained, Orus wrapped the end of the rope around his forearm and started to pull.

Movement, but not much.

Another great pull and another. Foul water began to trickle from the tunnel. One more, he thought.

He moved closer, winding in the slack on the rope, and then heaved with all his strength and weight (the latter, he reluctantly admitted, making far more impact than the former).

Inside the privy chute, the Shadow-wart bush came free with a jolt.

The rope snapped back and Orus fell, landing right in front of the tunnel mouth. In the darkness above him he could hear the rolling squelch of something horrible picking up speed as it rushed to meet him.

He tried to get up, but his old back was having none of it. The twisted nerve he had picked up last winter when shovelling snow from the castle courtyard chose this moment to paralyse him with pain.

Stuck, there was little he could do but jam his fingers into his nose, scrunch up his eyes, and wait for the bony foot of Fate to kick him square in the teeth.

The rolling squelch grew louder and louder, nearer and nearer, until Orus was sure it was directly above him. There was a popping sound, the light behind his eyelids darkened.

This is it.

But it wasn't. The shadow passed over his eyes. There was a splash behind him as something heavy landed in the moat. Then silence.

Ah, he thought, I know this game. There'll be a second wave. Bound to be. There's always a second one. It's waiting on me. I know it. I'll open my eyes and it'll drop right on me. Well, this old boy's wise to that trick.

The nerves in his back relaxed and he rolled to the side. Only when he was sure he was safely out of the danger zone did he open his eyes.

The chute was empty.

He took his fingers from his nose and turned to look back at the moat.

A huge dung ball, complete with a lattice shell of Shadow-wart branches, was slowly bobbing down the moat towards the river.

Marvelling at his good fortune, Orus dusted himself off and started to collect up his tools. Maybe his luck had finally started to turn. Today would be a good day.

No sooner had this thought formed in his head than it was knocked out again by a servant emptying the Prince's temporary toilet bucket over the top of the castle wall.

'Look out below,' came the world's worst warning.

That's more like it, thought Orus.

CHAPTER TWO

Orus trudged down Old Mill Street. With every step, water spurted from the soles of his boots. Standing under the water wheel was the closest to a shower he could afford. Normally it was pretty effective, but the way the busy street parted in front of him told him that memories of today would linger on for a while yet.

The town of Ditch got its name from what was left of the main street, or perhaps it was what was left *on* the main street. Every year, on the way to the winter pastures in the south, herdsmen would drive their charges through the town, along what was originally the High Street but was now known as Deep Street. Their cows would leave in their wake Ditch's main source of fuel for the cold months ahead. Once the beasts had passed, the townsfolk would rush out with wheelbarrows and shovels and collect up as much valuable manure as they could. The effect of all this frantic digging was that the road had been gradually scratched away until it became less of a highway and more of a low-way.

To reach Deep Street from the door of any of the shops and houses that lined it, took a five-foot ladder. More than a few of the original buildings had toppled into the trench and those left were braced against their opposite number with a tangle of wooden beams. A system of walkways had been constructed linking the fronts of the upper floors of the more popular establishments (and the rears of the less reputable ones), while in some parts the leaning buildings created a near canopy, casting an ever-present shadow across the street below.

This shadow was weakly held at bay by the sickly light of street lamps, themselves fuelled by manure, pulsating like barely contained boils. However, even with these, the crumbled remains of older buildings and the exposed but darkened basements of others, meant venturing into Deep Street without a keen eye, a big stick and a pair of shoes suited to fast sprints, was likely to end with you leaving with nothing at all.

Fortunately for Orus he already had nothing at all and everyone knew it. Even if he did have something, the smell coming from him would convince any thief it was probably contagious and he could keep it. Orus turned off Old Mill Street onto Deep Street and dropped into his designated slot in the social hierarchy.

The glorious smells that one only finds in the dark underbelly of towns (perhaps because what is making them is harder to enjoy when you can see it) assaulted his nose and even managed, for a moment at least, to mask his own distinctive musk. He picked up a steaming bowl of something orange and lumpy from Mrs Crumble (the chalk board menu by her stall read, as it did every day, "Better not to ask") along with a chunk of only slightly mouldy bread. Trudging along their familiar route, his feet took him through the winding warren of the ditch until they brought him to a stop, as they often did, in front of Wassermann's Armour Emporium.

He lifted his head for the first time that day and stared at the array of weapons and armour. All second-hand of course: Wassermann's stock wasn't exactly top of the range, not that this mattered to Orus. A sword was still a sword, and each one called out to him songs of adventure and daring deeds.

The shop was closed. He pushed his face close to the glass and peered inside. He wanted to see if there were any new pamphlets in. This was a change since his brief time as a hero. Tavern songs were all well and good, but printing had given heroes a way to spread news of their adventures to a far wider audience. Orus had heard that some of the new, younger lads even had whole books made up. He could never afford to buy something like that, so he stuck to the penny folds. These were short, single story publications, and mostly produced by the older, more traditional heroes.

Every so often he would find one about an old friend from Cromalot. Last month he managed to pick up *Golan Triple Axe VS the Muggie-Marsh Grobler*. Little Golan won as well: not bad for someone who failed his Wetlands Monsters exam three times in a row. Orus had thought about trying to write him a letter to see how he was doing, just for old times' sake. In the end he didn't. After all, what if Golan wrote back and asked what *he'd* been up to for the last twenty years? Would he tell him about the time the guards' fencing practice got out of hand and he'd had to replant a whole bed of daffodils? Or the fight he had trying to clear the bats out of the north tower before the Prince's grandmother came to stay?

Oh yes, I'm sure the hero of Muggie-Marsh would be very impressed.

Still, Orus thought, Golan was ages with him and he was still out there. There was still time. He just needed to wait for the right moment. Once he had finished all the jobs he had at the castle, and at the house, and finished the preparations for the next tournament, then he would go and give it one last try.

He drew himself up to his full height and stood so his reflection on the window filled a well-made leather cuirass.

'One day,' he whispered.

'What's that?' A hand landed on his shoulder.

Orus jumped more than he liked to admit. Turning his head, a face like an old peach (wrinkly, brown and with hair in strange places) jutted towards him. The face belonged to Old Grimmer, Ditch's resident retired hero.

'Oh, nothing,' Orus said. 'Was just thinking, that's all.'

'Don't want to do too much of that,' said Old Grimmer. 'It's bad for you, I hear. They hung a lad down in Drossan for it just last month. He started thinking, then all these other people started thinking and the king didn't like that. "They'd be 'aving ideas next," he said, "then hopes, then dreams, and that causes all sorts of problems." Na, better to stay clear of that thinking. Only leads to trouble.'

Orus turned back to the window. The proud warrior from a moment ago had gone, eclipsed by a fat, balding muck shoveller. Grimmer was probably right. Dreams weren't for people like him. They were for princes and kings, knights and wizards. Dreams were there to push along children until they reached the point in their lives where it was too far to turn back, where joy in what you had was replaced by frustrated desire for what you didn't. For people like him, dreams were there to break you.

'See, Orus, the trick is, don't think, just do. You can't wait for it. That's the rule I used when I was still a hero. Things work out in the end, and if they don't, you won't be in much of a position to complain anyways.'

Orus looked at Old Grimmer. Back when the old man had been Felgrim the Blade, he was one of the greatest heroes of the age. His adventures were legendary: he'd climbed to the highest plateau of the Inverted Mountain; he'd defeated Cragus the Wall in single combat armed only with a broom handle and a slice of melon; he'd even saved Speakleaf from the terrifying Blood Forest Octopus. He was the real deal.

'Yeah,' said Orus. 'Maybe you're right.'

'No maybe about it. If you want something, go get it. Time spent thinking is better spent doing.'

'It's not always that easy. What would Thunder say if you just up and left him to go back on the road?'

Grimmer's trusty donkey, Thunder, looked up from his hay bale as if to say: 'That would suit me just fine.'

What he actually said was '*You try sleeping beside someone who snores like that. See how much you miss him.*' However, much to his annoyance, no-one ever listened to him.

'He'd come with me. Loves an adventure, don't you boy?'

Oh yes. Carrying all that equipment. Hardly any sleep. Routinely being chased by things with more heads than legs. And not even a nice bale of hay at the end of it. What's not to like?

'Well, I'd better be going,' said Orus, turning to leave. 'I need to get an early night. I'm heading over to Rivercrook this weekend to wait for a shipment of Bolgovian Black Carrots for the Prince. Apparently, they make the weight just fall off.'

'Is that his new thing? Do they work?'

'So they say. He read about them in *High and Mighty*. The prisoners in the Bolgovian salt mines eat nothing else, and there isn't a pinch of fat on any of them. Not after the first month, anyway.'

'On the subject of food,' Old Grimmer cleared his throat loudly, 'do you plan on finishing that?'

'Oh, no. I shouldn't. Mavis'll have dinner for me.' Orus handed over the soup and the bread. 'Here you go.'

'Thanks.' The retired hero took the bowl and scuttled back to his leaky hovel. It was made from various bits and bobs he had collected over his heroing career. The fabric roof was a battle standard from an undead army he had defeated with a pack of hungry terriers, and the floor was covered by some old tapestry he'd swiped from a vampire's castle. He hunkered down on the seat he had made from a Night Knight's helmet, took out his spoon (itself melted down from a magical dagger that just wouldn't shut up), and started slurping up the unknown soupy chunks through the gaps in his teeth.

Continuing home, Orus thought about Old Grimmer sitting alone in his dank, damp memories. With all the towns he'd saved and princesses he'd rescued and gold he'd appropriated from the lairs of fallen monsters, by all rights Grimmer should have a castle of his own. Unfortunately, reasonable financial prudence was another subject not covered by Cromalot's curriculum. Orus knew life wasn't fair but sometimes he wished it would at least pretend.

Had he not been lost in such thoughts he might have noticed a messenger rush by him, heading towards Grimmer's hovel grasping a letter printed on strange, scaly paper. But he didn't, so he was unaware that his one day was fast approaching.

CHAPTER THREE

Orus pushed the gate, cracked his knee against it, swore, lifted it over the uneven paving slab, and made his way up his garden path.

His house was very much a 'do the best with what you've got' kind of place. Crouching in the shadow of the Prince's castle, it was humble with a small 'h'. The lack of direct sunlight had attracted all manner of strange vegetation, the sort normally only seen in caves and dark dungeons. Luminous toadstools pocked the walls, while straggly grey moss drooped down from the eaves like the eyebrows of a dusty librarian. Wooden beams propped up the east wall, where the foundations had started to slip. This tilt had led to an exodus of slates from the roof that he still hadn't found the time to fix. In fact, the only bit of the house that looked right was the small upstairs window and that was only because it was round.

And there was a light in it. That meant Tag!

Orus rushed to the door, bounded inside, remembered, went back outside and kicked off his muddy boots. Inside again, he leapt up the stairs. Reaching Tag's door, he stopped to catch his breath and to listen.

Quiet. Tag must be reading, Orus thought. Always reading that boy. Don't know where he gets that from, but it certainly seems to have worked out for him. Started way down here and now a mage's apprentice in the court of the Prince's own cousin, Duke Hector of Blackstone. And all through honest, hard work. Good lad.

He knocked twice and didn't wait for an answer. So many questions: 'Back already? Enjoying the job? How's the Duke? Is he treating you okay? Good house? How's the food?'

But the reply was only silence. The room stood empty, the only change from when Tag left it six months ago were the mice footprints in the dust on the floor. A yellow toadstool poked out from under the window frame, its pulsing light reflecting in the glass. Orus let out a long sigh. He stood in the doorway, lost in recent memories. Already so long ago.

It had been over so quickly. Nineteen short, short years. And now Tag was gone, off to be his own man. A strange mixture of sadness and pride gripped Orus in these moments. Part of him wished to have more time, or at least to have some of it back. Was that wrong? Probably. But knowing that didn't stop it.

A gentle hand gripped his shoulder. 'I'm sure he's missing you too.' Mavis stood behind him in the doorway. She noticed the smell coming off Orus, but didn't mention it. Such things pass, but pride takes much longer to heal.

'Oh hi, honey, I was just checking for gnomes,' he lied.

She knew.

Neither mentioned it.

'You know how they are. One gets in, then a whole family. Before you know it, there's a full cobblers' shop upstairs.'

They stood together in the doorway for a few more minutes, watching the loud empty nothing.

Mavis turned away. 'Dinner's ready.'

*

After dinner Orus got stuck into the washing up. He quite liked doing it at the end of a hard day. The warm water eased the calloused joints in his fingers, and there was something ritualistic, soothing even, about the whole process. He even wore Mavis's apron. It was from the Rugged Barbarian range and featured a print of a hugely muscled torso on the front. Every night, whenever he caught her looking, he would strike up his best exaggerated heroic pose. In return she would fan herself with the tea towel, playing up like the noble ladies who walk through the market square for an excuse to watch the blacksmith's apprentice hammering away. She would have faked a swoon, only she was far too sensible for that kind of thing.

Posing and fanning completed, quiet crept into the room. They didn't have Tag's groan of embarrassment to provide the closing music anymore,[3] and that gap at the end of the scene always drew their eyes to his empty place at the table.

'Do you know in the castle kitchens,' said Orus, stuffing the awkward silence into the cupboard under the sink, 'they've got trained water nymphs to do the washing up now?'

'Oh yes, and how would you know that?' Mavis wrapped her arms around his very round, printed six-pack. 'Not been in for scones and jam with the ladies again, have you?'

'No,' he lied. It was a far better place for his lunch-break than sitting in the stable and chewing that dried mutton Horin the Stable Master was always so keen to offer him. 'I had to go in a few days ago to check the rat traps in the wine cellar.'

---

[3] The idea that parents might have fun from time-to-time being offensive to teenagers across all strands of reality.

'Ah huh.'

'They're not very good though, the nymphs, I mean,' he said, trying to pull the conversation back from any hint of dietary infringements. 'They made a right mess when one of their water spouts got out of control. And Betty says her aunt in the kitchens in Steeplecroft has been having trouble with theirs too. Nearly drowned the whole place.'

'Well, if that's the case, maybe I should tell them about your talents. Who needs magic when you've got all this?' She gave his rear a cheeky squeeze and shot him one of her killer winks. You could bring down a charging ogre with one of those winks. Even after all these years of marriage, they still made Orus's heart stutter and skip. A flash of an eyelid and it was all there. Beauty you couldn't buy and love you couldn't fake.

Even though she worked long hours at her dress shop in the Ditch market, Mavis always kept her sparkle. That reminded Orus, he had promised to have a look at the Morphing Mannequin. Mavis had picked up the magical gadget last summer. It was supposed to mimic the size and shape of the customer perfectly, making for a much better fit. But last week it had burst three seams by jumping up a size, all for no reason. The other craftspeople were having similar problems with their magical timesavers too, Mavis had said. Mrs Tweedle, the fortune teller, thought there was a disturbance in the mana-fields, whatever that meant. Someone should sort it out, Orus thought, before things really go tits up, metaphorically speaking.

His musings on the matter were interrupted by a string of swears from outside. He really did need to fix that gate.

Orus opened the door to find Old Grimmer on the front step, rubbing at a bruised knee.

'Alright, Orus. Wow, been hitting the weights, have you?'

Orus whipped off the apron and threw it behind the door.

'Eh no, I was just...'

'I remember when I used to look like that. Now I've just got the skin and none of the stuffing.' He croaked out a laugh. 'Here, you said you're going to Rivercrook tomorrow, yes?'

'Yes, I am but...' Old Grimmer had never come round to Orus's house before. He never normally went out of eyeshot of his hovel, in case someone tried to nick something. Not that anyone in Ditch would be that stupid. It was probably all cursed.

The old hero rummaged in the pouch he kept on the thin belt that used to fit him.

'How'd you fancy lending me a hand? Here.' Grimmer thrust a large jade coin into Orus's hand. 'Can you take this to the All Seasons Tavern on the way?'

'The All Seasons?' Orus looked down at the coin. It just about filled his palm. A dragon's head was carved into the centre, and runic writing in a style Orus didn't recognise ran around the rim. 'Why? What is it?'

'Just a favour I owe some old friends. I'd go myself, but it's a bit of a trek for old bones. All you need to do is hand over the coin and they'll explain the rest. Nothing you can't handle.'

He could do it, thought Orus, probably, possibly. The Prince's shipment wasn't due until the end of the week and, even if he was held up for a while, no harm would come to the carrots by sitting in a warehouse for a few extra days. Plus, the All Seasons wasn't much of a detour, and he'd always wanted to go there. Back in his Cromalot days it had been legendary. Crouched on the banks of the Cobalt River, the boundary to the wild northlands, all the greatest heroes of the last century had sought shelter under its roof at least once in their careers. 'Will it take long?' he asked.

'I hope not,' replied Grimmer, casting a quick look at the cold sky above him. Orus didn't notice this worried glance. Instead, in the back of his brain, adventure stirred.

'Well...' Orus looked down into the face of the dragon. It stared back fierce and green.

'I'll loan you Thunder,' said Old Grimmer. 'He can carry back them veggies you're getting. What was it again, Bolgovian cabbages?'

'Carrots.'

'Even better. He loves carrots. Great. That's it sorted then. Come round in the morning and pick him up.' Old Grimmer turned to leave. 'You're a real hero, Orus. Remember that. A real hero.'

'Wait,' Orus said (but, it pays to mention, he didn't say it very loudly, and he didn't try to stop Old Grimmer either). 'How will I know who to give it to?'

'Don't worry,' Grimmer called back, negotiating the gate. 'He'll find you.'

*

It was a strange exchange, Orus thought as he lay in bed. Even by the normal standard of conversation with Old Grimmer, this was a weird one.

The jade coin lay on his bedside cabinet. He called it a coin, but it didn't look like the kind you bought your lunch with. He knew Old Grimmer had picked up his fair share of magical trinkets during his years as Felgrim the Blade. Maybe it wasn't a coin after all. It could be a medallion. Maybe it gave you some sort of special powers or protection. Dragon-proofing perhaps, or maybe even flight. Or it could be some sort of key. The kind that fits into a huge carved wall in a hidden temple and opens the way to untold treasure. Then again, it could just be a very fancy coaster.

The whole business was more than a bit odd. Faced with such intriguing circumstances, Orus jumped to the only reasonable conclusion a man of his age, leading the rather mundane sort of life he was living, would ever arrive at: this was clearly all part of some great and secret quest organised by the most powerful people in the land, and it was down to him to play the vital role and, very likely, save the world.[4]

He knew it. All the time spent slaving away in the castle grounds, digging irrigation ditches, chasing moles off the tournament field, defrosting the mechanism on the drawbridge, it had all been building up to this.

Mavis lay beside him, listening to his brain clicking away. 'Everything alright, honey?'

'Hmm, what?' Orus replied, his mind already rappelling down an ancient castle wall to where his trusty steed waited below.

'You've just seemed a little distracted since Grimmer came round. What did he want, anyway?'

'No, I'm fine,' Orus's voice replied, as his brain raced across the night, a secret coded message in hand, and the torches of his evil pursuers behind. 'Grimmer? Nothing, nothing important. He just came to offer me a lend of Thunder. For the trip to Rivercrook. To help carrying things back, you know.'

Best not to worry her, he thought. He would explain it all when he got back. They'd probably give him a medal, or some gold, or a big bag of jewels that magically filled itself up again whenever he spent one. Then he would treat her to something nice. She'd like that.

---

[4] Some readers at this point might find that a strange conclusion to jump to in the face of so little evidence but, in fact, it is a line of reasoning played out by middle-aged men almost every day. This is why management consultants from Richmond go on outdoor survival courses, it's why plumbers from Leicester consider learning to navigate by the stars, and why call centre managers from Cardiff buy large 4x4s with snorkels on the exhaust. Because they know, deep down, that one day they will be called upon to do something momentous, something they will go down in history for, and when they are, they are damn well going to be ready.

'That was good of him,' said Mavis, trying to read what her husband was really up to. 'I've made you up some food for the way. When do you think you'll be home?'

That was a good question. Originally, he had only planned to be away for four days. Two days there, two days back, if the ship came in on time. But now, how could he know? A week, a fortnight, six months? It was hard to tell with these kinds of things. Saving the world could be a tricky business. He might get captured, held prisoner, tortured even.

'No more than a week,' he said. He would get a message to her somehow if it looked like things were going to take longer.

'Well, make sure and be careful on that road. And no running off with any of those Rivercrook women.' She dug a playful elbow into his side. 'We girls talk, remember.'

He laughed off the last comment. After all, there were more important things to think about than sex. She was right about that first bit though. Even around Ditch, the roads could be dangerous. You never knew what could be out there in the wilds.

He would need to get ready.

CHAPTER FOUR

It is a truth universally acknowledged that men collect things. A real man never throws anything away. Who knows when you might need a spare wooden door knob or that old pair of water waders with the holes in the knees? One thing was for sure, there is no length of rope short enough not to be worth keeping – just in case.

To be fair, sometimes the sorts of things men keep really are handy. The problem is, with so much junk to search through, when a man finally needs something from his collection he inevitably can't find it. This, in turn, just reinforces man's belief that he should keep hold of things. That way, next time he'll be ready. In the meantime, most of these antiques of the future end up in a man-chest.

Orus had been searching through his man-chest since dawn. It was about an arm's length in breadth and half that in height and depth. The top was rounded like a pirate-chest and held down with a metal clasp. He was sure he had left it under the bed and was surprised to find it had moved. This had happened before. Once he had found it in the loft space. The time before that it was out in the wood shed. After a bit of searching, he asked Mavis and she, probably by some kind of women's intuition, knew exactly where it was. Strangely enough, she didn't question him as to why he needed to take such an essential collection of items from the house to go on a perfectly normal trip to Rivercrook. He hoped she wouldn't need anything from it while he was away.

He had already sorted the contents into two piles (one for things to leave behind and a much larger one for the bare essentials) when he found his old sword. He pulled it free from its wooden scabbard and took a tentative practice swing. The feel of the leather grip stirred long buried passions and the blade cut through the invisible bindings that had dragged on his spirit for so long.

He gave his body a shake to loosen the cobwebs and took up a guard stance, the blade stalking in front of him. A lunge, a stab forward. Then back, holding the sword high to catch the counter attack. Side-step, slash, forward, slash again.

Yes, still got it.

His imaginary opponent made a desperate lunge.

Foolish.

Orus darted left and brought his sword round in a high arc to deliver the fatal blow. The sword bit deep into the rafter above his head and he fell forward into the cupboard.

'Everything okay, dear?' Mavis called from the kitchen.

'Fine, honey. Just getting ready.' Orus sheepishly pulled the sword free from the roof and returned it to its scabbard. Taking one last look over the pile of rejects, he put them all back in the chest and decided to take the whole thing, just in case.

*

On the doorstep, with the food Mavis had prepared tucked safely in the man-chest and the chest tucked under his arm, Orus kissed her goodbye.

'You will be okay without me?' he asked.

'Me? No, I'll probably get kidnapped again by a mud-man from the Gobbling Bog, and some other burly hero will rescue me. Then you'll need to fight him for my honour and love. I'll cheer for you though.' There was that wink again. Like a rose delivered via crossbow. It nearly knocked him off the step, but he was glad to be taking it with him. He really did love Mavis, and Tag. It wasn't that his life hadn't been a good one. It was full of happy memories: Mavis and his wedding at the church in Trundle, Tag being born, Tag's first steps, his first word (spoon), Mavis getting her apprenticeship at the Seamstress' Guild, opening her shop, the camping holiday to Muely, teaching sports at Tag's school. It was just that, in all the memories, not one was his alone.

This though, was an adventure. This was what he needed. He was more than just a castle gardener, just a servant, they would see. The Prince and his friends might like to play at being heroes, loading themselves up with expensive swords and embroidered cloaks, but he was the real deal.

As he made his way down Deep Street and on to Old Grimmer's hovel, he felt lighter and more awake than he had for months. The dark shadows were a bit warmer, the dankness a bit fresher.

He found the old hero wrestling with a scraggly brown rat. Each had a hold on a strip of pork fat Grimmer had been given by the butcher's boy earlier that morning.

'Morning, Grimmer.'

With his free hand, Grimmer swung his begging stool at the rat. He missed, spun round twice, careered across the front of his hovel and landed in Thunder's water-trough. The rat collected its prize and made off into the foundations of the Ditch Tax Office.

'Bloody thieves!' Grimmer shouted, shaking his fist.

'Yeah!' agreed a passer-by, who had recently received a huge tax bill.

'That damn rat. I was gonna share it with him,' said Grimmer. 'Is that you all set, then?'

Orus helped his friend unfold his old bones and climb out of the trough. 'Yup. Got everything I need right here.' Orus patted the man-chest with his free hand.

'Ah, taking your man-chest. Very wise. Always best to have it, just in case.'

Grimmer collected his stool and set it down outside his hovel.

'And you've got that what I gave you last night?'

'Right here.' Orus held up the jade coin.

'Good. So all you gotta do is wait at the inn 'til the contact gets there. He'll explain the rest. Like I say though, nothing to it.'

'What's he look like?' asked Orus.

'Beats me. These friends of mine, they're a kind of secret order. Very hush, hush. But don't worry, he'll find you.'

A secret order! I knew it, thought Orus.

'Just wait in the bar. But best not to mention my name. Had a bit of a misunderstanding with some dwarves last time I was there. Not got round to paying for the repairs yet.'

'And what is it they need this for?' Orus looked down at the coin again.

'You mean the job? Just a quick bit of heroing. Nothing you can't handle. You got a sword?' Old Grimmer opened the flap of his hovel and tugged at a black handle behind his bed. The broadsword he pulled free was huge: double handed, its thick steel blade glowed with a dull green fire. ''Cause you can borrow Troll-Slicer if you want?'

'That's okay,' Orus said. A sword like that had "collateral damage" written all over it. 'I've got my own.'

'Ah, good lad.' The old hero replaced his sword, narrowly avoiding cutting the roof of his hovel in half as he did so. 'You'll just be needing Thunder, then. I haven't actually told him yet. Luckily, he isn't the kind to grumble.'

Grimmer hobbled over and took Thunder's bridle. 'You wouldn't mind going with Orus, would you, boy?'

Thunder didn't move.

Mind? Me? I don't suppose it would make much difference if I did.

Orus watched Grimmer pull and push and swear and poke and swear again until he finally collapsed against Thunder's back leg. Once the old hero had caught his breath, he stood up and whispered in Thunder's big ear.

Fine, I'll do it, but you owe me, again. A donkey never forgets.

'That's elephants,' said Grimmer.

'What's elephants?' asked Orus.

'Oh, you know, big grey things, trunk and tusks, that's elephants.'

Before Orus could question the statement, Grimmer thrust Thunder's bridle into his hand.

'Just strap the chest on his back. He won't mind.'

Yes, I will. And he better not think he's getting to ride me.

'Can I ride him?'

'Course you can.'

Great.

Orus hauled himself onto Thunder's back. He felt surprisingly solid for such an old donkey.

Grimmer gave Thunder a pat on the neck and handed Orus the reins. 'Look after him,' he said.

'Don't worry, I will.'

Don't worry, I will.

With that, Orus tapped his heels into Thunder's sides. Nothing happened. Then, very slowly, the greatest hero the world of Drift would never know, set off on another adventure.

Bet I still don't get any credit.

CHAPTER FIVE

The day's sun was well into its autumn years when the All Seasons Tavern came into view. With Thunder making little effort to provide a comfortable ride for his charge, it did so in jumps and bumps, slowly revealing itself, as if raised from the horizon on a ratchet. Orus didn't pause to take in the splendid view of the Cobalt River's snaking descent into Lower Andrus afforded by a look back from the Tavern's courtyard. After a full day of bruised buttocks, it was different liquid that drew the majority of his attention.

So distracted, Orus was not aware that his arrival had already been noted. From a small window on the first floor, a hooded figure checked the description he had been given.

A bit heavier than expected. Still, he met the criteria:

Old: check.

Riding a donkey: check.

The Grandmaster would be pleased.

*

Orus waddled into the stable and led Thunder to a stall between two lean looking mares. A third was tied up by the door. He took the man-chest from Thunder's back and left it in the stall. The jade coin was tucked safely in his pocket. Turning to leave, he thought twice and went back to cover the chest in hay. You don't leave treasure like that lying around in a place like this.

As Orus approached the main entrance, the Tavern's door-troll stared at him from under a moss-covered monobrow. Puffing himself up and putting on his best 'You know, it's me, I come here all the time,' face, Orus marched confidently towards the door.

"Alt!' growled the troll, looming over Orus like an avalanche. 'You got any weapons on you?'

'Only this,' Orus said, pulling his sword free from its scabbard, while trying to give the impression it was the smallest of his many swords. 'Not going to do much damage with a butter knife like this, am I?'

The door-troll reached out a thick finger and gave the blade a flick that made it ping violently back and forth. 'Hmm. You ain't wrong der,' it rumbled. 'Wanna buy somethin' a bit bigger?'

The troll turned with a noise like gravel crunching under heavy wheels and opened the cabinet on the wall behind him. Inside was an armoury that wouldn't be out of place in a city barracks.

'I gots swords, knifes, clubs, clubs wiff nails in, poison toad launchers, everthin'. How's bouts this for a little guy like you.' The door-troll took a spring-loaded bolt launcher down from its hook. 'Fits right on yer arm. Trigger's a bit jumpy, so be careful putting yer hands in yer pocket or yer might end up do'in yerself a mischief.'

'I think I'm fine with this actually,' said Orus, shuffling out of the line of fire.

'Fair 'nough,' the troll said, as Orus made for the door. 'Yer funeral.'

Had he been listening, Orus would then have heard a spring bolt thudding into the floorboards of the porch, followed by a distinctly gravelly groan. But at this point, he was taking in the atmosphere of the famous All Seasons Tavern. In fact, atmosphere was the wrong word. It was more than that. What the All Seasons had was weather.

Playing host to decades of drunken wizards, cursed princes and enchantment laden adventurers had caused magical energy to seep into the very fabric of building. This energy was the cause of the Tavern's famous meteorological manifestations. On this evening, ominous storm clouds hung over the bar, periodically casting tiny lightning bolts across the taps. At the very back of the room, a wizard's hat poked through a man-sized mound of snow while hail stones pelted noisily against the inside of the windows. In the centre, where a trio of small town thugs were playing a game of Cut Purse Poker, a rainbow leapt from the pile of gold coins in the pot and landed in the drink of the unconscious dwarf at the next table.[5]

Orus strode towards the bar, avoiding the puddles of rain water and making sure not to nudge into any of the easily offended looking types, which, in here, was just about everyone.

'One Head-drummer, please.'

The barman turned to face Orus. A smell of burnt hair surrounded the man, and the ends of his beard glowed like tobacco in a pipe.

'Nn-nn, nothing from the t-t-taps while the light, while the lightning's on,' he said, raising a jittery hand towards the crackling brass. 'You wa-want something else?'

'Oh, right.' Orus wasn't much of a drinker anymore. A man who was often called upon to unblock drains soon learned that hangovers are best avoided. Still,

---

[5] Some people believe that there is a pile of gold at the end of every rainbow. This is of course nonsense. The gold is always at the start. Others maintain that even this is not true, being that they have checked lots of rainbows and never found any gold to speak of. You should ask these people if they have ever checked both ends.

this was an adventure and ordering an apple juice might look a bit suspicious. Some of the other customers might take offence. 'Just a whisky then.'

'You wa-want an umbrella with that?'

Orus looked round at the grizzled faces of his fellow patrons. Eyes turned to fix on the newcomer, both singular, and in the more traditional pairs. 'No thanks.'

'Your choice,' said the barman. 'It'll probably rain later though.'

*

Orus sipped his drink and tried to work out what his next move should be. How would he know who his contact was? The dwarf hadn't moved since he came in, so he was pretty sure it wasn't him. Then again, maybe that was his cover. He didn't think it was the wizard, who was now swatting at the tiny sun orbiting his head. Members of super secretive cults tended not to dress in bright, multicoloured robes. They drew too much attention, and not just from the fashion police.

Orus casually looked around at the other patrons, until some of them started to stare back. Keen to avoid being asked to identify the object of his ocular survey, he turned to the crackling gaze of the barman.

'Barman?'

'Jerry,' replied Jerry.

'Sorry. Jerry. You haven't noticed anything strange around here today, have you?'

'How d-d-do you mean?' said Jerry, wringing out a small cloud into the sink before it could rain all over the bar. 'Strange for in here or strange in general?'

'More like, strange people.'

The forecast suddenly turned chilly. Jerry could see this remark had not gone unnoticed by his regulars. It didn't do to insult a man in his own pub.

'Someone,' Orus continued, oblivious to the parking of tankards on tables and the slow scraping of a roomful of chair legs, 'not from around here. Someone that looked like they might be in need of help?'

'I can th-th-think of one,' said Jerry, stepping sideways and hopefully out of the line of fire.

'Ah, great. Can you point him out to me?'

'Perhaps l-l-later,' replied Jerry.

Clever move, thought Orus. Too many unfamiliar ears in range right now. Old Grimmer probably had Jerry in on this too.

Jerry tried to pull the conversation onto safer ground.

'Do, you kn-know if Mavis's new autumn range is in?' he asked. 'My wife buys all her d-d-dre-dres, her clothes from her shop in Di-Di-Di, at the market. Lovely patterns, she always says. Floral. That's what she likes.' That seemed to have done it. His customers were returning to their drinks. Crisis averted.

'What do you mean?' asked Orus, going a bit flush.

'You're Mavis's husband, aren't you? The Prince's gard-gard-gardener? I've seen you around when I g-g-go in to collect orders.'

This wouldn't do. Orus didn't want whoever it was he was meeting to think he was some kind of amateur. They might not let him do whatever it was he was needed for. He was a hero now. 'What? No. I mean, I don't know... I mean, that's not me. That's Orus, he is my... brother.'

Jerry knew a desperate look when he saw one. He casually took the cloth from his apron and rubbed at a non-existent stain on the bar, then gave Orus a sly wink. 'Sorry, my mistake. Orus is a g-g-good head shorter than you.'

'True, he is the runt of the litter.' Orus laughed nervously and gave a quick nod of thanks.

'And balder!' came a shout from somewhere in the back.

'Again true. My brother doesn't have quite the mane I do.'

'And fatter!' came another unseen voice.

He didn't respond to that one. It would only encourage them.

'So,' Jerry came to his rescue again, 'What sort of work are you in?'

'Me? I am an adventurer, a swashbuckler, a hero. Protecting the weak, fighting monsters, saving the world, that kind of thing.'

'Oh yeah!' The shout came from one of the men playing cards. From the look of the collection of aces up his sleeve he cheated a lot. From the look of the collection of knives and fingers on his belt, people probably let him. 'Don't look like much of a hero to me. What's your name, then?'

Orus looked around quickly for inspiration and found none. People were staring. He couldn't pick the name of a real hero. They might know it. Something quick and easy to remember.

Then his voice shouted out before his brain could stop it. 'Morris!'

'Morris?' replied the cheater.

No going back now, he thought. It wasn't very inspiring, but then neither was he. 'Yes, Morris. Morris the Marauder.' He patted his sword to show he was the real deal.

'What are you doin' out here, Mr Marauder? Not plannin' on causin' any trouble, I hope. This is our turf.' The cheater gestured to his two companions. One was in the midst of pick-pocketing the still comatose dwarf, while the other was chewing on a tiny white whale he had just skewered with a cocktail stick as it swam through his pint.

'No, nothing like that. I'm just passing through on my way to do a favour for an old friend,' Orus said, loud enough for any hidden ears to hear.

'Well, you can't be that good. I ain't never heard of you.'

Orus should have let it go and finished there. He was supposed to be keeping a low profile. Maybe it was the excitement of the whole thing or his wish to show that he really was more than just a gardener. Whatever it was, pride got the better of him. 'Oh, you wouldn't have. I do most of my heroing down south. I don't come up this way often. Down there I'm famous. More than famous. Greatest hero in the land. Number one. Tip top.'

In the corner of the room, a booth table was nestled in thick mist. Only hints of shadows could be seen through the haar. Orus had assumed it was empty when he came in, and now his interest was elsewhere. But, at that last comment, a dark form condensed in the cloud. Like a ghost ship's black prow, a hooded face emerged from the mist, the grey fog still filling its cowl. This did not bother the stranger. He had grown up in dark far denser than this. He had a clear view of his target. A great hero – that clinched it. He was the one.

Back at the other side of the room, Orus (or Morris) was still trying to convince the other clientele of his heroic credentials.

'So what have you done then? Rob any temples? Steal lots of jewels? Stuff like that?' asked the pickpocket, while exchanging knowing glances with his friends.

Orus didn't recognise the meaning of these glances and so barrelled forward. 'What have I done? Now, that's a question.'

Drawing on his half-remembered education in heroic history and a list of place names from the very back of the atlas he had given Tag for his thirteenth birthday, Orus spun a tale that would make an octogenarian fisherman blush. Armies led into hopeless battles, princesses rescued, sorcerers slain, dungeons delved, demons vanquished, temples plundered. He had done it all. There wasn't a village or a town in the whole of the south that he hadn't defended from a terrible monster, evil queen or power-crazed community council.

The gamblers hung on every word until eventually one asked the question they had all been dying to: 'So, Morris the Marauder, with all that behind you, you must be pretty rich?'

'Rich?' In all the excitement, Orus hadn't really thought about expenses. He had only budgeted for the trip to Rivercrook, not this detour. Still, in for a penny, in for a pound. 'You could say that. I don't keep it all on me of course. You can't be too careful, if you know what I mean.'

'Of course, never know what kind of people could be about,' said the cheater. 'But enough to buy your new friends a drink, I bet.'

'Well...'

'Unless, that is,' the cheater's eyes narrowed, 'you don't count us as friends?'

'Not at all. Not at all. Jerry, three...'

'Whisky!'

'Three whiskies for my new friends here.'

'Coming up,' said Jerry. 'Anything else?'

'Scratchings! Pork if you got 'em,' said the whale chomper, 'or goblin.'

'And a bag of scratchings,' said Orus. So much for breakfast.

'Three bags!' the chomper called out, pointing to his fellow scroungers.

'Sorry. Three bags.' So much for lunch.

The rogues abandoned their card game and came to sit by their new benefactor. A thick arm clapped round Orus's shoulders. 'Cheers, buddy,' said the cheater. 'What are friends for ehh? Now, you were telling us about how rich and famous you is.'

And so the night passed with Orus plumbing the depths of heroic lore to satisfy his audience. He had to mix and match a bit. Luckily, since reading was considered a specialist skill in these parts, he was pretty confident no-one in the bar would know it was actually Torrin Frost-fist who had killed the Rampaging Rhinestone Rhino of Glort, or that the Belching Fog had in fact been driven from the city of Cannon-mouth by Grand Conjurer Ian.

By midnight there was still no sign of his unknown contact so, after getting in another round of drinks for his new friends, he asked Jerry for a room and turned in for the night. It wasn't long before he was snoring away, if a little poorer, still pretty happy about how things were going so far. He hadn't been killed, which was a good start in anyone's book, and when he woke up the next morning he would still be on an adventure. He was not to know that the adventure had already become a hunt and that he was the prime target.

CHAPTER SIX

The hooded stranger sat awake and alert at the end of his bed, waiting. He listened intently to the creaks and groans of the old pub until he was sure everyone had gone to bed, or was at least no longer conscious.

Confident that he would not be disturbed, he reached into the folds of his dark robe, drew out a roll of parchment and sat by the small desk. At the top of the paper were his instructions, now crossed out. Below these it was blank. He took the stopper from the pot of ink and began to write.

Grandmaster, I have found him.

He waited as the ink spread from his pen strokes, welling into the tiny cracks in the Pairing Paper.

The reply did not take long. It scratched its way across the paper, the ink rising up from the cracks in answer.

Good work, Initiate. And he is alone? He has not been followed?

The Initiate answered, keeping his writing small. He'd only been given one sheet and Pairing Paper was expense stuff.

Only the donkey, as you said. No sign of any other heroes.

Good. Don't hang about then. Bring him to me. And the token.

Yes, Grandmaster. I will not fail.

The Initiate allowed his last message to dry, then rolled up the Pairing Paper and returned it to his robes. His mission was almost complete. He admired the heroes, they led such interesting lives. It was a shame that he would have to be the one to stop them.

CHAPTER SEVEN

The sound of snores rattled through the flimsy door. A knife turned in the lock, and a dark figure stole into the room.

He snuck across the room to his quarry's bedside. Morris the Marauder coughed and rolled onto his back, making it all the easier to slide the blade up under the slumbering hero's flabby chin.

'Wakey, wakey,' he hissed.

Orus opened his eyes. A black silhouette hovered over him. He felt the point of something very hard and very sharp pressing under his chin and wished really hard that he would wake up again soon.

'Where is it?'

Orus searched his sleep-fogged brain for a way out of the situation, then felt the pressure of the blade increase.

'I won't ask again.'

Orus tried to speak without giving his mouth an overflow outlet. ''her is 'hat?'

'The coin, you fat fool. The treasure. Tell me where it is or I'll slit you, ear to ear.'

Orus cursed his wide ears. The jade coin was at the end of the bed rolled up in his sock. After all his wishing to be part of a great conspiracy, he was not enjoying it as much as he had expected.

The point under his chin pressed harder still and he felt a drip of blood ooze down his neck.

'Tell me, or this ain't gonna end well for you.'

He couldn't die here. Not now. Not with so much left undone. He had promised to help Mavis put up a new display rail in the shop for one. And there was that damn gate.

He managed a glance sideways. The attacker's hips were just above his left elbow. The words of Wee Mental Davey, Cromalot's close combat teacher, came back to his head: 'Every man has a weak spot – so hit him in them.'

All he needed was a distraction.

Behind the attacker someone cleared their throat. 'Erm. Excuse me. I don't mean to be a bother, but when you are finished, I would like to speak to Mr Morris, if that's okay.'

The attacker turned to face the new visitor and said, 'Who are yoooouarrrrch?' then toppled over onto the floor clutching his groin.

Orus rolled off the bed and grabbed his socks from the end of it. He fished out the jade coin and kicked the attacker's knife to the other side of the room. Then, with expert precision, he knelt heavily on the same weak spots and bound the groaning man's hands and feet with the socks.

With the door open and light from the hall pouring in, his attacker was revealed as the cheater from downstairs.

The other visitor to Orus's room still stood in the doorway, a bit like a man watching a husband and wife argue and trying to pick the best moment to explain his jacket was on the back of one of their chairs. He rocked on his heels and raised his hand to speak. 'Mr Morris, I am–'

'Be with you in a minute,' puffed Orus, emptying his pillow case, then refilling it with the cheater's head.

'Oh, sorry. Don't mind me. I'll wait.' After a few more seconds the stranger leaned over Orus, who was still making final adjustments. 'Do you need any help, perhaps?'

'No, no. I'm nearly done.' He was working on the cheater's boots now. They were the long kind that went up to the knee. He held them briefly against his own bare feet. 'Damn. Too big. Need some new boots?'

'Eh, no, thank you. My Order has provided me with adequate footwear.'

Orus looked at the second man's feet. Adequate apparently meant socks and sandals.

'Fair enough,' he said, pulling off the cheater's socks. 'I'll keep these, if it's all the same with you. Don't think I'll be getting mine back. Can you open that window for me?'

'Oh, yes, no problem.' Orus could see now that the man wore long dark robes, with a cowl. Pale hands pushed back the window. This side of the Tavern backed onto the river. Its rushing water flopped and dopped beneath them.

Orus strode over to the window and launched the cheater's boots out into the night. He felt more alive now than he had in years.

'You'll be after this, I bet.' Orus held up the jade coin.

'You have it. Excellent. The Grandmaster will be pleased. I thought it was you when I saw the donkey. I wanted to speak to you earlier, but I had to be sure we weren't being watched. I am to bring you back to the temple.'

'Ah-ha, a secret temple,' said Orus. Villains in the night, secret rendezvous, lucky escapes. Just as he'd expected. 'I knew it would be something like that. And you are Brother…?'

The monk moved into the light and dropped his hood.

'Initiate actually. Initiate Ambrose. I'm not a full Brother yet. I will be soon. Hopefully. My exams are coming up later in the year,' said Ambrose. 'Provided everything goes to plan, anyway.'

Ambrose wasn't exactly what Orus had expected in a secret messenger. The bits of his body covered by his robes had all the substance of a bundle of coat hangers, while the bits that poked out from the dark fabric were either too short, too long, too pale, or gave the impression that if you touched them they would be greasy. He reminded Orus of one of Tag's friends. The one that called him 'sir' and always seemed to be ill.

'Well, nice to meet you. I'm–'

'Morris the Marauder. Yes, I heard downstairs.'

This could be tricky, Orus thought. But best to play along for now. He could sort it out later. 'Yes, that's me. So, what is it exactly that you need help with? Someone stolen one of your relics or something like that?'

'Not quite,' replied Ambrose. 'You see, we have a rather serious problem concerning a dragon.'

Wow, thought Orus. This was big stuff. Secret plots were one thing. Big scaly, fire breathing monsters were a whole different animal.

It did explain the carved face on the jade coin. It was probably some sort of protection charm after all. He knew he had seen something like it before.

Still, a dragon was pretty big game. If the excitement of the night's adventure was not still crackling through his synapses, the rational part of his brain might have convinced him to opt out, take the monk's address and put this quest down as one to work up to.

A voice hissed in the gloom behind them. 'You taken care of him yet? Did you find the gold?'

The cheater's two partners were standing in the doorway, daggers drawn. The pickpocket slid into the room, the whale-chomper coming after him.

'Who's that with you?' asked the pickpocket, his eyes still adjusting to the dark.

Orus looked round for his sword. He had left it leaning by the door. The whale-chomper stepped in front of it, blocking any chance of retrieval.

'Who's that on the floor?' the whale-chomper added, pointing with his dagger.

Orus grabbed Ambrose by the arm and backed towards the window. Moonlight spilled around them, creating perfect silhouettes.

'Hey, that ain't the boss. He ain't that fat and he ain't that tall.'

'It's him – Morris! Get him!'

The rush of river filled Orus's ears. There was only one way out.

'I'd say that's time to go,' he said, scooping up Ambrose. 'Can you swim?'

'No.'

'That makes two of us,' Orus said, before leaping into the night.

*

The rushing water poured into Orus's ears and nose, as the current pulled them under the bridge.

The water was cold, really cold. Orus scrambled for his footing. The dark of the bridge made it impossible for him to see anything to grab onto. Flailing wildly, the biting cold began to loosen his grip on Ambrose's robe. He tried to clench harder but the force of the water pulled the fabric through his fist with irresistible inevitability.

Together, they crashed into a large rock, and to their surprise, it grunted, turned and picked them up.

The door-troll lifted the two sodden bundles onto the near bank. ''Ello again. Spot of midnight swimmin' is it?

You wanna be careful. If yer'd gone much further yer would have got cot up in me fishin' nets.'

Orus's teeth were chattering so hard you could have used them to mill wheat. 'Th-thh thhhankk-kkkk-kk you.'

Ambrose was trying to wring out his robe and bring the feeling back to his fingers.

'What's goin' on up der den?'

'J-j-just a b-bit of tr-tr-trouble with the locals,' Orus replied.

'Yer shud 'ave bot one of my weapons, like I saids.'

Above, the door of the Tavern opened with a bang. 'Find them! Under the bridge! Go!'

The voice belonged to the cheater. Waste of a good pair of socks. But no time to think about that now.

'I don't suppose you could hold them up for us?' Orus asked the troll.

Their granite saviour looked towards Orus, then slowly down to the south side of the bridge where the shouting was coming from, then back. He was going to ask how long he should hold them up for, but, rather rudely he thought, the two fleshies had already run off. He shrugged his shoulders and turned back to the pair of nice boots he just found.

Probably make a good set of horn warmers. The things peoples throws away these days.

Out from under the stone arch, Orus and Ambrose scrambled up the bank towards the back of the stables.

The old donkey was where Orus had left him, oblivious to all that was going on. The three brown mares however, which Orus correctly guessed belonged to their pursuers, were nowhere to be seen. It was almost as if someone had untied them, led them outside and told them there was some extra delicious grass about a mile back down the road.

Horses are so stupid.

Orus untied Thunder and helped Ambrose on board. The donkey tossed his head in disapproval.

His bony bum too. You must be joking.

Orus ran to the pile of hay where he had hid the man-chest and heaved it off the ground. He lifted it over to Thunder and pushed it into his companion's hands. 'Here. Take this.'

Thunder protested at the extra weight and lashed out with his back legs. His right hoof struck a water bucket, sending it barrelling across the stable. At the same moment, the pickpocket crashed through the stable door, only to catch the bucket in the face and go crashing back out again.

'Nice one, Thunder. Lucky shot,' said Orus, climbing onto his trusty stead.

Yeah, lucky.

Once they were well out of sight of the All Seasons, Orus turned back to his new companion. 'Sorry about all that. Comes with being a hero,' he said. 'So, where is this dragon you need me to slay?'

'No, no, no. Not slay. We need you to save it.'

'Save a dragon!' Orus gulped. 'From who?'

CHAPTER EIGHT

Conrad Von Strauss stood triumphantly over the still writhing body of the dying dragon. He gripped his shining sword over his head, poised to strike the final blow. The neck of his scaly foe was twisted back on itself as the dragon fixed its dimming eyes on the powerful hero who had bested it. Conrad's steely gaze looked deep into those eyes and promised no quarter.

'Fritz! More smoke!' Master Lenz poked his head round the edge of the canvas to shout at his assistant. A spotty youth rushed to the bellows and gave three good pumps. Blue smoke puffed from the mock dragon's head.

'No, no, no, Fritz. It's not smoking a pipe. Coils, boy, we must have coils. Long, gentle pressure.' Lenz rolled his eyes, cursed the lack of good apprentices and then returned his focus to his subject. 'I am sorry, my lord. He is new.'

'No matter, Master Lenz.' The real Conrad Von Strauss stood over the mock dragon, holding his most heroic, trouser stretching pose for this first sitting. From above his faux foe, he looked down on the shaking youth.[6] 'I will have some of my men flog him for you once we are done with the preliminary sketches.'

'Thank you, my lord. Your reputation for generosity is well deserved. However, given his gentle disposition, I am trying to avoid too much stress. A shaking hand is no use to us men of craft. Now, if you could resume the pose, I will continue.'

'Yes, of course. Like this?' Von Strauss lifted the wooden spoon which was standing in for his sword. The real one was far too heavy to hold still for so long.

'Excellent, my lord. You are clearly a natural,' exclaimed Lenz, resisting the temptation to add the words 'pompous ass' to the end of his sentence. Master Lenz was used to dealing with men like Von Strauss. The curse of being a master painter is that most of the people who can afford to pay your fee were about as likable as gangrene. He often thought about going back to doing landscapes. They were far more pleasant company.

You have to be a very particular type of person to pay someone to paint a massive picture of yourself wearing hugely impractical clothes and then hang it in your own house. In Master Lenz's experience they tended to be the sort of people who felt that mirrors lacked the talent necessary to capture such excellent form.

However, while his skill with the brush was expert enough that he could whip up a picture of a strawberry trifle so delectable people would try to take a bite out of it, he'd yet to master the process of reflecting the nutritional benefit of such subjects. Thus, not being able to exist on his art alone, he was forced to complete these rather boring commissions.

---

[6] This is partly because Von Strauss was standing on a table but mainly because he looked down on just about everyone.

But the painting wasn't a total waste. Behind the pantomime costume dragon and his vacuous subject rose a truly remarkable piece of geography. The Worm-mound was a solitary mountain that rose from the high steppe like a gargantuan red rock tree stump. Sheer-sided and flat topped, its plateau was known to hold a vast lake of molten metal that shone in the night like a celestial crown. On an island in the centre of that lake was the entrance to the temple of the dragon monks and somewhere inside that was The Dragon. The capitals in this case were fully deserved, as it was known to be the only dragon left alive on the whole Drift. If Conrad had his way, soon it wouldn't even be that.

'Thank you, Master Lenz. You don't mind if I continue with the book?'

'No, my lord. By all means, it is a great honour to hear the tales of your adventures first hand.' The canvas hid his groan.

'Capital.' Von Strauss looked across the crowd in his camp. Lifting his voice he shouted for his personal chronicler. 'Huggle!'

The various warriors, bodyguards, cooks, healers, magicians, masseuses, smiths, farriers, stable boys, pot washers, tent pitches, foragers and messengers that made up Conrad's considerable 'lone hero' entourage bulged momentarily and then spat out the portly scribe. Huggle clutched a hefty leather-bound manuscript under his arm. He stumbled forward, wiping the sweat from his brow with a well-used polka dot handkerchief. 'Here, sire.'

It had been Huggle's idea to hunt down the last dragon. He had been on the lookout for an exciting quest to top-off the seventh volume of Conrad's adventures when he learned of the creature's existence from a street urchin in Conrad's father's city. The boy had overheard an old missionary monk talking about it in the market. No hero had killed a dragon in over five years, and it was one of the few foes Conrad had yet to face. That it was the last one alive was the icing on the cake. The monk had already left by the time Huggle made it to the market. The boy, however, was thrilled to be granted an audience with the Drift's greatest living hero. He told Von Strauss of the Worm-mound and all he had learned about the monks that lived there.

As soon as Conrad heard of the existence of the beast he wanted it. In fact, it went further than that. He deserved it. He was entitled. He was the greatest living hero in all of Drift and here was the greatest living prize. For anyone else to receive the glory, the prestige, of slaying it… it just wouldn't be right. And, if Conrad was anything, he was a man driven to do what was right.

Having thrown the boy in his father's dungeon to prevent any of his heroic rivals finding out the location of the dragon, Von Strauss was very annoyed to find on reaching the Worm-mound that many of these rivals were already there. Heroes and adventurers from across the land had gathered at the mountain, their camp totally surrounding it as they tried to figure out a way to reach the beast inside. More arrived each day. This was entirely blamed on Huggle. It certainly had nothing to do with Conrad announcing to a packed city square the target of his next quest, before taking two weeks to decide on which of the monster hunter outfits in his walk in, walk around, walk upstairs, wardrobe best suited dragon slaying.

When they arrived, Von Strauss was even more annoyed to find that the Dragon Monks didn't feel inclined to let him into their temple to slay the beast. This too, he confidently summarised, was probably Huggle's fault. He would have to keep a closer eye on his assistant to avoid any further mishaps.

'Huggle, you are standing in the frame.'

Huggle looked down at the fake dragon's tail, passing between his feet. 'Ah yes. Many apologies, sire.'

He stepped back, careful not to tread on anything.
'Here?'

'That will do.' Von Strauss regarded him with disdain so deep it was almost philosophical. 'You see, Master Lenz; even the greatest hero in all the world cannot get good help these days. Were it not for men of intelligence, such as you and I, this land would fall into ruin.'

Von Strauss turned his attention back to Huggle, who was now standing ready with the manuscript open and quill in hand. 'Now, where did we get to last time?'

'The Ice Giants of Cainth's Point, sire.'

'Ah yes, the ice giants. Have you ever seen one, Master Lenz? Ugly brutes. You will enjoy this. Huggle, read the last section aloud so Master Lenz can hear how I vanquished those disgusting creatures.'

'Yes, sire.' Huggle drew in a deep breath and went into full saga mode:

'And lo, brave Von Strauss did steal entry into the fast frozen lair of the devilish ice giants,

Though the way was strewn with the frost covered bones of lesser men,

He did march forward alone and fear did not once strike his bold heart,

Reaching the vile creatures' inner sanctum, its walls adorned in savage symbols etched in reddest blood,

He, bravest of men, did put all three to death,

Striking with shining sword and righteous fire,

He sent them back to the evil from which they had spawned.'

Von Strauss glared at his scribe. 'Huggle, as always, your incompetence finds new heights every time you open your mouth. There were five giants in the cave. Any fool could slay three.'

Huggle set down the manuscript and reached inside his jacket for his small note book. 'Sire, begging your pardon, but my notes of the expedition clearly state that three bodies were recovered: the two infants and the old one-legged one.'

Von Strauss rolled his eyes and gave Master Lenz a knowing look. 'And were you in the cave at the time, Huggle?'

'No, sire, but Grundtal and Drömmar were—'

'And Huggle,' boomed Von Strauss, 'have you, little scribe, ever battled an ice giant?'

'No, sire.'

'No. Of course you haven't. So you are doubtless unaware that if you sever one's head from its body, it immediately melts.'

Huggle knew that he would lose this argument, just like all the other times, but he couldn't help taking the opportunity to help the master painter get a real handle on his exalted subject. 'I was aware of that, sire, though I have heard it is a myth.'

'And like most good myths it is also fact. Correct the manuscript this evening. Really, at this rate we will never meet the publication deadline. I shall dictate from here to save you further embarrassment.'

'Yes, sire. Sorry, sire. Please, when you are ready.' Huggle suppressed a grumble. Since he was going to have to rewrite it anyway he continued with the truthful version:

'Verily, did the Fearless [Cowardly bastard] Conrad Von Strauss return to the court of Baron Silt,
And was received [tolerated] by the adoring townsfolk with great joy.
Presenting the heads of the five [now unmelted] ice giants who had plagued the town,
He did recount the story of his latest great victory. [For some reason choosing to ignore the bits about him travelling the whole way in a heated carriage, getting lost in the ice giants' cave and being found hiding in a barrel of fish heads with his thumb stuffed securely in his mouth.]

'Truly inspiring, my lord.' Lenz came out from behind the canvas. 'It has given me great insight into your character. I shall certainly look forward to reading the volume when it is completed.'

'I shall have one specially autographed for you.'

'Many thanks, my lord. Your generosity is proven once again.' Lenz needed a good door stop.

'Think nothing of it. We can take the cost of it from your fee.'

'Why thank you again, my lord. But now I fear we shall have to end for the day. The light is getting poor.'

'Very well, very well. We shall resume tomorrow at midday.'

Von Strauss broke his pose, stepped down from the table and out from the mock dragon's coils. He slithered round to stand in front of the canvas and placed a manicured hand on the painter's shoulder. 'Do you know, Master Lenz, I think this may turn out to be your finest work. Have you thought of a name for it?'

Lenz resisted the urge to shiver under that well-oiled grip. 'I thought *The Worm* was fitting, my lord.'

Von Strauss looked at the canvas. It was a good likeness. He always knew his chin was sharper than the mirror claimed. And such good cheekbones. 'Perhaps *The Last Worm* would be better.'

Not really, thought Master Lenz. There will be plenty others just as wormy as you in the future.

Conrad's myriad of followers parted in front of him as he started back towards his tent. 'Huggle, if you would. I wish to go over the schedule for my victory tour.'

'Coming, sire,' said Huggle, trudging after the worm.

CHAPTER NINE

What had once been a grassy plain had now been trampled into a dry, dusty wasteland. In place of the fine lush grass, a sea of tents sprouted up from the sun-beaten soil. The multi-coloured canvases, their former brightness muted by the dust in the air, rippled as waves in the steady breeze and crashed around their central supports. Every so often one tent would push above those around it and reach upwards towards the sky. These larger tents were topped by flags bearing all manner of beasts and heraldry.

Von Strauss led Huggle confidently along one of the troughs in the canvas sea. Down here it was just as choppy as on the surface. Swarms of grimy, sweating servants moved between the tents in throngs, carrying water, weapons and supplies to their masters like long weary eels. The dust kicked up from the practice grounds met the smoke from the forges and decided to team up to give everyone a five-star dirt bath. Everyone that is, except for Conrad Von Strauss. He employed a team of wafters – tall men carrying large wicker fans – to walk in front of him at all times and beat back the dust, dirt and grime, lest he be confused by someone important for someone who was not.

Boards had been put down on the main thoroughfares in the camp to stop the dirt turning to mud. As Von Strauss marched his way along their route, the swirling mass of callused hands and dirty faces parted ahead of him, falling back in reverence to his fame. At least, that is what he liked to think. Huggle suspected it had much more to do with the eight heavily muscled, heavily armed and lightly brained bodyguards forming a protective ring around their master, just behind the wafters.

'And make sure the Emperor of Krum knows that the pillow of my bed must be of the finest downy feathers taken from two week old Pinnacle Grouse. The Duke of Grabos should... Are you listening, Huggle?'

'Yes, sire, Pinnacle Grouse. Noted. Continue.' Huggle trotted back to his place at his master's heel. The preparations for Conrad's victory tour had been taking up the majority of his time since arriving at the Worm-mound.

'Good. As I was saying, the Duke of Grabos is to give me the use of his bed-chamber for the duration of my stay. The one I had to use last time had the most awful carpet.'

'Sire, we could ask that they replace the carpet with something more tasteful.'

'No, no. I do not want to cause too much disruption to the Duke. I will have his bed-chamber, my servants can have the one he gave me last time and he can sleep in the castle barracks.'

'Very well, sire. I will send the dispatch out this evening.' That way the Duke should have cooled down sufficiently by the time we arrive, Huggle thought.

'Excellent. You know, Huggle, for a man of letters you really have a lot to learn about diplomacy. People skills are very important,' said Von Strauss, stepping over the crumpled form of a water carrier caught unawares by the advancing entourage.

'So it seems,' said Huggle, helping the man to his feet just in time for him to be crushed again by the bodyguards bringing up the rear.

'The next stop will be to—'

The bodyguards in front of Von Strauss had stopped.

'What is it now?' said Conrad. 'Move aside, move aside.'

The two behemoths leading the column parted to let their master through. Ahead, a crowd of youths clutching quills and parchment were gathered around the porch to a large, purple tent. All were trying to peek round the huge men holding huger axes guarding the entrance flap. With a ripple of shoulder tapping, nudging and head pointing, the crowd rounded on Von Strauss, Huggle and the entourage, then poured towards them.

Von Strauss switched to his public friendly persona and held his arms out to the crowd. 'Ahh, my adoring public. Thank you all for coming out. You are too kind.' He flashed a brilliant smile then leaned towards the nearest bodyguard and whispered, 'If any of them touch me you will all be cleaning out the latrines for the next week.'

'Yes, boss,' replied the bodyguard, his voice emanating from somewhere behind the kind of facial hair you could lose a badger in. A flurry of gestures followed and the rest of the guards moved to encircle Huggle and Von Strauss in an even tighter ring. Their charge secure, the guards advanced towards the crowd smiling and with weapons bared.

Von Strauss himself waved and winked and blew kisses to the crowd through the treacherous passes between his men mountains. Pieces of parchment were thrust towards him from all directions. Huggle sprang into action, the pre-inked CVS monogrammed stamp he kept with him for just these situations hitting each sheet with expert precision.

'Do not miss any, Huggle. I don't want my fans going away empty handed. It is the least I can do for these, eegh, fine people,' he said, skilfully weaving this way and that, to avoid getting any commoner on him.

Making it through the press, Huggle and Von Strauss reached the tent's porch. The guards formed up behind them and held back the crowd. Thin arms continued pushing squares of paper through the gaps in the wall of muscle like an evangelical giant squid armed with a never-ending supply of soul saving pamphlets.

Von Strauss lifted the corner of the entrance flap and looked back at the crowd. 'Is that not wonderful, Huggle? Simply by my presence I am able to distract these poor wretches from the pointlessness of their worthless lives. I dare say many of them will remember this day until they die.'

'Sire, I think you stood on one of their heads back there.'

'Did I? How excellent. Far better than an autograph. I am sure he will be the envy of all his friends.'

The scary thing, Huggle thought, is that he really believes that.

'However, nice as this is, it does not detract from the squalor I am being forced to live in due to those damned monks.'

Von Strauss ducked inside his tent.

Huggle followed. His stomach lurched forward as he was pulled through the magical portal hidden inside. He stumbled forward, his feet skidding across the polished marble floor. Not for the first time that day, he felt more than a little bit sick.

The Whizzabang-Go had been made to Conrad's exact specifications and was the latest thing in glamping chic. The mages at Wig-Wow! embroidered the canvas with a magical transportation spell which, when properly aligned, created a portal to Conrad's summer hunting lodge. It turned a five man tent into a four storey mansion with extensive grounds, a boating lake and a great view of Cherrybark Forest.

Von Strauss strode down the central passage, discarding his cloak and gloves into the hands of waiting footmen. 'Just look at this place. Marble busts went out of style months ago. I told Father the place needed renovating. I mean, these doors. Oak? What am I? A style deficient pauper?'

Half right, thought Huggle.

He caught up to Von Strauss in the study. One wall was lined with expensive leather bound books. Most had never been read, but then that wasn't what Von Strauss bought them for. Above these, the mounted heads of all manner of fantastical creatures stared down with glass marble eyes. The far wall was taken up by a huge stone fireplace. Von Strauss slipped into his Yeti fur slippers and sank down into his green wingback chair. His right arm rested on a Cyclops head, which had been set into a table. After his bodyguards dispatched the creature, Conrad had its skull made into his drinks cabinet.

'All this waiting is quite intolerable. Have we received any reply from our last message to the temple?' He pushed the eye of the Cyclops and the top of its head slowly swung open, revealing a crystal decanter of the finest Hebrian whiskey and a monogrammed glass.

'No, sire,' replied Huggle, taking up his place at the tattered old desk in the corner. It was so covered in unopened letters that it reminded Huggle of when he had worked in the complaints department of the Tyrant of Tuanington Spa (easily the most middle-class city in the land). There had been a big fireplace in that office too. One didn't need a pen, so much as a coal shovel.

'And how are the climbers coming along?' Von Strauss sipped on his whiskey. 'I trust they are still in the lead. I have not waited all this time to be beaten to the prize by the riff-raff outside'

'Yes, sire. Francis d'Rou was closest behind our team, however his men suffered a slight setback when one of their climbers woke up last night, forgot the tent he was in was hanging from the cliff face, and went outside to relieve himself. He didn't hit anyone on the way down, but it did take quite some time to clean up.'

'And how much longer till they reach the summit?'

'I received a message from Master Climber Bront this morning which said they hoped to be at the top in three days, barring any misadventure.'

'That is acceptable I suppose. But tell Bront if he does not reach the top by then I will send some of my personal guard up to provide a bit of extra motivation. If someone else kills that dragon before me, I will not look kindly on him. It is, after all, only right that the greatest prize go to the greatest hero.'

'Yes, sire.'

'And what of these rumours that the monks are trying to recruit a guardian for the beast? Has any fool taken up the position?'

'Not that I am aware of. I can't see them having much success filling that position. Every hero worth his salt is here already, trying to kill it. I doubt there has been a greater gathering of people so adept at removing heads from shoulders outside of the annual executioners' conference in Sorn.'

'Good.' Von Strauss polished off the last of his drink and set the glass back into the Cyclops head. The taste of glory was wet on his lips. He looked up at the empty mount above the fire. The plaque read 'The Last Dragon'.

'After all,' he added, 'suicide is such a waste of a life.'

CHAPTER TEN

Orus, Ambrose and Thunder had made good progress through the night, arriving at the Worm-mound a few hours before sun-up. They made camp on a small hillock overlooking the heroes' tent city. Its chaotic sprawl curled around the solitary mountain, the light from a thousand torches washing against the round rock face. Beyond the tents, scaffold towers gripped at the sheer wall. The sound of creaking timbers and ongoing building carried across the sky, mingling, as it did so, with the drunken singing of those heroes and bodyguards and mercenaries and hunters yet to turn in. High above it all, crowning the night in flame and fire, the plateau of the Worm-mound glowed orange and red.

'That's the lava lake,' said Ambrose, following Orus's gaze upwards. 'The mountain used to be a volcano. It's dormant now, but lava still bubbles up from the reservoir underneath and collects on the top. Our temple is inside, built from old channels in the rock.'

'Uh huh,' said Orus. While the idea of building a house of religion inside a volcano seemed pretty mad to him, looking out at the forces arrayed against him, he couldn't help but feel it was still saner than the challenge he was supposed to be undertaking. 'And how many monks did you say there were?'

'Thirty-three, including me,' said Ambrose. 'We'll be there to help you.'

Well, that was a start, thought Orus. Everyone knows that mystic monks hiding in mountain fortresses tended to be trained in all manner of mystical martial arts. 'And are you good at fighting?' he asked.

'Fighting? Oh, no. We won't actually be fighting with you. Our Order is bound by a vow of non-violence. That's why we need you.'

'So, when you say 'help'…?'

'We'll pray for you.'

'Great. I don't suppose you could fight this once, and then ask for forgiveness afterwards?'

'I don't think it works that way,' said Ambrose.

Shouldn't be a problem. In my experience, it doesn't work the other way either.

'But the dragon is in there?' Orus did have that going for him. Huge scaly monsters do tend to tip the other kind of scales in their direction. 'And it's the big fire breathing type, yes?'

'Ah,' said Ambrose. 'That's the other thing I need to tell you about…'

The knot which had been growing in Orus's stomach since their flight from the All Seasons Tavern took up the ends of his long intestine, ready to add another bend.

'…You see, the thing is, the dragon hasn't actually hatched yet. We are hoping it will soon though, if that helps.'

'When you say "hatched", are you using some kind of mystical religious metaphor?' asked Orus, feeling the knot tighten.

'In a way. The hatching of a dragon is a deeply symbolic event, representing cycles of creation and

65

destruction. But it is also a not-metaphor, in that, for the moment at least, you will be guarding what is, essentially, and exactly, an egg.'

Orus gulped as the colonic half-hitch tightened around his bowels. Deep down, he knew he really should have expected this. Deeper down, his stomach gurgled a familiar 'I told you so'. If life had taught him anything, it was that given the unlimited possibilities the future could hold, the chances of the one you get being the one you want were as close to zero as made no difference. If he was an optimist he might have found the unravelling of the infinite possibilities of the universe quite beautiful, but as he was more of a realist, he found it much more practical to ignore the majority of the cosmic quilt and focus on avoiding the strands that included him being smashed to a pulp or chopped into little bits.

There was still one option. He could just give up. He didn't have to admit it was because he was scared. Just come up with a good excuse, hand over the jade coin and slink off to find a more manageable quest. He was probably doing a much more worthy hero out of a job by continuing anyway. And, wasn't getting rid of dragons a good thing? They didn't have the best reputation.

'And,' he asked, tentatively testing the waters of cowardice, 'what if I fail?'

'Oh that's easy. The end of the world. Or, the end of magic at least. Which will mean the end of the world for a lot of people, and a lot of not-people,' replied Ambrose rather chirpily. 'I don't understand it fully myself, but the High Council and the Grandmaster are quite positive on that one. I'm sure they'll explain it when we get to the temple. But I doubt that'll happen. After all, this is nothing compared to some of the quests you told us about last night. If you can't save the dragon, no-one can.'

So that was his quest: save the world. How hard could it be?

You get used to it.

CHAPTER ELEVEN

Orus woke up early. If he was going to make it through the camp around the mountain he wanted to do it as quietly as possible. He approached Ambrose's prone form and gave it a nudge with his foot. The monk pulled the hood of his robe further down over his face and let out a groan.

'Five more minutes, master.'

Not even growing up in an isolated religious sect could break a teenage boy's natural aversion to early mornings. But Orus knew what to do. Tag had been a late riser too. Dragons he wasn't so sure about, but teenagers he could handle.

One impromptu shower from his water skin later and Ambrose was up and ready to go.

To Thunder's great relief, Orus decided it would be best to walk from here. He still had to carry most of their gear but after the previous day's burden this was a distinct improvement in his situation.

The sea of tents washed around the Worm-mound on all sides. The channels between the canvas were filled with servants rushing back and forth with plates of breakfast. Orus took a moment to scan across the camp to gain an idea of the task ahead. You could have filled two bestiaries with all the heraldic animals on display in the flags topping the biggest tents.

Back in his day hardly anyone had a standard, let alone their own coat of arms. A horse tail on a stick or a mouldy old goat skull on a spear was about as much trouble as anyone bothered with. Big flags only got in the way. But then, in his day heroes didn't have a standard bearer and heralds to carry the things around. And not just heralds. Most of the tents had guards as well. That wasn't right, he thought. What sort of hero has bodyguards? Might as well just bring an army and be done with it. Time to show them what a real hero looked like.

He hitched up his trousers, tried to suck in his gut and puffed out his chest. 'Come on then, the early bird gets the wor... sorry... saves the worm. Stick by me, lad. I'll get you back to your temple safe,' he said, slapping Ambrose firmly on the back.

After picking Ambrose up from the mud, they headed down one of the main thoroughfares leading into the camp. Seeing as none of the assembled heroes had made it up to the temple yet, and so didn't know what the dragon monks actually looked like, they were able to pass through the outskirts without much trouble.

Now that they were down in the meat and bones of the place, Orus realised camp wasn't really the right word for the settlement. It was far too sturdy for that. It was more like a town and an expanding one at that. On all sides of the road yet more tents were being erected. The morning traffic got thicker as they moved further in. A double line of wagons ran up each side of the street. On one side they were heading towards the mountain laden with everything from weapons and armour to cattle and poultry. On the opposite side empty carts rolled back up the slope and out of the camp.

Bouncing between the two lanes like bluebottles

stuck in a jar, street vendors buzzed around the new arrivals, trying to offload their own guaranteed dragon slaying sure thing.

'Here ya're, sir. For your master.' One of the entrepreneurs thrust a dripping brown slab under Orus's nose. 'Best there is, no word of a lie. Fix that dragon right up, this will. Only two pennies.'

The smell of honey forced itself so far up Orus's nostrils he wondered if the brown slab might be a very well-disguised bee. 'What is it?' he asked, pushing the slab back from his face.

'It's a flap-jack. Dragon size. Auntie Bunce's best. Just what you need against dragons.'

Orus reached out and gave it a cautionary squeeze. It had all the give of a well-fired brick. 'What do you do, hit them with it?'

'Na ya great lug. Ya feed it to them. Gets all in their teeth and they can't open their mouth. Then you just walk up and lop its head off. Easy-peasy.'

Orus thought about this for a moment and then thought about dragons. 'What about the claws? And the spiky tail? And the horns? Wouldn't it just kill you with them?'

The street vendor stopped for a second to consider this. Come to think of it, there did tend to be more to a dragon than just a big mouth. Still, he wasn't going to be put off. 'Never had any complaints.'

'I bet you haven't,' replied Orus. After all, it is very hard to write a strongly worded letter if your arms have been ripped off.

'What about some armour then. I've got a suit that'll see a dragon right. All covered in spikes see, so it can't get a hold of ya. Like a hedgehog. The more it tries, the more it'll hurt itself. Then you just walk up, give it a kick in the wotsits and ya're all done.'

Orus didn't know much about hedgehogs. One

point he was quite sure on, however, was that they were flammable.

'No complaints about that one either, I'm guessing?' he said, pushing past.

'Shouldn't you have told him you're here to protect the dragon?' asked Ambrose, with all the innocence of a cow that accidentally sat on a mouse.

The air around them took on the consistency of treacle. Orus felt the camp's collective consciousness swivel from the mountain to focus on him. He hadn't felt this awkward since he complained about his sore back at Mavis's pre-natal class.

'Ha, ha, ha.' He gave Ambrose another hearty slap on the back. 'Only until it is my turn to have a go at it. That beast won't know what hit it.'

That did it. The crowd turned back to its own business, satisfied that the small fat man did look mad, but not that mad.

Orus beckoned Ambrose down to a height where he could whisper in his ear. 'I think it would be better if we didn't let on about the protecting bit until we get to the temple. Seeing as I haven't been formally named as the guardian yet. It would be more, traditional, for your Grandmaster to make the announcement don't you think? Got to do these things properly.'

'Yes, yes. Quite right. Sorry. I was getting ahead of myself a bit. We shouldn't mention it until it is official.'

'Good. So until then let's just try and keep a low profile.'

'Right,' agreed Ambrose. 'Hey! Look at that!'

On the left, past the next tent, a large, flat open space had been left clear. On the right hand side, closest to the mountain, a group of troubadours were playing loud music, backed up by thumping war drums. In the centre of the practice area, rows and rows of bare-chested warriors were moving in time to the music.

At the end closest to Orus and Ambrose, the warrior Orus assumed to be the warband's leader was facing his comrades and directing their movements. If it was a war dance, it was like none Orus had seen before.

The crowd jumped up, stretching their feet wide apart and clapping their hands above their heads. Then they crouched down until their hands touched the ground before shooting their feet back until their legs were at full stretch. All at once, they brought their knees up to touch their elbows and then with a loud shout of 'Oooft!' they leapt back to standing. Over and over again they did this, all in time with the music.

The sweat poured off the warriors and the noise of grunting, clapping and straining filled the air. As Orus and Ambrose watched, the chief warrior led his band through other weird movements: running on the spot, then skipping sideways like a crab, squatting down and jumping up high. The effect of so many people moving together started to make Orus feel queasy (although the tight bright leggings the warriors were all wearing might have had something to do with this feeling as well). Ambrose looked at him excitedly. He was meant to be the expert. He'd better think of a reason for this behaviour.

'Must be a war dance. A lot of the island tribes down south do them before battle. Asking favours of the gods,' Orus said, proud of such a convincing deduction.

'Isn't it Strobics?'

'Strobics?'

'Strobics. The exercise method invented and endorsed by Conrad Von Strauss. I thought all heroes used it now. It's supposed to be great for your cardio.'

It was Orus's turn to look quizzical now. He'd never heard of Strobics, or this Von Strauss character, or a cardio for that matter. Time for a bluff. 'Oh, Strobics. So it is. Looks very similar to island war dances though.'

'I think it is the calve-buster routine. It's what he

used to get fit before chasing down the Unicorn of the Wandering Woods.'

'So it is,' said Orus, gently pulling Ambrose away and back to the road. 'I never liked that routine much myself. I always thought it was a bit unfair on the calf.'

*

Meanwhile, Huggle was at the foot of the mountain inspecting the night's progress. The wooden scaffolds were growing by the hour, reaching ever further towards the summit of the Worm-mound. The site was a hive of activity, not to mention health and safety nightmares. Great bundles of wood were being hoisted up to the tops of the towers by teams of mules trundling round a pulley wheel. Blacksmiths were hammering away at blunted and broken tools, while up and down the precarious scaffolds teams of builders scurried over every surface like ants across the wicker wall of a picnic basket. The noise was a chorus of braying animals, clonking tools and every kind of foul language you would expect from tired men working with big hammers.

The towers themselves were huge, rickety affairs, so tall now that they had to be attached to the rock face with thick metal staples. At the foot of each one, a flag bearing the heraldic symbol of the hero paying for it fluttered in the mid-morning breeze. Conrad's tower was of course the biggest, and had the biggest flag: an elaborate gold CVS monogram on a field of purple, held in place by two rampant lions, also in gold.

Huggle tried not to look at the tops of the towers. His job made him ill enough as it was. Bront's morning report should be on its way down. Von Strauss wanted to know when they were near the top so he could be there when they finished. He was to be the first onto the plateau.

The message would come down on the bucket chain. Mainly used for passing up nails and passing down broken tools, it was a great way of ensuring Huggle didn't need to scale the tower twice a day. They had tried dropping the messages down tied to a rock, but this had not gone well. Everyone on site was now required to wear helmets at all times.

As he stood and watched the mysterious world of manual labour, three figures appeared at the edge of the site. One fat, one tall and one donkey. Probably here to try and sell the beast to the pulley teams, Huggle thought. Still, there was something familiar about the tall one. Something about the robes he was wearing.

Before the wheels of his brain could clock into place the wheels of the bucket chain brought the morning report creaking past his face. He took out the capsule and retrieved the note from inside. The message read: 'Rock fall during night. Lost twelve yards and two men. Now in second place'.

Huggle sighed, reached for his handkerchief and dabbed his rapidly perspiring brow. How was he going to explain this to Von Strauss? He knew building the tower was dangerous work but he still hated messages like this. Second place. Conrad would tear a strip off him for sure. Or worse, he might be made to climb up and help. Huggle had no head for heights at the best of times. But if Von Strauss wasn't the one to slay the dragon their business strategy was finished. He hated working for the oaf, it was true. Still, if he kept at it, kept plugging away, it would all pay off in the end. It had to. Otherwise, it just wouldn't be fair.

Lost in dark thoughts, his padding feet took him away from the scaffolds and round to the other side of the mountain. There wasn't much round here. The craggy rock face wasn't suitable for climbing so it had become the camp tip. He flopped down on a discarded wheelbarrow, wrung out his handkerchief and then dabbed his brow again. What was he going to do?

The sounds of mumbled conversation broke him

out of his trance. There was no-one else around, as far as he could see. He strained his large ears to the source of the noise. It was coming from behind the dung heap.

'Thank the gods for that,' said one voice. 'I don't fancy going up one of those towers.'

'Now, where is that secret rock,' said another.

Huggle crept to the peak of the dung heap, trying to keep as much of himself off the surface as possible. Reaching the top, he looked down on the three figures from earlier. The donkey was just a donkey and the fat man looked like a servant, possibly a gardener, but the tall one: he had to be a Dragon Monk. He was dressed just like the boy in the dungeon had described.

The monk glanced back over his shoulder. Huggle pressed himself into the muck and held his breath. The monk turned back to the mountainside and took hold of a triangle-shaped rock. He twisted it until the triangle pointed upwards, then pushed it hard. The rock slid back, disappearing into the Worm-mound.

Nothing happened.

Then, slowly, with a sound of creaking ropes and rushing water, a section of the mountain the width of a small wagon split in half and folded inwards. Huggle watched the three figures enter the secret gateway, melting into the murk within. The doors closed after them, leaving no sign that they had ever been there.

So, that was how they did it. Since arriving, Huggle had been pondering how the monks survived holed up in a lump of rock all this time with no way of getting food or supplies. Some people said they had flying machines they used to go to towns in the mountains during the night but he had seen no evidence of that.

He had to tell Conrad.

CHAPTER TWELVE

'Not much farther now.' Ambrose pointed up the smooth stony slope that led up from the secret door. 'This passage runs up to the store room.'

It was a long trek from the bottom. Orus's feet were beginning to ache, his new socks rubbing against his old boots.

'Most of these tunnels were created by the molten rock pushing up through the mountain,' said the Dragon Monk. 'We had to finish them off, putting in places for torches, extending some areas, ventilation. But most of this engineering was done by nature. Quite amazing really. In some places you can actually see the magma flowing through the new channels just on the other sides of the walls. See, there.'

In the dim light ahead, a section of wall glowed dull red. Orus tried to calculate his chances of being able to outrun any sudden leaks. They were not good. Even the sewer pipe was better than this.

'Do you ever have any cave-ins?'

'From time to time. Normally when the alchemists have been playing about with things. The last one was a few years ago now. The ceiling of the Hall of Remembrance sprung a leak. Brother Tokus was very lucky. Well, sort of lucky.'

'Was he hurt?'

'Hurt, no. He's dead. He was sweeping up in the Grandmaster's alcove at the time. It is where previous Grandmasters are commemorated. He was brushing down a newly installed plinth at the time. Now he's the only person under eighty to be buried there. The lava preserved him quite well too. I'll show him to you later if you like?'

'No, that's okay.' Orus wiped an arm across his brow. It suddenly felt very hot in the long, bare tunnel.

They entered the main temple complex through the storeroom. There wasn't much to be said about it. It was a pretty dull room full of crates and barrels. They might well have been full of useful things, but really play no part in the rest of the story so aren't worth worrying about.

From the storeroom they entered the Great Hall. Orus let out a workman's whistle (the kind that can be roughly translated as 'Jeepers, this place is worth a fortune in re-painting contracts') as he took in the cathedral-size cavern. One end housed a semi-circular altar space. At the other, behind a half opened set of brass doors, stone steps led up to the plateau. The vaulted ceiling was held up by two rows of pillars, each individual construction carved into the shape of different species of dragon. Golden flames from the mouths of each of the stone beasts cast light out into the vast room.

Orus, Ambrose and Thunder entered from an archway a third of the way up the long wall to the left of the altar. Orus could see several other arched passageways leading off from the other side, each one throwing a shaft of torchlight across the hall. He had never been in a place quite like it. The Prince's banqueting hall could have fitted inside four times over. Even the Cromalot Mead Hall wasn't this size. It was the sort of building only someone with a lot of slaves, or some people with a lot of faith, could build.

'This must have taken decades. The flagstones alone. There must be thousands of them. It took me three days to lay a garden path,' he said, focusing on the only part of the construction he could closely relate to.

'Why were you building a garden path?' asked Ambrose.

'Oh, er… It was part of a quest, a long time ago.' Smooth going, Orus. You've only been here thirty seconds and you've nearly blown it. 'It was part of a set of trials I had to complete for King Philip of Macadamia.'

'Seems a bit of a strange quest?'

'Well, King Philip was a bit nuts. He trapped me in his castle and wouldn't let me out until I completed five trials. There was the path, then I had to fight off some giant birds roosting in the castle roof, the dwarf ghosts in the cellars that were undermining the walls, the castle gate which had been magically sealed shut. Oh, yes, then there was the bog monster that would cover the carpets in mud every evening.'

'That is a lot of curses. Did you beat them all?'

'Yes,' replied Orus. They were all on the to-do list, he told himself, so it wasn't really a lie, other than the castle bit. 'Although, sometimes the bog monster still gets in.'

Emerging from a passageway opposite, another Dragon Monk shuffled towards them.

'Initiate Ambrose, is that you?' This monk's robes had an extra band of gold around the cuffs. Like Ambrose, he was tall and thin. However, unlike Ambrose's floppy frame, the new arrival's figure was all exact measurements and sharp pointed corners.

'Humble greetings, Brother Amphis,' Ambrose said, bowing his head slightly. 'I am back from the outside.'

'So I see. How fortunate,' the other monk said in the sort of tone a dentist might use when saying 'this won't hurt a bit', before picking out the largest of his drills. 'I had started to think you might not make it back, what with all that is going on down there.'

'And I've brought the hero to defend our holy dragon.'

'I look forward to meeting him.' Brother Amphis turned to Orus. 'Is your master going to be much longer? Only, time is of the essence.'

The blood started to spread across the web of broken capillaries in Orus's weather-beaten face.

'No, no, Brother. This *is* the hero. He is the one the Grandmaster sent me for.'

'Is it?' Brother Amphis inspected Orus as if he were a piece of homework. 'Yes, I imagine that is correct. Forgive me, sir. You must be of great talent for our most wise Grandmaster to have such faith in you. And your name is?'

'Morris the Marauder,' answered Ambrose quickly.

'How quaint. Well, Sir Morris, if you could keep the marauding to a minimum while in the temple. It is such a chore to clean up afterwards.' Amphis made a noise that might have been a laugh, had he been the kind of person who laughed, which he wasn't. He turned his red pen gaze on Thunder and their supplies. 'And this must be your trusty steed. He looks very... experienced. However, I am afraid animals are not permitted in the Great Hall. You may leave him in the storeroom with the rest of your equipment.'

Equipment! Bloody cheek.

Once Orus had managed to convince Thunder to remove his hoof from Brother Amphis's sandaled foot and secured the donkey in the storeroom, the limping monk led them across the Great Hall to the Grandmaster's study.

'Sorry about that,' said Orus. 'I'm sure he didn't mean it. His eyes aren't what they used to be, and with the gloom in here and all.'

'Hmm,' said Brother Amphis. Thoughts of vengeance didn't suit a godly man. Then again, technically speaking, the Dragon Monks didn't worship a specific deity. The devil, Brother Amphis always found, was in the detail.

'I could take Morris to the Grandmaster myself, Brother, if you need to go down to the healer?' said Ambrose.

'No. I will take you. It is best not to delay. And the Grandmaster may need my input. After all, he is a very busy man,' replied Brother Amphis, this time going for the plaque scaling hook.

*

Grandmaster Argus Bach was indeed busy. All morning he had been wrestling with a problem that, if not solved soon, could bring all his important work to a grinding halt.

The new tea urn was stuck on full power, kept boiling dry and was currently in danger of blowing its top. It was a Brewmaster 5-40: supposedly the greatest step forward in tea technology since a grandmother in Spits had suffered a minor fit while knitting a woolly hat for her grandson, and ended up with a hole for a spout. But right now, this central pillar of Grandmaster Bach's administrative policy was bouncing about on its fittings so much it looked like it was challenging the surrounding volcano to step outside and let off some steam.

This being the case, the first sight Orus had of the revered Grandmaster was of a small, dumpy, white-haired man wearing light blue and yellow polka-dot oven mitts, battling through a cloud of vapour.

Brother Amphis limped inside the Grandmaster's study with a surety that suggested this behaviour was far from unusual for the head of the Dragon Monks. 'Your Reverence, I have brought Initiate Ambrose and his hero for your blessing.'

'Hero? Oh yes, yes, that. Come in boys, come in. Nice to see you.' The Grandmaster finished re-filling the urn then picked up a mallet from his desk and gave the pipes a good clanking.

'Be with you in a second.'

Clank, clank. Clank, clank, clank.

The steam retreated.

'There, that's better. Have a seat.'

The Brewmaster 5-40 gurgled one last call of defiance. The Grandmaster raised the mallet again and gave it a hard look. This seemed to convince the tangle of brass plumbing to submit for the time being. It hadn't given up though; revenge – it knew – unlike tea, was best served cold.

Orus sat down in one of the large chairs facing the Grandmaster's cluttered desk. He reached into his pocket to check the jade coin was still there. It was. Now all he had to do was explain why he had come rather than Old Grimmer.

That is, he would do, when he could get a word in.

This is because, as Orus soon found out, having a conversation with Argus Bach was a lot like shepherding a flock of anecdotes. You had to be careful not to let one get away from the pack, because by the time you'd tracked it down another four or five would have broken off up the track into a nearby field of warm reminiscences.

'Ambrose, Ambrose, back from the outside already, good, good. How was it? See a lot of interesting sights I'll bet. I remember the first time I went out of the temple. Did you know I used to be one of the missionaries? Yes, yes, wouldn't guess it now. Up and down the lands, spreading the good news, looking out for new recruits. I once had to walk all the way to Hornbach, in winter too. It was luck that saved my skin that day. Luck and soup. I was frozen to the bone and nearly out of food when I stumbled across a traveller's camp. An old grass witch took me in and gave me a bowl of warm nettle soup. Wanted to keep me too, she did. Ha ha. My vows were stretched that night, I can tell you.'

Brother Amphis winced at his master's lack of formality.

Argus Bach paused and began to pat down his robes. Not finding what he was after, he went to speak, raised a finger in thought, stopped, then decided he really did need whatever he was after and dived into his desk's drawers. 'Now, now, now. I know I left them here somewhere.'

Brother Amphis cleared his throat and leaned towards the Grandmaster.

'No, Amphis, don't tell me. Don't tell me. I know where I put them.' Argus Bach began sifting through the jumbled pile of scrolls on his desk. 'First I was doing the accounts, then the letter to them down below. Then I needed to check…'

As Argus turned to inspect his bookshelf, Brother Amphis retrieved the Grandmaster's glasses from the tea trolley and put them down in the middle of the desk.

'Then,' continued Argus Bach, turning back to his desk, 'I had to calculate the cooling time. Ah ha! Here they are!'

He picked up the spectacles, rubbed them on the sleeve of his robe and put them on.

'Thought I'd lost them again, Amphis, didn't you? That's much better. Now, who's this you've brought me, Ambrose?'

'This is the hero that you sent me to bring back. The one that's going to help us save the dragon.'

'Is it?' Argus Bach looked Orus up and down and round about. 'You're looking a bit different to how I remember you. Still, retirement will do that to a man I hear.'

Orus's stomach gave a nervous gurgle. Better to straighten this out now.

'Actually, I didn't get a chance to explain to Ambrose, but I'm not Felgrim the Blade. Neither is he, come to think of it, not anymore. He goes by Old Grimmer now, not that that matters. We're friends from Ditch. I was heading out this way already, so he asked if I wouldn't mind stepping in for him this time. I hope that is okay?'

Ambrose shot him a shocked glance but Argus Bach just leaned back in his chair and smiled.

'A stand-in hero. Yes, I think that could still work. Any willing volunteer is better than none, considering what we are up against.'

'Your Reverence,' Brother Amphis was not smiling. It was one of the many things he did not believe in. 'How do we know this man is who he says? He could be an imposter. A ruse by those in the camp below.'

Argus Bach leaned forward and looked over Orus again. 'He could well be at that. He doesn't look like he is. Still, he could well be. How do we know you're really friends with Felgrim?'

Orus took the jade coin from his pocket and held it up. 'He gave me this to give to you.'

'My coaster!' Argus reached over the desk and took the jade disc from Orus. He picked up an empty mug and slipped it underneath. 'I knew he pinched it. The dragon sigil keeps the tea warm. Great little thing.'

'He could have stolen it,' suggested Brother Amphis.

'Could have done, could have done. Did he come with the donkey?'

'Yes,' added Amphis, clearly trying not to preface his agreement with the word 'regrettably'. 'I have had the animal tied up in the storeroom.'

'Ha, ha. Well that settles it. A fast hand might get one over on Felgrim but no-one could make Thunder go along with them without his help. The last time that donkey was here we had to postpone the festival of the Stoor Worm for two days because he decided to have a nap in the robing room, stubborn old toad that he is.' The Grandmaster reached over and shook Orus's hand. 'Pleased to meet you, substitute hero. What's your story then? Traditional, I hope. Not one of this modern lot?'

'Traditional? Yes. You could say that. Old fashioned might be more like it. I trained at Cromalot when I was young, then went out and had a fair few adventures. I've been taking a break for the last little while. But I'm all ready to get back into the swing of things now,' Orus said, injecting slightly more confidence into the statement than he felt. He was starting to think that entrusting a dangerous – possibly deadly – world saving mission to a part-time hero might not be such a great idea, especially for the hero.

It was lucky then, that Ambrose stepped in to retell all the stories Orus had spouted out at the All Seasons. There were even more than he remembered.

'And, if that wasn't enough, he's already saved me from a band of vicious robbers back at the tavern,' Ambrose said with a final flourish. He had edged so far forward on his chair that it was only the front of the Grandmaster's desk that stopped him hitting the floor.

'Is that right? Well thank you for looking after him, Morris the Marauder. I don't normally let initiates out of the temple. All the missionary brothers are abroad at the moment, so I'm glad Ambrose had you to look after him.'

'Yes, it is good that you made it back, Initiate,' said Brother Amphis. 'I've been keeping a tally of the chores you have missed while away. If you would start by–'

'Not now, Amphis,' said the Grandmaster, waving away his assistant. 'Give the boy a break.'

'Initiates must complete their chores, Grandmaster. It is the rules.'

Brother Amphis loved rules. Next to himself, they were his favourite thing in all the world. He would have married them, had there not been rules against it. He had been sent to the Dragon Temple as a child after helpfully pointing out to his father and mother all the mistakes they had made in their tax return. There were whole sections of the accounts for the family shipping and cave tour guiding business not declared. Not getting the column of ticks and gold star sticker he had expected, he took his corrections to an expert: the local sheriff. But abandonment didn't dent his enthusiasm. On arriving at the Worm-mound he had dedicated himself to learning all the tenets, rules, bylaws and decrees of the Order off by heart.

It was only later that he found out Argus Bach and the other top monks didn't have quite the same respect for the rules as he did. Still, that would all change when he was Grandmaster.

'No time for that now. We're on a deadline.'

Brother Amphis did remember. The death of magic: he was not overly concerned. Magic, as far as he could see, was the ultimate rule breaker. It was for people who were too lazy to do things properly and had only come about because the first set of such people in Drift were the gods. Far better to be rid of it, he thought. Then things would finally start working properly. Given the obvious quality of the champion delivered to them, it looked like the end of magic was in safe hands.

'So,' Argus Bach turned to Orus again. 'You'll need to be hearing about the quest. Do you have the book, Amphis?'

'Here it is, Your Reverence.'

The Grandmaster took the scale-covered tome from Amphis.

'That's the one. See, handy to have around this lad,' he said, jerking a thumb over his shoulder while giving Orus and Ambrose a sly wink. 'Now, let me just get the right page. Yes. See lad!'

He spun the book round on the desk so Orus could see it.

'That is what this is all about.'

The picture was of dragons. Only these dragons were not doing the things Orus normally heard about dragons doing. No burning down villages or carrying off livestock. There were lots of different kinds too. Not just your general every day, run of the mill, giant, bat-winged flying lizards. In the centre of the scene, a brown, moss-covered dragon was shown under a hilltop forest. It was made of living roots, and water spewed from its mouth to nurture the trees above. Gnomes were living in the trees, busily building their stores for winter. In the sea, a dark green dragon, shaped like a stretched out tear drop, pushed an iceberg from the path of a family of water nymphs. In a cave, a black dragon with bright yellow eyes scratched gems from a rock face. From there they fell into a river and were collected by dwarves with pans and sieves. From under a ridge of mountains, a red dragon with a golden belly blasted magical fire out of the cone of a volcano. The ice at the top of the volcano melted and turned into rivers, feeding the lands below with water. Where the magical flames touched the rocks they rose up to become trolls. And in the dark sky over the sea, a thin silver dragon held a light to the stars, pointing the way to a ship full of sailors.

'A bit of a simplification,' said Argus Bach, turning the book back to himself. 'But you get the idea. You see, this world needs dragons. It needs them to keep going. The gods didn't do a very good job of putting it all together and their fix was magic. Only thing is, magic gets used up. Or maybe not used up. Changed. Dragons change it back. In their bellies they convert what they eat into food and energy. That energy, it's pure magic. Then they release it back into the world. Without them, there'll just keep getting less and less of it in the world. Magic will drain away, and once it's all gone we won't be able to get it back. That is why we need to save this one. That is why we need you.'

A loud whistle from the Brewmaster interrupted the explanation. The lid jangled violently and small jets of steam erupted from the pipe-work, intent on scalding any who dared tried to stop their breakout.

'Damn thing.' The Grandmaster sprang from his chair and started clanking away with the mallet again. 'Only had it a month and it's never been right.'

'Do you mind if I have a go?' asked Orus, sizing up the brass contraption. The Prince had the earlier model Brewmaster. Many was the time Orus had helped to retrieve it from the moat after it blew itself out of the kitchen window.

'It won't do any good,' said Brother Amphis. 'It must be a problem with the manufacturing process. I put it together personally, in exact accordance with the instructions provided.'

'Well that'll be your problem right there,' replied Orus. Instructions implied the world worked the way it was supposed to. A man like Orus knew they were not to be trusted.

An extra washer, a new hole drilled in the lid and some precision thumps with the mallet later, the whistling stopped, the lid calmed down and the jets of steam relented.

'See,' Argus jabbed Brother Amphis in the ribs with his elbow. 'The right stuff this lad. What did I tell you? Come on, boys, I'll take you to see the egg.'

CHAPTER THIRTEEN

Back at the foot of the Worm-mound a crowd had begun to amass near the manure heap. Groups of shifty-looking men stood in suspiciously nonchalant poses doing their best to give the impression that they definitely weren't up to something. And if you thought differently, one of the things they weren't up to would be knocking you about a bit until you forgot what you hadn't seen them not doing.

Huggle stood by the secret door, clipboard in hand, ticking off the selected members of Conrad's entourage. Once he had told his greased and diseased master about the secret entrance, Von Strauss had him gather up his most essential servants so that, in his words, he would have a suitable sized audience for his victory. The fact that half of these essential personnel were heavily armed warriors with enough weapons between them to decorate a large regimental museum was, Von Strauss explained, to ensure the safety of his other, more delicate staff.

As well as the warriors, Huggle checked off a team of sketchers working with Master Lenz, two chefs (in case Von Strauss needed to stop for a snack on the way up to the temple), four pairs of armour bearers each carrying a different set of supposedly dragon proof armour, three healers, one alchemist proficient in fire warding magic, the wafters, a hairstylist, and, finally, nine trumpeters, who were to play out his victory salute after he vanquished the beast.

As Von Strauss had told Huggle many times before, it takes a lot of people to be a lone hero these days.

Luckily, Conrad's roll call was of such size that he could spare these few servants and still maintain enough of a presence in camp not to give the game away to the other heroes. While Huggle was not very enthused at the thought of this quest as a whole, now that he had put so much work into it he was damned if he would let that fool mess it up.

So as not to arouse suspicion, he had convinced his master to carry out his daily routine as normal until all was in readiness.

The cockerel wrangler was the last to be ticked off the list. One of the merchants in the camp had told him that some species of dragon are terrified of the birds. Apparently caravans crossing the Cracked Wastes still carry a few of them to ward off any basilisks or sand dragons they might encounter. Apparently they were one hundred per cent effective. Not one single complaint received.

Huggle's ears caught the sound of a growing commotion. It was coming this way and he didn't have to strain his brain long to guess at what it might be.

He ran (well actually he more chugged – not being built for running, especially not uphill) up the path that led back to the sea of tents. Taking a sharp right onto one of the boarded walkways, he was confronted by the sight of his master's attempt at doing things quietly. This involved being followed by a large crowd of admirers and autograph-seekers, all of whom were cheering and shouting Conrad's name.

Von Strauss himself swaggered down the walkway towards Huggle in full purple and gold armour, blowing kisses at, and avoiding being touched by, his adoring fans.

Huggle chugged up to meet him, ducking under the accompanying wafters.

'Ah, my most trusted servant,' Von Strauss said using his public friendly voice. 'Just look at the multitudes that have turned out to wish me well for the quest.'

'I can see them, sire.' Huggle gave a quick wave before leaning in close to his master's ear. 'However, I thought that we had agreed to keep this quiet. We don't want your opposition finding out and stealing any of the glory.'

Conrad ducked under an outstretched baby before it could dribble on him. 'Do not worry yourself, poor little Huggle. By the time the others get here I will be well on my way to victory, and besides they won't be able to follow me anyway.'

'Sire, what if one of your lovely fans shows them the secret door?'

'Again, worry not my portly pen-pusher. Your master has thought of that too. You can be sure that even if those sluggish fools manage to open the way, they will not be able to follow me.'

'Why not?'

'Because you are going to stop them. Now wave to the people. That's it. Good. You won't see a day like this again.'

He was right, thought Huggle. If I have to stand in that doorway when all the other heroes turn up and tell them they aren't getting in, I won't see any kind of day again.

CHAPTER FOURTEEN

Argus led Orus, Ambrose and Brother Amphis back to the Great Hall. This took considerably longer than getting to the Grandmaster's study had, owing to Argus stopping to introduce Orus to every monk they passed. Every meeting was then followed by a story about the Grandmaster and the other monk swiping pastries from the kitchen when they were younger, or smuggling contraband back from missionary missions. And it wasn't just the people Orus was introduced to. Notable parts of the interior architecture were also a frequent cause for a halt, particularly those that served as places to hide the aforementioned stolen pastries.

'And if you leave all of these doors open and sit in the back left corner of the prayer room at morning mass,' the Grandmaster gestured down a corridor to the left, 'you can catch the most brilliant smell of the scones being prepared for breakfast.'

Brother Amphis's stern expression told Orus that he did not often sit in the back left corner of the prayer room.

They came back into the Great Hall and the Grandmaster led them to the altar. The semi-circular wall that faced it was covered in a long stone frieze. The carvings showed a world full of dragons. These were accompanied by what must have been the first Dragon Monks. Some were busy building temples, while others were studying at the feet of the creatures themselves.

'And this, Morris, is the history of the Dragon Order.' Argus Bach pointed to the frieze.

'The *secret* history,' interrupted Brother Amphis.

'Quite right, Amphis.' Argus smiled and clapped an arm around his starched assistant's shoulders. 'This, Morris, is the *secret* history of the Dragon Order. Long ago, when the world was young–'

'Your Reverence,' Brother Amphis stepped free of the Grandmaster's arm and came to stand in front of Orus, blocking his view. 'I meant to suggest that perhaps you should not entrust our secret history to this man. After all, he has already practiced a deceit on Initiate Ambrose and we know almost nothing about him.'

Argus paused to consider this. He turned to face Orus. The jolliness drained from his features and was replaced by a stern, cold look. He cleared his throat to show he was now being serious. He even took off his glasses to make sure the message was coming across. 'Morris the Marauder, Brother Amphis is correct. Before we go any further I must ask you this very important question: how do you like your tea?'

'Grandmaster!' snapped Amphis. 'This is serious.'

'That is why I am asking, Brother. I could ask him all sorts about his background but if he was a spy or a liar he'd just make it up, wouldn't he? Now, how he takes his tea. You can tell a lot from someone with a question like that. Where he's from, how he thinks, if he is married. Ask what type of biscuit he likes too and I could give you his whole family history. So hero, how do you like it?'

Orus wondered if this was a trick. Some sort of secret society test to find out if he was the sort of hero they

were looking for (and in a way it was). He tried to think
how Grimmer liked his tea, or some of the great heroes
from history. Sadly most of the sagas didn't go into that
kind of detail. 'With ale in it' would probably be the sort of
thing most of the heroes he had grown up hearing about
would have said. On the other hand, lying had not worked
out very well so far. Better to stick to the truth.

'Eh, bit of milk, bit of sugar, if there is any.'

'See,' said Argus. 'Adaptable, sensible, married –
the key is in the amount of sugar – economical. Probably a
dunker too, aren't you? I thought so. That all sounds good
to me. There, see Amphis, need to know anything else?'

'Quite, Your Reverence.'

'So, on with the story. This tells the secret history
of the Dragon Order and many of the great dragons of the
early ages. Great stonework, isn't it? It was made by Brother
Hestus. Long before my time, Hestus. He did a lot of the
early carvings. Must have had a steady hand. Anyway this
here...'

Argus Bach went on to tell the history of the
Dragon Order. To avoid the multitude of digressions and
anecdotes, a short summary will be presented: he explained
how the wars of the first gods had rained magical energy
down on Drift, creating the infinite variety of life. The
dragons were born of this and they fed on it, growing into
all different shapes and sizes, each matched to a particular
environment. When the head of the gods eventually had
enough of being kept up all night by the constant cosmic
bickering, he told his warring offspring that if they couldn't
share Drift, then none of them would get it. With the war
over, the rain of magic stopped and Drift settled into an
equilibrium, a balanced stew of equal parts magical and
normal. But with so many creatures, plants, animals,
peoples and even pieces of geography reliant on magical
energy and no new energy coming down from above,
dragons with their ability to extract magic from their food

and expel its raw form back into the world, became essential to the multi-coloured, multi-material, no two squares quite matching and some not even squares, patchwork quilt of creation.

Unfortunately this knowledge was gradually forgotten. As the peoples of Drift flourished they increasingly came into conflict with these scaly engines of existence. The Order was created to protect the dragons and to try to remind the world about the need for them. When dragons were killed, they would often leave young or eggs behind. The Order would collect these and look after them until they were ready to be released back into the world. In this way, they had kept the balance for thousands of years. Now, however, this new breed of heroes, each wishing to outdo the others, had hunted the creatures to the brink, even attacking the temples of the Order to get at the dragons sheltered within.

'So there it is,' said the Grandmaster, wrapping up his memory lane marathon. 'We haven't heard from another temple in over a year. Haven't heard of a living dragon in much longer. And by the looks of outside, no-one is going to be hearing about us if we don't pull our socks up and do something. That is why we need you, Morris.'

The Grandmaster took a stone peg from his robe and pushed it into a matching hole in the frieze. The wall slid back and a wave of dry heat rose up from the gap left behind. Orus could already feel bulbs of sweat forming on his head.

They stepped through the door and into a cauldron. They had entered the heart of the volcano. A vortex of molten rock and bubbling metal stretched from wall to wall. The churning veins of red and yellow twisted around each other like hot toffee on the spinners at the Ditch summer fare. Here and there, the slowing swirling mass would bulge in a great bubble, before bursting with a lacklustre pop, too hot to make a real effort, but still releasing a burp of superheated shimmering air.

Around the circumference of the cavern a precipitous ledge of rock jutted out across the fiery pit. From this platform, four chains held a glowing ball about the size of Orus's head suspended above the surface of the boiling rock.

The folding air made it hard to see properly, but it was clear that this was to be his charge. He hoped it came with some kind of heat-proof gloves.

Two monks approached from an alcove halfway around the ledge.

'Greetings and blessings, fellow Brothers,' said Amphis, bowing slightly.

'How do, Nidd? Alright Uff?' said the Grandmaster. 'Have you met Morris yet? Ha, no, of course you haven't. You two are never out of this furnace.'

Argus Bach turned back to Orus and Ambrose. 'I could tell you some good stories about these two. Nidd here is the grandson of the High Alchemist of Andrus. Now there was a sharp lad if ever there was one. We met, oh must have been fifty, no, fifty-five years ago, at the…'

The Grandmaster paused. Brother Amphis was fixing him with one of his PE teacher glares.

'… I'll tell you later. Anyway, this is Brother Uffington and Brother Niddhogg.'

Orus learned Nidd was an expert of dragon behaviour and had a sister in Meuly that sent him a new pair of socks every winter, while Uff was an expert in dragon biology but had a habit of forgetting to send his mother a birthday card.

'Hot down here, isn't it?' said Argus Bach. 'Could do with some ventilation I think. So Uff, Nidd, this is Morris. He's here to save the world.'

'Brave of you,' said Nidd, extending a blackened hand to Orus.

'Do you have a lot of experience looking after

dragon eggs?' asked Uff.

'I wouldn't say "a lot",' replied Orus.

'But he has nursed a thunderbird chick to adulthood,' said Ambrose. 'I heard him talk about in back at the Tavern.'

'What was that?' Orus tried to remember at what stage of the night that story had been invented.

Ambrose turned to the other monks. 'There was a cabal of witches and they carried Morris up to the top of a high mountain on their broomsticks and left him there to die. There was no way down until he found a thunderbird's nest. The mother was dead but the chick had just hatched. He nurtured it, catching creatures that lived on the rocks to feed it, until it was big enough to take his weight, then he climbed on its back and flew to safety.'

'You must have been up there for a long time,' said Brother Amphis. His eyes momentarily flicked to Orus's belly.

'Yes, well, I was a bit trimmer back in those days.'

'Excellent, excellent,' said Argus. 'See my boys, he's got fatherly instincts all over him. Now, Morris, Uff and Nidd here will go with you and the egg to make sure everything is okay. Lads, I think on this occasion I can absolve you of your vows of non-violence. That looks like a pretty nasty lot down below. I saw some dragon ivory hunters from Someto and you know how persistent they can be.'

'Reverence?' Uff and Nidd exchanged worried glances. They were inside monks, not missionaries. They never left the temple. The only fights they ever got into were with Brother Amphis over scorched library books.

'I heard that at one of the other temples, when those Sometos broke in and found there was no dragon they pulled out all the monks' teeth and tried to pass them off as baby dragon chompers. Nasty lot. Still, I'm sure Morris will look after you.'

'Actually Grandmaster…' started Uff.

'The thing is…' continued Nidd.

'We both,' they said together, exchanging glances to make sure they were staying on the same track, 'agreed to… help the Initiates… with cleaning out… the mouths of the dragon statues in the Great Hall.' The last word was almost shouted, so pleased were they that they had manage to come through as a pair.

Argus Bach scratched at his chin then slapped his hands together. 'Ah well. A promise is a promise. And it's good for the Brothers to show the Initiates how it is done. Very well. Brother Amphis, we all know how devilishly clever you are. Fancy taking on the horde below?'

For a second Orus thought Amphis might faint. Perhaps he did. He was so rigid and formal he didn't seem the sort to go in for actually falling over. Whatever happened, he recovered quickly.

'While you are of course correct about the unrivalled depth of my knowledge, yourself and the High Council excluded, I am simply swamped at the moment. It would be rather unfair of me to leave such a lot of work for others to pick up, so, I fear, for the sake of the Order, it would be best for me to remain here.'

'Yes, I suppose you're right. After all,' Orus thought he caught a wink cross the Grandmaster's face in the dark of the egg chamber, 'those library books won't reorganise themselves.'

'I'll go with him,' said Ambrose. 'I know the way to the Hatching Grounds and if Brother Uff will lend me a book on caring for the egg, I can read up on the journey.'

'Yes, that could work. Uff give Ambrose *Brother Coalgrip's Dragon Hatchery Handbook*. Nidd you fetch the egg and pack it up ready to travel. You'll need the dragon scale bag to keep it insulated. And make sure to put a set of my gloves in. Amphis you can cover Initiate Ambrose's chores while he is away. Morris the Marauder, as for you, I think it's time we had that tea.'

CHAPTER FIFTEEN

Meanwhile, in the winding tunnel, Conrad was struggling with the ascent.

He reached out through the curtains of his litter and motioned for the lumbering collection of muscles, weapons and scars to come closer.

'Grunka.'

'No, boss. I'm Skar. 'Cause of the scars, see.' The warrior pointed to the long vertical slice down the right side of his face. He could have picked the one under his chin or the criss-cross pattern on his chest with much the same result.[7]

'What happened to Grunka?' asked Conrad.

'Dead, boss. Remember, he got killed by that giant we fought in the Tumbling Pass. Got eaten while you was bravely hiding in that big empty cooking pot. It was lucky the monster choked on one of his knives. And my mum always said iron was an important part of your diet. Guess

---

[7] In fact, Skar's name suited him so well that nobody he met ever thought to ask what he was called before his face acquired its impressive geographical features.

that was too much. Did you put Grunka in your book like you said?'

'Oh yes. I remember now. Yes, I put a whole page in on him, just like I promised. You could get in the book too if you do well.'

'Really, boss. I would love that. My mum'd be so proud. The only thing that normally gets writed about me is 'Wanted: Dead or Very Well Tied Up'. When they do a new poster I always send her a copy, for her scrap book.'

'How lovely,' replied Conrad. 'Now could you tell your chum at the back to lift his end a little higher. Only my lunch keeps sliding away from me.'

'Will do, boss.'

Conrad ducked back inside. From the rear of the litter he heard a couple of deep voices, then the sound of something heavy hitting something hard. The apple on his breakfast tray rolled towards him, then stopped as the litter evened out at a new flatter position. He cut a slice from it with his dagger and popped it into his mouth.

He liked Skar already.

CHAPTER SIXTEEN

The Grandmaster led Orus and Ambrose back into the Great Hall and then to the storeroom to fetch a fresh batch of tea. They were greeted by the sight of a man so wrinkled he looked like a Shar-Pei in a robe. The ancient monk was leaning heavily on a thin white staff. With his other hand he rubbed Thunder's greying snout.

Ambrose bowed his head and whispered a blessing Orus couldn't quite hear.

Even the Grandmaster was surprised to see the tiny man. 'You don't see that every day. Come on, Morris. I'll introduce you to the real boss around here.'

Argus Bach gave a little skip and then double quick bounced over to the wizened figure.

'Isn't he the boss?' Orus asked Ambrose.

'Of the temple yes, but this is our Order's headquarters too. The very top of the Dragon Monks is the High Council, the premier authority on all draconic lore.'

'And he's a member of this council?'

'No. Not a member, not any more. He *is* the High Council. He's all of it, or rather it's all him. Originally, there were thirteen members. When a member died a new one was chosen by voting. It took seven votes to gain entry. The problem was, after a Council meeting was held in one of the northern temples five members died from pneumonia. After that it took the others so long to decide who to replace them with that by the time the shortlist was compiled another four had passed on from old age. Brother Vergil is the last one left now.'

'Couldn't they have changed the rules to let more people in?'

'Not without a two thirds majority, and that two thirds weren't in any position to be voting.'

'How does it work with just one?'

'Quite well actually,' said Ambrose, following after the Grandmaster. 'Far fewer arguments, and they don't get sidetracked by who gets to sit at the head of the table anymore.'

'Your Holiness,' Argus Bach bowed to the High Council. 'It's nice to see you out and about.'

The High Council's voice sounded as if it started moving up his throat a century ago. By the time it reached the open air it was the mere memory of an echo. 'Hello, Argus. I came to see who you had chosen for our saviour.'

Orus put a hand on Thunder's back.

'High Council,' said the Grandmaster. 'May I introduce—'

'No need,' came the quiet, gentle voice. The old man smiled and the wrinkles around his mouth pushed back like crushed velvet curtains. 'We have already met. Nice to see you again, hero.'

'Is he . . .' Orus started, but then stopped again to let the old man continue.

'You have found,' the High Council said, 'a champion of great stamina and courage. He will do well. I have seen it.'

Before Orus had a chance to muse on the old

man's words, Brother Amphis rushed into the storeroom.

'Grandmaster, Grandmaster, quick! We are undone.'

'Calm down, Amphis. What's this all about?'

'We are breached. Brother Borel has just returned from the supply tunnel. There are men coming up from the camp. Dragon Hunters!'

'That is a pickle.' The Grandmaster scratched at his chin. 'Morris, I'm afraid we'll have to leave that tea until you get back.'

'What do we do?' ask Amphis.

'Not to worry,' replied the Grandmaster. 'We just need to move up the schedule a bit. Amphis you go and find Uff and Nidd. Make sure the egg is ready to go and have them bring it up to the surface. I will escort the High Council back to his chambers. Ambrose, you take our hero and his trusty steed up to the launching platform. I will be with you shortly.'

'Yes, Your Reverence,' said Amphis, rushing out before the final syllable reached Orus's ears.

'Come on, get your things.' Ambrose helped Orus lift the man-chest onto Thunder's back again.

Thunder moved with his normal lack of speed. He wasn't afraid of dragon hunters. He was less sure about the phrase 'launching room'.

Just who exactly are we going to be launching?

No-one answered. Thunder had the feeling he would find out soon enough... and then regret it.

Ambrose ushered them back into the Great Hall and off towards the stairs at the far end.

Following at a much more sedate pace, the Grandmaster led the tiny form of the High Council between the towering dragon pillars.

The Head of the Dragon Order stopped under the shadow of a dragon with scales so long they looked almost like feathers.

'A good choice, Argus.'

'Yes, I thought so,' agreed the Grandmaster.

'But who is the round one with him?'

'Oh him?' The Grandmaster smiled down at his old friend. 'He is someone very special indeed.'

*

The dragon monk landed heavily on the floor.

'Found him hiding in the back, boss.'

Conrad Von Strauss checked his profile one more time and then snapped shut the clam shell mirror. He looked down at the pathetic bundle of robes lying in the dirt of the temple store room.

'Excellent, Skar.' Most of Conrad's truncated entourage had managed to squeeze into the store room. They formed a circle around their leader and the new captive. 'Lift it up so I may talk to it.'

Skar and one of his men gripped the monk under his arms and pulled him up to a kneeling position.

'Please, my lord, we are a peaceful order. Do not hurt me.' The monk's eyes darted back and forth.

'Hurt you? Do you really think the great Conrad Von Strauss would ever strike a man of the cloth? I am saddened by your low opinion of me.'

'I am sorry, my lord,' replied the monk. 'I meant no disrespect. I did not realise it was you. The light you see, and my eyes they are not what they once were. Forgive me.'

Conrad continued on without taking any notice of the monk's words. 'No, I would never hurt you. My associates however, well sometimes they forget their own strength.'

At a look from his master, Skar took the monk's wrist and gave it a sharp twist. The monk let out a gasp of pain. Conrad gave another signal and Skar let up some of the pressure.

'Now, I assume you know why I am here. Tell me, where is the dragon?'

'The dragon?' replied the monk.

'Yes, the dragon. This is the Dragon Temple, home to the last dragon in the land, is it not? You are a Dragon Monk, sworn to protect the beast. So where is it?' Conrad paced slowly around the circle of his men, one hand behind his back holding his cape for maximum theatrical effect.

'My lord,' the monk's eyes followed Conrad as he circled like an oily shark, 'I mean no disrespect, but I think there has been some confusion.'

Conrad gave a nod to Skar. With a cruel twisting of his face that may have been a smile, the bodyguard ratcheted the monk's hand through another notch.

'Do not lie to your better, monk. It is very ungodly. The combined heroes of the world have been camped at your doorstep for months. We know the dragon is here somewhere. We heard it from one of your own. Tell me how to find it and I may be generous enough to stop Skar from giving your limbs some extra corners. Where is the dragon?'

Conrad enjoyed watching the man squirm below him. The weak were such funny things.

He lifted a hand, ready to signal Skar again.

'The fat one!' gasped the monk. 'The fat one has it. They went to the launching room.'

Conrad spun on his heel and brought his face close to the monk's quivering form. 'What do you mean he 'has it'? How can a dragon be given to a man? Is it tamed?' Conrad hoped so. That would make it far easier to dispatch. He might even do it himself. He would have to make sure none of his entourage ever told anyone but that was easy. Poison was cheap and he could always get a new entourage. He had done it many times before.

'It's not a dragon.'

Skar twisted harder.

'Aaargh, I mean, not a dragon yet. It hasn't hatched. It's still an egg. They have to take it to the

Hatching Grounds.'

'Still an egg.' Conrad pondered this revelation for a second. That would be even easier than a tame dragon. He would need some sort of explanation as to why no-one could see the body after he'd killed it though. Huggle could come up with something, he was sure. This was all turning out quite well. All he needed to do was catch up to this 'fat one' and take it from him. He couldn't be a hero. They were all down below looking to kill the beast. Perhaps a specially trained monk then.

'And who has been entrusted with this task? One of your Order?'

'No,' replied the monk. 'He says he's a hero. Like you.'

'There are no other heroes like me. That is why I am the best. Now, where did he go?'

'They went to the launching platform. Through the Great Hall and up to the surface.'

'What did he look like?'

'Bald and fat.'

'He should be pretty easy to catch up with then. Thank you for your co-operation.' Conrad waved off Skar. He and the other bodyguard dropped the monk back to the dusty floor.

Then Drift's greatest hero took his sword in its gold scabbard from a waiting lackey. Drawing its shining blade, he turned to his men. 'Come on, men. Let's go and see what this *hero* does when he is confronted by the genuine article.'

Conrad hesitated. These monks could be tricky. There could be booby-traps or an ambush waiting for them. Still, that was no trouble for someone as clever and brave as him.

'Skar, you lead the way.'

CHAPTER SEVENTEEN

Emerging from the gloom of the temple, Orus shielded his eyes from the mid-afternoon sun. He was standing on the mountain's plateau, inside the arc of a wide semi-circular section of the upper temple walls, looking up at what appeared to be a boat. The boat was perched at the top of a wooden ramp and rested on six metal wheels. Once this ramp reached the plateau floor it levelled out, cutting across the lake of molten rock right to the very edge of the mountain. There it stopped.

Orus was not a seafaring man. However, in his limited experience of such things, one point he was very clear about was that normally these kinds of ramps should end in some form of water.

His stomach gurgled a bubble of nervous uncertainty.

I know. I have a bad feeling about this too.

A long sack of sewn up hides was attached to the boat by some complicated rigging arrangements. It was about the same length as the vessel below and was laid out on a scaffold some fifteen feet above the deck. Ambrose was currently pushing a long pipe in one end of the airbag. The other end of the pipe was attached to a giant version of Argus Bach's Brewmaster. The huge boiler was heated from below by a channel of molten rock cut from the lava lake. The brass danced with the reflected colours of the volcano's crown.

'Marvellous, don't you think?' Argus Bach gave Orus another good hard slap on the back. 'One of my lads had the idea when he was trying to fix the last urn. He'd taken his robe off to stop it getting dirty and laid it over one of the steam pipes. Well, that pipe decided it had had just about enough so it split in two, right where the robe was. The steam puffed up his robe in a second. Shot right up to the ceiling. It's made it much easier to get around. That tunnel is a bit hard on the knees after fifty years or so.'

Orus looked at the boat again, high on the ramp. He was starting to get a terrible rising feeling.

'All ready here, Grandmaster,' Ambrose shouted down over the growing rumbling and rattling.

'Come on, lad,' Argus Bach said to Orus. 'Uff and Nidd should be up with the egg anytime now. We'll make sure she is ready to go.'

'Does it work?' asked Orus.

'Sure. Don't worry. We use it all the time. It'll take you to the Kingdom of Harradin up in the Fang Mountains. That's where we get our supplies. From there it's not far to the Hatching Grounds.'

'And is it safe?'

'Oh yes. One hundred percent safety rating. So far at least. Ambrose knows how to fly it. It'll be like being back on your thunderbird chick. Not scared of heights, are you?' Argus added with just the hint of a twinkle in his eye.

'Me? Scared of heights? Hardly.' This much was true. Orus had fallen off enough dodgy ladders in Ditch in his time to know heights aren't the problem. It's the hitting the ground at high speed that you had to worry about.

'Good good, I thought not.' Argus turned and shouted up to Ambrose. 'Ready down here! Start filling her up.'

Up on the wooden scaffold, Ambrose gripped a large metal valve and gave it a full turn. A rumbling, bubbling whooshing noise was forced from the giant Brewmaster's cylinder into the twisting pipe-work. The steam clattered against the bends in the pipes as it raced through the copper maze, building up for a few seconds at the corners before barrelling forward once more. The wooden scaffold began to vibrate fiercely. The pipes shook in their mountings. At the far end, the sack of hides rippled like the blubber of a seal, if you slapped it just right.

As more steam pushed in, the sack even took on a seal-like shape: long, fat and round, tapering a bit towards the end. As it reached half-full the front end tipped off the scaffold. The rest slipped gracefully after it. Rather than come crashing down to the deck below, the sack hung in the air and, as the steam continued to push inside, it began to rise back up again, stretching out the rigging.

By the time Orus, Thunder and the Grandmaster had reached the top of the system of ramps that led to the ship, the air sack was full.

'On you pop, Morris,' said the Grandmaster. 'You too, Ambrose. I'll go and fasten up the end. When Uff and Nidd get up here with the egg, hit the release and get going. These misguided hunters are probably in the temple already. I hope they don't make a mess down there.'

Before Orus could ask any questions, Argus bounded off up to the higher scaffold. He seemed to be enjoying all this action and danger. Orus wondered if he would be interested in swapping jobs. Then he remembered the temple below was full of very armed and very dangerous, soon to be very disappointed, dragon hunters. Perhaps, he thought, a possible death by plummeting wasn't the worst thing that could happen to him right now.

'This is all terribly exciting, don't you think?' A great grin spread between Ambrose's spotty cheeks.

Orus had seen this look before. Tag used to get it when Orus told him stories of all the famous heroes who'd trained at Cromalot. Caught in the moment, he forgot to reply.

'Sorry. You've probably done this sort of thing loads of times. Do you think I'm ready for it, a real adventure I mean? You will tell me if I get in the way or do anything silly? I wouldn't want to be a nuisance. And I'll try not to get scared.'

Orus looked from Ambrose, with all his youthful enthusiasm, to the old Grandmaster, fearlessly scaling the scaffold, to the ingenious (and hopefully safe: please, please be safe) contraption under his feet, straining against the laws of nature. He thought about Mavis and her confidence in him. He thought about Old Grimmer and the promise he had made. He thought about Tag: all that his son had achieved and still hoped to achieve. If these monks were right, and Drift really did need dragons, all that was at risk. Orus had wanted a mission, a purpose. Well now he had it.

Time spent thinking, better spent doing…

'Scared? Being scared is what being a hero's all about. It's the doing things anyway bit you've got to master.'

Thunder, still laden with the man-chest, plodded on board after his charges with altogether less enthusiasm.

It's the being alive at the end bit that I like to concentrate on.

*

Master Bront's tower team had been making good progress, despite their earlier setback. He was confident they would reach the summit by the end of the day. The wind tugged at his clothes as it whipped past the mountain on its way to the higher peaks in the north. To either side of him, competing towers swayed as workers scrambled between the struts. They were moving fast, but his team were faster.

Far beneath him, the sprawl of the camp spread out across the plain. Things down there were strangely quiet for the time of day, but Bront didn't worry about such things. It would soon liven up when he told the boss everything was ready. Not far to go now.

*

'It's full!' the Grandmaster shouted down from the higher scaffold, his voice having to curl around the now fully inflated air sack. The hissing and whistling of the pipes tapered away, then stopped altogether.

The deck pushed up against the soles of Orus's boots as he stood by the wheel. An array of coloured levers stretched out to either side. Much to Orus's relief, there was even a spare handle in case one snapped. Whoever had built the ship clearly had a man-chest of his own.

'Once we're airborne,' said Ambrose, 'this lever releases the rudder sail. Then you can steer with the wheel, just like a normal ship. There's a small stove in the hold too, in case we need to top up the air sack.'

'And what's that one?' Orus pointed to a large red lever.

'That's the brake release. When we're ready to launch—'

A shout from below signalled the arrival of their charge. Uff and Nidd were at the foot of the launching ramp holding the egg between them, safe inside a dragon scale satchel bag. A yellow glow pulsed behind the green scales.

Before they could start climbing to the airship, Thunder let out a loud warning honk. A crowd of very large men with very large swords appeared at the temple entrance. The latter outnumbered the former by quite a way. At the head of the column, a man with impossibly shiny hair and even shinier armour was pointing at Uff and Nidd and shouting. The swords and their holders started to advance.

Uff and Nidd turned to face the crowd of muscle and steel bearing down on them. There was no way they could make it up to the ship in time. Not carrying the egg between them.

Thunder had taken all this in instantly. Grimmer's fat friend was standing frozen like a statue and the skinny kid didn't exactly look like springing into action. As usual, he would have to take charge.

He trotted up to the bank of levers.

Now which one was it? Ah, the red one.

Thunder opened his mouth wide to grip onto the top of the lever.

Time to save the day again.

But before his grinders could close on the handle, the worn fist of a gardener grabbed hold of the lever.

'Better hold on, Thunder. This could get bumpy.'

The donkey's surprise was momentary.

Hold on, he says. I'll loan you my hooves and see how well you hold on to anything. No-one ever thinks about the donkey.

Orus yanked the lever back as far as it would go. Somewhere beneath him something heavy went *clunk*. The bow of the ship tipped forward. The clear sky was replaced with the steep ramp. The sensation that followed was not unlike tipping back a glass for a long drink, only from the drink's point of view.

The airship raced down the ramp, sparks skipping from the steel wheels. Orus staggered across the rushing floor to the edge of the ship and looked down. Uff and Nidd stood at the end of the ramp, shaking in their socks and sandals.

'The egg!' Orus shouted. 'Throw it!'

The two monks looked up at the ship hurtling towards them. Then they looked at the collective eyes of the crowd of very scary men also hurtling towards them. Those eyes were fixed on the dragon scale bag and they didn't look like they belonged to the sort of people who would ask twice, or nicely, or at all. Together, Uff and Nidd decided the fat man's shout was the best idea they'd heard in a long time. As the lead warrior, his face a mask of scars, reached out a huge hand, Uff and Nidd swung the scaly bag and its yolky cargo high into the air and let go.

It soared high above Conrad's men, then started to fall.

The train of steel and muscle all tried to halt at once. They failed in their attempt. Those still standing tried to follow the tumbling bag back the way they had come. Near the rear of the column Conrad reached out, ready to seize the prize.

He smiled. 'Got you.'

A rumbling, squeaking whoosh sped past Nidd and Uff. From its wooden sides, two weather worn hands reached down and grabbed the bag tightly, lifting it out of Conrad's moisturised fingers. The ship flashed by the rest of Conrad's entourage, speeding towards the mountain's edge.

'Got you!' Orus shouted from his upside-down position, dangling over the ship's railing. Ambrose had hold of one trouser leg. Thunder had the other between his teeth. The lava lake bubbled and spat beneath him. 'Can you pull me up now, please?'

Below, and increasingly behind, Conrad boiled with rage. How dare that fat fool steal *his* egg. 'Archers!' he screamed. 'Shoot them!'

Conrad's archers spun on the spot and took aim at the airship as it sped out across the stone runway. Arrows leapt upwards from their bows and raced towards the retreating foe.

Back on board, Orus moved hand-over-hand back to the wheel, not that it looked like being of any use. Molten rock bubbled on either side and, even if it didn't, while they were still on the ground there was no way of turning the ship.

'Quickly,' Ambrose grasped a long blue lever. 'Help me with the wings!'

Together, Ambrose, Orus and Thunder pulled on the lever. There was a snap below. The deck surged upwards, lifting Orus's insides first. On either side of the hull, triangular wings trapped the hot air coming up from the fiery lake, sending the airship soaring into the sky. Arrows thunked harmlessly into the stern of the ship as it rose into the blue.

Below, the six wheeled carriage that had held the ship continued along its track towards the mountain's edge. Freed from its burden it bounced and bucked, hit a rock and spun. The first four wheels of the heavy cart skidded across the edge. Master Bront looked up just in time to see the last two clear the lip of the Worm-mound. He had planned for a lot of eventualities in his tower design. Traffic, however, was not one of them.

As Ambrose, Thunder and Orus watched from the stern, the carriage shattered Conrad's tower, splitting it in two. To either side, builders on competing towers scrambled for the escape ropes as the dominos began to fall. Dust from the collapsing scaffolds flowed up the mountainsides like wash from the sea, quickly blotting out the shrinking figures left on the plateau below.

'We made it!' shouted Orus, managing to just about hide the surprise in his voice. Energy and excitement flowed through him in a way he hadn't felt in years. He'd been proud of Tag and Mavis lots of times but this was the first time since defeating Garvock he'd been proud of himself. His 'one day' had finally arrived.

'That was amazing,' said Ambrose.

'Well,' Orus replied, stretching his hands out in front of him until his knuckles gave a satisfying click. 'That's the kind of thing you have to expect when you're hanging around with a real hero.'

'Yes, but, but, that was Conrad Von Strauss! Conrad Von Strauss was shooting at me. The other Initiates will never believe me.'

'The exercise guy?' said Orus. 'Some warrior he turned out to be. I doubt we'll be seeing him again anytime soon.'

As the two humans basked in their triumph, Thunder's attention was fully fixed on the single arrow poking out of the air sack.

I wouldn't be so sure of that.

CHAPTER EIGHTEEN

'Where are they going?'

His quarry escaped, Conrad targeted his powers of persuasion on Uff and Nidd. Refusing to dirty his own hands by laying them on the grubby robes of some grotty old book-botherers, these powers mainly consisted of asking the questions, loudly.

Luckily, Skar was there to help by using *his* powers of straightforwardly threatening large amounts of violence to make sure his master got the right answers. He was currently holding Brother Uffington upside-down, with a firm grip on each ankle. Skar found that if you shook people in this way for long enough, the truth would eventually fall out.

'I don't know,' replied Uff, the words tumbling out of his mouth and up his face.

'That is a shame. I bet you could guess though. Why don't you take a chance, before I raise the stakes?' A disconcerting smile curling at the side of Conrad's mouth suggested that the stakes he was talking about might not be metaphorical.

'They aren't allowed to gamble I'm afraid,' said the fattest and oldest of the monks. 'Temple rules.'

'Is that so?' Conrad turned to the Grandmaster. 'Well then, I suggest you help your fellow brother by removing him from temptation. Because, I can assure you, in a few minutes he will find my offer very, very tempting.'

With the casual ease that an experienced forager may reach through a bramble bush to get to a particularly juicy berry, the Grandmaster glided past the massed thorns of Conrad's guards and wrapped an arm around the hero's gilded shoulders. 'Now, now, young lad, I don't know if that would be such a good idea.'

'Do not try to intimidate me, you smelly old fool. I know you and your scrawny band have taken a vow of non-violence, and even if you hadn't I'm sure my men are considerably more than a match for a bunch of snivelling weaklings. All the fancy martial arts in the world won't stop a crossbow bolt to the face.'

'Ha, ha, ha,' boomed the Grandmaster. 'You're not wrong there, lad. Why I'm sure you could slaughter the whole lot of us without breaking a sweat. I mean, here we are, unarmed, outnumbered, trapped and surrounded. Totally defenceless, you might say. Then again, if you did, you would have to explain it all to them.'

Argus Bach turned Conrad by the shoulder to face the temple entrance. Emerging from the gloom, armed with all manner of quills and notebooks, came a crowd of bards and scribes, all eager to get the first interview with the slayer of the world's last dragon.

'And while dragon slaying is, unfortunately, all the rage, I doubt tales of butchering defenceless old men will do your image any good.'

Conrad forced a smile across his face as the approaching crowd drew nearer. How he hated them: leeches, one and all, trying to feed off his hard-won fame. The only problem was, it just took one to spit out some false poison and his fellow heroes down in the camp would seize on it. A reputation was a hard fought thing. People would kill for the level of fame he enjoyed. He should know, he had.

'You may think you have won,' he hissed. 'But you have only prolonged the inevitable. I will find that dragon and whatever fool you have guarding it. And when I have finished with them, I will come back here to pick up where we left off.'

Conrad snapped his fingers and Skar dropped Uff. Breaking free of the Grandmaster's grip, Von Strauss advanced towards the press flock with his arms stretched wide.

'You have missed all the action my ink scribbling friends, much like my poor comrades-in-arms down below. Not to worry though, I will fill you in on a tale of bravery and intrigue you will seldom hear.'

He found Huggle's huffing, puffing, sweating form in the crowd and pulled him close. 'Get back down to my camp and get everything ready to move out. Then we can talk about how exactly this lot managed to find their way up here.'

Huggle wiped his forehead with his handkerchief and looked back towards the temple. So many stairs…

CHAPTER NINETEEN

Ambrose and Orus stood at the bow looking north towards the growing wall of geography that was the Fang Mountains. The thick forest of the Grimwood ran in a murky band across the foothills, before giving way to the bare grey rocks and snow-capped peaks. From this height, numerous valleys could be seen cutting between the first wooded rises and the towering monoliths beyond.

'The Kingdom of Harradin is in the third valley to the right.' Ambrose pointed to the faint traces of smoke rising behind the foothills.

'And that's where the Hatching Grounds are?' asked Orus.

'No, they're beyond that, in the midst of the mountains themselves. But we have to go to Harradin first because the pass that leads to the mountains is protected by a great gate, to stop any of the wild creatures coming down and attacking the town. Only the King of Harradin can give permission for people to pass through.'

Now that he had time to catch his breath and the reasonable part of his brain had escaped from all his visions of grand adventure, Orus was starting to realise this quest was not going to be the refreshing holiday from his normal mundane existence he had expected. He knew about the Fang Mountains. Everyone did. And because everyone knew about them, very few ever had the inclination to visit them.

'Okay, so after we cross the valley full of the most dangerous creatures in the world, what then?' Presuming we get that far, Orus added to himself.

'Then we have to take the egg to the Hatching Grounds and place it in the sacred fire.'

'And then it hatches?'

'It should do. If we make it in time.'

'How much time do we have?'

'Hard to say. Let's have a look.'

Ambrose lifted the flap on the dragon-scale bag. Bright light rose from the egg like golden steam. It flowed down the sides of the bag and onto the monk's arms, curling around them, and then spread out across the deck in a thin, shimmering mist. 'Heat flows into the egg through tiny holes in the shell,' Ambrose said. 'The dragon draws the magical energy out of it, separating and consuming it, but if there's too much it breathes it out again.

'This,' Ambrose moved his hand through the golden cloud, 'is the Aurora Draconis. Pure magical energy.'

Orus ran his fingers through the magic. His skin tingled. It felt like feathers of silk, like a snow of suspended heat, delicate and warm. 'But why is there too much?'

'Getting the incubation temperature right is a tricky business. The fire we use in the temple is slightly too hot. It doesn't have the same level of magical energy as true dragon fire, so we compensate by turning it up a bit.'

'Can we take it out?'

'Best put the gloves on first. It'll be hot. They should be in the side pocket.'

Ambrose held the bag while Orus retrieved a set of the Grandmaster's oven mitts from within. This pair were designed to look like pigs, although one sow had a burn across the top of its nose. Orus put them on, then reached inside the bag. As he lifted it out, golden magic trailed behind it. The wind blew the comet's tail out across the prow of the ship, bending it into a thin wave that sparkled against the grey horizon.

'It's bright,' he said, turning his eyes away from the halo surrounding the shell.

'That's good. It means there's still plenty of energy for the dragon to feed on. It will get dimmer as that energy is used up. If it stops glowing altogether... well, I'm sure that won't happen. Not with you here.'

'Oh, yeah, thanks.' Orus turned to look at the egg once more. The golden strands of magic flowing down his arms reminded him of Mavis's hair. It tickled him the way her curls did when she fell asleep with her head on his chest. The end of magic would be the end of many things. Who knew what would happen? Whatever it was, thought Orus, it's unlikely to be peaceful. The egg felt heavy in his hands. He carefully put it back into the bag.

'So how long do we have to get there?'

'A few days at least,' said Ambrose. 'And we can top it up on the way. We just need a fire. It won't be as good as the one in the temple, but it'll be better than nothing. The book might have some more tips. I'll go and check.'

Before he could rummage through their supplies to find *Brother Coalgrip's Dragon Hatchery Handbook*, Thunder started nudging Ambrose with his nose.

The donkey had honked for a good twenty minutes after they had escaped from the temple. The excitement was probably too much for the poor creature, thought Orus. Donkeys were not the most aerodynamic of creatures. And given how much time Thunder spent lying on the ground, being this far from it must be a distressing experience. It certainly was for him.

'Morris, do we have anything we could give Thunder to calm him down? I don't think he likes being up here,' said Ambrose, rubbing the donkey's snout.

It's not the up here part I'm worried about. It's when we stop being up here and start being down there.

But no-one was listening. They never did.

To the west, the sun was beginning to graze the serrated edge of the long curve of the mountains. Its light rushed up through the blanket of cloud, turning the sky into the neat yellow rows of a wheat field.

In the shimmering dusk, Orus's eyes struggled to focus on the peaks ahead. The glare of the dancing light almost made them look like they were getting higher. Or the airship was getting lower.

'Ambrose,' he called out. 'How long did you say it would take to get us to Harradin?'

'Oh, I wouldn't think we'll be there until midnight, which might make landing a bit exciting,' said the monk returning to the bow, book in hand.

'And you're sure that we have enough steam to get all the way?'

'Plenty. We were totally full when we left. It's not as far as Brompile. That's where we normally go for supplies for the temple. We'll need to start letting some steam out once we get closer.'

'That's good. For a minute there I thought we were sinking. Or falling. Whichever is worse.'

Thunder gave out a long honk and again turned towards the stern.

'Don't worry, Thunder. I said I only *thought* we were sinking.'

No sooner had the words left his mouth than Orus's old friend Fate gave him a slap about the head to remind him of who was in charge on this boat. He surely didn't think everything was going to go his own way on this trip. Nope, ever since the dung ball and the sewer he had nothing but good luck. It was time to redress the cosmic balance.

It started with a whistle. Then there was a rip. Then they were falling.

Ambrose was thrown backwards as the stern dropped away from him. *Brother Coalgrip's Dragon Hatchery Handbook* fell from his grasp and skidded to the wheel deck. Sliding after it, he managed to grab onto the main mast with both hands.

Thunder started skidding backwards too. His hooves little use, he clamped onto the end of the monk's robe with his teeth.

Hold on, he says.

At the bow, Orus gripped the rail with both hands, trying to keep his footing.

Steam pumped out of the air sack with a volume and force reminiscent of when the Prince of Ditch had tried the 'all sprouts' diet. The wings slowed their terminal descent from 'terrifying plummet' to mere 'careering catastrophe'. In the end, however, Orus knew this would have little impact on the final effect (or affect on the final impact).

'We need to level out,' shouted Ambrose, the words just reaching Orus's ears through the up-rushing air.

'The secondary burner,' Orus shouted back. 'You need to turn it on.'

Ambrose looked over his shoulder towards the wheel deck. All he could see was Thunder's terrified form. The wheel and controls were somewhere behind the ass. If he let go he could probably catch them as he slid by. Probably.

'I think I can make it. Thunder you're going to have to let go.'

Not a chance.

'Come on, let go. We're going to crash!'

Still the donkey held firm and looked in no mood to shift.

While Thunder continued to struggle with Ambrose, the dragon-scale bag slid past them, heading towards the stern.

'The egg! The egg's going to fall!'

Orus saw it too. If it kept going, the bag would slide right under the rear rail, taking the future with it. If he was going to be a hero now would be a good time to start. Orus convinced his right hand to release its grip. His weight immediately pulled him round so that he was facing down the sloping deck, his back screaming in protest at the jarring impact. Scrabbling behind him, Orus managed to grip the rail again. He was now hanging in a crucifix position. Ahead of him was Ambrose and Thunder, clinging onto the mast and each other. Behind them, the satchel containing the egg was sliding towards the wheel deck. Beyond that was the stern railing and then nothing but air for 3000 feet.

Orus lowered himself onto his rear and stuck his legs out in front of him. It's just like when you took Tag sledging as a boy, he said to himself. Fair enough you don't have a sledge and the wooden deck is going to leave a few more splinters than your average snowy slope, but what's the point of all that extra cushioning you've got back there, if not this?

He shimmied along the rail until he was in line with the retreating bag, all the time the rushing air battering him back and forth.

A judder of turbulence struck the ship. One of Ambrose's hands came free from the mast and his feet slid out from under him. Orus could see the fingers in the monk's second hand were straining from the weight.

Here goes nothing.

Orus let go and started to slide. Fast. And getting faster. Too fast. He felt himself lifting off the deck. He tried to dig in his heels to slow his slide. It didn't work. He was still picking up speed.

He raced past Ambrose and Thunder, leaving a distinct burning smell in his wake. The dragon-scale bag was dead ahead. Orus scooped it up between the Y of his legs.

'Got it!'

His elation (and surprise) was short lived. His adjustment to reach the egg had lined him up with exactly nothing capable of stopping him. At this speed the railing across the stern would at best provide little more than a warm up to hitting the ground.

The wheel deck was fast approaching. Stretching as far as he could, he reached out for the bank of levers. His hand found one and latched on tight. He felt the skin of his palm rip and burn as he slipped to the end of the lever's handle. The weight of his body was pulled around with another jarring snap to his back. And then that was it. He had stopped. At least on one directional plane.

Orus let out a sigh of relief and looked back up at Ambrose. 'I've got it!'

'Not the black one!'

'What?'

'Not! The! Black! One!'

The black lever juddered in Orus's grip. 'What does it —?'

The lever sprung back. Inside the body of the airship something mechanical began to click and clank. The ship began to tip forward. It started to fall faster. Much faster.

'You've pulled the wings in! Push it back! Push it back!' Ambrose yelled as Thunder began to skid past him towards the bow, hoofs scratching across the deck.

Orus pulled himself up. He swung the egg and its bag over his shoulder. Taking the lever in both hands he pushed against it with all his strength. Thankfully, and in defiance of literary tradition, it did not snap and, after a brief moment and a considerable vertical distance, Orus forced it back into place.

They kept falling.

Ahead the forest covering the foothills was fast approaching. Orus tried to shout at Ambrose but the words were ripped past his shoulder.

How had he done it the first time? The release? It was the blue one!

Jamming his feet at the bottom of the wheel, Orus leaned over to the blue lever. He could make out individual trees now, each one a green spear ready to bring them to a very final halt. He pulled and pulled, the muscles in his arms burning. The lever wouldn't budge. He couldn't do it. He wasn't strong enough. He despaired. This was it. The end. All those who had called him fat and useless were about to be proved right.

Fat.

Maybe, just maybe. He wasn't strong enough, that much was clear, but he might just be fat enough. In the circumstances that would do just as well.

He collapsed backwards, letting his legs transfer all his body weight into his arms. The lever snapped back so suddenly Orus felt slightly offended. He wasn't *that* fat.

The wings snapped back open, catching the air rising over the foothills. The airship swooped low across the tree tops, regaining a level glide just in time. Beneath it, squirrels scattered across the canopy to avoid being crushed under the hull. This was a new experience for them – boats not being on their list of recognised natural predators.

The hull jerked and bucked. The sound of splintering wood filled Orus's ears and he gripped tightly to the wheel. They had stopped falling but they were definitely still crashing.

*

Victor Still was enjoying a bit of late night fishing. This was his favourite time to be out on the lake. Not just because the fish were getting careless, convinced they had made it through another day, it was the calm that came over the forest too. The animals of the day were heading to their dens and the creatures of the night weren't quite up yet. It was a truly peaceful time when he could just lay back in his old red boat and relax.

This being so, he was pretty miffed when his evening was interrupted by the sound of something crashing through the tree-line. Bursting through in an explosion of splintering branches Victor Still's wife ran out into the shallows, flushed and frightened, not even bothering to hitch up her skirt.

She cupped her hands around her mouth and shouted across the lake.

He turned his head and put his ear to shore. Still couldn't hear properly: something about a stoat in the hay barn.

Stoats weren't the worst thing one had to contend with in this place. The Grimwood could throw up some pretty unexpected visitors now and again, and the Stills had lived there long enough to see most of them. Even though, he'd better go and chase it out before it got any ideas about the chickens. With a long sigh, he started to reel in his line.

CHAPTER TWENTY

'We are very sorry, Mr Still.'

Victor hadn't spoken since he first set eyes on the undeniably boat-shaped construction stuck bow first into his hay store. He paced back and forth along the rut the airship had made as it came down in the clearing around the farmstead. The force of the crash had burst the walls of the barn outwards, leaving the whole structure flat on the ground, each wall having fallen straight back. It looked as if the ship had been packaged up whole and then delivered from on high by the gods' least careful celestial courier.

While Orus apologised about their unannounced visit, Ambrose was busy trying to lean a portion of the barn door against the side of the airship so that Thunder could get down.

'We would normally stay and help to fix everything, but we're in quite a hurry.'

'Yes, yes,' mumbled Victor, still unsure if this was all really happening or if he had simply fallen asleep out on the lake again. He approached the airship and knocked an arthritic knuckle against the hull. 'Clearly.'

'If it is any consolation, you can keep anything you salvage.'

The old woodsman didn't hear Orus. He started to pace out the rut in long strides, mumbling to himself as he did so.

'Mary?' he called to his wife. She was busy retrieving her bloomers from the prow of the ship, it having picked up the Still's washing line during the crash.

'The wings would make some good tanning racks if you prop them up. And the skins will be worth something,' added Orus.

Victor Still kept pacing out the rut. When he made it to the end, he turned back to look at the barn. He wasn't deliberately ignoring Orus. It was just that his mind could only process so much information at one time and the information in front of him was proving quite a lot to take in. He scratched his head once, twice, then looked over his shoulder. He'd lived in the Grimwood all his life and he was confident, had there been an ocean nearby he would have noticed it before now. Well that settles it, he thought, I must be going mad. It was bound to happen eventually.

'Victor,' shouted Mrs Still, bloomers successfully rescued. She was a squat woman, with the kind of wide hips that formed a natural shelf for balancing buckets of firewood on. 'Stop standing around like a fool and help these boys.'

'Yes, dear,' Victor replied, glad to retreat to the comfortable state of falling into line with his wife's orders. Ambrose was still struggling with the barn door. Victor gripped the free side and helped the monk lift the make-shift gang plank into place.

On deck, Ambrose found Thunder munching on a pile of hay collected in the course of the crash. The donkey looked remarkably calm, as if he had been through similar situations many times before (which, of course, he had). Ambrose, on the other hand, was shaking: the midnight flight from the All Seasons, escaping from Conrad at the temple and now this. It was the most adventure he had had in… in ever.

The Temple was not a place for excitement, especially when Brother Amphis was around. It was a place for reading, praying and chores. Lots of chores. Growing up, if he was lucky, one of the missionary monks might bring him back a penny fold adventure when they came back from preaching. Ambrose collected them, hiding the precious contraband under his thin straw mattress. They provided his only experiences of the world outside the cloisters. When he read them, late at night, using the smallest stub of a candle he could find, he imagined what it would be like to be on a real adventure: the excitement, the danger, the fame and glory. But then, like all dreams, in the morning these images would fade. His sweeping brush would stare back at him from across the initiates' dormitory and the reality of temple life would sink back in.

Now he had nearly died. Three times. It was great!

'I thought we were finished that time for sure, Thunder. Morris really is a great hero, isn't he? Just jumps into action.'

I'll admit there has been a moderate improvement. Although, I want you to know I had the situation totally under control. I wanted to let him have a go himself. It's the only way he'll learn.

'Come on. We'll get you down and then see what the plan is from here,' said Ambrose, looping the lead rope over Thunder's head.

We have a plan? That'll be nice.

Mrs Still approached Orus. En route, the bloomers disappeared into one of those parallel dimensions old ladies kept between the various layers of shawls, cardigans and blouses. Having raised three children, Mrs Still was used to discovering unexpected scenes of destruction. As a result, she had adjusted to the arrival of the airship much better than her husband. With the *What* sorted out, she moved on to the *Why*.

'So, where are you boys heading?'

'Harradin,' replied Orus. He turned a complete circle. The Still's cottage was set in a natural depression in the forest. The Fang Mountains were obscured by the thick curtain of trees. 'You don't happen to know which way it is?'

'Yes,' replied Mrs Still. 'It's about a day's walk from here. In fact, Victor's going up that way tomorrow to get in some supplies before winter. You must be in a hurry.'

'Why do you say that?' Orus had the dragon-scale bag slung over his shoulder. It glowed a pale yellow in the forest night. His hand gripped the strap.

'You'd have to be to get in a contraption like that. Lucky you came down here and not in the woods. There's all sorts of wee naughty beasties out there, especially at this time.'

'Really?' Ambrose's ears pricked up, sensing adventure. 'What kind of beasties?'

A deep rumbling reverberated around the clearing.

'What was that?' the monk said, turning to peer into the twisted boughs.

'Probably just a bear,' replied Mrs Still. 'They get restless this time of night. Always like a snack before bed. But don't worry, they don't bother us.'

The rumble rolled across the clearing again like underwater thunder. This time, Orus recognised the source.

'Sorry to have to ask. I don't suppose you have any food you could spare? Running a bit low of fuel I think.' He tapped at his belly, eliciting another rolling growl. 'We can pay for it. We have money. Then we'll be on our way and out of your hair.'

'Nonsense. You're not going anywhere tonight. We don't get visitors dropping in very often. Certainly not literally.'

The surrounding forest pressed on the edges of Orus's senses. The noise of something dying, quickly and violently, carried across the twilight. Perhaps waiting until morning wasn't such a bad idea.

*

As a gardener, Orus often heard people throw around the phrase 'the balance of nature'. The majority of people using it, he found, did so to invoke images of tranquillity and serenity. Nature was to them a dance: beautiful, graceful, delicate, and, above all, harmonious. They imagined frolicking bunnies, with eyes so wide and black they constituted a trip hazard, and trains of bobbing bumblebees in their fetching striped jumpers crossing flower speckled meadows. Every movement of every creature was directed by some unseen hand, every individual worked as part of the greater whole, consciously working towards a collective goal.

Orus knew better. Real nature was not a dance. It was a war. The Grimwood was testament to that. If it had to be compared to a human creation it would be the dynastic struggles of kingdoms. War, sex, violence, invasion, assassination. Thousands, millions of deaths, all played out in hundreds of different timescales simultaneously. Trees strangled their neighbours over hundreds of years, while amongst their roots whole civilisations of insects could be uprooted and devoured in a matter of minutes by a giant ursine paw. It was quick, it was slow, it was shocking, it was brutal, it was relentless and merciless, careless and calculating, but the one thing it was not was harmonious. Roses, after all, have thorns for a reason.

The Grimwood was also dangerous. Not dangerous in a targeted way. Things died there all the time, it was true. They often did so violently and painfully, but there was no malice in this. The forest could kill you in a thousand ways, yet it had no guiding purpose, no evil heart, no curse set on. There was no malicious spirit tugging at the silvery strands of spider silk that ran through the canopy. It simply was. And even though it was filled with dangerous creatures, the most deadly aspects of the Grimwood were not its residents. Most people who died there were not killed by wolves or carried off by giants to give extra body to a pot of goulash. They weren't lured into one of the many caves by will-o-the-wisps to be calcified and turned into stalactites. They weren't swallowed up by carnivorous moss men while they slept or plucked from their horses by snatcher vines to be slowly dissolved in the plant's innards (most mind you – these things did happen). No. Nothing so exciting. The fact was that the large majority of people taken by the forest died from normal, rather boring things like starvation, falling trees, slips into ravines or, and this was by far the greatest cause of death, pure stupidity.[8]

---

[8] After all, it is hardly the Grimwood's fault if someone decides to go giant mushroom picking without looking up which ones you can eat and which were the opposite kind (even then, the teeth should really give the game away).

CHAPTER TWENTY-ONE

Inside the Still's cottage, the smell of freshly-made stew filled Orus's nostrils with all the restorative effect of the brightly coloured herbal teas the Prince of Ditch was so fond of. As the tiny particles of marrow bone, rabbit meat, forest herbs, and nuts and vegetables rushed up his nose he felt the stress and anxiety of the last few days drain out of him. Even his back felt better. Those jolts on the airship had straightened it up pretty good.

Ambrose sat across from him in a large, squishy armchair. A set of knitting needles was pushed into one of the arms and coloured balls of wool were mounted up like scoops of ice cream in a basket by his feet. His fingers played at the arms of the chair and his crossed legs twitched along with them. The poor lad had really been thrown in at the deep end, Orus thought. Quite a change from the cloistered life. He would sleep well tonight.

Orus sat in another armchair, this one complete with footstool and pipe burn marks on the right arm. His eyes wandered around his surroundings. The cottage was a simple but sturdy affair. There was a pantry and kitchen, a living area — where they were seated — and, at the far end, two bedrooms. One was for Mr and Mrs Still, while the other, going by the trio of brightly coloured name plates on the door, must once have been for the couple's children. Brian, George and Sophie. Good, simple names.

The letters were a mix of red, green, yellow, blue, purple and pink. Victor must have carved them himself. Orus had done the same for Tag's room, and just like on that door back in Ditch, each name was set between a pair of rearing animals. Brian had a pair of cave bears, George had a set of centaurs and Sophie had two warty-grobblers, complete with dripping slime (Victor later explained he had first made his daughter beautiful silver unicorns — but she wanted something a bit more original). Tag's door back in Ditch was guarded by proud stags, antlered heads raised and watchful. Orus passed them every morning on his way down the stairs. Even though Tag no longer lived with them, he couldn't imagine he would ever take them down.

As he was slowly enveloped by Victor's armchair, Orus watched the old couple move around each other in a routine made graceful by years of gentle repetition. No sooner had Victor set his boots down by the fire than Mary had scooped them up again and held them out the door to bang off the dirt. Next the old woodsman wrestled off his coat, just in time for Mary to take it from his hand on her way back from the door and hang it on a hook beside her own. As she did so, she took Victor's fish fly box from the pocket and passed it back to her husband. He always forgot it.

Victor took the blackened iron kettle, just boiled, from the stove and poured the steaming tea into the mugs Mary had that very second placed on the kitchen table. Even the addition of a few guests didn't break the hypnotic rhythm, as before the second mug was full Mary was back with an extra pair.

'There you go, dearies. Get that warmth through you.' Mary handed Ambrose and Orus a mug each in turn.

Ambrose sipped at the tea. It was good and strong. The Grandmaster would have approved.

Orus offered to help but a kind smile from Mary let him know everything was in hand.

She turned back to the kitchen, pirouetting around Victor, he with an emergency chair in each hand. Victor placed the chairs at either side of the simple table. He went to sit down, only to be stopped mid-rest by a call of 'Victor, hands please.'

He gave Orus a 'how does she do it' look and nipped out to wash his hands in the water barrel.

As Victor nipped outside Orus noticed another similarity between the cottage and his own house. Moving up the frame of the front door were three sets of parallel cuts. He wondered how long it was since the Still's children had left. They had grown fast, going by the gaps between the cuts. Most children do, as he well knew, but the ascent to adulthood of Brian, George and Sophie must have been particularly rapid, not to mention high. The cuts kept going up the frame, eventually leaving it behind and stretching into the eaves above Orus's head.

Conditions would have been cramped, he thought. Victor and Mary were quite small, certainly below average. Not so their children. It looked like each one was seven feet tall by the time they were in their mid-teens. Not only that, the width of the seats and the sturdy construction of the emergency chairs Victor had set by the table suggested the children's considerable size was not constrained to their height. Had Orus not been so tired he might have noticed that the doors in the Still's cottage were also unusually wide and, while he had seen big wooden spoons in kitchens before, he had never seen a matching set of giant wooden forks.

The arrival of dinner battered any curiosity in his mind into meaty submission. Mary placed the great pot on the table just as Victor returned from outside. Orus and Ambrose took their places and stared hungrily at the huge sea of stew. Iceberg sized chunks of turnip rolled past carrot atolls, while rafts of rabbit trailed glistening oil slicks over the surface. If Orus was in any doubt as to how hungry he was, those doubts were now drowning.

'Thank you both,' he said, eyes fixed on the stew. 'And again, we're very sorry about the barn.'

'Don't worry about that. We're used to taking in the waifs and strays of the forest here,' said Mary. Both she and her husband's eyes flicked towards the bedroom door with its three multicoloured names. 'We've been meaning to downsize since the children left anyway. You were lucky you landed where you did, else you'd be in real trouble.'

'Not to mention pieces,' added Victor. 'Whatever possessed you to get in that mad machine?'

'We're on a quest,' said Ambrose.

'A quest. And what's that about?' asked Mary.

Ambrose spoke at a pace normally reserved for children on their first day back at school, full of stories of all their holiday adventures. 'We're trying to save a dragon. The last dragon. It's still an egg at the moment really, but it will be a dragon soon. We're going to take it to the Hatching Grounds up in the Fang Mountains, past Harradin. Otherwise the magic will seep out of the world and everything magical will die. Only Conrad Von Strauss, you know, the great hero, he is trying to stop us. He chased us out of the Dragon Temple – that's where I'm from, only, thanks to Morris here, he's a hero too you see, except he's on our side – we escaped on the airship but then it got shot by an arrow so Morris had to save us again. And that's when we crashed here.'

'Sounds like quite an adventure,' said Mary.

'Wouldn't have got me up in that thing,' added Victor. 'In my day, boats was for the water. Still are, I thought.'

'Oh it works in water too,' continued Ambrose at his double quick pace. 'If we had reached Harradin we would have landed in the great lake. Then we have to convince the King to let us through the gate at Pale Pass. But, as I said, Conrad Von Strauss's arrow put a stop to that. I think I'll get up early tomorrow and see if I can find it. The arrow I mean. What a great souvenir that would be.'

'Your boy's an excitable one.' Mary's words dragged Orus out of his meat and marrow meditation.

'Hmm, oh, you mean Ambrose? Oh, he's not my son. We're questing companions.'

'No madam, Morris is the hero. I'm just a guide.'

'Just nothing,' said Victor, through a beard full of stew. 'Ain't no such thing as just. Especially not just a guide. People don't get far in this part of the world without a guide.'

'A guide then,' agreed Ambrose, fighting his own modesty. 'Or maybe a sidekick.'

'Don't ever sell yourself short, lad,' continued Victor. 'That's what I always told my three. Plenty of people out there will try to put you down, without you joining in too. Everybody's got a role and ain't none more important than the rest. How far do you think a king would get without his cook, or a knight without his squire to help him into his armour? I could show you a tree out in the forest, biggest one for miles. Huge it is. All kinds of birds and other creatures living in it. But the only reason it's there in the first place is 'cause a few hundred years ago some tiny mouse forgot where he'd buried the seed. Ain't that right?' Victor looked to Orus. 'I mean, how far would you get in the forest out there without a guide?'

'Is it dangerous?' asked Orus.

'Dangerous? The Grimwood? That depends on you. There is certainly a lot of ways to die out there if you're not careful. If you don't have your wits about you or your brain turned on. But dangerous? Only to the reckless.' Victor paused and took a big spoonful of stew. 'Not seen a dragon for a while though. Not for a good long while.'

'Well you wouldn't have. This is the last one. That's why we've got to look after it,' said Ambrose.

'But it is still an egg, you say?' asked Victor.

'For the moment.'

'And it's the very last one?'

'Well when it hatches it will be. Until it has eggs of its own I guess.'

Victor leaned back in his chair with a slight smile on his face. 'Is that right? And who has asked you to do all this?'

'Grandmaster Argus Bach. He's the head of my temple.'

'Smart man,' said Victor. 'Sounds like quite an adventure. I'm going up to Harradin tomorrow to get supplies for winter. You can come along with me. Better than striking out on your own.'

'Is it really that dangerous?' asked Orus.

'Like I said, depends on you. As long as you show the forest a bit of respect, you should be fine.'

CHAPTER TWENTY-TWO

'Huggle, what is that ghastly smell?'

Von Strauss and his vanguard had arrived at the edge of the Grimwood just before night did. Behind them, snaking out across the steppe, back towards the Worm-mound, the rest of the mass of men and horses that made up his single-handed dragon slaying expedition trudged after their fearless leader.

It was not one of those woodlands that gradually snuck up on you, first a few trees, then some more, tighter in, then gradually closing in around you. The boundary between what was and what was not the Grimwood couldn't have been clearer. The grass plain ended, there was a strip of barren earth two strides across, then the ranks of dark, swollen trees rose like a wall. In the canopy the branches intertwined in a tangled mess, constantly trying to block invasions from their neighbours and push through to the best of the light. The trunks below, having spent all their energy carving out precious space on the forest floor, were bloated like gout ridden kings, while the forest floor itself was smothered in snot coloured moss. This crawled over rocks and roots alike, making walking a tricky business.

Skar's scouts had found an old trail leading into the heart of the wood and it was from here that a waft of stale, musty air was channelling out onto the plain. The whole place smelled like it had been left for a long time in the back of a leaky garden shed.

'I believe that is nature,' said Huggle, trotting up to his master's side.

'It's revolting.' Conrad clicked his fingers and the wafters took up positions in front of him. 'Skar, are you sure the airship came down in there?'

'Yes, boss. Dead sure. My scouts saw it crash. It's quite far in, but we should catch up to them tomorrow. That's if they survived the fall.'

'Oh I do hope they did, Skar. It will make killing them far more satisfying. Lead on.'

The trail the scouts had found was more of a tunnel than a road such was the thickness of the branches overhead. It did not look well used. Arched roots heaved against the ground. In places the mossy mulch swallowed up the path completely. But it was not the conditions under foot that worried Huggle. People rarely came this far north. When they did they kept to the highway with its rangers and safe coach houses. He stared into the murky forest and, in a break with tradition, it didn't stare back.

Somehow, he thought, that is worse. Total indifference. Just like death.

He wiped his brow with his handkerchief. 'I have heard, sire, that it is not wise to travel through the Grimwood at night. Perhaps we should camp here and continue on in the morning.'

'And risk the thieves escaping? I don't think so, little scribe. Doubtless my competitors will have started on the trail by now as well. It was a good idea of mine to have you announce that fake press conference so they would all wait at the mountain, but I'm sure they will have figured it out by now. We can't risk them overtaking us in the night. A few more hours, then we will find somewhere to camp. Worry not, no harm will come to me, I assure you. Isn't that right, Skar?'

'Yes, boss.'

Had he not known himself to be such a coward, Huggle would have explained to his brave master it was not him that he was worried about. Nor was it Skar and his men, who looked like they would probably enjoy a nice fight before bedtime. It was the expedition's other personnel that he was worried about. These included the cooks, farriers, smiths and messengers. Not to mention Master Lenz, his assistants, the people who looked after Conrad's wardrobe, the horses who carried Conrad's wardrobe and – most importantly of all – himself.

'Are you sure, sire? Even on the highway they don't travel after dark.'

'Huggle, I did not get to be the world's greatest hero by being afraid of the dark.'

I know, Huggle said to himself. You got there by lying, cheating, stealing and murdering. And spending a whole mountain of your father's money on a huge publishing campaign.

'That egg is rightfully mine,' Conrad continued, 'and they have stolen it from me. In return, I plan to steal some things from them. I haven't quite made my mind up on what exactly, but I'll start with their hands and see where the feeling takes me. So unless you would like to join them on the begging step at the nearest temple, perhaps we could continue.'

'Yes, sire,' sighed Huggle.

'See, Master Lenz,' Conrad called back to the old painter. 'You see here the difference between the hero and the coward.

'Onward to glory.' Conrad drew his sword and pointed into the heart of the deep dark wood. Then, rather more quietly, he added, 'Skar, you and your men go first.'

CHAPTER TWENTY-THREE

With dinner finished, Orus borrowed a lantern and made his way back out to the crashed airship, explaining to the others that he was going to collect some hay for Thunder. However, if someone had been watching him (this being the Grimwood there were plenty of *somethings* watching him) they would have noticed his path back to the flattened barn was strangely zigzagged and what he was collecting was not hay at all.

Like Ambrose and his arrow, Orus was after souvenirs. The airship had shed parts of itself across a wide area as it bounced across the clearing and, being a practical man, Orus reckoned there was a good chance many of those parts could come in useful further down the line. He wouldn't take any bits of the barn. That would be stealing. The bits of the flying machine on the other hand. That was recycling.

He retrieved the spare lever from the wheel deck, along with some of the fabric from the wings and the pulley system that extended them and was storing it all in the man-chest, when he heard a man's scream echo across the forest.

It was not one of those long screams that gradually retreat into the distance. It was the other kind: the sort that stopped very abruptly and, for those close enough to hear, were often followed by the noise of grinding teeth, then slurping, then burping, then a full and satisfied sigh.

Thunder heard it too. He poked his head out from under the makeshift shelter Orus and Ambrose had constructed from airship wreckage.

'I'm glad we decided to stop here until tomorrow,' Orus said to the old donkey. 'You wouldn't want to be out there at night.'

Thunder looked around what was to be his bedroom: flimsy walls, no doors, nowhere to hide, nowhere to go.

Oh yes, I feel much safer here.

Orus turned to leave, and then stopped. He looked back towards the shelter.

'Actually,' he said, walking back to the old donkey, 'probably safer inside.'

I thought you'd never ask.

'There we go,' said Orus, heaving the man-chest onto his hips. 'Don't want a gang of gnomes carrying all this off in the night. Not after collecting up so much good stuff.'

Glad to see you've got your priorities right.

Thunder plodded to the back of the shelter and hunkered down against the hull of the airship. Another scream lifted across the canopy, before being cut off by a wet squelch.

At least I don't have to listen to him snoring.

*

Inside, Ambrose was sitting in front of the fire in Mary Still's chair reading through *Brother Coalgrip's Dragon Hatchery Handbook*. The dragon-scale bag lay empty over the knitting basket.

'Where is it?' asked Orus, setting the man-chest down by the side.

'In the fire. I'm giving it a top up.'

The egg sat amongst the coals of the hearth. Orange flames danced across the glowing orb. Orus stared at it. For a second, he thought caught a glimpse of a dark shadow moving behind the shell. Then the brightness began to sting his eyes and he had to turn away.

'Have you ever seen one?' Orus eased back into his host's armchair, the light from the fire spilling between them. 'A dragon, I mean.'

'Me? No. Plenty of pictures,' said Ambrose, thumbing through the book, 'but never a real one. How about you?'

'No. I don't think I know anyone who has. I always assumed that was because most men that did see them didn't live long enough to talk about it. I guess it's actually the other way round.'

'I wonder what ours will look like. I can't wait to see it.'

The imaginative, adventure-seeking part of Orus's brain was still wrestling with the logical, rational bit. The crash landing had given the latter a boost and, for a while, it had locked the former in a mental full-nelson. But logic and reason hadn't figured for the tag team effects of Ambrose's undentable enthusiasm and imagination. Dreams and wonder were making a come-back.

'Me too,' said Orus. 'Me too.'

Behind them, the fire cast light and shadows on the back wall of the cottage, projecting flames from floor to rafters. Had they turned from their chairs to look at that image, they would have seen a dark shape in the centre of those flames.

Claws and wings, tail and neck. Twisting. Coiling. Stirring.

*

By morning the fire had reduced to charcoal and white ash, but the egg was still burning. It glowed in the hearth and the air shimmered around it. Even so, its brightness had noticeably lessened since leaving the temple.

'Such a small fire just doesn't have the energy to charge it up completely,' Ambrose noted, using the heat-proof oven mitts to lift the egg back into its protective bag. 'A blacksmith's forge or a really big bonfire would keep it going for a while, but it needs dragon fire. We have to hurry.'

After a good breakfast, Mary Still saw them off. With Victor leading the way, they plunged into the tree tunnels of the Grimwood. The old woodsman picked his path carefully, so as to disturb the forest as little as possible. The trail he led them down was little more than a channel of squashed moss and undergrowth. By the multitude of different kinds of footprints and the varied range of droppings that stood along it like Nature's mile markers, it was clear that most of the traffic was other than human. Every so often the forest would shudder with a distant roar or crashing branch, while below their feet the leaf cover was constantly shifting as hidden rodents rushed on their busy ways.

As they continued deeper into the wood, Orus caught sight of scratch marks in the bark of many of the trees. The biggest ones bore scars all the way up their trunks – each one marking out ownership by a different citizen of the forest hierarchy. Like the marks in the Still's cottage, the deep claw marks of the most successful creatures advanced up the trunks. The whole life of a particular animal could be read in those marks. They would go up and up and up, only to suddenly stop and be replaced by another set, wider or narrower claws, longer scores, sometimes higher up, sometimes lower down.

Their party continued on until the early afternoon without incident, until the trail skirted the edge of a dim clearing.

'Have you always lived out here?' Ambrose asked Victor.

'All my life,' he replied. 'My father was a woodsman, his father was a woodsman, his father was part of a travelling cabaret – you'd be surprised how common that is around here – but then his father before was a woodsman.'

'And in your experience,' Ambrose had stopped walking and was staring into the clearing, 'is it normal for the trees to move?'

'Of course they move. Wind and all that.'

'Yes, but is it normal for them to walk around? On legs?'

'The trees? No. They tell me their roots go far too far down for that.'

Orus got the feeling that the 'they' Victor was using was not the normal sense of 'they' people use when making statements like that. It was far more personal, like the 'they' in 'they asked us over for tea' rather than in 'they say rubbing mandrake root on your feet is a good cure for warts'.

'There's a lot of things that look like trees that walk though: dryads, moss-men, sylvans. Sometimes you'll get a troll that lies down for a nice hundred year nap and wakes up to find a bush growing out of his back. All sorts out here in the wilds… At least there used to be. You don't see as many of the magical creatures around nowadays, not like when I was a lad.'

'And which of those is that?'

Orus followed Ambrose's gaze to the creature approaching them through the clearing. It didn't actually look like a tree. It was more than that. It looked like a sort of walking forest. It covered all the bases, root to tip. Its main skeletal structure was made of wood, with different species of tree intertwining around each other. Leaves, buds and fresh sprouting stalks covered its shoulders, neck and back like a cloak, while its legs were coated in mud and earth from the knees to the ankles. Under these it walked on hooves of bedrock, themselves webbed with tiny thin roots. Its head was a woven mass of branches, with leaves for eye-lids and a stack of mushrooms on each side, which Orus guessed were ears.

The most remarkable thing about the creature, however, and the thing that was drawing Orus's attention, was the waterfall where its stomach should have been. Rather than a solid central trunk, its body split in two, just under the chest. The wooden structure bowed outwards on either side before joining again at the hips. The bowl shaped hollow of its pelvis held a pool of water and, into that, a rumbling, tumble of water gushed from an opening in the bottom of the apparition's rosewood heart. The water must have been circulating in some way as the pool wasn't getting any fuller. In its centre, sitting on a rock, a small frog wiped spray from its bulbous eyes with a sticky front foot.

'That's a Sylvan,' Victor said. 'But it's more than a which. It's a who.'

'Hello, Trickle. What news?'

Trickle raised a hand in greeting. He smelled of fading summer and when he spoke it was with a voice of cracking branches.

'Hello, Victor Still. Nice to see you. Who do you have here?'

Now that he was up close, Orus could see that the frog in Trickle's stomach wasn't the only thing hitching a ride. From the caterpillars on its leafy shoulders to the centipedes weaving between the branches that made up its arms and the bees nesting in a hole in its leg, the Sylvan's entire body crawled with life.

'These chaps are heroes, or so they say. This is Morris, Ambrose and Thunder.'

'Hmm.' Trickle looked down on them with cold expression. 'More heroes. Just what we need.'

'What do you mean 'more'?' asked Victor.

'Didn't you hear it last night? Men travelling through the forest. Smashing, cutting, burning. When they finally stopped they cut down a whole family of fresh plum trees, just to clear a space for a big tent.' Trickle's body shuddered and the multitude of insects disappeared from view. 'They ran into a spot of trouble after that, or such is the word on the vines. Not undeservedly so. They claimed to be heroes too.'

'It must be Conrad,' said Ambrose.

'The one that's chasing you?' said Victor.

'Well,' Victor turned back to Trickle, 'this pair aren't like that. And there won't be any cutting or burning of anything still living while I'm around.'

'That is good to know.' A second right hand emerged from Trickle's body. He extended one each to Orus and Ambrose and shook a greeting with them at the same time. 'It is nice to meet you, friends of Victor Still.'

'Ehh, hello there,' said Orus.

Ambrose could only manage an 'Uuuuh.'

'You should stick close to Mr Victor Still. The Grimwood can be a dangerous place for those who are not careful.'

'Thank you,' replied Orus, slightly distracted by the small bird that had perched on Trickle's shoulder mid-way through the Sylvan's sentence. It snatched a fat yellow grub from a hole in the creature's bicep, then flew off with its bounty gripped in its beak.

'Do you know where this other group were heading?' Victor asked, looking back the way they had come.

'I believe they are heading towards your cottage. Is Mary there alone?'

'No, no. The kids are coming round for lunch today. They should be there any time now.'

'I had heard they had left home. You are a true friend of the forest taking them in as you did, Victor Still.' Trickle's third arm rejoined his body while he reached up with his left and scratched at his mossy beard. 'Perhaps someone should warn them.'

'The heroes?' said Victor. 'Oh no. If they're as bad as these lads say they are, they've got it coming.'

CHAPTER TWENTY-FOUR

Conrad strutted purposefully in front of the porch but the old woman continued to pay him only the bare minimum level of notice required by polite behaviour. She rocked back in her chair, knitting needles still clicking methodically away. Von Strauss was doing his best to be gentlemanly, but Huggle could tell by the way he wrung his gloves behind his back that this woman was about to step off the precipice of his master's shallow patience.

'Madam, it really is very important I catch up with my friends. I have news for them essential to the success of their endeavour. If you could just tell me the direction they went, my colleagues and I will be swiftly on our way.'

Mary Still looked up from her knitting only momentarily. She'd seen enough rats in her days to spot one easily enough, even if it was all dressed up in fancy clothes. 'Seems an awful lot of you just to deliver a message.'

Conrad looked back at his amassed entourage. Even with the last night's losses it was still a small army. 'It is a very important message.'

'Quite a few swords on show too,' she said, surveying the band with a careful eye.

'Important messages must be protected. These are dangerous lands after all.'

'Are they? Never had much trouble myself. I tend to find people bring trouble with them rather than the other way round.'

Huggle thought back to the horrors of last night. By the time they had stopped to camp they had already lost three wafters to giant spiders, a pack of wolves had chased off half of the horses, and one of Skar's men had gone for a pee in a bush only to find the bush was growing out of the back of a very angry troll. Then just when they managed to clear enough space to put the Whizzabang-Go up, a huge ogre burst into the camp shouting something about its plum trees. Then it started hitting people, with other people. And, to top it all off, they woke up this morning to find gnomes had nicked half of their bacon supplies. Given all that, Huggle couldn't help but feel that a woman who lives in such a place was not one to get on the wrong side of.

'A wise observation,' Conrad said through gritted, recently whitened, and perfectly aligned teeth. 'However I feel it is often the other way round. Some people bring trouble on themselves when there really is no need. As I said before, it is a very important message. You could even say it was a matter of life and death.'

The great hero punctuated his last word with a sharp stare to make it clear just whose death he was referring to.

Mary ignored it and kept on knitting. The garment across her lap looked to Huggle like a large quilt or throw, red and green and big enough for a double bed.

'What are their names?'

'What does it matter? Tell me where they went!' Conrad put his boot down on the end of the chair's rocker, lifting Mary's sweet round face to eye level. 'Now!'

She didn't even flinch.

'What does it matter?' Mary said, setting down her knitting. 'It matters because if they are your friends surely you know their names. Heck, who is the message addressed to? I wouldn't want to send you after the wrong people, would I? Not with such an important message.'

'Do not play games with me. The people who fell out of the sky in that.' Conrad released the rocking chair and pointed at the hulk of the airship, now colonised by the Still's chickens. 'Where did *they* go? You might think me a gentleman and that I would not strike an old woman and you would be right. However, I assure you, Skar here has no such restraint.'

There was a cough behind Huggle. The fierce warrior was standing in a pose normally reserved for a child about to explain to his PE teacher that he had forgotten his kit, hand raised and eyes down. 'Eh, begging your pardon, boss, but not a woman. My mum always said tha–'

Conrad closed on Skar with the cold finality of a coffin lid. 'You will do exactly what I tell you to do. Do I make myself clear? I own you until such time that I no longer need you. Unless you want to quit? Is that what you want? No place in the great saga for Skar. What would your old mum say then, to her failure of a son?'

Skar scuffed his feet and rubbed at the heart-shaped tattoo on his shoulder. 'Still don't think it's right.'

'How lucky for you that what you think doesn't matter.'

'You should listen to him,' said Mary. 'It's bad luck to hit a lady.'

'I do not deal in luck, old woman. I deal in facts and the facts are you are all alone out here and if you do not start being more helpful then very shortly *we* will be all alone out here.'

Apart from Conrad's hissing breath, the forest around the clearing became eerily silent. No birds chirped in the trees and no animals rustled through the undergrowth. Even the wind seemed to be holding its breath. Turning to look along the edge of the clearing, Huggle could see nothing out of place. All the same, he couldn't help feel the forest's attention was slowly turning inwards.

Mary continued to rock back and forth on her chair. 'Oh, I'm not alone out here. My children live out in the woods. Going by the look of your men you might even have met one of them already.' She lifted her knitting to inspect it.

Huggle could now see that what he had taken for a bed throw or quilt was actually a huge, ogre-sized jumper, complete with smiling snowman on the front.

'I'm doing this for my youngest, Brian. He's always complaining about the cold. Do you like it? His brother and sister will be coming too. They'll be very hungry I would think. I told them not to bother with breakfast. Mum's in charge of cooking today. I would ask you to stay; only it gets quite cramped with even just them to worry about. And, since you have such an important message to deliver...'

CHAPTER TWENTY-FIVE

The town of Harradin stood bare-chested against the cold
north wind, daring it to come and have a go. It was built on
a hook-shaped spur of rock that rose from the scrub on the
edge of the Grimwood, before curling back on itself to face
the towering peaks of the Fang Mountains. The King's Hall,
known locally as the Broch, stood at the extreme end of the
spur, its back to the city gates and its front looking up to
the wild lands it was charged with keeping in check. In the
crook of the rocky spur, the end of a deep lake resisted
freezing by virtue of pure stubbornness. This was despite
the glacier at the far end keeping it stuffed with ice-bergs.
The other side of the crescent was open to the wild,
Harradanians not being the kind of people to hold much
truck with hiding behind walls. Their style was much more
the charging madly forward in a mass of huge axes and
huger beards.

Orus had heard of it of course. Most people had.
The students at Cromalot were taught to revere and respect
it as the true home of the traditional heroic values.

Everyone else was taught to avoid it, or at least not to make any sudden moves around it.

It was founded by the barbarian warrior and all round dirty fighter Big Yin Belter. This came about after the then King of Andrus, a master of reverse psychology called Simon the Thick, explained to Belter that sacking the city of Andrus was far too easy. A *real* blood-crazed, muscle-brained manic, King Simon suggested, would go north and fight the hordes of monsters that periodically sallied forth from the Fang Mountains. In fact, the King added, what would really scare people, and show the rest of the world how tough Belter and his men were, would be to live up near the mountains permanently. As it is known that a man without fear is mad, and only a truly crazy person would even visit the Fang Mountains, to actually build a town there was surely the best way to show just how brave and fearless the Big Yin and his men were.

So that is what they did. Harradin was the result and, while it had mellowed somewhat over the last century, it was still more of a bar-fight than a town. Almost everything was decided by force of arms (or pokes in the eyes and kicks to the unmentionables), from the price of milk right up to who got to sit on the throne. The chance to become a king through martial skill and prowess (or through hitting someone really hard) drew heroes to it like students to a free buffet. Not only that, but its place as the last bastion of civilisation (if not civil behaviour) before the wild wastes of the north meant it had served as a stopping off point on some of the greatest sagas ever told.

It felt good to have finally made it. Many of Orus's most famous classmates from Cromalot had travelled through Harradin. Now he was there too. Next time, maybe it would be Golan Triple Axe reading about *him* in the penny folds.

Okay, he thought, so the hardest bit was still ahead, but he'd been doing pretty well so far. Maybe he really did have it in him. Maybe he really could've made a life of it, if he'd been dealt a different hand. That's all he really wanted to know.

But even Orus's high spirits at reaching Harradin and joining the trundling lane of carts, pack horses and travellers that grumbled, whipped and swore its way towards the town, were eclipsed by the youthful excitement of his companion.

'Can you believe we're here?' said Ambrose, poking his head out of the neck of his robe like a curious tortoise. 'Those gates were the first sticker I got for my *Heroes of the North* album. I never thought I would actually see them for real. The other initiates are going to be so jealous.'

The gates certainly were impressive. Fully twenty feet high and always kept wide open. Not built for security, their main purpose was to provide a place to display the town motto to any would be attackers; it hung on a banner above the gates and read: "Come and have a go if you think you're hard enough!"

'Just remember,' said Orus, 'there'll be plenty of heroes in here that would love to be the one to kill the last dragon. We'll need to be careful not to draw attention to ourselves.'

Much like the lake, the ground in Harradin refused to freeze, instead remaining a crackling mud with a varying strength of crust. Lighter loads would pass steadily over the top, while heavier ones broke through to the mush below. As such, Ambrose had gained a couple of inches on Orus by the time they reached the threshold of the town proper, while Orus had gained some wet feet.

A commotion halted the channel of traffic. Two of the towering carts of fur swayed then sunk into the mud at a lean as something heavy bashed between them. Shouts and grunts fed down the line, punctuated by the heavy thuds of fist on flesh.

'Looks like trouble,' said Victor, straining to see what was going on.

'What's happening?' asked Ambrose.

'Just some friendly neighbourhood fisticuffs,' Victor replied, stepping out of the main line of traffic. 'Probably some trader not wanting to pay the toll. Or caught smuggling. Or caught smuggling and not wanting to pay the bribe.'

Orus followed Victor. Ahead a familiar circle of men was gathering in the street. In Orus's experience this signified that somewhere in the centre of the circle, if not blood, then at least teeth were about to be spilled.

'Come on, lad,' he said, directing Ambrose forward. 'I'm sure they'll sort it out themselves.'

'But shouldn't we go over there? What if one of them needs help?'

'Bet on the other one,' suggested Victor.

The crowd ahead parted, spitting out a rolling mass of mud and fists. Orus grabbed Ambrose and yanked him out of its path before the young monk could become collateral damage. The two men brawled past them and out of the gates, followed closely by the jostling crowd.

'Get him, Eric!'

'Smash him, Shug!'

'In the kidneys!'

'Stop bawling, it's only a finger. You've got eight more.'

Ambrose stepped in front of Orus and Victor. 'We can't just walk away.'

'Best to let these things run their course,' said Victor.

'But shouldn't we at least call the gate guards?'

'Those were the gate guards.'

CHAPTER TWENTY-SIX

Victor was staying with some family down on the waterfront, but he recommended an inn to his new friends. The Hairy Flagon certainly lived up to its name. Everyone had a beard. Even some of their beards had beards. The dog sleeping by the big hearth seemed to be entirely made of beards, so much so that it was a wonder it could see where it was going. As if this wasn't enough, all of the other patrons were swathed in thick furs; not the kind that a beautiful heiress might wear to a fancy do, these were the kind of furs that doubled up as bed clothes and were designed to stop bits of their owners dropping off when it got really cold.

The two beers that Orus purchased from the Yeti-ish barman collected an intricate lattice of fibres by the time he made it back to their seats. He manoeuvred his own personal insulation under the table and slid along the bench.

Victor had been right about the Flagon being quieter than the inns near the gate. There weren't any fights in it, yet. However, there was an accordion player sitting in the corner unpacking his instrument. Dancing in Harradin was a full contact sport. The style favoured was like that found at a Scottish rugby club ceilidh at 2am, and resulted in a similar number of hospitalisations.

Ambrose reached hesitantly for his flagon, watching Orus carefully. Orus had seen enough young lads in Ditch sneaking into the Overhang Bar to know when someone was having their first drink. 'You'll want to scoop that out first,' he advised, pinching the hairs out of his beer's frothy head.

Ambrose did likewise and looked around for somewhere to deposit the bar's namesake. He tried to wipe it on the bench but came back with more than he started. Following Orus, he wiped that on the leg of his robe.

'Cheers.' Orus reached forward and the two clashed mugs. Orus took a large gulp of the cold beer. An earthy taste. Backed up by cool crisp mountain water. 'Not bad, not bad.'

The young monk followed suit with an ambitious gulp. He swallowed hard. His face turned inwards, he coughed, once, twice, then padded his tongue on the roof of his mouth. 'Mmm,' was about all he could manage.

'A bit strong for you, eh?' Orus smiled.

'No, no it's not that.' Ambrose reached into his mouth and retrieved a long silvery hair. 'Missed one.'

'It's a sad day when your drink has more hair than you do.' Orus rubbed at his surviving archipelago of hair. Out of the cover of the Grimwood the cold was biting. Before heading further north they would need to find some new clothes and buy some supplies. And he should send a message to Mavis, to let her know he was alright.

'How's the egg?'

Ambrose lifted the heat-proof bag onto the table. 'Fine I think.'

The monk pulled open the flap to reveal the dull red glow. It wasn't nearly as bright now. Orus could see the shell's surface, pocked with tiny pin prick indentations. But the light was still enough to draw unwanted attention. Considering they already looked out of place, being the only people in the bar not dressed as their favourite winter animal, and as he had no wish to repeat their adventure at the All Seasons, he quickly flipped the top back over the bag and placed it on the floor between his feet.

'Do you think we'll have enough time?'

'We should do. The innkeeper says there's a stove in our room. We can put the egg in that overnight to warm it up again. I bought an extra bundle of sticks so we can give it a real boost. It's only another day to Pale Pass and then about another half day's walk to the Hatching Grounds. We should just about make it. So long as nothing gets in our way. But then, I guess that's what you're here for.'

That *is* what I'm here for, Orus thought. The confident masculinity in the air was rubbing off on him. Here in Harradin. On this quest. To save the world. He was no longer a servant. He was a leader.

'That's right,' he said. 'We'll get some rest tonight and then go to see the King tomorrow morning. I don't want to hang around here long. Von Strauss will still be after us. He didn't look like the giving up easily type.'

'Oh no, he isn't,' replied Ambrose excitedly. 'He once chased a griffin all the way across the Twilight Wastes, alone, all because the first time he tried to slay it the creature swallowed his favourite sword. Afterwards, he had the carcass stuffed and given as a gift to the Empress of Krum. She loves birds you see. I never understood how he managed to carry the body back with him, but then I guess that's why he is such a great hero.'

'Sounds like quite a guy.'

'Oh, he is. I'm surprised you've never come across him. He has a whole chapter in my sticker album. He's been the top hero for a few years now.'

'Until we came along.' Orus nudged at Ambrose with his elbow.

Ambrose went flush at Orus's plural pronoun use. 'Until *you* came along.'

'Hey, if it wasn't for you I'd probably be back in the All Seasons trying to scrape together enough cash for a new everything. And you made a daring escape from the Temple, travelled through the Grimwood unharmed. I'd say that's some good heroing behaviour.'

'I suppose. But I'm just an initiate – not even a full monk yet. I'm ordinary.'

And I'm just a gardener thought Orus, but what does that matter?

'Ordinary people can be heroes too,' he said, thinking about all the late nights Mavis spent working on new orders to pay for Tag's schooling, all the other servants at the castle who slaved away day-in day-out to keep Ditch going, the ones that never got rewarded, that never even got noticed unless something went wrong. He thought about the young stable boy who slept in the hay store so he could save money on rent and send the extra back to his ailing mother. He thought about Jenny in the kitchens, who would gather up the leftovers and make them into pies and pastries for the street children. He thought about the guard captain that gave up half his pension to support the wives of men that had died in the line of duty. He thought about all the people that did the things that no-one asked them to, the people that so many depended on but so few acknowledged. The people that did the things that had to be done, not because they particularly wanted to, not because they were paid to, certainly not because they thought they might get rewarded to, but because someone had to and they were someone – even if the rest of society never noticed it. They were his people. They weren't the people that made the world go round, but they were the ones that made it a worthwhile ride.

'In fact,' he added. 'Most of them already are.'

*

That night Orus couldn't sleep. His mind was full of visions of daring deeds, great sagas, parades in his honour, Mavis and Tag with admiration and pride in their eyes, and, above it all, the wings of dragons cutting through the clouds. He knew he had a long day tomorrow so tried to block these visions out. It didn't work. He tried to count sheep but the dragons kept chasing them away. He tried to think of waves gently lapping at a distant shore but they soon turned the colour of ale and sloshed and slapped over the sides of tankards as their owners sang songs of his adventures.

Eventually, he gave up altogether. He wrapped himself in his itchy blanket and went to sit by the stove. The flames cracked and popped as they chased down air pockets hidden in the logs. Ambrose had left the egg on a grate above the fire. Its glow was already getting brighter.

Such a strange thing for the fate of my world to rest on, Orus thought, as he watched tongues of fire curl around the base of the shell. A black shape twisted and moved under the surface. Then it was gone, melting away like a ship in the fog.

I guess you're probably thinking the same thing.

The moon passed by the window and Orus's eyelids began to droop. Before they could close completely, the flames in the stove began to stretch upwards. Orus shook himself awake. He slid forward on his chair and stared at the fire. The flames were losing their familiar pointed tear drop shape, becoming uniform along their length. Like magnetic spaghetti, they were being drawn up from the coals and directly into the egg. As they channelled heat from the heart of the fire into the shell, it began to glow brighter and brighter.

The strands of light danced across Orus's face. They surrounded the egg, protecting it, warming it. It raised itself from the iron grate and hung in the air, spinning slowly. After a time, the wood in the stove burned down and the pasta strings of heat grew thinner. Eventually, they started to detach themselves from the shell and it resumed its place on the grate. Orus remembered the extra bundle of sticks. He put on the fire proof mitts and pushed some new logs into the stove. Soon the thermo-magnet started up again and the dance of the flames continued.

As the heat in the room increased, Orus felt himself slip away into sleep.

CHAPTER TWENTY-SEVEN

Ambrose was already wide awake by the time Orus roused from his seat by the fire. The fire in the stove had burned out but the egg blazed more brightly than any time since they had left the temple. It was so hot that they had to borrow a pair of tongs from the innkeeper, the Grandmaster's mitts not thick enough to provide the necessary protection. In the rush and the half-haze of pre-bacon roll wake-me-up, Orus forgot to ask about the strange happenings of the night before.

Before heading up to the King's Hall, they went to Strathy's Furs, as Victor had suggested, and picked out some winter clothing. Going for substance over style, Orus bought a simple, thick wrap around cloak of mountain goat, some hard wearing boots, and a hat to stop his head getting frost bite. He was particularly happy with his purchases as he had bought them with a stash of Harradanian dollars he had kept in the man-chest for just such an eventuality. They had been given to Orus by a merchant after he had helped to fix the man's wagon when it threw a wheel on Deep Street. Mavis had told him to get them changed into Ditch money, but the exchange rate was criminal. Better to keep them, just in case.

Score one for hoarders, he thought.

Orus caught a glimpse of himself in the store window as he left. Swathed in wool, with the light snow falling around, he was really starting to look the part. He sucked in his belly and puffed out his chest, the latter almost overhanging the former for the first time in a long time. Next, he went to the Messengers' Guild and paid for a note to be sent to Mavis via pigeon. In it he explained that the Prince's carrot shipment had been delayed and he would be a few days late. He hated to lie to her, but he would tell her everything as soon as he got back. Then he and Ambrose went back to the Hairy Flagon and left their new supplies with Thunder in the stables.

Striking out for the Broch, the sun cast long shadows across the dark lake to the west as the town climbed the rocky spur to the summit. The majority of the buildings were built on the sloping side of the spur leading down to the water. Like the people that owned them they were stout, square and hairy on top. Further down, thatched roofs gave way to the wooden warehouses of the waterfront. It was jammed with ships and echoed with the sound of nautical terms, which Orus didn't understand, and the colourful language of men at work, which he did.

On the rocky side, the buildings were grander, growing increasingly so the higher Orus and Ambrose went. These were the halls of the great clans of Harradin. Outside each one stood a banner pole bearing the family crest. Most included a very large weapon backed with a field of the family colour (although in one instance the field was full of bodies – that family's colour presumably being red). All the way up the main street Ambrose stopped to point out famous landmarks from his favourite heroing adventures.

'And that is The Burning Ship,' he said, directing Orus to a small tavern. Around its door the snowy imprints of the previous night's patrons' unsuccessful attempts to stumble home were still visible, not yet having been trampled over by the morning rush. 'That's the tavern where Ulfric Suresight became Ulfric One-Eye.'

Orus made a note in his head: one to avoid.

'And that,' Ambrose pointed to a huge double headed battle axe embedded in an anvil, 'that is the axe that Hoth Steel-Toe dropped whilst fighting Sky-Claw, King of the Snow Eagles. It is said that after losing it Hoth beat Sky-Claw to death with his own boot. He drowned in the lake when it fell from the sky, but they say he was still laughing when he hit the water.'

Orus knew these stories as well. The great sagas were recited nightly at Cromalot and tales from Harradin were always popular. Lots of his classmates talked about going there when they graduated. Maybe when he had finished this quest someone would write a saga about him. Maybe he could go back to the school as a teacher. Not all the time of course, Mavis and Tag still came first (and second), but a couple of weeks here and there. He could be Visiting Professor of Survivability.

As they neared the top of the town, the cliff to the west became too steep to build on, allowing for a great view of the ice filled lake. Harradin had a proud nautical tradition. Many people lived in their boats and most were buried in them too. It was far easier than digging in the hard frozen ground. Orus and Ambrose stopped to watch the fishing fleet threading through the charred, up-thrust masts of the funeral ships crowding the floor of the bay.

Rounding the final corner, the spur opened up and its rough cobbles gave way to fine cut flagstones. The slabs were laid out in a great octagonal arena. In its centre the town symbol, a towering mountain bear being kicked between the legs by a Harradanian warrior, was set out in black on white. This was where the King met his challengers.

A rather forward thinking place in some ways, Harradin prided itself on being a meritocracy. It was just that the merit it was particularly interested in was a talent for violence. Just as the poor man can stay in the finest castles if he is scary enough for no-one to argue with him, any person can wear the crown of Harradin. He only needs to kill the previous owner and survive long enough to arrange his coronation.

'Do you know,' Ambrose stood in the centre of the arena, 'I heard last night that the current King has defeated thirty-two challengers. Only Big Yin Belter survived more. I can't wait to meet him. Do you think he'll let us through the gate to the mountains?'

'What?' Orus pulled himself back from imaginary duels in front of cheering, baying crowds. Maybe instead of Cromalot he could come back here and have a go at taking the throne. 'Oh, the King? I expect so. He is supposed to stop things getting in, not out. Still, best not to mention the egg. If Conrad turns up we don't want him knowing we've been here.'

'Good idea.' Ambrose patted at the pouch by his hip. Even with all the insulation, a gentle wisp of steam rose from it in the cold morning air. 'What about this?'

'We'll say we're going hunting. That's our soup. Freshly made this morning.'

'Do you think we just go and knock?'

'Probably, I don't think this is the kind of place where they stand on ceremony. Enemies maybe, but not ceremony.'

A bank of stone steps rose from the arena, levelling out in front of the entrance to the Broch. The main building was a large long house, its roof shaped like the keel of a ship. It rested on a raised stone platform. This in turn had smaller doorways set into it, leading to the servants' levels.

Two guards flanked the main doors.

They crossed their spears over the doors. 'State your business.'

Orus pushed out his chest again. 'We're here to see the King. We wish permission to travel north, into the mountains.'

'You sure?' replied the guard on the left, giving each of them a look up and down. 'It's pretty dangerous.'

'Not for the faint-hearted,' added his partner.

'If I see any, I'll be sure to mention that,' replied Orus.

'Can get pretty hairy,' said the first guard.

'The wilds hold no fear for me.' Orus gave himself a big tick for such a fine piece of hero speak.

'Not the wilds,' replied the first guard, jabbing over his shoulder with his thumb. 'His Majesty isn't really a morning person.'

The walls of the Broch reverberated with a loud bellow. The guards stepped quickly to each side of the doors in a well-practiced motion. As they did so, a sword blade burst through the wood, showering Orus in splinters. Its point had penetrated a good three inches and was staring directly at Orus's head. He reached out a hesitant finger and gave the blade a ping.

The old Orus started to creep back up into his stomach. 'We, eh, could come back later,' he said, 'when he is in a better mood.'

'Not much point,' said the guard on the left, reaching for the large iron door ring. 'He ain't an afternoon person either.'

'Or evening,' added the other.

On pulling the door open, Orus and Ambrose were greeted by the King's aid.

'Cribond. Some visitors to see the King.'

'Oh excellent, excellent. Ferrip, if you would be so kind.'

The guard called Ferrip took hold of the sword pinning Cribond to the door by his green cloak and yanked the blade free from the wood. The pale servant dropped to the floor like a snake lowering itself from a tree. He coiled back up to a standing position, dusting himself off as he did so.

'Please excuse me. Occupational hazard.' Cribond's long pale fingers closed in a lattice in front of his chain of office. 'Please come in. Always happy to have visitors. Heightens the odds you see.'

Ferrip held out the sword to Cribond. 'Will His Majesty be needing this back?'

'Oh no, I think we can leave that out here for now.' Orus stomach settled.

'He has plenty more,' continued Cribond. 'This way please, gentlemen.'

CHAPTER TWENTY-EIGHT

In some of the kingdoms of Drift, power rests behind the throne. It was hard to tell if this was the case in Harradin since the size of the man *on* the throne made seeing behind it quite a challenge. If the rest of him was anything to go by, King Tyran probably had muscles on his teeth. Other than the long black hair that fell across both of his massive shoulders, his only coverings were a loincloth, a pair of boots and a thin coat of what might have been wood-varnish.

As the party approached the throne, the King clapped together hands that coal-shovels could only aspire to. 'Back so soon, Cribond? I didn't nick you did I?'

'No, sire. Not this time,' replied Cribond.

'You must be getting faster.'

'One hopes.'

'Perhaps I will try it with my eyes open next time.' King Tyran lifted his huge head, bucket chin first, and smiled with the good side of his face. 'What have you got here, Cribond? Breakfast I hope. You, fat one. What have you made for your King?'

'Actually, Your Majesty...' Orus decided to ignore the fat comment in view of the large collection of weapons leaning against the Tyran's throne. Not that he was sure he would have challenged the huge man if they weren't there. Something told Orus he was probably the type who enjoyed working with his hands just as much. '... we are here to ask—'

'To challenge me?' the king roared, hauling himself to his feet. 'I accept. Both together is it? Very well. To the arena.'

He slapped his fist into his other hand.

'Cribond! Call up old Jones from his workshop. He'll want to measure these two up for a box.'

'Actually, sire, they're not here—'

'Not! Not what?'

A knife struck the ground where the servant had been standing. When he spoke again, Cribond was on the other side of the throne.

'They're not here to challenge you. I believe our visitors were looking to talk to you.'

'Talk? How boring.' Something about King Tyran's voice poked at Orus's brain. He was sure he had heard it before. He tried to ignore it, preferring to keep his mind concentrated on the monarch's throwing arm. 'What do you want then?'

'We,' said Orus, 'that is, my friend and I, have come to your kingdom—'

'Great kingdom,' nudged Cribond.

'Your great kingdom, to ask permission from Your Majesty—'

Tyran's hand moved towards a nearby sword pommel.

'Most wise and powerful,' suggested Cribond.

'From Your Most Wise and Powerful Majesty, to be allowed to pass through the gate to the Fang Mountains. If that is not too much trouble.'

The King looked down on Orus. Being close to seven feet tall it was a look he had a lot of practice at. Suddenly, he clapped his hands together like two battle lines at full charge and let out a booming laugh.

'Ha, ha, ha. You? You and him are going into the wilds. Ha, ha, ha. Cribond are these the new jesters I asked for? A good start, little clowns.'

Blood began to rush along the cracked lines in Orus face. It was one thing to call him fat, but to laugh right in his face. Maybe the old Orus would put up with that. Not anymore. He was done being laughed at. He was a hero now. A real hero. Why shouldn't he go to the Fang Mountains? 'We're not jesters,' he said. You might not have said there was steel in his voice, but the words at least had a good iron count. 'We mean to go into the mountains and we are here to ask permission to travel through your lands.'

The King leaned forward again. When the word came it was cold and hard and suspicious.

'Why?'

Stick to the plan. He has no reason to refuse.

'I am taking the boy hunting.'

'With no weapons?'

Orus looked down at his empty sword belt. After the furs there had been no money for weapons.

'They are back at our lodgings,' he replied. 'We wouldn't bring weapons into your hall. We came only to talk. Nothing else.'

'In my experience, there are only two kinds of people who don't carry weapons: fools and spies. And you've already said you're not fools. Have you been sent to watch me for your master, so he can try to find out how to beat me? What a coward. Maybe I'll send you back to him, over a couple of months, small bits at a time.'

'We aren't spies or fools. We just want to go hunting.' Orus's iron tongue was beginning to melt under the King's bronze gaze. His mouth was going dry and his face was getting hot.

'You are serious then, fat man?' The King scratched at his chin. 'Well, if you insist. Who am I to deny the wolves a hearty meal so close to winter? Cribond better call Jones after all. I doubt these two will even make past the tree-line. If they even get to the gate. Fatty looks close to a heart attack already.'

The King let out another booming laugh. Cribond, always conscious of his position, oozed out an accompanying smile.

'You're sure you don't want me to finish you off here?' King Tyran lifted a sword from his collection and looked down its blade at Orus and Ambrose. 'It'll save you the trip. That road is quite steep going.'

Orus clenched his fists tight. The old Orus might have put up with this but not now.

'I mean look at you,' the King continued. 'Nice furs. A sheep in sheep's clothing. Like lambs to the slaughter. Ha, ha, ha.'

That's it. Orus stepped towards the King. He had had enough of this.

'How dare you!'

The King stopped laughing immediately. The words were out before Orus even knew he had said them. It took him a further instant to notice this was because he hadn't. The gurgling in Orus stomach shot up into his throat. Ambrose had stepped to the foot of the King's throne and was pointing at the massive monarch with a skinny finger. This was not going to end well.

'Do you know who you are talking to? This is Morris the Marauder. He is one of the greatest heroes who ever lived. You should watch your tongue you, you big bully, or Morris might just, well, he'll, he'll do something not very nice to you and you won't like that, I can tell you.' Ambrose jabbed a finger back at Orus. 'He escaped Conrad

Von Strauss and survived the Grimwood and he has been heroing for twenty years all over the world so you better just watch it.'

Much to Orus's surprise the King did not cut them both in half. Instead, he sat very still, calm as a volcano. Cribond had disappeared altogether, no doubt retreating to some kind of emergency bunker. When the King spoke the words came slowly, as if great effort and thought was going on somewhere inside that massive head. 'What did you say his name was?'

'Morris,' replied Ambrose. 'Morris the Marauder.'

'Morris… Morris,' the King turned the name over in his mouth. He turned his gaze on Orus and stared hard. 'But that's not right is it?'

Tyran was off the throne and advancing towards Orus. As the King moved forward into the light the little niggle Orus had felt earlier broke through and slapped him with a firm hand of realisation.

'That's not right, is it?' Standing before Orus now wasn't just the King of Harradin. It was also Cromalot's premier bully, Tyran Sarus: owner of the school record for Best Olopian Burns, highest Bolgovian Wedgies, and the creator of a hundred repressed memories. He was older than Orus. They had only been at school together for two years, but in that two years they had become very well acquainted. They would often go out for runs together. Sometimes Orus even managed to get away. But only sometimes. 'Hello, Orus. Long time.'

'Hello, Tyran. You've grown.' Orus shrunk back from his old nemesis.

'So have you.' Tyran delivered his usual five finger greeting straight to the gut.

Orus doubled over. The punch was hard as an iceberg and already he was getting that sinking feeling. Bits of his brain were rushing to the lifeboats, while cold reality drowned the fire in his engines.

Ambrose rushed to Orus's side.

'So, this is your little brat. Oh we all heard about you and that girl. First quest as well. You know you're supposed to clear off when that happens. I've probably got dozens of waifs dotted around, driving their mums crazy. Unless, did she beat you up too? Make you stay. Ha, you always were a weakling.'

'Come on, Morris,' Ambrose tried to lift him up. 'Don't let him get away with this. You've taken on bigger before, like the Yellowknife Leviathan.'

Tyran let out another great laugh. 'Him? The Yellowknife Leviathan. Have you been telling porkies, Orus? That's not on, you know. Stealing someone else's glory. It's against the Cromalot Code remember? They string you up for that sort of thing round here.'

Orus tried to muster an answer but all he could do was gulp down air and pain.

'Morris killed it.' Ambrose was red with rage. 'A spear right through its eye. Didn't you? Didn't you?'

Orus turned away, shuffling on his knees. He had been a fool to think he would even get this far.

'Boy, the Yellowknife Leviathan was killed by Aslaf the Sabre about four hundred years ago. Though you'd have had to have gone to a hero school to know that, eh Orus – his name's Orus by the way. No bards sing Aslaf's saga anymore. Bit old fashioned. But they still tell it at Cromalot. Tradition and all that. What else has he told you, boy?'

'He, he, sank the Tattersail Armada, he killed the Roggle Stomper of Black Pine Forest, he defended Olop from the Clockwork Squid.' Ambrose ran through all the embezzled tales Orus spouted out back at the All Seasons but Tyran only laughed harder and harder. When he had finally finished, the King wiped a tear away from his eye.

Orus, meanwhile, sat on the floor in the middle of the great hall, thoroughly crushed.

'What a saga you've spun for yourself, Orus. Not bad for a lowly gardener. Oh yes, I know about that too. We royals talk you see. The Prince of Ditch was telling me what a good job you did on the roses last year. Didn't get scratched I hope. Those thorns can be dangerous, so I hear.'

'What are you talking about?' asked Ambrose, still clinging on to hope.

'He is not a hero. He's a gardener, a servant, and he has been for years. He's a nothing, a loser, a failure. Isn't that right, Orrrussss?'

But Orus was beyond words. Even being cut up by Conrad and his lackeys would have been better than this. At least then he wouldn't have to go home a failure. Back to Ditch. Back to cleaning out drains and shovelling up after the horses. Back to all those people who treated him like a nobody. And this time, he'd know they were right. Tyran would make sure all his old friends knew too, all the crew from Cromalot. He could bet on that. What would Golan Triple Axe think then?

'Well, what does that matter?' Ambrose stood between Orus's huddled form and the King. 'Gardeners can be heroes too. Do you know what this is?' Ambrose lifted the dragon-scale bag up for the King to see. 'In here is a dragon egg. The last dragon egg. And with it, Orus is going to save all of Drift. I bet you and your friends have never done anything that big.'

'Did you say an egg?' The King snatched the bag from Ambrose's hand. 'Still haven't had my breakfast. How are you at cooking, Orus? The kitchen's just down those stairs. No, best not. There's lots of knives down there. Wouldn't want you getting hurt. Then who'd trim all those hedges, eh?'

The King let out another great laugh, before bellowing for his aide.

'Cribond! Get in here.'

Without any sound or hint of movement, the clerk was back at the King's side.

'Yes, sire?'

'Have the cooks boil this.'

Cribond took the egg from the King. He stared at it for a moment. His eyes flicked to Ambrose then back to the egg. 'Sire, is this—'

'An egg. Yes it is. Good for building up muscle. Just what the doctor ordered.'

'Indeed, sire,' replied Cribond. His eyes lifted from the egg and fixed on Ambrose again. 'Indeed.'

'You can't do that,' protested Ambrose. 'The egg must be taken north. The world depends on it.'

Ambrose's protest was useless. Although no-one would have been able to pinpoint the exact moment he moved, Cribond had already disappeared into the shadows of the hall.

Tyran looked down at Orus's broken, weak form. 'More of his lies, little fool. Any idiot could tell that is a snow eagle's egg. Very tasty they are too. Now get out of here.' The King took one final look at Orus and spat on the floor. 'And take that gardener with you. We have no need for his kind in Harradin. Too cold for pretty flowers up here.'

CHAPTER TWENTY-NINE

Orus stared into his mug. A tired, worn face stared back from the surface of the ale. Even with the extra hair afforded by the Hairy Flagon's unique ambience covering his bald spot, he knew it was not the face of a hero. Not like the ones he'd grown up hearing about: no battle scars, no piercing eyes, no grim determination. Sure, it was a worn down face, but it was the other kind: the sort that, if repeated and dressed appropriately, could form a crowd of any number of unremarkable dead-enders, in any city or town in the world, all toiling away, stoking the fire for someone else's barbeque. It was a defeated face. A servant's face. A loser's face. The bottom, that was his place and he'd been a fool to think otherwise. He'd made it this far by the skin of his teeth and when it came to a real test he collapsed faster than a two legged stool. No doubt Fate was laughing somewhere above. The old trickster had got him good. Just like the Shadow-wart bush. Let me think I've won, give me hope – that way, slapping me down again is all the more fun. Yeah, I know your game. I just don't remember asking to play.

'So what do we do now?' asked Ambrose.

Orus picked a long grey strand from his ale and took a sip. The poor lad didn't even know it was over.

'We go home,' he said.

'But the quest. We need to get the egg back. We aren't finished.'

'No we don't and yes we are. It's over, Ambrose. Even if we could get it back, we can't cross the gate to the mountains, and even if we could, we'd still be dead within an hour anyway.' Orus glugged down another mouthful. The ale wasn't making him feel any better, yet. 'Can you fight giant wolves and white orcs and snow snakes? 'Cause I can't.'

'But we can't just give up.'

'It's not giving up if you were never going to win.' The face in his drink came back again. Orus took another swig. He didn't need reminding of who he was. Not now. He knew. He was nobody. 'People like us don't save the world. How could we? It barely even notices us.'

Ambrose sat back in his chair and looked at the broken figure in front of him. He looked like he'd gained ten years in the walk back from the King's Hall.

'Why did you lie to me?'

'Would you have trusted me with the egg if I hadn't? Anyway, it wasn't you I lied to. It was me.'

Orus drained his tankard and shuffled out from the table. 'Now, if you don't mind, I'm going home. My wife is probably worried sick for her selfish husband.'

'But the dragon,' Ambrose grabbed Orus's arm. 'The world will be destroyed.'

Orus paused, but only to brush off Ambrose's hand. 'Well,' he said, 'that'll probably be a weight off a lot of people's minds.'

*

Ambrose was left in the Flagon, surrounded by the noise and tension of pre-fight drinking. He felt scared. With

Morris here, or Orus as he was now, he'd felt secure, confident, invincible even. They would never get into trouble Orus couldn't get them out of. Whoever heard of a hero getting bumped off in some backwater bar fight? Lonely foreigners on the other hand…

With this security blanket of narrative necessity gone, the Hairy Flagon suddenly became a much more threatening environment. It was the mid-morning rush. The heavy hitters from the night before had battled off enough of their hangovers to make it back in the ring, while those who never made it home in the first place were stirring under the tables.

The young monk glanced around. One of the patrons stared back at him from the midst of a huge ginger beard. He did not look friendly. He didn't even look liked he could spell 'friendly'. The monk turned back to his table, hoping to avoid any excuse for trouble. Not being used to bars, he was unaware that when trouble came, it tended not to bother with such formalities.

He tried to think about the egg and the dragon – how to get it back, what to do then – but it was all too much for him. He had no mind for planning. He didn't know how the real world worked. He needed help.

Reaching into his cloak, he pulled out the roll of Pairing Paper. He tried to write small. He had a lot of explaining to do.

Grandmaster, are you there?

Hello Ambrose. Still alive I see. Good, good. How goes progress?

Not well, Grandmaster. In fact, I fear all may be lost. I have failed. The King of Harradin has taken the egg and the man I brought you is not the great hero I thought he was. He has confessed to being a fraud. All his stories are stolen from other heroes, long dead. He is just a gardener. A servant from the town of Ditch. Nothing more. And now he has left.

How do you know all this?

The King knows him. Knew him. They used to train together at Cromalot. But Orus, that is his real name, quit after only his first quest to raise a child. He hasn't even used a sword in twenty years. He isn't a real hero at all.

The Grandmaster was obviously thinking hard. When he answered he was writing in tea rather than ink. Brother Amphis kept telling him he should put the ink well and the mug on opposite sides of the desk.

That is why we picked him Ambrose. Because he is not a real hero, at least not the kind you mean. If he was, he would have been building one of those towers up the side of the Worm-mound, just like all the rest. You need to remind him of that.

I will try, Grandmaster.

I don't know how, Ambrose thought, but I will. What other choice do I have?

As for the egg, it is with the King?

Yes. I think he means to eat it.

Well that at least gives us some time.

How so?

Have you ever tried to boil a dragon egg?

CHAPTER THIRTY

Down in the kitchens of the Broch, Tyran's head chef, Dimble Shanks, gripped a long pair of tongs he had borrowed from the blacksmith. The outburst of kitchen shorthand that followed his first attempt at picking up the strange egg had drawn a crowd of other servants. With his scorched hands bandaged up, he was ready for another go. The other kitchen staff peered cautiously over his shoulder as Dimble pushed back the top of the protective bag and exposed the glowing shell of the King's breakfast. The chef's handprints still pulsed on the surface of the egg, giving off a whiff of burnt skin.

The air shimmered as the egg was uncovered and a sweat sheen spread across the chef's forehead. Moving with the care of a vet reaching into a hissing cat box, he lowered the tongs over the egg and began to squeeze.

'Lid off, now!' he called out.

Behind him, a kitchen boy lifted the top of a large pan of boiling water.

After a quick check of his escape route, Dimble dropped the egg into the rapidly bubbling water.

'Close it!'

The kitchen boy slammed down the heavy pot lid, trapping the egg inside. For a second at least.

It started with a rumbling. Then there was a rattling. Then steam punched at the lid from below, escaping in angry puffs. The kitchen boy shook as vibrations travelled up his arm. He looked for support from his colleagues. It was not forthcoming. Most were in the process of hiding behind varying pieces of cookware.

Reaching from behind an extra thick chopping board, Dimble Shanks turned over a miniature hourglass. 'That's it, boy. Hold it there. Just three minutes more. The King likes a runny yo—'

An eruption of steam lifted the lid, and the kitchen boy, high into the air. The other servants dived for cover as flying shards of metal filled the room.

Once his ears stopped ringing, Dimble Shanks used the tongs to lift the remains of the pan off the heat. The egg was still in one piece, glowing defiantly.

'Briban,' he called to a colander headed chef peeking out from one of the large, thick-sided sinks. 'Can you go and get me the shoeing hammer from the stable. I think fried might be a better option.'

*

In the stable at the Hairy Flagon, Orus was fastening the man-chest to Thunder's back. He hoped Mavis hadn't needed anything from it while he had been away.

He tightened the straps under Thunder's belly. It pulled to the next hole in the leather. 'And I've dragged you along too. You must think I'm mad.'

Not just you.

The old donkey dipped his head and took a big mouthful of hay. He wasn't looking forward to the return journey, even if it was downhill most of the way.

'People our age should be taking it easy. Not going off on adventures,' Orus added, patting Thunder between the ears.

If you really thought that, you could always leave that junk here.

If anything, Thunder thought, the man-chest was heavier than when they had set off. Almost as if, all along the journey, someone had been collecting things that might come in handy, just in case.

Thunder eyed Orus suspiciously. The gardener of Castle Ditch was inspecting a bucket handle left in a neighbouring stall.

'That'd be alright if you brushed the rust off,' said Orus, tucking it into the chest. He didn't notice the groan from below. 'Come on, hopefully we can make it back to the Still's cottage before sun down.'

Orus turned to the exit. Ambrose was waiting for him. 'It's no use,' Orus said. 'I'm finished with this. Don't try to change my mind. He's right. I'm no hero, just a servant. An ordinary person. A nobody. At least in Ditch I was a useful nobody.'

'You said ordinary people were heroes.'

'I'm a liar too, remember.'

'But we can't leave him with the egg. He's going to kill it!'

'If not him, someone else. You saw all those hunters at the temple. Do you really think they'll give up when it hatches? Anyway, storming the Broch in the middle of the day is a bit extreme, even if I was a real hero. There must be twenty guards around the walls. Nobody could get in there without a fight.'

The door to the stable swung back again and clattered against the first stall. A messenger brushed snow off his purple riding cloak and gestured to Orus.

'You, stable boy, bed down my horse and take my bag up to your best room. I have an urgent message for the King and when I return I shall need lodging for the night.'

'Do I look like the stable boy?' asked Orus. Tyran might get away with demeaning him but this snotty little grot could stuff it.

The messenger unclipped his cloak and threw it at Orus. 'Servants all look the same. You can't expect a messenger of Conrad Von Strauss to spend time determining which basement level of the social ladder you happen to cling to. Just get the horse. If you're lucky they'll be a shiny coin in it for you.'

Orus looked down at the cloak. He looked at himself. Then he looked at the messenger. An idea was forming. Maybe there was a way back into the Broch after all.

He folded the purple fabric carefully over his arm. 'Why certainly, my lord,' he said, approaching the messenger. 'Just out here is it?'

'Yes, the bay. And be quick about it or there'll be trouble.'

Orus's fist lifted the messenger high into the air. He came crashing down a moment later, laid out in the mud. 'Trouble? We wouldn't want that, would we?'

Ambrose looked down at the crumbled figure. 'I don't think they'll fit either of us.'

'What?' Orus rubbed his knuckles. They hurt. In a good way.

'His clothes. So we can get into the King's Hall again. That's the plan isn't it?'

'That would have been a good idea. Not what I was thinking though. Help me get the chest off Thunder. We're not done here yet.'

'So you're back on the quest?'

'It certainly looks that way. Let's go get that egg.'

'How do we get past the guards?'

'You heard him.' Orus prodded the downed messenger with his foot. 'All us servants look the same.'

*

There was still a great guard in Althor somewhere. Incompetence in guardsmen doesn't start straight away. It builds up over years, like rust and resentment. Back when he started in the King's Guard he had been keen and attentive. He followed all the procedures. He'd learned all the proscriptions. He kept himself fit and alert, ready to break into a daring rooftop chase at a second's notice, and his salute was so sharp he could've used it to the cut the cheese for his sandwiches. Then he got stationed at the servant's door.

Having been brought up on stories of the King's Guard defending the town against the terrible monsters of the mountains, and spent his formative years practicing swordsmanship and small unit tactics, a life of checking the various lower orders in and out of the Broch was not what he had envisioned for his future. There hadn't been a big monster attack on the town in over a decade and, from what he heard from the northern outposts, the mountains were getting quieter every year. As if this wasn't demoralising enough, like a camel crossing the desert, every time he managed to heave himself up under the burden of his frustrated ambition, Life took it as an invitation to add another problem to the top of the pile.

So today, as he looked out along the line of servants queuing in front of his lectern, with their sacks of turnips, barrels of ale, obscure rodent killing devices, fish baskets, bread baskets and washing baskets – same as yesterday, and the grey infinity of days before that – going through every item and checking every pass against the daily work schedule was not at the forefront of his mind.

That prize went to his daughter's new boyfriend, or, more precisely, to his wife's feelings about his daughter's new boyfriend. Althor had actually quite liked the lad. His customised long-ship was a mean piece of kit, and the inkmanship on his runic tattoos was very impressive. Luckily Althor's wife didn't pay much attention to his opinion on such subjects. This was because she was too busy telling him her own opinion, and asking what he planned to do about it. Add to this distraction the fact that last week he'd been passed over for promotion again – this time so some rich nobleman's thick son could have an excuse to waltz around in a sergeant's uniform – and that as of this morning he was sure the funny brown growth on his neck was getting bigger, it becomes easier to understand that when presented with two blokes lugging a big chest towards the door and saying something about unblocking drains, he wasn't too fussy about checking their particulars.

CHAPTER THIRTY-ONE

Safely inside, Orus and Ambrose kept moving deeper into the Broch's under-tunnels until they found a quiet store room to collect their thoughts.

It was full of turnips, their peppery smell mixing with a hint of moisture and mould. Along one wall there was a long table with a plethora of heavy, sharp knives on top and rows of deep buckets underneath. Probably for the servant's dinner, thought Orus. They wouldn't keep the animal's food in somewhere so damp.

'See, I told you we could get in.' Orus put the chest down and stretched his back, letting out the sort of cracks and pops normally reserved for breakfast cereal adverts. 'Oh. That's better,' he said. 'Now we just need to find the kitchens.'

'And if anyone questions us?'

'Stick to the story. They've got drains in the kitchen. Makes sense we'd need to do them too.'

They ventured back into the tight corridors of the under-keep with the man-chest still held between them. Orus should have been surprised at how little attention the various guards and clerks paid to them as they waddled through the passageways, but he wasn't. You don't just carry a heavy box around the dark of the servant's levels for no reason. Probably the only more convincing disguise would be if they each brought a brush. No-one questions a man with a brush. He wondered if any thieves had stumbled on that handy piece of information.

Turning a sharp corner they came into a wider passage. This one was big enough for three to walk abreast and many passages branched out from it. Along one wall a large tapestry depicting Hoth Steel-Toe's battle with Sky-Claw hung between burning torches (he was laughing, just like in the story). At the far end, a large archway led to a set of stone stairs. The stairs disappeared into the floor above. A guard stood at the end of each banister. If Orus's internal geography was correct, those stairs took you to the throne room.

As Orus and Ambrose approached the guards, a young boy in a chef's smock struggled out of a side passage, a heavy iron hammer in his hands. His face was bright pink and a smell of burnt hair travelled in a cloud around him. The boy headed for a door just in front of the two guards, pulled it open and melted into the cloud of steam within.

Bingo!

Orus started down the corridor, shaking the chest a bit to give them a clumsy wobble. The guards pushed their shoulders off the wall and stood up straight.

'Can you catch the door, boss?' Orus called out, putting on a rush.

Sure enough, one of the guards obliged and caught the heavy door before it could swing shut. Inside guards aren't there to interrogate people. That's what outside guards are for. If anyone has gotten this far they must be bonafide. And, if not, it was someone else's fault.

The guard held the door open for Orus and Ambrose. A smell of fresh bread wafted through from the other side. This was definitely the right place.

Orus smiled a half smile to the guard. 'Thanks.'

'Hurry up,' was the gruff reply. 'And you better not knock anything with that junk.'

'No, sir,' Ambrose added.

'And tell that lot to hurry up,' said the other guard. 'He's getting rowdy up there.'

'Will do, boss,' said Orus, as the door closed behind him.

Turning a sharp bend they entered into chaos. The kitchen looked like it had just taken part in a full scale naval assault. Two long preparation tables ran the length of the arched room. Both were studded with metal shrapnel. A thick bed of steam hung across the room like gun-smoke and the only sign that there was anything underneath it came from the muffled groans of the wounded.

Half way up the room, in front of what had until recently been a stove, two kitchen hands were trying to dislodge an unconscious third from a swinging pan rack. As Ambrose and Orus watched, some of the walking wounded began to emerge from the steam, their white chef's smocks showing up their poached pink faces all the more.

The sound of clanging iron reverberated across the kitchen. Through the mist and clearing carnage they could just make out a pair of cooks engaging in what looked like a spot of black-smithery.

'Hold it tighter, tighter,' said the large one with the bandaged hands. He was holding the iron hammer, getting ready for a swing.

The smaller, thinner cook held the egg with two large leather gauntlets. They looked like the kind of things the Prince's hound handlers wore when training new dogs.

'Okay, okay. Just watch my fingers,' the smaller cook said.

'Never mind your fingers,' replied the larger one. 'If we don't get the King his breakfast soon, it'll be your neck you'll need to be worrying about.'

The chef raised the hammer and brought it down on the egg with a clang.

Ambrose's hands went to his eyes.

A shower of sparks flew into the air. There they mixed with steam and swears. The hammer pinged backwards, ripping free from the chef's hands and cartwheeling over his shoulder. A collection of pink faces ducked back beneath their various improvised shields as the hammer flew across the kitchen, finally striking a large frying pan on the opposite wall.

The resulting gong wobbled through the steam in visible waves.

The cook holding the egg was left shaking like a plucked harp string.

Only the egg was unaffected. Its angry surface shrugged off the blow and looked up at the head chef, daring him to try it again.

Orus pulled down Ambrose's fingers. 'It's okay. They haven't broken it.'

Relief escaped from Ambrose in a short sigh.

'Hold it there,' the head chef barked at his helper, 'I'll be back.' He waded through the steam to retrieve the hammer. Absorbed with the task in hand, he didn't notice the two strangers loitering in the doorway of his kitchen.

'Ah ha.' He raised the hammer triumphantly and spun it round in his hand so the claw end was facing forward. 'Let's see how you get on with this, Mr Egg.'

Orus took the measure of the man, and, more importantly, the measure of the butcher's knives on the rack behind him. They were both worryingly large. Force was not a good way to go. The egg's dragon-scale bag had been left unattended on the closest prepping table. Orus grabbed it, then took hold of Ambrose with his free hand and dived under the steam.

'Come on,' he hissed, crawling between the table legs. His legs protested heavily and he wasn't sure they would lift him up at the other end, but it was the only way to get close.

Ambrose shuffled along beside him. Through the haze they could both make out the four legs of the head chef and his helper. They were standing facing each other, between the two long tables.

'Right.' It was the head chef's voice. 'I'm going to make a small hole in the top and then we'll just pour it into the pan. Okay? Hold on to the bottom so it doesn't fall through your hands.'

'Gotcha,' replied the egg holder. From down on the floor Orus could see his knees knocking.

He nudged at Ambrose and motioned out the plan with his hands as best he could.

You…

Lift? Raise? Push.

Push!

Finger? Point?

Up!

Okay, okay. You push the egg up.

I. Catch. In. Bag.

I catch it in the bag!

Okay, got it.

They each nodded in what Orus hoped was shared understanding. He leaned out from the eve of the table. Looking up, he was directly under the egg. He turned back to his companion and started counting down on his fingers.

Five, Four…

Above the head chef had started his countdown too.

'Three, two…' Dimble Shanks lifted the hammer, eyes fixed on the target.

One!

'One!'

Above, the hammer came racing down.

Below, Orus shoved the gloved hands up.

The egg lifted free from the thin cook's grip. The boy's eyes widened. The head chef saw it too. But he was too far into his swing to stop now. The egg and the hammer passed each other in opposite directions. One started down again, the other made a crunching contact with the thin cook's fingers.

Ambrose reached out with the bag. The egg dropped inside. Above the steam, the room filled with squeals of pain.

Ambrose gave Orus a thumbs-up and, like a pair of mice after a successful smash and grab raid on the cheese larder, they scampered back under the table towards the door.

Above, confusion had usurped carnage and was laying out his programme for government.

'What did you do that for?' Dimble Shanks shouted.

'I di-dn't,' said the thin cook, the words emerging around a mouthful of bruised fingers. 'It 'umped.'

'Eggs don't jump!'

'They don't flash boil water or blow up pans either,' said another cook.

'Shut up. Where did it go?'

'I an't se it.'

Dimble Shanks took off his hat and started beating away the steam.

At the far end of the room Orus and Ambrose extracted themselves from under the table. Orus flicked up the lid of the man-chest and pushed all his treasures to one end. Ambrose made sure the egg was snug inside its protective bag and fastened the flap down. He placed the

195

package inside the chest, fitting it between a broken drinking horn and a set of white candles.

'You're sure it won't burn through,' asked Orus. 'Some of that stuff is quite valuable.'

'No, the bag will hold the heat in. It should be safe.'

'Right then, let's get out of here.' Orus snapped the lid shut and together they heaved the chest up from the floor.

Escaped again. Chew on that Tyran.

'Oi! What are you two doing here?!'

Or not.

Orus turned to see the head chef marching towards them, hammer in hand.

'It's not there, Dimble,' shouted one of the other cooks.

Dimble Shanks eyed the kitchen interlopers suspiciously. 'What's in that box?'

'De-bunging rods,' offered Orus, 'from the drains…'

'Oh really. Funny that.' Dimble Shanks eye's narrowed and the pink on his face started to darken. 'The drains were cleaned out last week.' The chef picked up a fat meat cleaver with his free hand. 'What are you really doing down here?'

Orus and Ambrose looked at each other, then at the door.

'Leaving!' they both said together. They rushed at Dimble Shanks, striking him in the gut with the man-chest. The chef tumbled backwards into the steam. Quickly, they turned and sprinted for the door. Racing up the stairs they heard his bellow of rage behind them.

The guards in the decorative corridor had heard it too. They stepped forward to block the passageway.

'Hey, what's going on down there?' one asked, reaching for his sword.

Orus jabbed a thumb backwards, 'Assassins!' he shouted. 'Dressed as cooks! You'd better stop them.'

'Right. Stand back. Leave this to us.'

'Yeah,' said the second guard, taking up a fighting stance. 'Better get out of here quick. No place for servants now.'

'Couldn't agree with you more.'

CHAPTER THIRTY-TWO

Ambrose and Orus ran back to the servant's door, lugging the man-chest between them. They pulled up to a walk just before they reached Althor and his lectern.

The guard's head was down, studying next week's rota. How'd Tauk managed to get three days off? That's the sort of lucky breaks you get when you're the captain's nephew. Now he was stuck doing two nightshifts, then straight back on the door for the rest of the week. So much for going to Jilly's school show. At least it gave him a nice conversation with the wife to look forward to for the rest of the day.

Althor briefly looked up as the lads that had come to unblock the drains trotted past. They looked like they were in a hurry, but then who could blame them? He had seen the state of the toilets on the lower floors. He'd be racing for a bath too.

Back out in front of the King's Hall a large group of guards was practicing drill on the arena. Each uniformed movement and change of direction was accompanied by a sound like a prize-fighter hitting a punch-bag full of pennies.

Beyond the marching guards, the main street was full with the busy life of the town. If they could make it into the crush they'd be lost, just two more nobodies in the crowd. Then, down to the Flagon, load up Thunder, and get out of town as soon as possible. Once word got back to Tyran he'd have riders out on the roads for sure. The King might let them off with humiliation for pretending to be a heroes; stealing from him was a different matter. They had challenged his authority and Orus knew from his Cromalot days that Tyran Sarus was not the kind of person to bury the hatchet, unless it was in his enemy's back.

No, the roads were out. The lake on the other hand: that could work.

They could barter passage on one of the fishing boats and sneak out hidden in the hold. The lake ran almost all the way to Pale Pass. The boat could take them most of the way there then it would be a quick trek through the forest and they would almost be finished. They didn't have Tyran's permission to pass through but Orus was confident he could find a way. He had just broken into a royal palace.

Ambrose stumbled and the jerk on the chest crushed Orus's fingers against the handle. The pain brought his focus back to the job in hand.

'Okay back there?' he hissed to Ambrose over his shoulder.

'Yes,' replied the monk through clenched teeth. The weight of the man-chest was dragging at his arms. But he wasn't about to let up and let Orus down.

Orus's arms were starting to burn from the weight too. He was impressed with the stamina of his skinny, bookish companion. More than a bit of fight in the lad.

The metallic snap of fifty right boots on blood stained stone brought a crown of sweat to Orus's head. The massed ranks of the guards turned to face them.

Just keep going, he thought. Don't look back, don't look worried.

They were halfway across the arena. So far there were no shouts from the door behind them. So far...

'Company advance!' The short stamp of the guard captain's voice battered Orus's ears from behind, shaking the sweat from his head and sending it down his back like a ball of needles. His muscles tensed and his brain begged him to run.

The chink of chain mail on leather jangled towards his back like a steel snake. Any minute now he expected to feel the foot-long fangs pressed against his skin.

'Company, arms!'

There was the rattle before the strike. If they dropped the chest now they might just make it. But then they'd be back to where they'd started.

'Company, charge!'

The steel snaked hissed and Orus's sweat speed reached hitherto unknown velocities. He braced himself. He expected fear to race through his body, but it didn't. Instead, he thought about Ambrose. He thought about the boy's future. He'd got the monk into this situation. It was his fault they were here. The kid was young, young like Tag, and Tyran didn't have any beef with him. He could still escape, given the chance.

Orus stopped walking. Not one day.

He turned to face the coming wall of steel. The guards' spear points lowered to full charge position.

A shudder moved through his old muscles as adrenaline flowed into them.

Here goes.

The guards let out a battle cry.

Ten feet, eight, seven.

'What are you doing?' Ambrose said, fear audible in his voice.

'When I give the word you drop this chest and run.'

'What? What are you planning to do?'

'Just do it,' he said. 'Go find Victor, and don't look back.'

Orus got ready to drop the chest and launch himself at the coming massed death. This was it.

'Halt!'

The captain's shout nearly knocked him flat. With a stamp, the guards stopped on a button, the points of their spears only a foot away from Orus and Ambrose.

'Bloody servants!' The captain strode along the flank of his troops. 'You. Are. Messing. Up. My. Drill!'

'Sorry,' called Ambrose and pushed his end of the man-chest into Orus's back, setting him going again. 'We'll just get out of your way. Won't happen again. Sorry.'

'It better not.' If anything the captain's quiet voice was even worse than his shouting. His words were emphatically pointed, as if they'd been sharpened on a grinding wheel before he hissed them out. Without any signal Ambrose could see, the guards all turned back to face the Broch and began marching. Ahead, the press of the town streets opened to admit their escape.

We might actually get away with this, thought Orus. Wait. No. Don't even think it.

A shout from behind them. Orus didn't need to turn around to know the chef and his cooks had caught up with them. He didn't need to look to see them each carrying bigger knives than the last and he didn't need to listen for the shout to the guard captain or for the answering stamp of an about face.

He just thought, bugger it, and ran.

*

Rushing down Harradin's main street with the guards and chefs in hot pursuit, Ambrose still managed to call out the location of important heroic landmarks through gasped breaths. Orus on the other hand was fully taken up with not adding to the tally of fateful final footsteps.

'And that,' puffed Ambrose, skidding around a fisherwoman, 'is where Olifa Reeds, challenged a whole, pirate crew, to an, arm wrestling contest.'

A group of guards appeared from an alley ahead. Orus dug his heels in to stop but the combined momentum of Ambrose plus the man-chest brought the monk swinging past him. Orus was nearly pulled from his feet at the point of pivot. All Ambrose could do to stop from falling was continue down the hill in reverse. Together they pirouetted around the startled line of spears, before Orus's weight advantage brought him back to level pegging with the Dragon Monk.

The guards turned to give chase, but before they could, they were barged into the mud by Dimble Shanks and his angry kitchen staff.

'Don't let them get away,' shouted the chef, skidding past the confused blend of cooks and guards. 'Get after them, or it'll be your necks on the block.'

Another two guards were running uphill towards Orus and Ambrose. There was no way the egg fugitives could stop the heavy chest's drive downwards. The approaching guards realised this too late. The chest caught them just under the hips, flipping them head over heels into the mud.

The street turned sharply ahead. Orus sprinted, trying to regain the lead over the chest so he could prepare for the turn.

A long snake of children holding hands emerged from a side street.

'Stop! Stop!' Orus shouted.

Ambrose saw them too. He dug his heels into the slippery mud. It slowed them down, but not enough.

Orus leaned back. The chest barely noticed. It had a momentum all of its own now and it wasn't stopping for anything. It scooped him up and continued on regardless, throwing up sparks as it skidded down the street. He was now riding on top of the front end as Ambrose hung desperately to the back.

The children hadn't seen them. When they did it would be too late.

There. At the apex of the corner the handle of Hoth Steel-Toe's axe stuck out into the street.

'They say,' Ambrose shouted, 'only a true hero, can pull it free.'

Orus wasn't thinking about the prophetic reputation of the weapon. He was focused on the equally legendary stopping power of anvils. From his speeding steed he reached out with both hands, ready to bear the brunt of what promised to be a very sudden halt.

With typical good timing, the universe chose this moment to recognise his claim to true hero-ship. The anvil released its charge with all the resistance of an ill-set jelly. Caught unawares, the handle slipped through Orus's hands and the axe launched itself spinning across the street.

Sorry kids.

The front corner of the skidding chest caught a rock, sending it spinning past the wide-eyed children.

The spin finally wrenched the handle from Ambrose's grip. He was thrown across the street, landing sprawled in the mud. Orus, on the other hand, hung on tight. The world blurred around him. It was as if he was standing in the wheel of a picture lantern. His eyes lost all focus. People and streets were reduced to a smear of colours.

Gradually, his spin slowed.

He brain caught up with his eyes. The streets began to take shape. The scene appearing in front of him was not a happy one. With each revolution a crowd of guards and angry cooks clicked forward another step. Even worse, at the opposite pole, a familiar form began to congeal from the multi-coloured mash. In the midst of the brown and greys of Harradin, flashes of purple and gold.

Conrad Von Strauss was standing outside the Hairy Flagon talking to the messenger Orus had left in the mud. His extensive train of servants and bodyguards was amassed behind him.

The messenger raised a hand to point towards Orus and, in answer, a crooked and wholly bad intentioned smile spread above Conrad's chiselled chin.

'That's him,' said the messenger, rubbing his bruised chin.

'He doesn't look seven foot to me,' said Huggle.

'Well, he was a lot closer to me at the time,' replied the messenger.

'Not important.' Conrad drew his sword. 'We can sort out the details of your cowardice later. Skar, seize the fat one.'

'Yes, boss.' The hulking warrior motioned to his equally hulking colleagues and together, the five of them hulked towards Orus and the chest.

Orus was a little hurt by the speed with which it was deduced that he was the fat one in question. This thought didn't linger long in his mind. The prospect of becoming a lot more hurt in the near future channelled his brain to more constructive avenues.

Like how to get out of this one.

Luckily, a man riding a large wooden chest down Main Street while being pursued by the King's kitchen staff is not the kind of thing that happens every day in Harradin. They had drawn quite a crowd.

While Dimble Shanks and the guards tried to push through the gathering citizens, Ambrose caught up with his friend and helped him to his feet.

'Are you okay?'

'Ask me again in a few minutes,' Orus replied. Skar and his men were fanning out in front of them, blocking off the street.

Ambrose caught sight of their old adversary. 'Wow! Conrad Von Strauss! He found us. He really must be the best tracker outside of Speakleaf.'

The children that had narrowly escaped being crushed by the sliding chest gathered round Orus, each craning their necks to see what was going on. This, and Ambrose's unquenchable enthusiasm for their murderous pursuer, gave Orus an idea.

He cupped his hands around his mouth and shouted as loud as he could. 'Yes! It is! Look everyone! It's Conrad Von Strauss! I'm going to get an autograph!'

The air pressure around him dropped a few isobars as the children collectively drew in a deep breath. As one, their heads swivelled on their necks and their eyes spread wide across their faces. Like the first deer to start running on hearing the wolf break cover, the slightest twinge of a muscle in one child's foot sent the herd racing forward en masse, ready to stampede Von Strauss and his men in a frenzy of enthusiasm.

Helpless to fight against the tide, Skar and his men were carried back the way they came. Behind, Dimble Shanks and the other cooks were buffeted by the rest of the crowd of townspeople as they surged towards Von Strauss.

The forward rush of the mass of children revealed an alleyway on the lake-ward side of the street. Orus saw it. Time to go

'The chest.' Orus lifted his handle and tried to run. The chest refused to move.

Orus turned back to his companion. Ambrose was digging in his robes frantically.

'Come on, Ambrose. We have to go.'

With a triumphant flourish, the Dragon Monk pulled his autograph book free from an inside pocket.

'What are you doing?'

'I was just going to... Oh, right.' He stuffed the small book back into his robes. 'Nothing. The chest. Got it.'

'This way.'

They raced down the alley, away from the commotion of their creating and towards the docks.

CHAPTER THIRTY-THREE

The sound of rushing feet, people shouting and fists thumping on the flimsy wooden walls of the Hairy Flagon's stables roused Thunder from his pre-lunch nap. He had been dreaming about carrots, so this rude awakening did not put him in the best of moods.

With the press of bodies blocking him in his stall, he couldn't see the drama unfolding in the centre of the room. But he could hear it. And with ears the size of oven mitts, it didn't take him long to pin down the familiar voice of Conrad Von Strauss.

'The next time something like that happens, please try and remember that you have swords for a reason.'

'But, boss, they is children.' The voice came from higher up. It had a hard edge but sounded soft on brains. Probably one of Conrad's bodyguards.

'I don't mean kill them,' Conrad continued. 'Just scare them off. Rough them up a bit.'

'Not to interrupt, sire,' a new voice now, hesitant and meek. 'But roughing up children would not lend favourably towards your public image.'

Conrad's cape swished across the floor in answer to the new speaker. No doubt he was in full peacock strutting mode.

'Do not think, Huggle, that I have forgotten your part in this mess. The guards didn't even know I was coming. If they had, those two fools could have been caught by now.'

'And how is that my fault?' the one called Huggle bit back.

'Because most things are! I can't be expected to keep track of all your inadequacies. I was rounding up. Now get out there and sort this out.'

I don't suppose you'd mind quietening down. Some of us are trying to sleep.

No-one listened. And so many people stuffed into the small outbuilding he couldn't even lift his hind legs to give one of them a good kick.

Oh well, don't say I didn't warn you. Biological warfare it is.

CHAPTER THIRTY-FOUR

Orus and Ambrose had ducked into an open fronted storehouse down on the waterfront. With a twin sigh of relief they set down the heavy chest. Outside, wide shouldered dockers steamed in the cold mountain air. They were busy carting cargo on and off the lines of long ships with only hard work, hairy backs and colourful language to keep them warm.

Ambrose shook the strain from his arms before crouching down to check the egg.

'What have you got in here?' he asked, looking through the contents of the man-chest.

'Just the essentials.'

'Like this?' Ambrose held up the winch mechanism from the old castle well.

'Still works. Could come in handy at some point.'

'I thought this was full of all your heroing gear. Is there even a sword in here?'

'You can get a sword anywhere.' Orus looked out onto the pier, checking for any guards. 'That stuff is hard to find. You don't throw away things that are hard to find.

They don't make winches like that anymore. Never know when you might need it.'

Ambrose picked up the egg's satchel and checked over their charge. It was still hot to the touch but the glow was noticeably dimmer. 'And have you needed any of it recently?'

'That's not the point. Plus, some of it could be worth something in a few years. Look at how much people pay for old paintings and furniture and stuff.'

'If you say so.' Satisfied it was still in one piece, Ambrose returned the egg to its temporary nest among Orus's antiques of the future.

Looking around the storehouse Orus could see the touch of a man just like him. It was there in the cargo crane hook made from an old horse shoe, and in the window prop – previously half a broom handle – and in the crate trolley, the wheels of which looked very similar to the centre sections of much larger cart wheels, only with all the spokes broken off. This one impressed Orus the most. Goodness knows how long its builder had to endure questions as to why he was keeping three broken cart wheels, before that last one brought his master plan together.

Orus poked his head out of the door again. It wouldn't be long before the guards started searching all the warehouses. Tyran was not the giving up type and, with Conrad here, he'd have extra muscle to call in. A new hiding place was needed.

Sure enough, a group of guards was being led into the first storehouse by one of the dockers.

'We need to move,' said Orus. He looked out across the busy waterfront. All along it men were loading crates and cargo onto ships ready for the afternoon sailings. This was when there was the best light and it was easier to pick through the treacherous waters of the bay. Most of the ships were filled with crew, checking ropes and stowing rations. But, at the very end of the dock, a lone ship stood unguarded.

'Where to?' asked Ambrose.

'There,' Orus pointed to the lone ship. 'We'll hide down in the hold overnight, then find a fishing boat heading off in the early morning and hitch a lift.'

'What if it sails off?'

'Doesn't look like there are any crew on board. Probably laid up for a refit.'

As they scampered down the boardwalk, Orus felt even more confident of his choice of hiding place. The ship was well past its prime. The main mast looked half rotten, the deck was covered in bird droppings and a seagull was busy making its nest in the anchor rope. No-one was going to be sailing this anytime soon. In this condition it wouldn't even make it out of the bay.

In the bustle of the busy docks no-one noticed another duo of workers lugging their chest up the gangway.

CHAPTER THIRTY-FIVE

The stable doors at the Hairy Flagon were thrown open in fits of coughing and gagging as Conrad and his entourage stumbled into the fresh air, noses held and eyes streaming.

'Yaargh! The smell!'

'God, it's still going! Move!'

'Out of the way, pleb!'

'Air! I need air!'

Inside, reunited with solitude Thunder got back to the important jobs of the day. Top of the agenda: finishing the carrots dream.

In the street, the crowd that had trapped Conrad and his men in the stable was being held back by a semi-circle of Harradanian guards. Conrad, Huggle, Skar and the other survivors of Thunder's odorous assault wiped the tears from their eyes, and did their best to avoid throwing up. Most were successful.

As Huggle dabbed away the chunks with his handkerchief, a great laugh boomed like cannon fire from the middle of the guards. His eyes waterlogged and blurry, Huggle had trouble making out the source. After a few moments he decided the voice's owner must be somewhere behind the large standing stone he had failed to notice when entering the town.

It was a strange standing stone, in that it was walking towards them, cracking its knuckles.

'Well, well. The fearless Conrad Von Strauss,' said King Tyran, compressing his fist in his other hand. 'This is a day for old faces. Finally decided to challenge me, have you? Interesting training technique. Or are you trying out scents for your next cologne? You could call it Pompous Ass.'

'Yes,' replied Conrad, standing up straight. 'I had the idea when I had to sit beside you at the Emperor of Krum's daughter's wedding feast.'

The chanting and shouting coming from the crowd grew. Here were the world's two greatest living heroes, together, toe-to-toe, face-to-massively-muscled-chest. Harradanians loved to see their King challenged. If this was why Conrad was in their city, and if the tales of his adventures were anything to go by, this would be one for the ages. Mixed with the barked commands of the guards, the cheering was so loud only those within the ring of shields could hear the exchange between the two men, as Conrad and Tyran both well knew.

'Oh, that was you?' Tyran sneered. 'I thought it might have been one of your look-alikes. You know, like the one who won the jousting competition for you the next day, then mysteriously vanished before he could collect the prize money.'

'I don't recall that myself. I do remember one of my servants telling me he saw *your* men steal all the wedding presents, the cake and two of the bridesmaids? I hear the Emperor is still quite angry about that, and desperate to know who was involved.'

'That was never proven,' replied Tyran. 'And it was three bridesmaids. Not that it matters since, if you're here to challenge me, the only other monarch you're likely to be meeting any time soon is the one that sat on my throne before me. I'll introduce you before the match. I keep his head on a spear in the Broch, for old times' sake.'

'Much as I would enjoy teaching a brute like you a lesson,' said Conrad, confident that with the crowd watching Tyran wouldn't do anything rash, 'I have better things to do than rule over this dung heap. I am in the middle of a quest.'

'Ah, still doing the lone hero thing.' Tyran cast an eye across Conrad's extensive entourage. 'Are you planning on stopping overnight? I would offer you the use of my barracks but I don't think it has enough beds.'

'That's okay,' said Conrad, taking a moment to look over Tyran's men, still red-faced from the chase down from the town's summit. 'Your guards look like they need the rest. Spot of trouble today?'

'Just a couple of thieves. Nothing we can't handle.'

Conrad's eyes hardened. It made sense. They were here and they had form.

'Hmm, thieves, yes. A lot of that going around. It wasn't by chance a fat man and a monk?'

'You know them?'

Conrad nodded. He hated Tyran. Heroes like him were an embarrassment. Little more than peasants with big swords. They had no right to the title. All that death or glory rubbish: honour, courage, self-sacrifice – that stuff was all well and good when heroing was for amateurs, but now it was different. He was a professional. Heroing was a business. You wouldn't expect the owner of a mine to be down in the dark whacking at rocks with a big hammer. Why should he get his hands dirty? The brand was the important thing, not the actual deeds, and he had the income receipts to prove it. Tyran and his lot could plunder a hundred temples and not make half as much gold as he had on his last book tour.

However, since his own efforts had so far failed to capture the thieves, maybe a bit of extra manpower would help. And manpower was something Tyran was famous for.

'Perhaps we could pool our resources for a while. When we find them, we can split the glory.'

Tyran picked his nose and flicked the results of his excavation to the ground. He hated Conrad. Fops like him gave heroes a bad name. Spoilt rich kids that think the world owes them respect. All because daddy has a nice castle and mummy spends all her days in fancy frocks and jewels. Money: that's all the high-borns were interested in. Who has it, how much, and how they can get more while doing the least possible work. Sure, he had stolen his fair amount of treasure over the years, but only as a means to an end, or because he wanted to, or because it was lying around after he had killed the previous owner. But he never, ever counted it.

Still, as much as he hated to admit it, Von Strauss did have a reputation for coming up with the goods. And this situation could not be let go. It had gone far beyond Orus's initial deception. Stealing from him was a challenge to his pride, even if the thing stolen wasn't his to start with. It made him look weak and it demanded vengeance. Letting them escape was not an option. In the circumstances, a temporary alliance might not be the worst idea ever, provided he had an opportunity to hand out the king's justice.

'A good plan,' Tyran said, cracking his knuckles again. 'But I want the fat one.'

'Ah,' Conrad's smile twisted up in the way it didn't when he was thinking of nice things like puppies and kittens. 'Actually, when I said "split" I was thinking of half each.'

Tyran boomed another loud laugh. 'I like that. Maybe you ain't so bad, for a fop. It is agreed. My men are surrounding the town right now. They won't be getting out.

Come up to the hall and my captain will organise the search. In the meantime, some drinks. And we can watch the fireworks.'

'Fireworks? Are you having a celebration?' asked Von Strauss.

'No. More like a final send-off.'

CHAPTER THIRTY-SIX

Sitting in the dank hold, Orus listened to the slosh of the water moving up and down the outside of the ship. They had tucked themselves into a stall at the bow end. Most of the ship was empty. Going by the old musty turnip lying against the dividing panel and the smell of mouldy bread that infused the tight space between floor and deck, this is where the food had been kept.

They would stay here until nightfall, then he would go to one of the dockside taverns and see if he could buy passage on a fishing boat heading out for the early sailing. They still had no way of getting through the gate at Pale Pass, but Orus reckoned they could use the servant trick again. If the guards were still looking for them in the city, they could reach the pass before word of the pursuit got that far. Hunters sent out to find some rare creature for their master or something like that. After all, the gate was to stop things coming in, not going out.

The man-chest made a semi-comfortable seat, so he leaned his head back against the hull and let his eyelids dip.

Ambrose had gone to explore the rest of the hold and Orus was happy to let him.

Not that there was much to see. Ambrose wandered along the ship's length. The sun was dying outside. He lit a small lantern he found hanging by the stairs.

Looking stern-wise, on the left there were more stalls and then a few rows of water barrels. Ambrose opened one to get a drink. The water was stagnant and had a murky sheen to its surface.

Perhaps not.

He replaced the lid and went on with his exploration. Some of the compartments had hammocks in them. They gave off a faint whiff of a more populated time, but the cobwebs hanging between them suggested this time was not recently. The more Ambrose saw, the more he felt the crew would be better scrapping the whole ship, rather than patching it up. The lights of the town poured through a fist-sized hole in the hull, only a foot above the water line, and the walls and decks were slick with seepage.

Turning back, he approached the only significant piece of cargo left on board. Covered in a dull sheet, two long rectangular shapes, each one about a foot longer than Ambrose was tall, were laid out on a wide table. The sheet was free from dust. It must have been moved on-board recently.

Strange, Ambrose thought, that they would move these in while everything else had been taken out.

He lifted a corner of the sheet to have a peek.

The planks above his head creaked under the weight of a pair of boots.

This was closely followed by a thump and another creak as someone else dropped the short gap from the gangplank to the deck.

Ambrose let go of the sheet and dropped to a crouch. There was no reason for this, as the people on deck couldn't possibly see him, but it just felt like the right thing to do. He closed the hatch on his lantern and listened.

The two sets of feet were making their way across the ship. One was carrying a lantern of his own. As they advanced towards the mid-ship the light fell in sheets through the gaps in the deck. They were speaking to each other. Ambrose strained to hear. It could be the crew, or some of the dockworkers. Maybe the stuff under the sheet had been loaded on this ship by mistake.

'... the front. Take this...'

The front. That was where Orus was. And the egg.

He needed to warn his friend. The stairs were between them and the light from above was moving that way. Ambrose thought about making a run for it. Get to Orus. But the men above would surely hear him.

The light moved across his upturned face and he caught a whiff of the conversation.

'Two of them,' said one of the men.

'They're down below,' said the other.

Ambrose pressed his eye against the low roof, peeking through the boards. The light flowing down made it hard to see properly but the silhouettes gave away all they needed. The shaft of a spear rested on the deck by one man's foot. A sword hung by the other's hip.

Guards!

'... Tyran was really angry. Even more than usual.'

'Said he'd kill them both...'

The feet started moving again, the curtains of light advancing in a wave towards the stairs. Ambrose scanned the hold for something that could be used as a weapon. He had never had to hit anyone before. But he couldn't rely on Orus to save him all the time. It was time for action, as much as he wished it wasn't.

The light moved forward. He saw the glint of something metal sticking out from under the sheet. He moved to the table like a teenager sneaking past his parents' bedroom after a late-night party – hoping the floorboards wouldn't give him away. His hand found the handle of a large curved sabre. Now, if he could just spend a few months learning how to use it, they might get out of this alive.

The sword gripped in shaking hands, Ambrose slid across the deck towards the foot of the stairs. The lantern stopped at the top of them. Its orange light dribbled down the steps. Ambrose could just make out Orus, standing in the shadows, the musty turnip raised above his head, ready to throw. Always there, thought Ambrose. They nodded to each other as the first foot creaked on the top step.

Ambrose held his breath and tried not to make a sound. Surprise was their best chance.

The feet continued down. Heavy boots thudded on old musty wood. Then it was knees, then chainmail covered thighs, then the handle of a sword. Worn and stained by sweat, it looked well used.

Ambrose flexed his hands on the grip of his own sword. It felt slick and slippery, cold and unfamiliar. Like holding someone else's fish.

'Found it!'

Ambrose tensed. He was still holding his breath. The call came from the other guard, the one still on the deck.

The legs on the stair stopped.

Ambrose's face was turning red as the air in his cheeks punched at the sides of his mouth. Slowly, ever so slowly, the guard's feet turned.

'You got enough?'

'Yeah, there's a whole big coil up here. Plenty.'

The light of the lantern retreated up the stairs and continued along the ship towards the bow. There it stopped. Orus kept the turnip raised just in case. More curtains of light dropped between the planks, illuminating shafts of dust, as the guards moved back and forth, working on something at the point of the bow.

There was more talk above. Something about ropes. And getting a tow. That was all they could make out.

The guards stayed at the bow for the longest minutes of Ambrose's life. He kept his breath held. He was starting to feel woozy and the walls were going all fuzzy but he didn't let the air out in case they heard him.

Eventually, they finished whatever they were doing and turned to leave. The curtains of light moved back up the ship, passed the stairs and headed for the gangplank.

When the fourth boot lifted off the deck, air rushed from Ambrose's head and he collapsed against the hull. Orus set down his turnip and went to check on his friend.

'That was close,' he said, helping the monk up. 'Where did you get that sword?'

Ambrose looked down at the weapon in his hand. His arms were shaking. He never thought they would be so heavy. It wasn't just the metal. There was something about it being a weapon that gave it extra weight, like it was aware of what it was meant to be used for. Somehow, he knew if he had swung it, he would have regretted it.

He passed it over to Orus, glad to be rid of it. 'Over there,' he said, pointing back into the main body of the hold.

The sheet on the big table was flipped up at one corner, where Ambrose had pulled the sword free. Underneath it, Orus could see the ends of two pine boxes. What had Tyran said about measuring them up?

He picked up the free corner of the sheet and yanked the whole thing off, throwing up a cloud of dust from the deck in the process.

Ambrose returned with his lantern, now relit, and together they peered into the gloom.

The coffins were open, and each one was surrounded by the late occupants' effects: weapons, shields, helmets and armour. The bodies were bound and wrapped in grey cloth, ready for burial. Only their faces were exposed. Their skin was pale and in parts even looked slightly transparent, as if death had hollowed them out.[9] A silver coin covered each eye socket.

Ambrose lifted his lantern to spread more light over the grizzly scene.

'Errgh. They should hurry up and bury these. It's not very hygienic to leave them in here.'

Before Orus could answer, the rotting ship gave a groan from bow to stern, then lurched forward, out onto the cold lake.

---

[9] In fact, Tyran had done most of the hollowing in the arena.

CHAPTER THIRTY-SEVEN

Huggle sat with King Tyran and Conrad on the royal balcony, watching the funeral ship being towed out across the dark waters. The sky was clear of clouds and the crescent moon laid a shimmering path across the bay. By its light, the twin ships threaded a path through the charred, ice-flecked masts that marked the final resting places of past kings and failed challengers.

'Isn't it expensive, burning all these ships?' Conrad asked, pretending to take a sip from the extra strong mead Tyran insisted they both drink. When the King turned to watch the spectacle on the lake, only Huggle saw his master tip some of the drink over the edge of the balcony.

'Na, not really,' said Tyran. 'We only use dead old ships. That hunk-a-junk's worthless. Would probably sink on its own, even without the fire.'

The rhythmic jangling of the guard captain's armour announced his arrival on the balcony. He approached Tyran, swept his helmet from his head and bowed.

'I hope you're here to report the successful capture of our soon to be late-fugitives.' The King took a swig of mead a small child could drown in.

He didn't turn to look at the guard. He didn't have to. Had Tyran allowed such airy-fairy, wicker-witch, fluffy stuff as talk of auras in his town, one might say his massive bulk was surrounded by varying hues of impatience and violent impulses. What it was actually surrounded by was a collection of his favourite weapons (freshly sharpened), large quantities of alcohol, a blank death warrant and a list of possible replacements for the position of guard captain.

'The search is progressing as planned, Your Majesty,' the captain replied. 'The town is surrounded and with the assistance of Lord Conrad's men we should have the thieves apprehended shortly.'

'So you're saying you haven't found them yet?' asked Tyran, retrieving an estimate of the captain's funeral expenses from the papers in front of him.

'It is only a matter of time, my king. They cannot escape.'

'For your sake, Captain, you better be right.'

'Sire.' The captain snapped salute to the King and made to return to his men by way of a life insurance broker.

'So hard to find good men nowadays,' Tyran said, turning to Conrad.

Von Strauss cast a glance to where Huggle was sitting. 'Yes, I know exactly what you mean. It is the curse of the exceptional to be continually disappointed. Which reminds me, I must apologise again for not giving proper notice of my arrival. My scribe decided to trust the news to a moron rather than a messenger.'

Huggle fumed. Had Von Strauss not insisted that they travel no faster than a trot, lest his hair be put out of shape, they would have arrived in plenty of time to catch up with their quarry and this whole business would be over and done with.

'And why is it that the great Conrad Von Strauss is chasing nobodies like these all the way to my town?'

'A relatively small matter. You have heard of the last dragon?'

The King's adviser, Cribond, was at his master's side. He had not appeared suddenly, as that would have drawn attention. This was something Cribond did his best to avoid. Rather, he had simply not been on the balcony a few moments earlier and now he was.

'Yes,' replied Tyran. 'I would have gone after the beastie myself. But a king's got to look after his kingdom.

'That'd be your first dragon, wouldn't it? I've already done a few, so, you know, no big deal to me,' Tyran added, rolling his huge shoulders. Just because they'd agreed to work together didn't mean they'd signed a full truce. 'Surely those two didn't slay it before you?'

Conrad chuckled at the absurdity of the suggestion. 'The only way that fat fool could slay a dragon is if he sat on it. No, it's worse than that. They stole it.'

Cribond's fingers formed a steeple in front of his chest.

'How'd you steal a dragon?'

'A lesson in never trusting rumours and hearsay. You see, it isn't a dragon, not yet. It's still an egg. The monks at the temple were trying to make it hatch. By the time we found out what was going on, those two ran off with it.'

The steeple of Cribond's fingers lowered to a cage and his lips crawled into a smile. He knew it wasn't an eagle's egg. This could make things very interesting.

Tyran rolled out one of his full naval broadside laughs and slapped his hand on the stone balcony. 'That's the last dragon! Ha ha. Well, well. Orus was telling the truth after all. I was going to have it for breakfast you know, before they stole it from my kitchens.'

225

'Sire,' Cribond leaned to his master's ear. 'Might I have a word with you, quickly?'

'You may have two, Cribond: Shove and Off. I'm busy.' Tyran lifted his tankard and shook it to emphasise just how busy he was. 'I'm sure whatever boring clerkly stuff you want to warble through can wait 'til later. When I'm asleep would be good.'

'But, sire—'

'Shut up, Cribond!'

Tyran's dagger flew from what Huggle was sure had been an empty hand. It thrummed a deep bass chord as it struck the wooden wall behind the exact point where Cribond was no longer standing. Like the knife, Huggle never saw him move. The job of king's aide clearly rewarded those who are quick on their feet.

Tyran turned back to the lake. 'They're ready. This is the best bit. Watch.'

Down in the bay the lead ship let go its line and turned back to port, leaving the funeral ship alone on the cold black water.

Under the balcony, a spit of rock extended over the edge of the cliff. Heaving himself up, Tyran leaned down over the edge and bellowed to the company of archers below.

'Ready!'

The lead archer led his troop forward. A brazier of coals burned brightly and each man plunged a pitch-covered arrow-head into the flames until they dripped and crackled like marshmallows in a scout's fire.

The archers set the burning barbs in their bows.

Tyran leaned forward even further, trying to get as close to the action as possible.

'Aim!'

The archers lifted their bows and drew them back until their calloused fingers were level with their ears. The smell of burning pitch rose in the cold night air and curled up Huggle's nostrils. The funeral ship turned slowly on the current, helpless and alone.

'Fire!'

CHAPTER THIRTY-EIGHT

Two shadows, one pencil thin, the other more than moderately less so, stretched out across the deck of the funeral ship as the brace of orange orbs arched into the cold night. As the flaming arrows reached the top of their trajectories, they paused for a brief moment to reflect on the journey of their lives so far. They couldn't help but feel they had peaked early. From here, the only way was down.

'Quick, behind the hatch!' Orus grabbed Ambrose and ducked behind the hold's trap door.

Two dozen fiery barbs rat-a-tatted into the hull. The rotten planks into which they sank blackened, smouldered, then took flame. The seeds of a growing conflagration sprouted from the deck with angry red stems.

Orus ran to the nearest arrow and tried to pull it out. Before he could get a good grip on it, the shaft succumbed to the flames crawling up its length and snapped. The burning stub of pitch and iron stuck fast into the body of the ship like the head of a virulent tic. The sticky pitch bubbled and popped. He thought about stamping on it. Then, remembering the pain incurred when one of Tag's metal toy soldiers violently ambushed him on the way to the outhouse, and the flammable nature of the furs and wools he was wearing, he decided that this was not a good idea.

But they had to do something. Orus looked up at the cliff top. Another volley was arcing down towards them.

'Water!' Ambrose shouted. 'There's water in the hold. Come on.'

They rounded the hatch and leapt down the stairs, Ambrose taking them three at a time and Orus taking them quite fast too. The monk lifted the lid of a water barrel as the second volley thudded home.

'What do we carry it in?' Orus looked around for a suitable vessel. There wasn't much to choose from.

Ambrose ran to the coffins and, after a quick prayer for disturbing the dead, wrestled free the occupant's helmet. 'Here. These. You get the other one.'

Orus pulled the helmet off the other corpse. It was a twin horned job. It took quite a twist, and a crack, to pull it out of the coffin. The former owner's head dropped out and rolled towards the hull, stopping only when it lost the momentum to push over the kick-stand of its long nose.

Smoke was flowing down the stairs. Orus dunked the corner of his fur cloak in the water barrel, held it over his face with his free hand and raced back up to the deck. The fire was spreading quickly, bursting wood-worm in their tunnels and burning deep into the structure of the ship. The stern blazed. More orange orbs dropped from the sky.

Ambrose rushed to the closest waltz of flame and tipped the contents of the helmet onto it. The flames hissed and bowed under the water, but it wasn't enough. They stretched back up again, just as strong as before.

'More!' shouted the monk. 'Quickly!'

Orus gripped Ambrose by the shoulder and turned him back to face the stern. It was engulfed. The flames burnt through the support for the rotten wheel, sending it tumbling from its mount. It rolled across the listing deck and crashed through the charred railing. Smoke blotted out the lights of Harradin behind them. Orus looked down at the helmet full of water.

Barely enough for an octogenarian's birthday cake.

'We're going to need a bigger bucket.'

'It's no use. We'll have to swim for it,' said Ambrose.

They ran to the bow, still flame free for the moment, and looked out across the dark water.

Orus could see a group of seagulls huddled together for warmth on a passing iceberg. A brief wink from the moon showed up the sparkle of ice on their feathers.

They were dead. Frozen solid.

'We'd be corpses before we got twenty feet,' said Orus.

A corpse. Ambrose looked down at the dead man's helmet in his hands. That was it.

'A bigger bucket . . . Or a smaller boat. Back downstairs! Quick!'

Without time for reverence they tipped the corpses out of their resting places and dragged the two pine boxes off the table.

'Paddles?' Orus asked.

'These?' said Ambrose, holding up a pair of shields.

'Better than nothing.' Orus grabbed one of the shields and threw it in the coffin. The 'the' was very important. He wasn't ready to think of it as *his* coffin just yet.

They each dragged their new boats towards the stairs, then stopped.

'The egg!'
'My man-chest!'

Both dashed to the front of the hold and retrieved their precious cargo.

Reaching the stairs again, smoke was pouring from the deck above like a slinky of storm clouds. The air was full of bright, glowing embers. The sound of the deck collapsing under the strain of the fire competed with groans from the keel underneath. The ship was dying.

Orus batted away the smoke and tried to haul the pine box up the first few steps. They groaned and creaked. The smoke bit at his eyes. It was no use. The top of the stairs was already aflame. There was no way they could go back up that way. They were trapped, cooked, finished.

A rush of thick smoke engulfed Orus, sending him staggering back down the stairs. He put his hand out to brace against the cabin wall behind him. The rotten wood gave way to his weight and he crashed through. Landing hard on the deck, Orus looked up at the him-shaped hole in the flimsy planking.

To his left, the man-chest was rattling, almost bouncing on its ends. He ignored it. A memory was returning to him and, with it, a plan.

Orus ran back to where the coffins had lain and grabbed a double headed war-axe from the table.

'What are you doing?' Ambrose called over the roar of the flames.

'One time, back in Ditch,' Orus said, inspecting the inner hull, 'the Prince's cat, Tornado, was chasing rats in the stables. It fell.' Orus knocked on a plank with his knuckles. It sounded about right. 'Fell right between the wall and the end of a stall, down in the gap. It was stuck. Couldn't get it out. But we couldn't just leave it, not Tornado.' Orus hefted the axe onto his shoulder and took a step back. 'So you know what we did?'

'Euthanasia?' asked Ambrose, eyes on the axe.

'Made a hole,' said Orus, swinging the axe with all his strength.

Splinters flew.

Steadying his feet as the ship tipped back and forth, Orus kept slamming away. In four good strokes he made it through to the open air. He couldn't tell if the sweat spreading across his back was from the axe or from the fire above. Not that it mattered. In this case, hard work really would be its own reward.

A few more strikes and Orus had opened up the start of a decent escape route. Together, they kicked the edges of the planks free from the ribs of the ship. Soon there was a hole big enough to push the coffins through.

'Good idea,' said Ambrose. 'Maybe—'

'Don't say it!' Orus tried to clamp his hand over Ambrose's mouth but it was too late.

'—we'll get out of this after all.'

Exactly on cue, without even a prod from the celestial stage director, the bottom of the burning foremast crashed through the deck. It stood perfectly upright for a few seconds — burning like the main bar of a Scottish pensioner's electric fire the day their winter fuel payment arrived — before crashing down through the side of the ship, dragging a curtain of flame across the escape hole in the process.

'You really shouldn't say stuff like that,' said Orus. 'It makes them think you're winning.'

'"They" who?'

'Does it matter?'

'What now?'

Orus looked back at the stairs. They were fully ablaze. Ahead, the flames from the mast stretched from floor to what had until recently been ceiling. There was no way through.

'Euthanasia?'

Ambrose stared at the flames. He was used to hot. The temple, the Worm-mound, there were parts of it that would put the inside of a freshly baked sausage roll to shame. This, however, was something different. The heat didn't burn, it scorched. The air choked his lungs and parched his throat. Even his skin, normally covered in a greasy sheen of adolescence, was beginning to crack and gasp.

He had been taught to control fire. It was one of the skills of the Dragon Monks. He could conjure small flames and twist them into different forms. It was handy for reading his contraband hero stories late at night. But this fire was too much, too fierce. Even the Grandmaster, even the High Council, wouldn't be able to control the furnace the ship had become. That would take magic far greater, far more powerful, far hungrier.

The man-chest's rattling reached a peak. The lock split and pinged off, burying itself in the far wall. From inside, its fierce glow filling the body of the box, the egg rose into the air with the hum of a thousand beehives.

It lifted itself into the shimmering air. The dragon-scale bag fell back into the man-chest. Orus turned to look. There was a change in air pressure, like a deep, deep breath. The egg was drawing the heat of the fire towards itself. Just like in the Hairy Flagon the night before, tendrils of flaming spaghetti energy reached out to it from the surrounding inferno. They came from all sides, the egg stealing fire from the timbers in long, red coils, twisting the pure elemental power round itself like promethean bolognaise.

A thick strand curled past Orus's shoulder, coming between him and Ambrose's startled form. Another snaked through his legs and reared up to connect with the spinning shell. Orus jumped back before it could touch him. Following the tendril's route back to the source, he saw the curtain of flame across their escape hole being drawn back. A gap had opened.

'Wow.' Ambrose stood and stared. Flame strands coursed around him. 'It's, it's, absorbing them. Drinking them up.'

The hole was almost totally clear now. Orus grabbed the end of the first coffin and slid it into position. He pulled Ambrose away from egg. 'Get in.'

'Hey, maybe we will–'

Orus grabbed the monk and pushed him down into the coffin. 'Not this time!' He shoved the makeshift boat out of the hole as hard as he could.

It landed with a splash and a half-heard call of 'Sorry.'

If he left it here, Orus was pretty sure the egg would drink up every flame on the ship. Even the hull was starting to bend and buckle towards it. But that would do no good in the long term. The dragon needed real dragon fire to hatch, that's what Ambrose had said. This was just an appetiser. The egg would consume it all and then sink far out of reach. With it would go all the magic in the world.

Not on my watch.

Orus dashed forward, ducking under the tangled strands of burning energy. A thick rope of flame bucked and scythed through the air, singeing off the scant amount of hair that had still been clinging to the left side of his head. Reaching the man-chest, he dug his hands inside until he found the Grandmaster's oven-mitts and the dragon-scale bag. The egg was rotating above him, somewhere inside a glowing halo of fire.

Much like when it came to pulling Tornado from the hole in the stable wall, he knew this was going to hurt, no two ways about it. Best get it over with.

Oven mitts on, he sprung upwards and flipped the dragon-scale bag over the egg. Flames burned his arms and blackened his face.

The magic resisted, leaving him hanging by the bag's handles, toes brushing the floor, eyebrows curling back from the inferno. The heat was too intense. It blasted him, burned him, scorched him. Cut off from the shell, a ribbon of flame lashed down his back. It was like being splashed with hot oil. But he held on. He had to.

The egg submitted. Orus fell to the deck, rolling on his back to smother the flames burning through his cloak. Above the spaghetti flames whipped backwards, crashing through the remaining partitions before splashing across the hull.

Orus didn't hang around. He wrapped up the egg in its bag and stuffed it back in the chest. Then, having heaved his most prized possession into the second coffin, he took its back edge in his hands and pushed towards the hole in the hull. The edge approached. Then it was gone.

He landed inside just as the coffin crashed onto the cold waves below.

The coffin held fast. Luckily, old Jones, the Harradin undertaker, was not one to skimp on quality, even if all his hard work was to go up in smoke. After some careful shuffling, Orus gained a steady paddling position. Digging the borrowed shield into the water he pulled himself after Ambrose and free from the burning ship.

*

'Shoot them!' Tyran slammed his fist on the balcony. The two tiny boats moved awkwardly out of the conflagration, heading out into the body of the great lake.

'Out of range, sire,' called back the lead archer.

Tyran let out a bellow of rage as he vaulted from the balcony. Snatching the lead archer's bow, he shoved him to the ground. The King plunged an arrow into the flame, notched it and drew the string across his huge chest until the wood was bent into a perfect crescent. Hair-thin strands of wood pinged from the front of the bow under the massive strain as Tyran lined up his shot.

The arrow burst into the air and the bow exploded into a thousand splinters.

The flaming barb scorched skywards. Tyran's distance was good and for a second it looked like he might hit his target. Like a shaft of kamikaze stardust, it plunged into the dark water just to the left of Orus's coffin boat.

A miss, although not without some success. The next day a crab out for a morning scuttle would find an appetising kebab skewer of three fat fish buried deep in the silt of the lake bed. The impressiveness of such a feat would be lost on the crustacean but it was grateful for the free meal nonetheless.

Back above the water, the King threw the tattered remains of the bow over the cliff edge and roared curses into the night. They were not eloquent curses, not the kind gentlemen used before a duel when they tried to make the first cut with their words, nor the kinds of curses playwrights liked to put in the mouths of barbarians to show the nobility of the savage. Tyran's curses consisted mainly of the F-word, shouted very loudly, in varying tones of extreme annoyance, accompanied by a lot of stamping of feet and punctuated by punching any of the archers stupid enough to stay within range.

Conrad was equally enraged at having seen his prize escape yet again. He, on the other hand, expressed his anger with a cold simmer, twisting his gloves into an ever tighter coil in his hands.

'What now?' asked Huggle, while trying to suppress the hint of an inkling of a clue to a smile. He was starting to quite like these egg thieves.

'I should send you out on a rowing boat after them.' Conrad turned on him, striking him across the face with the gloves. 'This is all your fault, remember. If you had searched that damn mountain properly when we first arrived we would've had the egg before that fat oaf ever got involved.'

'My fault?' With Skar not around Huggle found his anger with his master gaining a foothold over his fear of the repercussions. 'We would have caught up with them before they ever got here if we didn't have to bring your entire wardrobe with us. I wonder what the King would think of the great hero's salon tent?'

Conrad's stare hardened. 'You should choose your words carefully, scribe. It is very difficult to write if someone cuts off both your thumbs. Go and find Skar, hire one of those ships and get after them.'

Tyran's huge hands slapped onto the balcony ledge and heaved the rest of him back over the parapet. 'Don't bother,' he said, striding to the door to the Great Hall and pulling his long dagger from the wall as he went. 'There's no wind. And anyway, I know where they're going. Cribond! Get the horses ready.'

'Yes, sire.'

The King's aide was by his side again, not that Huggle had seen him move. Even when he followed Tyran inside, Cribond didn't so much fall into step as slither noiselessly behind. As they passed through the door Huggle caught a hint of a hissed whisper.

'And if I could, in the meantime, have a word...'

'Huggle!' Conrad called out as he followed the King into the Broch. 'Get the men together. And find something to ride. I'm not waiting for you to huff and puff along behind.'

*

Down in the stable of the Hairy Flagon, Thunder shuddered. A familiar feeling of impending backache ran through him.

Just when I was getting comfy.

237

CHAPTER THIRTY-NINE

In the Broch's handsomely stocked armoury, King Tyran was casting swords and axes over his shoulders like an enraged porcupine that has just seen its favourite football team lose the big derby match to the stuck-up hedgehogs from the next valley. The really big weapons were at the back and when he caught up with Orus and that other skinny weed, Tyran wanted to be sure he got his point across. And through. And out the other side.

Behind him, oscillating from the path of the flying blades, Cribond was trying to get the King's attention.

'Sire, if you could just stop for a moment—'

A two-handed broadsword scythed through the patch of air Cribond had been standing in, before burying itself deep into one of the room's supporting beams.

'I think you will want to hear this.' This time the clerk's head sunk tortoise-like into his robe just in time to avoid a spinning axe. 'It relates to your recent difficulties.'

Tyran stopped his metallic barrage. Standing up straight his hand went to his back. 'What recent difficulties? You mean this.' He twisted to look at the recently sewn-up wound over his left kidney. 'It was a lucky swing. Just a scratch.'

'These scratches are becoming more common.'

'So what? I still won didn't I? A knick in my hide isn't going to be much comfort to those challengers now that they're at the bottom of the lake. I'm still the fastest, the strongest, the–'

'Oldest.'

'And? What does that matter?'

It matters, thought Cribond, because those last two challengers had their own scribes. Just like that idiot Von Strauss. That's the way with these new heroes. They don't just come on their own. They have staff. And he had not spent the last thirty years serving the Kings of Harradin, using the power of his position to build up a massive personal fortune, complete with a palatial house on the sunny side of town and an extensive estate on the far side of the Grimwood, to have some young pencil pusher poking his nose in the town's books, exposing all his hard – illegal – work. It had taken a long time to climb the tower of power. If found out, he'd be booted back to the shack behind the Hairy Flagon's outhouse without a tax skimming scheme to his name.

Tyran wasn't perfect, but he was the kind of king Cribond needed: not stupid, just disinterested. He didn't like to get bogged down in details like staff salaries or where all the bribes went and that provided opportunities. Cribond was not about to put that all at risk, especially not when he had been gifted such a fortuitous chance to extend the current king's reign.

'What I merely wanted to explain is that this dragon egg may be more valuable than you think.'

'I don't care about the egg. Dragon or no dragon. What does it matter?' Tyran said, digging back into the pile of weapons. He lifted out a spiked mace before changing his mind and casually tossing it out of the nearby window.

'It's Orus I want. And his little friend. No-one makes a fool of me in my city. No-one.'

'Granted, sire. And I'm sure when we catch them your thirst for revenge will be well quenched, but you should not discard the egg so lightly. Perhaps you are not aware of its special qualities.'

'Like what?'

'I have heard it said that a dragon's egg, if consumed, can restore one's youth and vigour to a remarkable extent. Perhaps not immortality, but another generation of would-be challengers might find the aging warrior-king of Harradin not quite what they were expecting.'

'Hmm.' Tyran passed his coal mitt hand through his hair. Some of the dark dye he used to cover the expanding grey came off on his skin. Of all the foes he fought over the years he was becoming only too aware that age might be the one to plunge the final knife. 'I like this idea, Cribond. You're sure this is not some myth? I know how much you wordy types like to exaggerate these things.'

'I am very sure. When the monk said it could be a dragon egg I went to do some reading in the library.'

'We have a library?'

'Yes, sire. Quite extensive in fact. Anyway, the properties of such an egg are well documented. Now that it has been confirmed to be of draconic origin, I'm sure it will work. There is just the problem of what to do with Von Strauss. He won't want to give it up lightly.'

Tyran turned back to his oily aide. The sword he held before him was gigantic. It was Tyran's favourite and he could wield it with mathematical precision – in that he used it to turn people into fractions.

'I'm sure I'll think of something.'

'I thought that you might.'

CHAPTER FORTY

With the departure of the man-chest, Thunder had hoped his next journey might at least involve a smaller load. This was not to be.

The scribe, Huggle, was if anything even fatter than Orus, and he had been lumbered with the saddle bags containing Master Lenz's painting props as well. Add to this that he was immediately downwind of Skar and Tyran's chief ranger, neither of whom, Thunder had quickly learned, could boast of excellent, or even just non-infectious, personal hygiene levels, made for an altogether miserable trek up the lake edge. He would have held his nose, if he could.

Bloody humans. Don't know how lucky they are.

The preparations for the pursuit from Harradin had been a rushed affair; like most things done in a rush, it had taken about twice as long as it should have done. The blame for the delay would have rested squarely on Conrad's shoulders, had he not expertly shrugged it onto Huggle's instead. Apparently, the scribe's poor organisational skills had meant that Conrad was forced to take two hours to decide what should be taken for his brunch tomorrow. In addition, his total lack of foresight or common sense meant that he failed to anticipate that the riding britches of Conrad's winter forest huntsman ensemble would clash terribly with the colours on the King's standard.

By the time they had left, stopped, sent Huggle back to collect Conrad's other winter forest hunter outfit, waited for him to catch up again, and then for Conrad to change, which of course meant pitching the changing tent, there was no question of the column apprehending the two fugitives that night. The road bent away from the lake up into the mountains and to pick through the forest back to its shore would risk missing them in the dense woodland. Instead, they were making straight for Pale Pass. There they would lie in wait for the egg thieves.

'So why is it called Pale Pass?' Skar and Tyran's chief ranger were getting on pretty well, each keen to find out if their hired muscle job was as good as the other's. 'Is it full of ghosts or wraiths or wispy stuff like that?'

'No,' replied the ranger, passing his wine skin over to Conrad's enforcer.

'So is it 'cause of the colour? With the snow and everything?'

The trip north had brought them off the foothills and into the knobbly knees of the Fang Mountains. Snow was thick on the ground, crunching under hooves and the trees had grown denser, huddling together for warmth.

'Nope,' said the ranger, taking back the skin.

Huggle wasn't offered any, not that he would have drank it. Perhaps pretended, lifted it to his mouth and made the appropriate noises. He had a feeling that what it contained would be enough to send him marching to the front of the column to give Conrad a piece of his mind, and the skin off his knuckles. While he no doubt would have enjoyed passing on that message, the hangover would be a killer.

'So why is it called that then?' Skar continued.

'It looks like a bucket.'

Behind them a groan announced Huggle's feelings on the current education standards.

'He's not really what I thought he'd be like, your boss,' said the ranger.

'Na, me neither.' Skar lifted himself up on his stirrups to get a view of the road ahead. His wide shoulders blotted out most of the sky and eclipsed Huggle completely. 'But he's much better in his books. Really impressive. Good memory too. Some of the stories have whole big bits that I must have forgotten about. He might tell us some tonight, if we're lucky.'

'That must be great, being in a book.'

'He says I'm going to be in the next one,' said Skar excitedly. 'I'm learning to read e-specially for it.'

'Yeah? You're lucky. That's like immortality. I'd love to be in a book. It'll never happen though. No-one ever writes about guards, unless someone is killing them, or running away from them, or bribing them. In most of the stories the bards sing, the guards don't even have names. Nope, no-one really cares about us. Even though we do most of the work. Guys like me barely even get a mention. I mean when this is all done and some scribbler writes it all up, I bet they won't have a chapter about Chief Ranger...'

The hooting of an owl distracted Huggle momentarily from the conversation, but he picked it up again quickly and didn't seem to have missed anything important.

'I can't wait to show my mum when I'm in the book,' said Skar. 'She'll be so proud. Always said I would do great things.'

'Hey, maybe they'll put you on a trading card. Like the ones of Conrad you get in boxes of matches.'

The idea of such an honour raced around Skar's brain like a ferret in a football. 'Hey! I'd never thought of that. Maybe they will. I mean, I have done most of the fighting so far. Yeah, that'd be great.

'Hey, 'Uggle,' Skar never could get his name right. 'When this is all finished, do you think I'll get to be on a trading card like the boss?'

This put the scribe in a difficult spot. Previous experience told him that not only was Skar unlikely to be made into a trading card, he was also unlikely to feature in Conrad's next book. He was, however, very likely indeed to be arrested by Conrad's father on return to Castle Von Strauss and thrown in a dungeon with all the rest of his men. And the only thing his mother was going to get to read containing any reference to her son would be a letter, signed by Von Strauss (but written by Huggle), describing how, despite the valiant attempts his master had made to save him, poor Skar died just before all the important stuff happened and Von Strauss had to save the day on his own again.

'It's possible,' he said, feeling thoroughly wretched from skin to core. He tried to pretend to himself this wasn't quite a lie. There was at least a small chance their master would break with tradition this one time. Stranger things had happened. Like when the Island of Rang decided it was tired of sea views, upped-bedrock and moved to the centre of the Distressed Swamp.

'Wow!' The hulking warrior gasped, his mind filling up with sticker albums and action figures.

It's easy to lie with your mouth. It's impossible to do so with your rear. Thunder could feel the tell-tale squirm of the fibber on his back.

Figures. Bet I don't get a trading card either.

CHAPTER FORTY-ONE

Out on the lake, the coffin boats were holding up well. They weren't the easiest things to manoeuvre, but their sturdy construction kept the water out and they didn't rock about too much. Orus and Ambrose had made it through the tangled forest of charred masts clogging the exit to the bay and were slowly making their way along the body of the lake.

At the far end, was the head of a huge glacier. This river of ice started many miles into the Fang Mountains, grinding its way along thousands of years of valleys before it reached the lake. Once there, the water would cut slices off its ever advancing front, like giant geological fingernails. These chunks of ice clogged that end of the lake, filing themselves against each other until they were small enough to escape from the churning mass. Any ship venturing that far up would quickly be crushed to kindling.

Nevertheless, the glacier pointed the way. Somewhere across its shifting flows and centuries old waves were the Hatching Grounds. To get up to it, Pale Pass was the only option.

'We should try to get as close to the top of the lake as we can,' said Ambrose. 'That way it'll be a shorter trip to the Pass. The Grandmaster warned me the forest here can be dangerous, more so than even the Grimwood.'

Orus laid down his shield paddle and gave his arms a much needed shake. He'd taken off his scorched cloak to stop himself getting too hot while rowing, but now that their pace had slowed he was feeling the cold creep back into his joints. He flexed his fingers back and forth, then stuffed his hands under his armpits for good measure.

'We could do with some light,' he said, watching a small iceberg drift by. The bobbing blocks were becoming more numerous and spotting them in the darkness was anything but easy.

'Let me try something.' Ambrose lifted up a tattered flag he had snatched from one of the up-thrust masts and wrapped it around the handle of the axe Orus had used to cut the hole in the ship. Holding the torch in one hand he started to whisper words of power.

He could only do a small flame but it would be enough to light the flag and get a torch going.

Sweat started to form on Ambrose's brow, sinking into the reddening furrows as he tried to force the spell. The young monk was not a real wizard, this being only a very basic spell, but he had not had this much trouble with it before. He said the words again, focusing his mind on images of fire. Still nothing.

After a few more minutes of trying he stopped, defeated.

'It's not working. I got all the words right, I'm sure.'

'Could it be the cold?' Orus suggested, blowing on his numb hands.

'No, I don't think so. It feels like there just isn't enough magic in the air to get it to catch. The Grandmaster said this would happen. Without the dragons to put the energy back in, magic is draining from the world. This must be a barren patch. Our missionaries have been reporting more and more of them.'

'So, is this it starting?'

'No,' said Ambrose. 'This is it ending.'

*

Ambrose was right. All over Drift magic was draining out of the world. In the navigator city of Olop, the Wind Wizard, normally able to raise gusts that filled the sails of the biggest ships, couldn't even pull together enough puff to turn the decorative windmills in his rooftop garden. This was nothing compared to the problems being experienced by the caravan town of Al Kahari. The magical engines that powered the town's hundreds of plodding legs seized up, stranding it in the middle of the desert. As if this wasn't bad enough, the caravan chief's iced drinks cabinet had broken down as well.

Even the runic magic of the Dwarves of Copperbottom and Tinpot was wearing thin. Last week, a whole legion of automatic hammers marched out of the mine, chanting something about not needing any more mind control, and a group of self-powered mine carts formed a union, refusing to move until a proper system of rest days, regular maintenance and lighter loads for carts with bad backs was agreed.

Ditch too had not escaped the effects of this thinning of Drift's cosmic fabric. Mavis's Morphing Mannequin had been playing up again, setting her a good day behind on an important commission.

That wasn't even the worst of it. Only yesterday, Mavis had watched from her shop window as one of the micro-cows high society ladies had taken to carrying in their purses ran out of magic and reverted to its true, massive-snorting-bull form. Luckily it had been inside Ms Ping's China Shop at the time. A careful business woman, Ms Ping was well aware of the dangerous nature of her trade and was covered by the full range of bovine-related insurance policies.

Still, a raging mass of meat, muscle and horns crashing through the market square was not the sort of thing that attracted customers, no matter how many pink bows it had on its tail or what colour its hooves had been painted. Mavis didn't sell a single thing all day. Not only that, a woman who had just bought a fetching red shawl returned it, citing a rapid change in local fashion.

CHAPTER FORTY-TWO

Huggle was also having difficulties of a magical nature.

'What do you mean "not working"?'

Conrad glared at the scribe from between the biceps of Skar and his deputy, Rägrund. The joint expedition had arrived at Pale Pass half an hour ago. Now that Von Strauss had partaken of his post-ride massage, restyled his hair and changed his outfit from *Winter Expedition* to *Northern Warlord* – complete with black bear fur cloak and silver wolf tooth necklace – he was ready to retire to the Whizzabang-Go for an evening meal.

'It's the portal, sire,' said Huggle. 'I can't get it to connect to the lodge. There doesn't seem to be enough magic to sustain the connection.'

'Why not?'

'I don't–'

'Huggle, if you say "I don't know" I will have Skar cut off one of your toes. It is your job to know. If you are not able to do your job perhaps I need to find someone who is better suited to the position.'

Fat chance, thought Huggle. There was no-one else for this job. It had been made for him, he was sure of that. It was his punishment for crimes committed. His own special hell, ordered up long ago and delivered to him like a sweet honey pastry from a celestial pâtisserie that specialised in just desserts.

The first time he encountered Conrad he had thought the slimy worm was his saviour, ready to rescue him from a life of disappointment, disillusionment and financial destitution.

He'd been so sure of himself when he was young. He knew how his life would play out. His father was a clerk in the local castle, his mother a noble woman's handmaiden. Good jobs, respectable jobs, but not the jobs for him. There was a whole world out there to explore and he wanted to see it. Lacking any of the martial skills required to become an adventurer, he decided to become a bard and a scribe. He would journey with a famous hero and chart their great adventures, weaving daring deeds into bold new songs and sagas. He would be the toast of the courts; people would come from far and wide to hear his music and he would make a nice bit of money out of it all too.

His parents used every last penny of their savings to send him to the Bards College. He excelled there, just as he knew he would. He quickly learned all the classic songs and sagas, as you were supposed to, but his real passion was composition. It was the new that excited him. Stories never told before or old stories told in new ways. That is what he loved and he couldn't wait to get out into the real world, beyond the college's walls, so he could start adding tales of his own making to the well-known favourites. He would have to work his way up, he was ready for that. You didn't get taken on by a travelling hero just like that. You had to prove yourself. Make a name for yourself. But that wouldn't take him long. After all, this was his destiny.

Unfortunately, he quickly found out that his love of the new was not shared by the beer halls and taverns where a new bard has to start out. Why listen to something new and risk it being rubbish when you could shout for the saga of Teger Crotchpunch and the Burping Orc, and belch along with the chorus.

Sure it was frustrating, but it wouldn't be for long. Just a few months, maybe a year. That's how it worked. Put in the hours, try hard, sacrifice, then he would get his big break, find the right hero to team up with, the right quest, and write a hit – a new favourite everyone would cheer for. If he didn't, if he tried and tried and tried and got nowhere, well, that just wouldn't be fair.

And he had been right. Okay, so it had taken a bit longer than he'd planned, and he'd had to supplement his barding income with numerous other jobs, but finally he came up trumps. Or at least he would have done, if he had only remembered to take down the hero's name. That Garvock incident had fallen right in his lap. It was perfect, it had everything. It should have been his ticket to the big time and he'd messed it up.

He'd never get a chance like that again, not in a hundred years. But what could he do? A story without a hero was nothing, useless, worthless.

It was while he was retracing his steps, making his way back to Trundle in the hope of tracking down the mystery hero, that he first met Conrad, or Conrad's father to be precise. The Marquis Von Strauss was returning from market with a train of fresh non-volunteers for his vast network of gold and silver mines, when Huggle was nearly run over by his carriage train.

After the scribe had dusted himself off and entertained the Marquis' entourage with some choice old classics, the head of house Von Strauss asked Huggle how he had come to be so far from civilisation. The young scribe then recounted his recent woes. Conrad's father,

Tyrone to his friends, played a gold coin across his fingers. As Huggle reached the end of his tale, the Marquis flicked the gold piece at the scribe's feet: it just so happened he had a solution to the scribe's problem.

Here was a story with no hero. He just so happened to know a hero with no story. If Huggle would write the story, making the Marquis' young son the lead, the Marquis would reward him greatly and take him on his staff at a handsome salary. They could tour the noble courts and Huggle would finally have the chance to make a splash in the barding world.

That was his pact. The hook that caught him and the shot that sunk him. It would set his life on a falsehood and by stealing the mystery hero's rightfully won glory he would be breaking one of the oldest rules of barding. His honour would be forever stained.

And what use, the Marquis has asked – with a voice as slick and shiny as a gallon of detergent – had his honour been to him so far? Surely he knew many of the old stories were not as they actually happened? Great traditions were often built on little lies. If no-one knew, where was the harm in that? If stories truly reflected real life they would be boring. They already skip bits and squish bits, add things and change things. Why else are the sizes of armies always nice round numbers? And why are none of the maidens that get rescued just okay looking? How many simple farm girls of truly astounding natural beauty can there really be? He would not be doing anything countless others hadn't done before.

That was it. That was the tipping point. Huggle was sure now. That had been his great test and he had failed. Everything else that followed, lies upon lies, the ever deepening hole, was his own fault.

Sure the new composition had been a great success. They had made a good bit of money from it and, thanks to the Marquis paying for a tour of the courts of neighbouring lords, its young star was catapulted into the spotlight.[10]

Fame, however, demands to be fed. Conrad quickly saw that he could not live off one adventure for long. Huggle had initially suggested they go out looking for more quests to complete so that Conrad could have a story that was really his own. This idea had been greeted with a tirade of abuse from the direction of the Von Strauss castle hot tub. Why go to all the trouble of risking his life when Conrad could just pay someone else to do the hard bit, then kill them and swap his name into the story? Far easier and far less chance of anyone important getting hurt.

The Marquis agreed. A fine idea. Of course, Huggle didn't have to go along with it if he didn't want to. It was entirely up to him. Then again, were he to refuse and word got out he had stolen a story for money, debasing his artistic integrity for a bag of gold, his reputation would be forever ruined. He'd be back to belching along with the Burping Orc for the rest of his days, but at least his conscience would be clean. Until the Marquis' assassins caught up with him that is. Then it would probably pick up a few stains. Throats are such messy things when cut.

So Huggle had kept going. The lies that let him sleep at night got bigger and the hole he was digging himself got deeper.

Conrad didn't have these problems of conscience. The only thing he needed to get a good forty winks was a triple mattress, silk sheets, pillows stuffed with the feathers of endangered species, a glass of warm milk and the soothing calls of the magical miniature whale he kept in a fish bowl by the bed. He had all of these things through the portal in his lodge, along with a whole team of chefs, each

---

[10] Often literally, Conrad not being one to miss out on making a dramatic stage entrance and catapults being easy to get hold of in a pre-gunpowder society like Drift.

one of which had been specially trained to prepare dishes that met his exacting dietary requirements.

'I've got the mages working on it,' Huggle said. Before Conrad arrived back at the tent the mages had got the portal to open for a few minutes. The problem was, they explained, it wasn't properly aligned with the lodge. If Conrad tried to use it, he could be stretched to spaghetti by the magical vortex and end up in some demon's pasta bowl.

Right at this moment, as Von Strauss moved past Huggle and stuck his face through the open tent flap, the portly scribe was having difficulty remembering what the downside to that was.

'And how long do they think it will take to fix?'

'They aren't sure, sire.'

'When are mages ever sure?'

'I could give them some motivation, boss,' Skar said.

'No, Skar. It is not wise to knock mages about. It can make a terrible mess. But we are still left with the question of where I am supposed to eat tonight.'

'Tyran's men has got a table set up by the big fire,' Skar suggested. 'There looked like plenty of room.'

A shudder ran through Conrad's well moisturised cheeks. Eating with common people was a trial he preferred to avoid. They seemed to pride themselves in spraying as much food over the person sitting opposite them as they got into their mouths. He did not want to get grease stains on his expensive wolf-skin jacket. Then again, this was a quest, and he was the world's greatest hero. It was only proper that he endure some hardships.

CHAPTER FORTY-THREE

'That is a fine tale, Your Majesty,' Conrad said while doing his best to avoid the spurting juices that erupted from the edges of the King's mouth every time he took a bite out of his chicken leg. 'It reminds me of my last adventure before this: *The Twelve Ice Giants of Cainth's Point.*'

Time to redraft the manuscript again, thought Huggle. Maybe he should just push it up to twenty ice giants to save time.

'Unfortunately, I can't recount it here tonight. Publisher's embargo you see. I owe it to my public that they get to hear it first,' Conrad continued.

'Must be a bit boring, all that writing.' Tyran bit down on his dinner, sending another gush of fat Conrad's way. 'I only have to do death warrants mostly, but even they bore the socks off you after a while.'

'Actually, Your Majesty,' Huggle leaned forward to look up the table, 'I do most of the writing.'

'What's that?'

Before he could respond, Conrad cut Huggle off. 'I'm afraid my little scribe sometimes gets ideas above his station. He merely scribbles down notes on the way. I then make these notes into the stirring epics you are all no doubt familiar with. I have to add bits in of course, where poor Huggle here has been so frozen with fear that he cannot remember them. They are a delicate breed, these men of letters.'

All the guards and bodyguards at the table cheered at this cheap shot and clashed tankards at Huggle's expense.

He'd love to tell them all what Conrad was really like. Maybe he could tell them the tale of his daring assault on the Bone Beast of the Gobbling Bog, when Von Strauss heroically sent wave after wave of mercenaries into the creature's lair until it went for an after dinner nap, presenting the perfect opportunity for our hero to sneak in and blow it up with a barrel full of Pengian fire powder. Or his defeat of the Gorgon of Sqeltch, slain singlehandedly, after it had been thoroughly mauled by sixty blind mongooses.[11]

But what would be the use? Everyone knew Conrad was the world's greatest hero and once everyone knows something, they aren't going to stand for someone telling them different. Makes them look stupid. Ignorance is bliss, so pity the poor chap that tries to shine a little truth on the situation.

'I know what you mean. He's like my assistant Cribond.' The King looked over his shoulder then decided just to shout. 'Cribond!'

'Yes, Your Majesty?'

'Conrad and me were just saying what a cowardly lot you are.'

'You mean Conrad and I, sire.'

'Are you sure, Cribond?' asked Tyran, casually flipping his knife end over end.

---

[11] Not being able to find a sufficient number of naturally blind mongooses was not a problem Conrad troubled over for long.

'No. My mistake, Your Majesty. I shall make sure to inform the city clerks of their long years of grammatical error when we return.'

Tyran let out a great laugh and jostled Conrad on the arm. 'See. I've seen more backbone in a bowl of porridge.'

'True, true,' said Conrad, discreetly brushing chunks of chicken flesh from his sleeve. 'But I'll bet it's Huggle that is the most spineless of all. I'm surprised he's made it this far. Can you ask your men to make sure and keep the fire going all night, only he does get rather scared of the dark.'

The table had a good laugh at that one too. All except one.

But Conrad wasn't finished. 'It's because of his teddy bear, you see. Ever since he lost it, he's never been quite the same. Grubby little thing. What was its name again, Huggle?'

The laughter erupted again.

That's it. Huggle pushed his plate away and got up. Conrad could go and get stuffed for all he cared. He'd didn't need a job this bad.

Just see how long that fool lasts when he doesn't have someone to save him from all the stupid messes he so loves to create. They could send all the assassins and thugs and brutes they liked after him. See if he cared.

No-one talks about Mr Snuggles that way.

CHAPTER FORTY-FOUR

He won't last one day without me.

Huggle stuffed a bottle of brandy into his pack for the trip back to Harradin. From there he could barter a ride on a trading caravan back to civilisation and get a simple clerk's job. Something without any heroes, without any adventure, without any excitement whatsoever: like accounting.

See how the great Conrad Von Strauss would get on then.

Huggle looked around his own modest tent. The manuscript lay on a small table by his bedroll.

Hang it, he thought, *let him have the damn thing. I've carried his lies around long enough.*

He shouldered his pack and ducked through the tent flap, back into the cold night. The sound of drunken laughter drifted across from the far side of the camp. They wouldn't find Von Strauss quite the same draw tomorrow, he fancied.

Huggle was almost tempted to stay and watch. See what this lot thought of their mighty hero when he is defeated by the complexity of his sock drawer. Almost.

In the camp stable, Thunder was sleeping soundly and dreaming his favourite dream: he was currently chasing a herd of giant carrots across a spring meadow. Carrots not having legs, he had managed to catch quite a few already.

While he enjoyed his dreams, Thunder was a realist at heart. Reality was rarely so nice to him. As such he was not surprised to be woken up by the thud of a pair of heavy saddlebags landing on his back.

However, not being surprised didn't mean he was happy about it.

'Oww!' Huggle managed to stuff his fist in his mouth before any more elaborate exclamations of pain could give announcement to his flight. He tried to pull his foot out from under the donkey's hoof with his other hand, but couldn't.

Heavy, isn't it?

The scribe shoved at Thunder's flank with his shoulder to no noticeable effect. Something like 'Hmmmvv, yrrrr, fooo,' escaped from the gaps between fist and lips.

Now imagine that, but with you on top too. Not fun is it?

The ridge on the donkey's hoof pressed down on Huggle's foot, pushing the blood into his frozen toes. They felt like high pressure sausages, ready to burst at any moment. Holding back more curses, he bent down and gripped Thunder's leg. He tried to haul it up.

He failed.

After Thunder was satisfied justice had been done, the donkey allowed his hoof to lift just enough for the scribe's boot to slide free. He did this quickly, without warning, sending Huggle reeling backwards into the water trough.

'I was,' Huggle said, shaking the water and strands of straw from his sleeves, 'going to walk back to Harradin. But since my foot is now thoroughly squished . . .'

Just try it.

Huggle eventually left the camp leading Thunder behind him. He fed the sentry a line about delivering a message from Conrad back to Harradin. It worked. The bleary-eyed guardsman hadn't even mentioned the muddy hoof print on his shirt.

*

Meanwhile, Orus and Ambrose had abandoned their boats at the lake edge and struck out for Pale Pass on foot. With no path to break through the dense, snow-covered woodland, it was slow going. Orus's hands were frozen numb from grabbing onto frost covered branches in an effort to stop slips becoming falls. This was an effort that was only partially successful and the hit rate was reducing as tiredness set in.

Dusting himself off after one such fall, he looked around to find the cause of his slip.

'Are you okay?' Ambrose stood on the edge of the circle of snow that had given way under Orus's heavier steps.

'Fine, I think. But if you've got any of your Grandmaster's tea, I think my hands could do with a cup about now.'

Orus was used to working in the cold. It didn't snow that much in Ditch, but when it did Orus was normally recruited as courtyard-shoveller in chief. He'd also go and do old Mrs Patch's path, and the one at the school. He hoped it hadn't snowed while he'd been away.

But up here in the Fang Mountains the cold was different: dry, stubborn and relentless. His fingers pulsed with it.

'You can hold the egg for a while, if you want?' Ambrose passed him the satchel. 'It's cool enough to handle now.'

'Thanks.' Orus plunged his hands in the bag and spread his fingers around the egg's protective cover. Ambrose was right. It was still warm, but it wasn't what you'd call hot. They were running out of time.

'You didn't keep that axe from the ship by any chance, did you?' Ambrose asked, looking down at Orus in the depression of snow.

'No, why?'

The boy was scared. Orus looked around him. The snow under his feet was packed hard. Another thinner layer must have blown over the top and that is what caused him to fall. The crust having now collapsed, Orus could see the depression he was in was about three feet across. It was round, apart from the three pointy bits that extended from one side. There was another similar looking hole to the left of him and they continued that way, step after step, disappearing into the darkness. Unless you were trying your best not to picture a huge, monstrous creature trudging through the woods around you, they would have looked very much like footprints.

'No reason,' said Ambrose, reaching down to help Orus up.

With the kind of timing Orus knew only from horror night at the Ditch Amateur Dramatics Society, a crash of branches and a crunch of snow ahead signalled the approach of something large. He scrambled out of the not-a-footprint to get a better view of what was coming.

There was a dark shape moving this way. It was not a shape Orus recognised, despite his long hours spent memorising the wild creatures of the Drift while at Cromalot. He would liked to have pretended that he couldn't be sure if this fact made things better or worse, but in his experience the answer was always worse.

'Do you think it's seen us?' Ambrose whispered.

'Even if it hasn't, I think we should get out of its way.'

From the twilight, the creature let out a loud and unmistakably angry growl.

'Over here.' Orus pulled Ambrose over to a thick pine tree. The conifer's skirt of needles had stopped the snow falling around its base, creating a funnel. There was a small gap between the top of the drift and the bottom of the branches. 'Come on, get in.'

Together they slid through the gap on their bellies and ducked down in the trench.

Hidden in the tree's moat, Ambrose peeked out into the forest. The creature could still be heard, but they could no longer see it. Not that they needed to: the sound of its bulk being pushed through the undergrowth, and the continuing cries of rage, made it clear it was still heading towards them.

'I can't see it,' whispered the monk.

'I hope that works both ways.'

'Did you get a look at it? What is it?'

'Nothing I want to meet.'

The crunching footsteps were drawing nearer and nearer.

'Is there anything in there that we could use to fight it off?' Ambrose nodded to the man-chest.

Orus thought about this for a moment.

Maybe the… No, that won't work. Or. How about? No. If I rolled it up first? No, probably break after one hit. Unless…

'You don't happen to have a spade handle and a size four crank wheel?'

'No.'

'Then no. Not really.'

'Is there anything even remotely useful in that box?'

'It's all useful. Very useful in fact. You just need to wait for the right sort of problem to come along.'

'So you keep saying.'

Another loud crash cut them off. The creature was much closer now, only a few feet away.

Orus moved up to the lip of the snow drift. In the shadows he could just make out parts of the monster. Legs: six of them at least. Thick bushes obscured the body. Sticking out above them was a pair of pointed horns. Trailing behind he could see a long tail, as thick as a python, dragging through the snow.

All sorts of weird creatures amalgamated in Orus's imagination, each more terrible than the last: a horrible mountain beast, some scuttling forest demon, a twisted chimera made up of parts from both.

Just then, the monster honked, swore loudly and then its head fell off.

'Thunder!' Ambrose pulled himself out of the hole around the tree. 'How did you get here?'

Same way I get anywhere, entirely against my will.

'Are you alright down there?'

The head of the creature, which Ambrose could now see was actually a man, was pinned between the heavy pack on his back and the circumference of his belly. The monk held out a hand to help Huggle up before realising this wasn't going to work. Instead, he rolled the scribe onto his side first, allowing Huggle to get some purchase on a nearby branch, and then lifted him to his feet.

Crystals of snow clung to the scribe's eyebrows and his plump face glowed with cold. 'Thank you, good sir. It took me ages to get up the last time.' Huggle shot a glare at Thunder. He had set off from the camp fizzing with anger and the rate of this effervesce had only increased when he had quickly become lost. The experience of battling through the tangled roots, all the while dragging his stubborn companion along with him, had caused this anger to boil over completely. In such a state, with his brain power mostly taken up with imagining terrible fates befalling his former master for taking him to this godforsaken corner of the world, he didn't realise he was in the company of the very people he had spent the last week looking for. 'I am rather perplexed though, as to why you are out in this damnable place. I only hope your route has been less stress inducing than mine,' he continued, dabbing at his head with his well-worn handkerchief.

Orus heaved himself back out onto the snow and crossed the clearing. Huggle might not have recognised him, but he knew the scribe. He was all ready to make up a convincing lie when Ambrose saved him the trouble.

'We're on our way to Pale Pass to deliver a dragon egg to the secret Hatching Grounds in the mountains above,' he explained with a friendly smile. 'Of course, that's provided Conrad Von Strauss doesn't catch us first.'

Huggle's eyes bugged out of his head before anatomical suction pulled them back in. 'You. You are the egg thieves?'

'Egg rescuers,' said Orus.

'Well, yes, granted. What I mean is, you're still alive.'

'Last time we checked.'

'I thought you would have frozen out on the lake for sure. How did you cross it?'

'Oh, you know,' said Orus, hoping to keep a bit of mystery about the adventure. 'Just luck and hard work.'

'We escaped in coffins from the funeral ship, then rowed them, using shields as paddles, as far as we could up the lake and walked the rest,' helped Ambrose. He was poking around Thunder's saddlebags. 'What is all this stuff?'

'Just supplies.'

'And this?' Ambrose lifted up the tail of Master Lenz's dragon model. The tail had fallen out the pack and was trailing behind Thunder.

'That? It was in there when I packed them. It's a model for that idiot Von Strauss's next portrait. You can throw it away actually.'

'Idiot?' Orus eyed the scribe suspiciously. Why would he be out here on his own? Was it a trap to lure them out? Tyran knew where they were going. Maybe they had teamed up.

Orus scanned the forest gloom for any sign of Conrad's men. 'I'm sure your master wouldn't like to hear you call him that.'

'I could call him a lot worse: coward, pompous ass, arrogant, pig headed, lying, back-stabbing bile inducing blowhard.' As he sounded off, Huggle's hands twisted his handkerchief tighter and tighter. Even when he wasn't there in person Conrad infuriated him, and this fact annoyed him all the more.

'You can't be serious.' Ambrose was still rifling through the saddlebag, pulling out more and more of the dragon model.

'No, you're right. He's much worse than all that.'

'This is Conrad Von Strauss the great hero?'

'No, this is Conrad Von Strauss the great fake. The great weasel.'

'Don't you work for him?' Orus took a step back. The little man looked angrier than a prize winning pimple on prom night and Orus didn't want to be in the firing line when he popped.

Instead of bursting, Huggle collapsed inwards and fell into darkness. Sitting down on a large flat stone he put his head in his hands and pressed his twisted hanky to his forehead. 'Don't remind me.'

Shudders ran through his hunched form, accompanied by soft, wet, sobs. This was not what Orus had expected. He had read lots of heroic adventure stories and heard lots more sung by bards in taverns. None of them ever involved men crying.

So he drew on experience from his own life. He even recognised the type of crying. He had seen it a lot during Tag's teenage years. The sniffing, the shoulder shrugs, the wobbly lip. He gently put an arm round the scribe's shoulder and waited for the inevitable exclamation.

'It's not fair! I just wanted to be a success. Is that so bad? I didn't know what he was like. I do now. You'll see soon enough, if you keep going with whatever it is you're doing.'

'What is that meant to mean?' asked Orus, in rather softer tones than before.

'He's waiting for you. That psychotic king too. They're both up at Pale Pass, along with a bunch of guards.'

'So, why aren't you there?'

'I quit, that's why. Although, ran away is a more accurate description. I couldn't even find the courage to do that right.' Huggle broke into sobs again. He blew hard into his handkerchief. 'He's a fake you know. None of it is true. The books, all the stories, sure there's a grain of truth in each, no more than that. He's never done a heroic act in his life.'

Orus walked to the edge of the clearing and looked north towards the mountains. Fake or not, there were still forty-odd well-armed, hardened soldiers out there. There was no other way into the mountains and if Conrad and Tyran knew they were coming, the servant trick was out of the window.

The egg was losing heat with every hour and Drift's magical field was wearing thin. They couldn't wait for Tyran and Conrad to give up. If they were going to succeed they had to get through that pass and they had to do it tonight.

'Could you take us back to the gate?'

Huggle looked up. Tears and mucus trials from his nose glinted in the moonlight. 'Why? Didn't you hear me? They'll kill you. Slowly and painfully.'

'Because we've got to, that's why,' replied Orus. Because of Mavis, because of Tag, because of Old Grimmer and Mr & Mrs Still. Because somebody has to do it, even if that somebody was a nobody.

'Have you seen this thing?' Ambrose had laid the whole dragon model out on the snow. It was big, at least eight feet long, not including the tail. The body was fat: fat enough and tall enough to fit a few men inside. 'It's great. So detailed. Can we keep it?'

'We don't have space for it. It's junk,' said Orus, rather more sharply than he intended. 'What do you want it for?'

Ambrose shrunk back at Orus's snap and directed his next words more at his own feet than anything else. 'I just thought, never know when it might come in handy.'

Orus looked at the dragon model again. Then he looked at the man-chest. In his head 'An Idea' began to form. It didn't take long to grow into 'A Plan'.

'Ambrose,' said Orus, walking over to the monk and slapping an arm around his shoulders. 'You are a genius.'

'What? Why?'

'Huggle, lead us back to the pass please.'

'If you're sure. But what are you going to do when you get there?'

The man-chest called to Orus. He knew its contents backwards. He had everything he needed. The design was quickly taking shape inside his head.

And they had all said he should throw that stuff away. Useless was it? He would show them.

'They want a dragon. Let's give them a dragon.'

CHAPTER FORTY-FIVE

Conrad, down one scribe, had transferred the administrative duties of the expedition onto the most literate of Skar's men and was busy dictating his latest update for his publishers. With the Whizzabang-Go still broken he was forced to do this outside. Despite King Tyran strutting around in only a loincloth, boots and a cape, it was starting to get very cold indeed. The wind blowing down from the Fang Mountains didn't so much bite as chomp, each gust swallowing up another good ounce of body heat. Luckily, Von Strauss had his own private fire, fuelled by his favourite cinnamon scented logs, along with the comfy chair from his litter.

Tyran could show off as much as he liked. Conrad knew comfort was the sign of the civilised man.

The servant he was resting his legs on twitched in fright as a spray of hot sparks erupted from a crackling log. The smell of burnt hair lingered momentarily, making Von Strauss stop and consider his improvised footstool. He should have him turn round soon, that way any scarring would at least be symmetrical.

'Rägrund, take this down,' he said, stretching his legs toward the fire and getting back to business.

'Dear sirs,' Conrad continued. 'I write this to you as I come close to the end of my great quest, and not a moment too soon for I say that this is truly one of the most arduous adventures I have ever undertaken.'

Rägrund raised his head sheepishly. 'Sorry, boss, but what's ardi-us spelled like?'

Conrad shot the bodyguard-turned-scribe a dark look (not an easy thing to do at night, but Conrad was well practiced). He made a mental note that once he was finished with this dragon, he would track down Huggle and invent a new and extra-painful torture especially for him. 'Just say "hardest".'

'Okay, boss,' replied Rägrund. He touched the quill to the page and then hesitated, mouthing out the word silently.

Conrad put his hand to his head. 'H.A.R.D.E.S.T.'

'Thanks, boss. Got it.' Rägrund began scratching away again.

'As I was saying: This is truly the HARDEST quest I have ever under...' he eyed Rägrund again, '... gone on. It is now two days since I last ate.'

'Boss, boss,' Rägrund's face beamed like a puppy expecting a treat. 'That's not right. You ate only about an hour ago. Remember, you had that steak with onions and potatoes. I'll change that bit, shall I?'

Huggle would pay for this. 'No, Rägrund. I was speaking metaphorically.'

The bodyguard looked back at him blankly.

'That means cleverly. Great heroes do it a lot. But don't worry, you don't need to understand. Just write it as I say it.'

'Okay, boss. So, does that mean earlier when you were talking about being all alone on the quest, that was metal-forkily too?'

'Yes, Rägrund. Exactly right.'

'Oh good. For a bit I thought you might be trying to write me and the boys,' Rägrund paused, 'sorry, the boys and I, out of the story. You know, and take all the glory for yourself. Glad that's cleared up.'

'Not at all, my studious scribe. It is merely a stylistic feature. Nothing for you to worry about. You can be assured, confident… clear that you will all get what you deserve at the end of this.' He was glad that Huggle had sorted out all of the arrangements for the homeward voyage. Once he had killed the dragon, or at least smashed the egg, killed its two protectors, and once Skar's men had killed Tyran and his guards in what would go down in history as a cowardly betrayal by the muscle-brained king, skilfully averted by our brave hero, he would meet his ship in the great lake. This would take them back to Castle Von Strauss, where his father had arranged some new, permanent residences for this expeditions' entourage. A letting agent would probably call them 'cosy' and 'rustic', whereas a human rights commissioner might call them 'inhumane'.

'So, as I was saying,' Conrad went on. 'I have not eaten in two days, but finally I have tracked down the violent beast in its lair. Though my arms are tired from the trials that it took to reach here, and even with the frost biting at my toes as I write… Another log on the fire please,' he shouted to another nearby servant, before turning back to Rägrund. 'Don't write that bit.'

'Metal-forkily again?'

'Yes, why not?'

A change in the wind brought the smell of the forest to the air and pushed away the band of cloud that had been trying smother the grey face of the moon under its pillowy mass. The gasping light it released shone down on the trees beyond the camp.

Conrad continued his dictation. 'But have no fear. The last dragon will soon fall by my hand.'

'Except for that one,' said Rägrund.

'What was that?'

'The last dragon except for that one,' he repeated, pointing with his quill to a rocky pinnacle that protruded from the forest canopy.

Conrad turned to look. There, surrounded by moonlight, a huge dark-green beast prowled along the rock. Its long whipping tail curled above a dark, scaly body. Its black wings blotted out the stars behind. All in, it was longer than his father's carriage and wider than a pair of oxen. The slope of the outcrop hid its feet from view, but the business end was all too visible. Supported by a neck easily big enough for a man to be gulped down, a diamond shaped head surveyed the camp with bright, glowing eyes.

'Are you gonna slay that one too, boss? Boss?'

Conrad's lip began to wobble like a prize-winning trifle.

CHAPTER FORTY-SIX

Orus looked out of the dragon costume through his peep hole. All across the camp men were turning to look, and then wishing they hadn't. Some looked to their weapons, others looked to the horses, most looked to the person next to them and tried to gauge who was the faster runner.

Above him in the neck section, Ambrose was pouring brandy from the bottle Huggle had swiped for the journey back to Harradin into Master Lenz's bellows. 'Now?'

'Now!' Orus called.

Orus turned the broken spade handle that controlled the dragon's wings as quickly as he could. The pulley system made from Mavis's old laundry bars and several lengths of rope so short various people had assured him he might as well throw away, spun into action.

Outside, the dragon's wings spread across the night. At the same time, Ambrose released the catch on the mouth, letting it hang open. He pushed the bellows into position behind the small lit candle then squeezed the

272

handles together as hard as he could, sending a long gout of flaming brandy arching from the creature's jaws.

*

This blast of flame revealed the beast fully to those in the camp. Conrad's footstool stood up to get a better view, sending his master tumbling into the mud. Those who had decided to fight ran for their weapons, and those who had decided their job wasn't worth this sort of trouble ran for their lives. Very quickly the two groups ran into each other. In the resulting scramble many forgot which group they had even been in to start with.

The dragon's great head turned to stare down at the camp. Its smoke-wreathed jaws let go another jet of flame. This one engulfed the Pale Pass Guards' whiskey store. Barrels blasted across the camp like rocket-propelled flower tubs, sending Tyran and Conrad's men diving for cover.

Inside the fearsome beast, the dragon's guts were getting ready to find out just how much guts they had.

'Wings at full,' said Orus, locking the spade handle in place. 'Ready?'

'Ready,' replied Ambrose from the head.

'Ready,' added Huggle, from the rump.

Why do you even ask?

'On three: One…'

The dragon's legs took a collective step backwards. 'Two…'

Orus gripped tight to the internal frame.

'Three!'

Altogether they ran, quickly building up speed along the narrowing finger of rock.

There was the edge.

And there it went.

Just like the airship, the wide wings caught the air current pushing up the face of the mountains and slowed them enough to stop their glide becoming a fall. It wasn't as graceful as soaring and you wouldn't have said it was flying, but the only thing that mattered to the occupants was that it wasn't crashing.

Burning whiskey barrels bounced off the sides of the dragon as it passed over cowering heads. While most of the warriors shrank away, one figure stood in the path of the diving dragon and did not run. Skar hadn't come all this way to be scared of some big lizard. He ate lizards for breakfast. Growing up in a place as reptile-infested as Bogmire there hadn't been much choice. A good source of protein, his mother always said. He grabbed a spear from the trembling hand of a Pale Pass Guardsman and planted his feet.

Crossing the burning whiskey store the dragon closed in on Skar fast.

He stood firm and waited.

The head passed over him.

He thrust his spear upwards.

The spear point punched through the fabric hide between Orus and Thunder. It wasn't enough to stop them, but it did give the donkey quite a fright.

Despite everyone knowing dragons have claws, Skar has always maintained that this one definitely had hooves. But then head injuries do funny things to you.

The kick knocked the huge warrior sprawling backwards and he collapsed into Huggle's abandoned tent. The whole construction fell inwards, wrapping him up like his old comfort blanket.

With the bravest of their group dropping faster than a troll from the 10 metre board, the rest of Conrad's men decided discretion was the better part of valour – and as for honour and glory, if they wanted to die in some fire-lizard's belly they could damn well fight it themselves.

Orus released the lock on the wings as the ground came up to meet them. He frantically worked the handles to bring the whole contraption into a mostly controlled landing. Skar's spear was sticking through the costume's flank, its head having stopped a spider's whisker from Thunder's nose.

I hope you're seeing this.

Twisting his body and pulling on various ropes and pedals, Ambrose moved the dragon's neck and head around until he could grip the spear and pull it free with the mouth.

'Where now?' he called down the throat.

'Everybody! Left!' Orus replied.

Huggle, Thunder and Orus all shuffled round to face the great gate. As they turned, the creature's thick tail struck a trio of Pale Pass Guards, sweeping them off their feet and into the mud.

Ambrose squeezed the bellows and the dragon let go another shot of flame.

Caught in the chaos, Conrad's horse broke free from its post and kicked out hard at another guardsman, launching him with crippling speed into the stone wall.

Barrels from the whiskey store had set off the brandy store, adding to the large amount of wood flying around.[12] As toppling tents came crashing down in a rush of feet through guide ropes, the dragon turned in a wide circle in the centre of the camp, scouting for its next victim.

Orus directed them towards the remaining guards. None were up for a fight and before long all were either hiding under some piece of camp debris or fleeing into the twisted boughs of the forest. It is amazing how quickly a man can access their evolutionary memory and re-learn the finer points of tree climbing when a two tonne fire-breathing behemoth is biting at their backside.

Ambrose, for the first time in his life feeling brave and strong and powerful, had forgotten all about being a

---

[12] Stuck between two of the most dangerous areas of geography in the land, drinking was a popular habit for most people in Harradin and a competitive sport for the Pale Pass Guards.

nervous, gangly teenager and was ready to settle some old scores.

'Right, right, right,' he shouted, lining the dragon up with a tall mercenary that bore a striking resemblance to Brother Amphis. Or at least enough of a resemblance to serve as a vehicle for some displaced retribution.

The young monk stared out from the dragon's jaws and thought of all those hours of so called character building exercises, which tended to mean building the kind of character that did all of Brother Amphis's chores for him. The young monk pushed hard on the bellows, releasing another spray of flame to make sure the might-as-well-have-been-Amphis know he was next on the to-do list.

'Charge!'

As they had reached full speed their target dropped his sword and quickly convinced himself it was high time he gave up being a mercenary and got a nice safe job working in a haberdashery.

In all the excitement the puppeteers almost forgot the objective of their plan. With the camp cleared they turned their scale-covered attentions to the great gate. Or at least they would have done had Huggle not noticed a familiar pair of monogrammed slippers poking out from behind a large pile of straw. He reached forward and drew the offending articles to Orus's attention.

Orus didn't need to have seen them before to recognise the owner of such a fine pair of sitting room shufflers.

'Can we?' Huggle asked.

A wry smile curled up Orus's cheek on its way to rendezvous with a mischievous twinkle in his eye. 'I think we can spare a moment or two for such a special case. After all, he's a very important man.'

Conrad cowered as only a man of his standing could: completely and shamelessly. He lay in the dirt and mouthed offerings to all the gods he could think of, if not for escape then at least for a handy servant he could throw in the beast's path. A shadow passed over his hiding place and he hoped that his prayers had been answered.

But when he lifted his head there was no readily available dragon fodder.

What there was, was a long, diamond shaped head, a set of long, pointed horns, two burning eyes and one huge mouth.

Conrad scrambled backwards through the mud. 'Hello, nice dragon.'

The beast advanced on him. Von Strauss got up and ran between the supply tents. He pulled over crates and boxes as he went, throwing anything not nailed down into the creature's path. The dragon kept coming, battering through the hurled obstacles like a Gran Torino in a 1970s car chase.

Conrad slipped and fell face first into the muck. He rolled onto his back. The dragon was there already. The smoke from its nostrils obscured its face, but he could still make out the pointed teeth silhouetted against the night. 'You don't want to eat me,' he said, crawling backwards. 'I'm on your side. I was just coming to warn you about all these nasty men coming to kill you. And I wouldn't taste very nice either. Wouldn't you like some nice horses instead? Mine is over there. You can have it. They're supposed to be good for the digestion. There is a donkey around here somewhere too. It's very fat.'

The dragon ignored his offer (and somewhere around the small intestine one of its members took particular offence at the suggestion of equinicide).

'I just remembered, nice Mr Dragon…' the beast snapped at Conrad as he stumbled over his expeditions' scattered supplies, '… or Mrs Dragon. It's a real pain, but I can't stay as, as, I've got a hair appointment in the morning and it's taken ages to get a booking.'

277

The dragon's jaws opened wide ready to strike. In a flash Conrad was up and sprinting across the camp, his slippers flying off as he went. Reaching the oxen paddock he didn't even break his stride. He leapt over the fence, diving headfirst into the manure pile.

'Do you think that will make it into his next book?' Orus asked Huggle.

'I'll make sure of it.'

Throughout the chaos and the destruction there was one person who sat quite unmindful of all that was going on, casually drawing a sharpening stone along the edge of the largest of his many swords. King Tyran had seen plenty of battles and fought many dangerous, deadly creatures. The bigger the better. He was not afraid. He was, however, suspicious.

There was something odd about this creature: the way it ran as if the front was trying to catch up with the rear, the way it didn't blink or breathe, the way it hadn't noticed that its tail was on fire.

Having enjoyed watching it see off that fool Von Strauss, Tyran looked on as the creature turned on the spot and waddled towards the great gate. He crouched silently behind a tent as the beast moved passed, noting as it did so the strange collection of foot prints it left in the mud.

Well, well, Orus. Found some more friends have we?

Tyran raised his sword in both hands and brought the point down on the trailing tail, pinning it into the ground.

Not that anyone inside noticed. They took the slight tug to be a stumble by one of the others and pushed on towards the gate. Even the ripping of the fabric was lost in the huffing and puffing of the forward momentum. It wasn't until Huggle looked up and noticed the sky full of stars that he stopped.

'Orus?' he called out. 'We have a problem.'

'What's that?' But he need not have asked. Turning back to Huggle it was not the puffed face of the scribe that Orus was focusing on. Rather, it was the twisted smile of his old school nemesis as he held up what looked very like the back half of their dragon skin in his coal-mitt fist, which drew the majority of his attention.

Much like the illicit lover who jumps from the balcony to escape a returning husband, only to find himself face to face with a hungry guard dog with nothing but a pair of silk boxer shorts for protection, Orus suddenly felt naked, scared and worryingly edible.

'Come on,' called Ambrose from the head. 'What's the hold up?'

Tyran's sword sliced through the wooden frame right in front of Orus, sending Ambrose and the head crashing to the ground.

'Behold,' the warrior king lifted the dragon's head and shook until Ambrose tumbled out of the bottom. 'I have killed the mighty beast.' He threw the empty head into the burning ruin of the Whizzabang-Go. 'I'm surprised it could fly after such a hearty meal.'

He better not be talking about me.

'Now,' the King continued, 'should I kill you one at a time or all at once? Maybe I should wait until the guards come back. I'm sure they'll want to meet the people who destroyed their winter drinking rations. That comes out of their wages.'

Orus and Huggle clambered free from the dragon's broken frame. They looked for abandoned weapons or even a sharp stone to defend themselves with, but there was nothing to hand.

'D'you know why you'll never be a hero, Orus?' Tyran spun his sword in wide arcs as he advanced on the gardener from Ditch. 'It's 'cause you're not selfish enough. You let all these wimps leech off you. Even worse, you feel responsible for them, as if keeping them in one piece was anything to do with you. You're thinking they make you stronger but they don't. They make you weak. Your armour's all full of holes. Every one of them's another way to get to you. A real hero must be hard. Stand alone. You've got to be driven. You've got to know. And you've got to be ready to step on ones like these to get ahead. Climb the pile, that's what it's about. Climb the pile, do it alone, and never worry about who's gettin' kicked back to the bottom.'

Tyran lifted his sword to strike the deadly blow.

Ambrose lined up a swing of his own.

'And who'd want to be like that?' said the monk, bringing a tent pole down on Tyran's head. It had never occurred to the monk that this wouldn't work. Being free of such doubts he hit the King far harder than even he thought possible.

The huge warrior stumbled at first, the sensation taking a few moments to work through his thick skull. Then, eyes rolling back into their sockets, he toppled forward like a seven foot stone domino.

Orus let out a sigh of relief. Ambrose's face filled with a great smile. Huggle fainted.

Amateurs.

But good amateurs. I've got to give them that.

'That was some strike,' said Orus, patting Ambrose on the back. 'I didn't know you had it in you.'

'Neither did I,' replied the monk. 'Do you think he'll be okay?'

Orus had to hand it to the young lad. Even when people were trying to kill him, the monk was still nice to them. He wouldn't have been surprised if, before swinging, Ambrose had tapped Tyran on the shoulder and said, 'excuse me, sorry, this might hurt a bit.'

'Unfortunately, yes. But we won't be around to find out.' Orus crouched down by the fallen king and retrieved the gate key from around his neck. 'We'll tie him up, just to make sure. Then we better get going.'

'What will we do with Huggle?' Ambrose looked down at the scribe's gently snoring form. 'We can't leave him here.'

Do you have to ask?

With the gate open, Tyran lashed to a prop in the stable, and Huggle draped over Thunder's back, the party prepared to cross the threshold of Pale Pass and enter the wildest, most dangerous part of their journey yet.

Orus looked at Ambrose. The legendary peaks loomed ahead. He pictured all the terrible creatures that might be waiting for them, then smiled. They didn't stand a chance.

CHAPTER FORTY-SEVEN

With the gate open and Huggle's prone form securely strapped over Thunder's back, Orus and Ambrose began to climb the pass into the Fang Mountains. After rising steadily from the gate, the trail turned a sweeping left, round a jutting toe of bedrock, and brought them behind the first set of peaks. In this valley, blocked in on all sides by towering slopes, they walked through the remainder of the night. The morning did not reach them until the sun was high in the sky.

Orus's feet were both throbbing with pain and burning with cold. But he knew they couldn't stop. Tyran was probably free already and he wouldn't waste any time chasing them down. With no paths running off the pass, there was no chance of hiding.

Forward was the only option. Forward and fast.

'Do you know how to find these Hatching Grounds?' Orus asked Ambrose. The monk had led the column all the way from the pass. They had barely stopped once, yet he didn't show any signs of being tired.

Orus, on the other hand, creaked and crunched so much that he half thought the sound of the grinding cartilage in his joints might bring down an avalanche.

'Not too far, according to the book. This valley should open out soon. Then it's just the glacier to go,' said Ambrose, as if describing a jolly walk through a meadow. 'Some beautiful rock formations up there, don't you think?'

Orus tried to remember if he had been so incurably interested when he was young. Probably. Before life had worn him down. Tag was like that too. Nothing was boring, everything was an adventure and every adventure was full of wonder. For the young, new experiences were exciting, something to be sought out and enjoyed. At his age they just got in the way of all the boring but necessary challenges of everyday life. He'd been grumbling along like that for so long now it had become his automatic setting. Here he was on a real adventure, a quest to save the world, and all he really wanted was to be sitting back in his house, in his comfortable chair, with a nice cup of tea.

Suck it up, he told himself. This is what you wanted after all. No use moaning about it now. Better than having your knees hurting because you've been crawling around dead heading roses all day. And if you don't finish this, who knows what will happen? There might not be a comfy chair to go back to. Without magic to hold it together the whole of Drift might start, well, drifting off, unravelling, falling to bits. Think of the mess that will make. And think who'll have to clean it all up.

'How's the egg looking?' he asked.

Ambrose checked the satchel. There was no glow when he opened the flap now. It had dimmed a lot over the last night. There was still a core of orange heat spiralling around itself under the shell but it was fading fast. 'Not great. We need to hurry.'

I thought we were hurrying.

'Come on, Thunder, nearly there now.' Orus tugged on the donkey's lead rope to little effect.

You know I could go faster if someone else carried him for a while. Or we could just leave him. He's got plenty of insulation. I'm sure he wouldn't freeze. Not quickly anyway.

As usual, Thunder's good ideas weren't picked up by anyone else.

Story of my life.

CHAPTER FORTY-EIGHT

Before long they reached the edge of the glacier. Huggle woke up just in time for a late breakfast made of very cold leftovers swiped from the Pale Pass camp.

After that they set out onto the frozen sea. Ambrose was in the lead, checking Brother Coalgrip's directions. The old missionary had wisely used the mountains as his landmarks, rather than the moving mass of ice.

A good few hours trekking later, Ambrose found what he was looking for.

'Over there,' he called out to the others. 'That is Dragons Watch. The whole mountain was hollowed out by dragons thousands of years ago. The Hatching Grounds are in there.'

Orus looked out across the frozen plateau. The mountain Ambrose was pointing to lifted steeply from the glacier. It looked like an ant mound, only the ants must have been twelve feet high and armed with a large array of power drills. The sides were sheer to about half way up. From there to the summit, it was pockmarked by hundreds of caves. The smallest were not much taller than a man, but you could have parked a large farmhouse in the biggest. All around them the mountainside was scored with dark cuts where dragons had presumably scrambled on their claws from cave to cave.

It boggled Orus's mind to think of how many dragons it must have taken to make Dragons Watch. What amazing creatures they must have been. So powerful, so strong, and yet here they were, with the fate of the species in the very hands that have driven them to extinction.

Ascent was out of the question, especially since they had used up all the spare rope in building the dragon costume and even more especially since Orus had never climbed a mountain in his life. A person of his girth had to be mistrustful of gravity: the forces of attraction between them were strong, but any intimate relationship was likely to be short and very painful.

'How do we get in? There is no way we can reach those caves.'

'Servant's entrance,' replied Ambrose, with a wink. 'Where else?'

Reaching the foot of Dragons Watch, the young monk led the party off the glacier and made for a gully in the rock-face. The sides were covered in walls of icicles. Orus pulled his furs tighter across his body and tried not to think of what could have melted so much snow in a place that was always so cold. Looking up at the pinnacle of rock, he could see the gouge marks in the cliffs and the shining lips of the caves where the rock had been melted by magical fire. Those dark pits stood sentinel, staring down.

'It says in here,' said Ambrose, 'that when guarding their young, the dragons would keep watch from their caves. Anyone trying to get in this door that they didn't like the look of could be incinerated from above in an instant.'

'Did they like the look of many people?'

'It doesn't say.'

'I thought it wouldn't.'

Orus's foot knocked loose a round, bone coloured stone from the snow. He watched it roll forward and come to rest facing him.

No, not facing him, he thought. Stones don't have faces and this was definitely a stone, no matter what an anatomist might say.

Huggle, being well used to avoiding noticing uncomfortable realities, didn't see the skull either. 'You could've have kept that to yourself, at least until we got through.'

'There's nothing to worry about. If there were any dragons here they wouldn't need us. We might have to be careful on the way out. This little guy will be pretty hungry when he hatches.'

'I meant to ask you about that,' said Orus squeezing through a tight section of the gully.

'Yes.'

'After it hatches, what do we do then? I mean, it's going to be an orphan. Do we have to feed it or look after it until it is bigger?'

'No. Dragons are very self-sufficient and they grow up fast. Very fast. It's the magic in them. But it will be hungry.'

'What does the book say to do after it hatches?'

Ambrose flicked ahead a few pages to the chapter titled 'Postnatal Care'. It was a short chapter. He read it aloud.

'It says "Run away bravely."'

'Great.' Orus's feet hurt bad enough from the trek up here.

'It also says, "A new baby dragon will assume anything in its nest has been put there by its mother for eating."'

'And if its mother hasn't put anything in the nest?' asked Huggle.

'I guess it must go looking for something.'

Thunder looked at Huggle and Orus.

I think I'll wait here.

With that head start he should outrun at least one of them.

'We could feed it that goat over there,' suggested Huggle, pointing at a grey, old goat, chewing on a patch of rock moss.

'No, you bloody well won't,' replied the goat.

'That goat can talk!' said Orus.

'That's amazing!' added Ambrose.

'Incredible!' exclaimed Huggle.

Show off.

'And I'm not a goat neither,' said the not-a-goat. It stood up on its hind legs and shuffled across the gorge. It picked up a long staff that had been leaning against the rock and turned to face the new arrivals.

Despite its protest to the contrary, it looked a lot like a goat, if now a bit more vertical. It had a goatee head, complete with long goatee ears, curled goatee horns and a long goatee beard at the end of its big goatee chin. It was only the gold chain around its goatee neck – the sort of thing you'd normally see on a town mayor rather than a piece of livestock – which marked it out as perhaps not actually a goat.

That and the talking.

'Nope, there will be no feeding of me to anything. You lot look like you've eaten plenty much already anyway, expect you maybe.' The not-a-goat pointed a hoof at Ambrose.

'Forgive us,' said the monk. 'We're just a bit surprised. We've not met an animal that talks before.'

The not-a-goat cocked its head and looked over to Thunder.

The old donkey shrugged.

Don't look at me. Doesn't make sense to me either.

'Is that so?' continued the not-a-goat. It hobbled forward on its stick and inspected Ambrose. It sniffed at his robe and then whipped a chunk of fabric from the monk's sleeve and began to chew. 'I'm a faun,' it said, moving on towards Orus and the others. 'Would have thought a Dragon Monk would know that. What's Argus teaching you lot nowadays? Not what he should be, I'll bet.'

'A faun! Wow! And you know the Grandmaster?'

'Yes, yes, I know him. He's been up here a few times to see me.' The faun circled Huggle, sniffing at his pockets. 'And a bard. Interesting. Interesting. He's not been here for a while, your Argus, mind you. Starting to think he'd forgotten about me.'

'Do you live here?'

'Course I do. Wouldn't be much of a guardian if I didn't.' The faun poked at Orus's belly with the bottom of his crook. 'What's this one?'

'Gardener,' said Orus.

'Hero,' said Ambrose.

'Mmm,' the faun looked him up and down. 'A gardener hero? Thought you felt a bit mixed up. Still, that's not a bad way to be in my experience. I don't suppose you have any carrots or a nice turnip on you, Mr Gardener-Hero?'

'Did you say you're a guardian?' asked Ambrose.

'Not a, *the* Guardian,' it said, moving on to Thunder. 'Not too sharp, this lot you've got with you.'

Parts of them are. Even through the saddle.

'That's what I meant,' said Ambrose. 'You're the Guardian of the Hatching Grounds, right? I read about you. Didn't mention the goat part.'

'Not a goat,' said the Guardian.

'Sorry. Didn't mention the faun part, I mean. I was expecting a man.'

'Well, that's sexism for you,' the Guardian replied, scratching at its udder.

Ambrose reached into the satchel and lifted out the dragon egg. Its glow was all but gone. 'You have to help us. We've brought this.'

'Better late than never. I've been wondering when you would turn up. Best not wait around then. This way boys.' The Guardian ushered them forward with its crook.

'Amazing,' said Orus, pulling Thunder along behind the others as the faun disappeared around a bend in the gorge.

You won't be saying that when you wake up tomorrow and she's eaten everyone's boots.

CHAPTER FORTY-NINE

The Guardian led them through the cut in the mountain and into a wide cave. It was two cart widths across and about ten feet high. Six pairs of metal braziers, blackened through centuries of continual use, lit the way ahead.[13]

A large door with an arched top sealed the cave's far end. It was probably bronze at one stage, but the combination of so much burning coal and the in-rushing wind meant that, like most things in the cave, it was covered in a thick layer of soot. On the left, half way between the entrance and the once-bronze door, was a small passage. This was where the Guardian took them.

The roof in the faun's home was lower than the rest of the cave. Orus and Ambrose stooped slightly to fit. In keeping with its owner, it was somewhere between a cottage and a cattle steading. On one wall a stack of shelves clung onto a rather meagre collection of long lasting food stuffs: various pickled vegetables, nuts and dried fruit. A

---

[13] Such places were often lit in this way. It didn't do to ask where the coal came from.

stone trough at the far end collected melt water from a channel in the roof, and on the other side of the room a thick bed of straw and dried grass was spread out a safe distance from the fire. There was a small table in the centre, on top of which was an earthenware jug filled with a large bunch of mountain flowers.

'You can leave your things in here if you want,' said the faun, leaning its crook against the wall by the fire. The curved handle of the staff was unlike any shepherd's crook Orus had ever seen before.

The Guardian saw him looking. 'Dragon claw. From a hatchling. They shed them when their proper claws start to grow.'

'And how old would that have been when it lost this one?'

'If I remember right, he was seven.'

'Seven. That's good. For a second there I thought you said it was from a hatchling.'

'Yes, seven hours old. They grow up very fast. It's the eggs you see. They're bigger on the inside. They have to be, in order to store enough magical energy. Otherwise the pressure would be too much.'

'So how big are dragons when they hatch?' Orus asked, unsure if he really wanted to know.

'Big enough that you don't want to wait around to weigh it and give it a slap on the rear.'

Orus's stomach gave an awkward gurgle. The claw was at least two hand spans long. He tried to remember how many toes dragons had, then he decided it was better not to. Ignorance is bliss after all.

'I was just going to have lunch, if you're hungry.' The Guardian pulled what could have been a milking stool over to the table and sat in front of the jug of blossoms. 'These wilt quick, so best to have them while they're fresh.'

'I don't suppose you have anything less floral?' asked Huggle.

'There is a leather belt I've been making my way through. It's hanging up on the shelf. It's good for a chew. Don't eat it all, mind you. I've been saving it.'

Told you.

'Errrr...'

'Or you can help yourselves to the fruit over there if you want.'

'Ah, that might suit me better,' said the scribe.

'And there are some carrots in that sack by the water trough. They got a bit damp, so there is a bit of mould on them, but that just adds to the flavour if you ask me.'

Now you're talking.

Huggle went to the larder and picked out a bowl of dried apples. He sat down at the table and fished his notebook out of his pocket. One thing that had always bothered him about the traditional stories he'd had to learn at the Bards College was how one sided they were. It was always from the human's point of view. It made writing difficult. Sure, he could compose an exciting tale about Conrad slaying the Voracious Megatroll of Shrouded Mountain, but he never really felt he could got to grips with the Megatroll's motivation. Why was it so voracious? Did it have an eating disorder? Was it the result of a damaging period in its childhood? Had it tried counselling? And had it always lived on the Shrouded Mountain? Perhaps, earlier in its life it had just been the Little-bit-on-the-chubby-side Megatroll of Moonsparkle Meadow. After all, monsters were people too. There was a gap in the market. If he wasn't going to do heroes anymore, maybe this could be his new angle. It might even make him feel a bit better for helping out Conrad for all those years.

'So,' he said to the faun, 'how long have you been the Guardian here?'

'A while. We fauns don't really count in years like you do. I've seen a good few generations of dragons come and go.'

Ambrose turned back to the faun. 'A few generations?'

'Yes. Seven or eight. Maybe nine.'

'That would make you,' Ambrose tried to calculate the faun's age but gave up once he got into five digits. 'I mean, you must be at least…'

'Tch, tch. Doesn't Argus teach you boys manners anymore? Not nice to talk about a lady's age.'

'But dragons can live for ten thousand years.'

'Mountain air keeps you looking young,' she said, before biting the head off a large yellow flower. 'And I eat healthy.'

'How did you get into it?' Huggle pressed on with his interview. 'The job I mean.'

'Raising babies isn't a job, nor's keeping them safe. Much more important than that.'

'Dragons though. I mean, big scaly beasts and small furry mammals don't normally go well together.'

'Says who?'

'I guess nobody says it. It's just good common sense.'

'Nothing common about good sense. What do you know about dragons anyway? The only time you hear about them is from these stories you write. Big brave hero saves village by killing scaly beast. You ever stop to think who was there first?'

'No, I guess not.'

'Do you know what dragon means, the word I'm talking about? Guardian. Not big terrible monster. Dragons don't go looking for trouble. In my experience, it's only people that are that daft.'

'Okay, so how did you become Guardian of the Guardians then?'

'Ah, now that is a story. Long time ago, there I was up in the mountains looking after my own kids, when this young dragon turns up. He's looking half-starved, all scale and bones, and he's fixing for making a meal out of my little ones.'

'So what did you do?'

'I set him straight is what I did. There's one thing every living creature's got in common: Beast or man, doesn't matter, they all have a mother. They might not know her, might not have ever even met her, but somewhere, somewhere deep down in their heads, there's a little bit for mothers. And when a mother talks, if she talks right, they listen. So I set him straight. Told him he wasn't getting any mutton here today, but if he washed himself up, scrubbed behind his horns, brushed his teeth and stopped slouching, I might let him share some supper. Either that or he can go an' eat snow, 'cause he won't be getting any meat here. So he does, and I do. He hangs around for a bit until he's put some weight back on then heads off.

'A good while later he comes back saying he's all in a fix. Now he's got kids of his own, but their mum's been stuck up on some human's wall. Some hero did it,' the faun gave Huggle a hard stare. 'Said they needed a mum and would I help. By then my kids were long gone. I was a mother and they needed one. That's all I needed to know. Been guarding this place ever since.'

'Amazing,' said Huggle, scribbling down the last of his notes.

Ha, that's nothing. I could tell you some stories that would blow your mind. Now, where to start... Oh, yes. Wait until you hear this. When I was a kid—

'We better be getting on,' said Ambrose, rising from his chair. 'We don't have much time. Guardian, we're ready to finish our quest. Can you show us the way to the Hatching Grounds?'

'Sure, I can show you,' said the Guardian, finishing off the final mouthful of purple rock weed. 'The question is: Can you make it?'

'What do you mean?' asked Huggle. He had been quite hoping this was the adventure over.

'Not just anyone can waltz in. Wouldn't be much point in there being a guardian then, would there? I can't let you in until you pass the challenges.'

'Challenges?' asked Orus and Huggle together.

'Oh yes,' Ambrose retrieved Brother Coalgrip's book from his robes, 'there is a chapter here on challenges.'

As the young monk read through the relevant section, the Guardian clipped and clopped over to the water trough.

'Drink?' she asked Thunder.

Thunder pushed past the humans.

Thanks.

He slurped up the cool water from the trough.

So what are these challenges?

Well, said the faun, *Just a few little tests to make sure the wrong sorts don't get into the Hatching Grounds.*

Let me guess. Three tasks. Each one more difficult than the last. Courage, strong will, smarts and skill. High chance of death. Many have tried, few succeed. That kind of thing.

You've done this before?

You could say that.

What do you give their chances?

Hard to say. They aren't exactly your conventional heroes.

The faun dunked its snout in the trough and sucked up some of the cool water. It scissored its white beard between a cloven hoof, flicking the water droplets to the floor. *Aren't exactly your conventional challenges either.*

'I thought this Coalgrip guy had been here lots of times?'

Ambrose put the guide book on the table at the chapter marked 'The Three Challenges'. The others looked over his shoulder. Orus reached over and flipped the page.

'There's nothing there. Just the names. *The Heart of the Dragon, The Wings of the Dragon* and *The Blood of the Dragon.* That's it. There must be more.'

'That's all it says. Three challenges to test worthiness,' said Ambrose. 'The way into the Hatching Grounds is a valuable secret. He wouldn't just put it down in black and white for anyone to find. What if someone like Conrad got his hands on it?'

'Can you tell us about these challenges?' Orus asked the Guardian.

''Fraid not. Against the rules.'

'Your Grandmaster's been here before,' Huggle said to Ambrose. 'Didn't he tell you what to do?'

'He didn't get the chance. I don't know if you remember but we had to leave in a bit of a hurry.'

'No time for fighting.' Orus took the book and closed it. He had experience in the lead up to a birth. If it wasn't scary, full of unknown horrors, and involve an encounter with a terrifying monster ready to take your head off at the first wrong move, you were probably in the wrong place. 'Don't worry,' he said. 'I've done this kind of thing before.'

*

The Guardian led them back to the main cave and the bronze door. It looked like it hadn't been opened in a long time.

'And you're sure there's no other way in? We are trying to do the dragons a favour here,' Huggle asked.

'Nope. Only way in, for humans at least. Unless you fancy climbing up to the caves. You're sure you're ready?'

'No,' replied Orus. 'But we're going in anyway.'

'Good.' The faun lifted its staff horizontally and lined it up with a round hole in the door. It pushed the claw end of the staff inside, then twisted.

A low rumble shook the cave from the floor up. There was a sound like the hungry rumbling of a deep belly and, for once, it wasn't coming from Orus. Parting on either side of the staff, the doors slid backwards, powered by some unseen engine.

Inside was perfectly dark. From the depths came a whiff of dust and dead eons.

The party all leaned forward to try and see what they were getting themselves into.

The air in the cave was sucked past them, down into the depths. Orus hoped it wasn't by a pair of scale covered lungs.

Silence held court.

There was light.

There was fire. Fire coming right at them.

The tangled metropolis of a thousand generations of spiders were vaporised as the fireball roared with ever increasing fury up the dark tunnel.

It stopped about fifteen feet from the entrance, blasting Orus and the others with its blinding heat and leaving the patter of hundreds of melting icicles to fill the cave in its wake.

The tunnel ahead was now lit by parallel rows of coal braziers. Their orange glow revealed a long stone passageway. It was floored with flagstones and sloped down deeper into the mountain.

'Off you pop.' The faun stepped aside to let the others pass.

'And you're sure you can't tell us anything about what is down there?' Huggle asked again, managing to just about hide the fear from his voice.

'Oh I could tell you lots about what is down there. But it wouldn't help you much. The three challenges you will face are there to test whether you can be trusted in the Hatching Grounds. Knowing about them won't help. You have the names from the book. That should give you a clue.'

'*Heart of the Dragon*, *Wings of the Dragon* and *Blood of the Dragon*.' Huggle tried to picture what each one could refer to, then wished he hadn't.

'Could be worse,' said Orus, hitching up his belt.

'Really?'

'At least it's not *The Claws of the Dragon* or *The Mouth of the Dragon*,' Orus said, stepping forward into the tunnel.

'Or *The Stomach of the Dragon*,' Ambrose suggested helpfully, rolling up the sleeves of his robes and following on.

'I'm glad everyone is in such fine form,' said Huggle, stepping into the tunnel after them. 'Face death with a smile, isn't that what they say?'

Thunder and the Guardian were left standing between the huge bronze doors.

Soooo, said the faun, completely failing to pull off nonchalant. *Is there a Mrs Thunder? It does get quite lonely up here in the cold.*

They might need my help. I better go catch up.

CHAPTER FIFTY

After a few hundred yards the tunnel levelled out. An arch opened onto a large cave and the sound of water cascading from a great height drummed into everyone's ears.

Orus crouched and picked up a skeletal arm. He pulled the sword free from the white hand and let it fall back to the floor with a clicking of knuckles.

'Doesn't look very sharp,' said Huggle helpfully.

'Sharper than your fist.'

'Good point. Can you use it?'

'I know a few moves.'

'I hope they're better than his.' The scribe kicked at the bony remains. 'Looks gnawed.'

Ambrose moved into the cave. Sunlight shone down from a hole in the ceiling. A fat tube of water poured over the lip into the cave. It formed a rushing column that disappeared into a well in the floor, vanishing into the heart of the mountain.

Orus joined him by the edge of the well and peered down.

'Where do you think it goes?'

'No idea. Down, I guess.'

The water was the loudest thing in the cave, until the bear started roaring.

It padded out from the rocky overhang that was its den, dinner-plate sized feet kicking through the remaining remains of the sword's previous owner. It was huge and white (at least its teeth were white, and, to be fair, they were the aspect that captured the vast majority of Orus's attention).

'Is this one of the tests?' said Ambrose, trying not to move any of his facial muscles lest the bear take offence.

'Well I hope it's not a warm-up.' Orus looked over to Huggle, and Thunder. They appeared to be choosing which of them was best to hide behind.

He gripped the sword tightly.

Okay Orus, put up or shut up. Time to be a hero.

Here is what he hoped would happen:

He bravely pushes Ambrose behind him, sets his feet wide and brings the sword up in front of him in a suitably heroic pose. Perhaps a stray shaft of sunlight breaks through the cascading water and illuminates him like a saintly figure in a church window. The bear circles the edge of the cave, its black eyes fixed on his unwavering form. As it closes in, he lets out an inspiring war cry and rushes forward. The bear, terrified by this heroic visage re-evaluates its position in the cave pecking order and slinks back to its den. Orus leads the others onwards and everyone lives happily ever after. At least until the next challenge.

Here is what actually happened:

The bit at the start played out just as Orus imagined, except that stretching his feet elicited a series of cracking sounds from his lower back, the sword was much heavier than in his vision, there was no illuminating shaft of heavenly light and, as the bear approached, rather than letting out a great battle cry, his head was filled with the noise of grains dropping through the hourglass of his life.

It didn't sound like there were very many left. Rather than the whoosh of sand he had been hoping for, each fell on its own with a solitary, distant plop.

The bear kept coming forward, taking a few heavy steps then roaring loudly. Its warm breath stank of rotting fish. Orus shuffled to face it, crushing something under his boots. He kept the sword held out in front of him. The grains continued to plop through his head.

He didn't think Wee Mental Davey's secret attack worked on bears, but his trademark full frontal assault with extra yelling might just scare it off. Orus dug his heel into the ground and gritted his teeth, ready to launch.

Plop, went another grain.

He lifted the sword high. He thought about Mavis. He thought about Tag. He tried not to think about being eaten. He was ready. At this moment, the bear reared up on its back legs, filling the cave.

Its roar shook the whole mountain. Orus drew in a deep breath and prepared to return fire with a roar of his own. He stepped forward. He slipped. He fell.

Plop.

The sword dropped from his grip.

He put out his hands to cushion his fall.

As he struck the cold wet floor, something sharp jabbed into his palm.

Plop.

Plop, plop.

He looked at his hand. A neat row of needle-like bones were sticking into the flesh of his palm. He looked around about him. There were more. Lots more. Spread over the cave floor like tiny white combs. Some still had heads and tails.

The waterfall was directly behind him. He turned towards it, just in time to see a flash of silver drop past and disappear into the well.

Plop.

It was followed by another and another. More flashes of silver. More plops.

Mountain salmon!

The bear lifted its forepaws high into the air. It tried to step forward but it quickly crashed back onto all fours, shaking the floor and sending the fish bone carpet into the air. From his lower vantage point Orus could see the bear's rear paws. As the beast moved forward it limped on its back left leg, hardly putting any weight on it at all. A realisation came over him. He grabbed the sword again and pushed himself to his feet.

'Stand back,' he warned Ambrose.

The monk moved out of the way as the bear took another laboured step forward. It swung a bone cracking front paw at Orus. He jumped back, narrowly missing the swipe, and landing with his feet on the very edge of the well.

Orus twisted the sword in his hands so the flat of the blade was showing and waited for the perfect shot. He'd only get one chance.

The bear roared. Orus swung. The flat of the blade pushed through the water and struck home with a fleshy thud.

Nailed it.

The skipping salmon landed between the bear's front paws. It had never fallen sideways before and that wasn't its only new experience of the day. It would remember this as a day of firsts, if it could have remembered it at all.

The bear gobbled up the salmon with voracious speed. Finished, it lifted its head and looked at Orus expectantly.

He took aim again, watching for the flash of silver. His swing was good. Another fish was slapped from the tumbling torrent. All those evenings teaching Tag's primary school rounders team were paying off. He batted four more fish from the waterfall in quick succession, each one landing just in front of the guzzling bear.

Spoilt by this sudden bonanza, it gracelessly sat back on its rear end, leaning its back against a rock, picked up the fish from between its outstretched hind legs and began to dine.

'Nice going, Orus,' called Ambrose. 'Hey, look!'

Sticking out from the black pad on the bottom of the bear's left paw was an iron arrowhead.

'No wonder it's hungry,' said the monk. 'It mustn't be able to reach the water.'

'It would have come from,' Orus grunted as he swung again and knocked another fish into the bear's lap, 'the skeleton. Before he was a skeleton.'

'Is it safe to come out?' Huggle whispered from behind Thunder. 'Will it let us pass?'

Behind the bear's munching hunch the tunnel continued deeper into the mountain. They could probably sneak through. Orus had managed to pile a good number of fish and the bear appeared more than satisfied to let them go. One challenge down.

'I think so,' he said. 'Just don't get too close.'

Huggle emerged from behind the donkey and, together, they started to cross the cave.

I hope you realise that this means when we get to the dragon, it's my turn to hide behind you.

Orus shook out the strain from his arms. He looked at the bear's wounded foot and its drawn in flanks. He felt a stupid idea pushing its way through his brain. He knew it was stupid, but, annoyingly, he also knew it was right and once it arrived with that label attached he knew he would have to do it.

'You go on ahead. I'll catch up.'

He put down the sword, doing his best to keep quiet.

Once, during the annual cattle drive through Ditch, a large bull had broken free from the herd and charged down a side street. It ended up getting its head stuck in a scaffold. Orus had helped the drover free it. Moving towards the bear, he approached it in the same way, making sure to stay in its eyeline and holding up his empty hands, hoping to keep it calm.

'Orus,' Ambrose whispered. 'What are you doing?'

'Fatherly instinct,' he replied, not turning around. 'You'll understand one day.'

With sliding steps pushing through the carpet of bones and scales, he reached the bear's wounded foot. The arrow head was dug in to about half of its length and the bear's pad was stained with dried blood.

The bear stopped eating its fish and stared down at the round little man crouching by its toes. Orus could see himself reflected in the black of its eyes. He moved his hands slowly from side to side, palms facing outwards. The bear watched him, following the hands. Then, apparently satisfied he was no threat, or as tasty-looking as fish, it returned to its meal.

With a slow hiss of out-breath, Orus crouched to one knee. The joint creaked loudly and he froze.

The bear didn't look up. It was busy.

Orus leaned forward. Slowly, he reached out and gripped the arrow by the stub of broken shaft. The bear shuddered briefly at his touch, but didn't move.

Thunder and Huggle had made their way to the other side of the cave and were waiting by the tunnel. Orus looked back at Ambrose. With his free hand he motioned for him to join the others.

He looked up at the bear again. He could hear its giant teeth crunch through the backbones of the slippery salmon. With the bull, after they freed it, it had chased him and the drover across two fields and up a tree. He checked his escape route. There were no trees to speak of. However, the next section of the tunnel would be a tight squeeze for the bear. He hoped.

One.

Two.

Three.

He yanked the arrowhead, falling backwards as it came free from the bear's paw. The bear roared louder than ever, but Orus was already up and running.

'Go, go, go!' he shouted to the others.

The bear dropped its fish and rolled onto its feet. It bounded after Orus, crushing unfinished fish under its paws.

Ambrose and the others turned and sprinted down the passageway. To their surprise, Orus quickly overtook them, only he wasn't running, so much as rolling. The tunnel led steeply downwards and Orus had tripped on the lip. He careered past his friends before colliding with a thunk against another heavy bronze door.

Reaching the bottom, Ambrose helped him up. The bear was still coming, its recent period of starvation allowing it to squeeze with some effort down the tunnel after them.

Huggle pushed against the door but it wouldn't budge. He moved his hands across its surface looking for a mechanism. There was nothing. Only a small hole in the shape of a six pointed star.

'It's locked! It needs a key!'

The bear was halfway down and picking up speed. The tunnel opened up in front of the door. It would have plenty of space to commence its second course unless they could get through.

'What key?' asked Ambrose, dropping Orus in the process.

From the floor, Drift's only gardener-hero held up the arrow head he had pulled from the bear's paw. Its head was a six pointed star, tapering to a sharp point.

Huggle grabbed the key and pushed it into the lock.

The bear roared again, then lunged forward.

The door swung open and all tumbled through. Thunder lashed out with a kick and slammed it shut before the bear could follow them. Its front paws thudded heavily against the bronze. The metal shuddered but held. They heard it roar one last time before it trudged up the tunnel to finish its pile of fish.

CHAPTER FIFTY-ONE

They were in another cave now, but whereas the last one had been long and narrow, this one was impossibly large.

The bronze door had opened onto a ledge which stretched about thirty feet out over a chasm of pure darkness. It was vast, bigger even than the great hall in the Worm-mound. The only light in the whole expanse came from a narrow cave opening high above them. The dark hung like a curtain after the edge of the ledge. The other side was barely visible: the crags of a vast canyon wall continued endlessly in both directions. Beneath them was only darkness.

Orus picked himself up. 'Is everyone okay?'

You mean okay apart from being stuck inside a mountain with two more rounds of possible, probable certain death? 'Cause in that case, yes. Just peachy.

'That was amazing.' Ambrose stared wide eyed at Orus. 'How did you know the arrow was the key?'

Amazing isn't the word I would use.

'I didn't. But I couldn't just leave it there to die.'

'*The Heart of the Dragon*,' the young monk said.

'I'm sure you'd have all done the same,' Orus said, turning to the precipice, in part to see what they were up against now and in part to hide his modest blush. He wasn't used to people being impressed with him. He wasn't sure it suited him.

Huggle said nothing. He'd had enough trouble with the donkey.

'Is there a way down?' Ambrose joined Orus at the edge.

'Doesn't look like it.' The chasm was dizzying to look at, solid with blackness. 'What is the second challenge called again?'

The dragon monk held the egg in his hands. Its glow had reduced to the barest whisper of light. He looked out into the expanse of night. '*The Wings of the Dragon*,' he said quietly.

'So, what? We have to fly across. How?'

'Could we make a rope?' asked Huggle. 'Climb down?'

'I don't think so,' said Orus. He picked up a small rock and let it fall over the edge. The black swallowed it silently. 'It must be hundreds of feet deep. There might not even be a bottom.'

'Build a bridge?'

'With what?'

'Just trying to be helpful.'

Try harder.

While Orus and Huggle (and Thunder) were talking, Ambrose made his way to back to the bronze door. An idea was forming in his mind.

Everyone knows dragons can fly, but Dragon Monks know they shouldn't. Not shouldn't because it disagrees with their stomachs. Physically shouldn't. The monks of the Worm-mound had discovered this while working out the calculations needed to design and build the temple's airship. The ratios were all wrong.

Dragons have dense, strong bones and thick scaly hides. They come in a vast multitude of different (mostly large) shapes, the only common factor between these being a distinct lack of aerodynamic streamlining. Most do have wings, this is true. Big wings. Wings so big that they should never be able to beat them fast enough to generate the required amount of lift to move such a massive creature off the ground. Much like the bumblebee, for the dragon flight should be filed away in a box marked impossible.

But impossible to a dragon was nothing. As had been explained to Ambrose during Brother Nidd's lectures on Dragon Behaviour and Anatomy, huge mythical creatures do not put much time into the study of physics. They do, however, spend a lot of time and effort on being incredibly terrifying. So while nature may say that they can't fly, she does so quietly, from a distance, preferably while they are sleeping.

Dragons fly through strength of will. They manage it because they expect it and believe it and never doubt it for a second. Impossible or not, they're going to do it anyway, and just you try and stop them.

Ambrose looked down at his long gangly arms. He looked out over the black chasm. Impossible, he thought. Last week, impossible was imaging he would be in a bar fight in the fabled All Seasons Tavern. Impossible was being chased from the temple by Conrad Von Strauss. Impossible was beating up the King of Harradin at the edge of the Fang Mountains. Impossible was a rule. It was for people like Brother Amphis. It kept them safe, kept them right, kept people in their place.

He lifted the dragon-scale bag over his head and set it down by the door. He had no time for impossible, not anymore.

Orus was considering the possibility of making a rope from their clothes. Huggle was searching the far side of the ledge to see if they could get around somehow. Only Thunder noticed the monk start running.

The donkey thought about shouting a warning to the others...

What's the point? They never listen.

It wasn't a graceful approach to take-off. More baby swan on ice than soaring eagle, but Ambrose's long limbs quickly covered the distance. He flashed past Orus at full speed, reached the edge, and leapt.

He stretched his arms wide. The long sleeves of his robe caught the air.

I'm doing it. I'm really doing it!

Then the blackness pulled him in.

A sickly movement in the pit of his gut signified the moment when the strength of his jump lost its fight with gravity, suddenly and badly.

He started to fall.

Even then Ambrose did not doubt. He knew it. He believed it. He believed.

There was no point looking down. Forward was the only way. He would make it. He had to make it.

I can do it. I have to. I have to.

His feet slapped against something hard. Suddenly he was stumbling forward, his legs sprinting to keep up. He fell and his hands slapped against cold stone.

Tiles. Hard ground.

From this new perspective, the illusion shattered. He looked down, then up. He was standing on the abyss. The crags of the far wall were laid out flat in front of him. It was a painting. The walls of the canyon, the dark chasm, it was all painted onto tiles. The joins were so fine they were barely visible. But from here he could see it. The cavern wasn't huge, it was barely forty feet across. He turned back to the others. The hole that Orus had dropped the rock down was a thin gap, only two feet across.

A barrier of fear. And he had beaten it. Not because he was special, not because he had magical powers or incredible talents, but because he knew he could. All his years of nervous worrying – about not being good enough, not being smart enough, not being talented or brave – he'd always thought fate held him back. He had been made that way and there was nothing he could do about it. Now he knew: it had been fear all along. Plain old fear.

Well guess what, I'm not scared anymore.

Orus ran to the false edge. 'Are you mad? You nearly gave me a heart attack!

CHAPTER FIFTY-TWO

After some encouragement, several attempts at bribery, a few threats and finally a good shove, Thunder joined the rest of the party on the painted floor. His hooves cracked the tiles as he landed, revealing the grey dirt of the cavern floor below.

From this angle they could see that what appeared to be a solid wall at the rear of the room was actually two walls, one overlapping the other. Turning between them they found themselves in front of a familiar looking bronze door. This one stood open and once they stepped through it, they were greeted by an equally familiar voice.

'You made it.' The room they were now in was made of bare red stone. In its centre was an altar and behind the altar stood the Guardian. 'And faster than I expected. Well done.'

'I thought there was no other way down,' said Orus, approaching the faun.

'I'm sure you never tell any lies, Mr Gardener. This is my job. Wouldn't be very good at it if I just said "oh and by the way there's a secret passage behind the sack of potatoes".'

Ambrose approached the final set of doors. They were ten feet tall and flanked by two huge stone dragons. Just like those in the Dragon Temple, their mouths held burning coals and cast flames on the engraved doors.

'We've made it. We actually made it. See Orus, I knew you could do it. Right from when I first saw you.'

'What about the final challenge?' said Huggle. 'We've only completed two.'

'Maybe we've done it. Getting this far, crossing the Grimwood, making it over Pale Pass, not giving up. Maybe that's it. We endured. The blood of a dragon is the blood of a hero.'

Huggle liked the sound of that. He'd had just about as many challenges as he could take. The only thing he felt like battling right now was a cup of tea and a nice hot fire. But not too hot, he thought quickly, looking up at the towering stone drakes. He was more than a bit disappointed when the Guardian pricked this balloon of optimism.

'No, that's not it. That would be silly. Still one more to go to prove you're worthy.' The faun ducked down behind the altar. 'Just a minute.'

'Silly? This whole process is silly,' said Huggle. 'We're trying to save this dragon. If we wanted to kill it we didn't have to come all the way here. What do we have to do now: arm wrestle an octopus, race a badger, beat a rabbit at cards?'

'No. There is a rabbit involved, though.' The faun lifted a cage onto the altar. Inside was a small tundra rabbit. 'But you don't have to play it at cards. The last challenge is a sacrifice. Just kill the rabbit on the altar, the blood drains through these holes and when they're full the door catch releases and the way opens. Easy.' The faun placed a long knife on top of the altar.

'You want us to kill a rabbit?' Orus looked at the faun for traces of a joke.

'Yes.'

'Why? What has it done?'

'Done? Nothing. It's just a rabbit. And I want you to sacrifice it. Not just kill. If you are to release this dragon you must know about sacrifice.'

'I know plenty about sacrifice already, thank you,' Orus replied.

Huggle looked at the little bunny in its cage. He had done a lot worse in his days, maybe not personally, but he had certainly let it all happen, and made money out of it later. He was an expert at repressing the protests of his conscience, softening them up with comforting claims of necessity then bludgeoning them into submission with his wage packet.

Not anymore.

He had tried going along with things just because someone told him to and he was done with it. That the little voice on his shoulder was right every time. And it didn't go away. It just sat there, reminding you of what you should have done, over and over. From now on he would try it the other way, the right way.

This challenges nonsense had gone far enough. It wasn't worth one life and especially not a fluffy bunny.

'No,' he said, cutting through Orus and the faun's discussion.

'Sorry?' The faun's left ear twisted towards the scribe, followed by the rest of its head.

'I said "no". It's stupid and we won't do it. Just let us through. We're done with all this rubbish.'

'You must. It is part of the challenges. It is the circle of creation. Dragons are the embodiment of cosmic fact. Death leads to life. The two are intertwined. You must prove your acceptance of this fact. I cannot let you into the Hatching Grounds until it is done.'

'Yes, you can. You just don't want to. But you're going to have to. We're not playing anymore.'

The flames from the dragon statues grew dim. A bitter wind twisted through the cavern, stinging at Huggle's eyes and forcing him to raise his hands to keep his balance. The faun's voice grew deeper.

'The builders of this place picked me as guardian for a reason. I warn you, if you do not complete the challenges you will not leave here.'

But Huggle knew this routine; he had seen it plenty before. He ignored the Guardian and approached the altar.

'Okay, so we need to fill these holes then,' he took up the sacrificial knife. 'Fine.'

The scribe opened the rabbit's cage and lifted it out. It backed off at first then, as his hand gripped it, it froze in terror.

It needn't have worried.

'Off you go, little guy,' Huggle said, setting the bunny down on the floor and giving it a gentle nudge. 'Now for those holes.'

A braver man might have cut his own arm and filled the balance that way. Braver and stupider. Huggle preferred knowledge and a clear head to painful displays of masculinity. He took out his water skin and cut the top off.

He poured the clear water directly into each of the holes, until each one was full to the top.

'There,' he said, throwing the dagger back onto the altar. 'Holes full and nothing had to die. How's that for your great challenge?'

Something heavy within the great bronze doors clunked. The locks turned and the doors began to swing back.

The rabbit hopped over to the faun's foot. The Guardian lifted it up and patted its head. 'The blood of the dragon answers to no one,' it said with a smile. 'You have passed the challenges. Heroes, the way is open.'

'Well done, Huggle,' said Ambrose.

'I still think all this is stupid, just so you know,' replied the scribe.

CHAPTER FIFTY-THREE

Stepping through the final door, Orus stared in wonder. The cave in front of him pulsed with life. Set within a gigantic bowl-shaped cavern, the Hatching Grounds were a lush meadow of green grass and bright mountain flowers. Sprouting from the ground, giant luminous fungus stalks rose like tree trunks, their wide-brimmed caps catching moisture that dripped from the roof. And what a roof. The cave walls were stone and rock, albeit covered in climbing vines and multicoloured moss. But when they reached the ceiling the rock walls stopped. Grinding across them, an azure streaked firmament, the underside of the great glacier sparkled with ice-filtered sunlight. There was moonlight too. The silvery hue of its rays fell more softly than their daytime counterparts, changing the shade of the grass from bright emerald to soft turquoise.

'The light gets lost you see.' The Guardian came to stand by Orus. 'Stuck in the ice, bouncing between prisms and crystals. Day and night, you can get both at once down here. Sometimes the whole meadow is black, then you can see the stars, only they're all in the wrong place, get mixed up on the way through.'

'It's incredible.'

Tastes pretty good too.

Thunder chomped through a couple of green clumps.

A rabbit hopped in front of the party, heading down into the centre of the cavern. At first Orus thought it was the one from the last room, but then he saw it catch up with another one. Then there were three. He scanned the tall grass again and this time he could make out the ears sticking above it. The meadow was full of them. And that wasn't all. The underground river that they had seen in the bear's cave fell in a great waterfall from the left hand wall, throwing up a fine mist of water droplets as it did so. The stream descended through a series of wide pools then flowed across the grasslands and out through another cave on the far side. Mountain salmon gaped in the slow draining pools, resting after their escape from the ursine-gatekeeper above.

In stark contrast to the musky, cobweb crowded composition found in the tunnels behind them, the air was fresh and clean.

'That's enough dawdling. This way,' said the Guardian, setting off down the green slope.

'But how?' asked Huggle, catching up with the faun. 'How did the dragons know this was here?'

'Didn't,' said the faun. 'Legend goes that the first dragon to find this place did it by mistake. It was up in the mountains, just finished a big meal, when it laid down for a nap. Curled up in this depression. The glacier was pretty far away so it didn't worry about it. Wakes up two millennia later and it's stuck under the ice. Meantime, the heat from its body's been melting the ice above, so all this grows. It had to dig through the mountain to get out, see over there.' The faun pointed to the far end of the cavern. A great tunnel had been cut from the bedrock, its sides smooth with melted stone. 'Then afterwards, it figured this was a good place to raise its young. Nice and out of the way. When they were grown up, they did the same. That's why it's the Hatching Grounds.'

*

While the Hatching Grounds were rather unique, much like a lonely grandparent who only keeps one extra mug out for the occasional visit by a family member, they were not used to large numbers of visitors. The challenges took a long time to reset and the Guardian hadn't expected any more company. Thus, when King Tyran arrived there was nothing to put pause to his enraged pursuit.

He didn't stop to inspect the curious entrance way with its stable/kitchen ante-room. He raced past the dozing bear in the first chamber. He paused momentarily in the chasm chamber, but the tiles broken by Thunder's hooves shattered the illusion. He leapt forward and sprinted across the painted floor. In the final challenge room even the sight of a small white rabbit nibbling at the moss between the toes of a dragon statue didn't give him pause for thought, and Tyran really hated rabbits.

*

Pushing through an orchard of giant orange mushrooms, Orus, Ambrose and the others were confronted with a circular hillock. Its sides rose at a uniform incline, but stopped short of forming a pointed summit. A sulphurous wind flowed down to the base and it was crowned with shimmering heat haze.

'That's the nest.' The Guardian motioned with her crook. 'Same one as the first dragon made. Same one they all used. That's where you need to put the egg. There's a crater filled with dragon fire. Never goes out. It'll be all the energy needed to hatch this little one.'

Stinks a bit.

'Show some respect.'

'Who? Me?' said Orus.

'What?' said the Guardian. 'No. I mean, yes. Everyone. This is it, boys. You've made it.'

Ambrose opened the flaps on his satchel. The egg's glow was almost totally gone.

Orus's hand rested gently on his shoulder. 'Looks like your Grandmaster chose well.'

Ambrose smiled back at his friend. 'I'll be a bit sad to let it go. I know it's only an egg, but still…'

'I'd tell you that it gets easier,' Orus thought of Tag and the light in his small round window, 'but it doesn't. That's just part of the deal.'

*

Tyran sprinted from behind a moss-covered rock, then skidded to a stop under an orange cave mushroom. The thieves had started to climb the nest. They were only a few hundred feet ahead. He almost had them.

The donkey stopped and made to turn.

Tyran ducked back.

He wasn't afraid of them. Who would be? He just didn't want them to see him before he was close enough to attack. Cowards that they were, they'd run again, and he wanted to get all of them.

*

'What is it, old lad?' Orus turned back to Thunder.

The donkey was staring back at the orange cave mushrooms.

'I wouldn't try eating any of that,' Orus said, tugging on Thunder's lead rope.

Probably nothing.

The crater of the dragon nest was free from grass, the stalks on the rim blackened and burnt. In the centre, the pool of dragon fire shimmered in a haze of orange, red and yellow. Every now and again there was a hint of blue, the odd splash of white and a few flashes of green. It looked more like liquid than fire, churning in a great whirlpool.

321

Heat rolled up the crater's edge, striking Orus above the knees then flowing up his body like a thick quilt being pulled from legs to chin.

'How does it work? Do we just roll it down there?' he asked.

'That's what the book says. It survived the hammer remember. And you wouldn't want to go down there yourself.' Ambrose was carefully lifting the egg free from his satchel. It was cool enough to hold with his bare hands. He held it tight. A thin veil of golden energy flowed around his fingers. It was warm. It was comforting.

'Well, this is it, little guy. Please don't eat us when you come out.'

The dragon monk put the egg down on the lip of the crater. He checked it had a clear path. Then he looked over to Orus.

'We did it.'

'We sure did,' said Orus.

Damn straight.

With a gentle push, Ambrose set the egg rolling.

As the soon-to-be-dragon picked up speed going down, King Tyran was picking up speed coming up. His huge legs powered him up the slope, bound after bound.

Thunder's expansive ears picked up his approach and he let out a loud warning honk.

The party turned.

The King's sword flashed in the shimmering light. 'You're mine, Orus! Nowhere to run now!'

One thing about being a bit on the heavy side is that you gain an appreciation of the rules of momentum. Not being one to throw things away, Orus was very familiar with that particular rule book.

'Yes there is,' he shouted back.

It only took a few steps down the steep slope of the nest for Orus to reach terminal velocity. And he wasn't the only one. Huggle and Ambrose were just a few steps behind. This was a team effort, right to the end.

Tyran raised his sword above his head with both hands. He fixed on Orus's head, ready to sweep it off the fat gardener's shoulders with one stroke. This was his first mistake.

As most of the people Tyran fought were trim and in shape, he didn't account for the extra foot of reach extended to Orus by his belly. Even with the exertion of the last few days it still maintained quite an overhang.

Tyran was still on the down stroke with his sword when Orus barged his gut into the King's midriff. Tyran's feet were pushed backwards, his face went forwards and his body fell with a thump into the grass.

Orus skidded to a halt. The winded king tried to get up, only to be clotheslined by the joined arms of Ambrose and Huggle. They caught him under the hips, sending him head over heels and back down to the dirt.

'Now what?' Ambrose pulled up beside Orus, shortly followed by a panting Huggle.

Tyran was picking himself up. He did not look happy. In fact, he looked much like an orc might if he came home from a hard day's pillaging to find that you had eaten his tea, cleaned his cave, painted pink ponies on his best armour and replaced his ear wax collection with a selection of scented candles.

'I hadn't really thought that far ahead,' Orus admitted.

'Orrrrrruuuussss!' Tyran pushed himself up on his sword. 'You coward! Will you ever stop running?'

Two grey furry streaks shot past the King, sending him spinning a third time. Thunder and the Guardian didn't stop when they got to Orus and the others. They disappeared into the grove of cave fungus, heading back towards the entrance way.

The ground rumbled under Orus's feet. Something in the nest was stirring.

Tyran recovered. He rolled his massive shoulders and picked up his gigantic sword. 'See! No better than a timid beast. I always knew you were a coward. Are you done running, or do I have to chase you down again?'

Orus pushed Huggle and Ambrose behind him. 'Not done running yet, Tyran. See, I might not have had a hero's life, and I might not be a good swordsman, or a king, but I have learned some things that you'll never know.'

'Oh yeah. Like what?' Tyran kept coming forward. It never occurred to him to look behind him. Why would it? He was a head-on kind of guy. Looking back was for wimps. Thus he never saw the long tail whipping back and forth above the rim of the nest. He never saw the clawed talons grip its edge or the green head rise up between them. He did catch a quick glimpse of the shiny white teeth as they closed about him, but the image didn't linger long in his memory.

'Children: they grow up so fast,' said Orus.

The dragon gulped down the King of Harradin without even chewing. Orus watched as it clambered out of the nest pit. When it was free it turned its head to the glacier above and let out a blast of pure magical energy.

'Beautiful,' Ambrose said.

'That's our boy.' Orus clapped an arm round the monk's shoulder.

'As much as I hate to break up this proud parenting moment,' said Huggle, 'can we please run away now?'

Ambrose watched the dragon as it paced around the rim of the nest, stretching out its wings and whipping its tail. 'Just a little bit longer.'

CHAPTER FIFTY-FOUR

They ran across the Hatching Grounds and back through the great bronze doors. Behind, the dragon's roar reverberated against the icy ceiling. The Guardian led them up the secret passage from the final challenge room. Narrow stairs twisted upwards through the mountain. After the first twenty or so steps the party slowed to a steady climb. This wasn't because they felt this was a safe distance. It was largely motivated by Huggle's need to avoid a heart attack.

Through gulped breaths, the scribe just about managed to exhale understandable words.

'You... could have warned... me... about... that.'

'Which bit?' asked Ambrose.

'Which bit!' he gasped.

'I think he means,' said Orus, lending the scribe his arm, 'the "one minute it's an egg the size of a melon and then suddenly it's thirty feet long and chomping people up with giant white teeth" bit.'

'I did say it would be hungry.'

'Yes, but hungry and six inches long and hungry and bigger than a house are fairly different warnings.'

'He wouldn't have eaten you,' said the Guardian.

'Are you sure? It didn't seem overly picky.'

'Quite sure… Well, mostly sure. Certainly not all of you.'

How reassuring.

'What happens to it now?' asked Orus.

The Guardian had reached the top of the staircase. It pushed open the door and stepped through. They emerged into the faun's pantry.

'It'll stay in the Hatching Grounds until it has absorbed all the dragon fire in the nest, then it will climb out through the top of the mountain and set about restoring the balance to the magical fields. It'll probably stay here for a year or two until it finds a lair of its own. I'll look after it until then.'

'Will it be safe?' asked Ambrose. 'It is still a baby.'

Huggle nearly choked on that.

'That is out of your hands, Dragon Monk. You have done what you can and that is your part finished. But I think it will be. After all, only one species I know would actually be stupid enough to go looking for a dragon.'

'I don't know,' said Orus. 'Those other hunters won't stop just because it hatched. Most didn't even know it was an egg to start with. What if one of them tracks it down?'

The Guardian tugged her long goatee. Her eyes fell on Huggle and, to the scribe's surprise, what followed wasn't an insult. At least, not entirely.

'Perhaps that is where the waddling writer might come in useful.'

'How so?'

'You are writing about the death of the last dragon, yes?'

'I was.'

'So finish. Write the story. The dragon is dead, so no one needs to look for it.'

'But people will want proof. A skull, bones, something to show it is definitely gone. Heroes always take trophies.'

'Simple.' The Guardian snapped the dragon claw from its crook.

Orus, Ambrose and Huggle looked at one another. It did make sense. Sort of. With Tyran gone and Conrad having fled, there was no-one else to question them.

'Tell people you fought it up here on the glacier. It was slain and its body fell into a deep crevasse. It tried to hang on but you chopped its claw off and it fell under the ice.'

Orus took the dragon claw in his hand. That could just work.

A wave of relief washed over him. They had actually done it. He had saved the world. He really was a hero. And now, more than anything, he wanted to go home.

There was one last thing that niggled at the back of his head but he chose to ignore it. Life was too short for niggles. Home: that was the important thing.

CHAPTER FIFTY-FIVE

They said their goodbyes to the Guardian and left her in the cave. In the gorge outside Dragons Watch sunlight was creeping down the side of the rock.

It was not the only thing creeping.

As they squeezed their way back along the cut in the mountain they did not notice the shadows that crowded its mouth, nor did they hear the scraping of foot on rock high above them. Conrad's men seized Orus first, grabbing him the moment he stepped out of the gorge. Ambrose and Huggle froze, only to quickly melt at the touch of the spears behind them.

Soon all were gathered at the edge of the ice field. Dragons Watch cast a long shadow over the circle of figures in the stalling light. Von Strauss, decked out in a new grey wolf skin ensemble and holding a long stiletto dagger, approached his captives like a smiling cat closing in on a pair of soon-to-be claw punctured trousers.

'What a merry little chase this has been.' He crouched by Orus, face to face at last. 'Unfortunately, it looks like you have finally run out of stamina.' He prodded

Orus in the belly with the knife. 'I must say, I'm surprised you made it this far.'

'Well, it's more tiring if you actually do the work yourself,' Orus replied. Tyran might have been a bully, not to mention a dangerously unhinged psychopath, but at least he had earned his crown. Conrad was a fake through and through, and Orus was done taking stick from his kind.

Conrad struck him hard across the face. Blood welled up in his mouth and he spat it onto the snow.

'Not that it appears to have done you much good,' said Von Strauss. 'Don't worry though. This next part I'm going to do all on my own.'

'It'll be the first day's work you've ever done.' Huggle bounced in his ropes as defiantly as possible (which was not very defiantly at all).

'Ah, the deserter speaks. Tell me, Huggle, how is your new career working out? Not quite how you imagined? It is a shame that it's come to this.' Conrad paused. 'Although not entirely unsalvageable. I understand that an artist's work becomes much more valuable when the author dies. You'll finally be rich, just like you always wanted. Don't worry. As your employer, I'll keep the money safe for you.'

'Go ahead and kill us then,' this was Ambrose, the spell of Conrad's virtue well and truly broken. 'It doesn't matter now anyway. The dragon has hatched. You've lost.'

'Oh, I wouldn't say that. I haven't seen the beast leave yet. Now that you've shown me where it is I can add the final piece to my trophy collection. The real thing will be better than that egg anyway.'

Ambrose struggled against his bonds. 'You wouldn't dare. You're a coward, whether the rest of the world knows it or not. It'll snap you up in two seconds flat.'

'Is that so? In that case perhaps what I need is some bait, something to sate its appetite. I imagine all of you would make a decent main course. I'll fill you up with some poison first, just to make sure. Then my men and I will finish the beast off. It will be a team effort.'

Conrad's bodyguards nodded in agreement.

'He's lying to you, you know,' Huggle shouted to them. 'You'll not make it into the book, or any songs. Once you get back to the ship you'll all be arrested and thrown in a dungeon. He's done it before. Loads of times.'

Conrad struck Huggle, hard.

'Silence! I have warned my loyal friends of your snake tongue.' Conrad turned to his men. 'Did I not say this is what he would do? Fear not. When we are done here everyone in the world will know your names. Your stories will be told in taverns and beer halls across all the kingdoms of creation. Just like mine.'

Conrad's bodyguards cheered and clattered their weapons together.

'And,' Conrad continued, 'to show that the glory on this quest is not all for me, I will let each of you try to best the dragon before me, so that the greatest prize of all will be to he who deserves it.'

Another cheer went up at this.

That should reduce the overcrowding in father's dungeon a bit, thought Conrad.

'Liar!'

The shout came from the direction of the glacier, outside the circle of guards.

'Liar, liar, liar!'

Conrad turned away from his captives. 'What is this? Who said that? Come and face me, coward.'

'I know that voice,' said Huggle, though he couldn't quite believe it.

'Liar, liar, liar,' the voice growled through the parting crowd.

Skar gripped Huggle's manuscript under his arm. He made straight for Conrad. 'He is lying to yous all. And I can prove it.'

Now it was Conrad's turn to look scared. 'Now, Skar, you know your reading is not very good. Give that here and let me read it to you properly. You probably got confused. You're in there, I promise.'

Skar ignored his master and turned to his men. He opened the pages of the manuscript and began to read in a slow careful voice.

'Listen to this: And, then, with sword, in his, virtue-ous, grip, Conrad, did, strike down, the Giant Gaulblot, which had terro, terro, terro-sized, the village of Verde, for the last, f,f, four years.'

'Hey!' A bodyguard carrying a large spiked club pushed to the front of the crowd. 'That was me. I killed the giant. He just watched. Said it was too easy for him.'

'Ahh, now, Molger,' Conrad tried to make a grab for the book but Skar shrugged him off. The huge warrior held it up out of his master's reach. 'That is still just a draft. I was going to put you in the final cut.'

Skar ignored Conrad and flicked to another passage. 'And, while, all about him, were, in panic, brave, Conrad, took up a sling, and, from, two hundred paces, struck, the Telescopic Cyclops, between its noses, killing, it, stone dead.'

Another of the bodyguards, this one with a notably deformed shoulder caused by a life's worth of slinging, threw his weapons in the dirt. 'What! That was me. That cheating bugger. Hey Skar, does it say about me at all?'

'Yup Drälla. It does actually. I ain't done reading this bit yet.'

'Now, I think that's enough.' Conrad jumped to try and snatch the book. 'Really, he is taking it out of context. You remember, Rägrund. It's all metaphorical.'

'Try this for metal-fork-i-ril.' Skar raised his voice again and mouthed out the words carefully. 'With, the Cyclops, van-squished, brave Von Strauss, was able, to rescue his friend Drälla–'

'See, see. You are in it.'

'I ain't finished!' Skar's shout bounced off the surrounding rocks like a thunderclap high fiving a war drum. '... His friend Drälla, who, had, hidden, from the beast, in, a, tree, so terry-frying was it.'

'You sneaky little git.' Drälla started towards Conrad, rolling up his sleeves as he did so.

They were very wide sleeves. They had to be to fit over Drälla's massive arms. On them, between the scars, were tattoos of all manner of terrible creatures. Each beast was followed by a series of tally marks. Orus wondered if there would be a Conrad-shaped one joining the ranks in the near future.

'Now, there's no need to look at me like that. I can explain this.' Von Strauss started to back away. 'If you would all just wait until we get back to my father's castle, we can straighten this all out.'

The other bodyguards closed in after Drälla.

'This is clearly a trick by, by...' Conrad's eyes were wide with panic. He thrust a jewelled finger towards the captives. 'By Huggle! He wrote it all! He must have changed it before he betrayed us. It was him.'

Drälla continued to advance on Conrad. 'You said back at the Pass that you writes it all. He just does the notes, that's what you said.'

'Yeah,' said the other bodyguards in chorus. Cracking knuckles provided the backing percussion, while long, long swords being drawn from scabbards hummed like strings.

'Ah, well, I did but...' Conrad retreated from the ominous music of impending violence. He held out his dagger. A stone from Drälla's sling knocked it from his quivering hand. He looked frantically for an escape route. He turned back to face the mountain. 'Dragon! Dragon!'

The bodyguards craned their necks upwards. They had very thick necks so this took a few moments.

Nothing.

When their heavily scarred heads lowered again Conrad was sprinting back towards the glacier.

Drälla and the others watched their ex-master's stumbled flight. Von Strauss tripped over his cloak and fell into the snow. He was up in an instant, discarding the rich fur and making all speed for the path back to Pale Pass.

The bodyguards looked to Skar. Skar looked to Huggle. Huggle nodded.

Skar closed the manuscript and drew his finger across his throat.

The pack sprung after their old master, each of them with one thought in their mind. Killing a dragon was all well and good. Killing Conrad Von Strauss however, that would get your name in the history books and no mistake.

Skar picked up Conrad's knife and used it to cut Orus free from his bonds. Orus watched the huge warriors lumber across the snow after their prized prey.

'What will they do to him?'

'Depends. I'd probably tie him to my horse, drag him back to Harradin and make him tell everyone what a big liar he is. Then I'd rough him up a bit.' Skar's scars made his broken smile all the more sinister. 'But some of those lads aren't as forgiving as me."

CHAPTER FIFTY-SIX

Some semblance of order had returned to Pale Pass by the time Orus and the others emerged from the mountains. But with Skar at the head of their column, and Huggle's persuasive patter, it was no trouble to get through. In fact, once news of Tyran's death spread, the guards each made their excuses about today being their annual beard trim or having left the cat in the oven and, after a few casual steps in the direction of the vacant throne, the whole lot broke into a full sprint back to the city.

'Do you not fancy being king?' Ambrose asked Skar.

'Na,' said Skar, watching the guards disappear down the trail. 'I never held with the monarchy much. Kings and princes and dukes and all that. All they ever do is fight. Violence never solves anything, that's what my mum always says.'

'Wise woman,' said Ambrose.

The only other person left in the camp was Master Lenz. He approached, a bundle of rolled up parchment under his arm. 'Hello, friends,' he called out. 'Glad to see you back safe.'

'Hello,' replied Huggle. 'Have you been waiting here? I thought the dragon scared everyone off.'

'Me? Run off? Hardly. I knew the beast was a fake from the outset. I'd be a rather poor painter if I didn't recognise my props. I caught sight of our previous master making his glorious return by the way. Surprising stamina.'

'The right motivation will do that to you,' said Orus.

'Yes, indeed. I may have to paint it one day. But here, look at this.' The painter pulled the roll of sketches from under his armpit. 'This new piece, it just had to be started straight away. It would be a crime to let it wait, lest the vividness of the scene faded in this old mind. I have completed my preliminary sketches. Here.'

Master Lenz held up the topmost sheet of parchment. It showed a Conrad-shaped apparition struggling from the mud and manure of the Pale Pass oxen paddock like a warthog after an immersive spa treatment.

'I am thinking of calling it *The Brave Hero Rises*.'

'I don't know much about art, Master Lenz, but I think you've captured your subject perfectly. I'd love to see it when you're finished,' said Orus.

'See it. You shall have it. I will do copies for each of you. Such a picture deserves to be shared.'

'I happen to know the publishers of several sets of heroic trading cards,' added Huggle. 'I'm sure they'd be very interested in a print for their next run.'

*

Conrad's ship was anchored halfway along the lake. Once Huggle had explained the situation to the crew they were very happy to go along with the new arrangements. This, Huggle was sure, had nothing to do with the fact that Conrad kept several barrels of the finest brandy in his personal cabin. And so with their bodies filled with a few measures of extra insulation, the ship stumbled across the water, heading for the start of the Cobalt River.

'It was supposed to take him on his victory tour,' Huggle said to the others. They had all gathered at the stern to watch the night rise over the towering mountains. 'A bit of a waste on the administrative front. On the other hand, I imagine those due to take up hosting duties will not be overly disappointed.'

'Can it take us all the way?' Now that the pressure of delivering the egg was gone, Orus had a great urge to be back home. He'd had a similar urge during most of the last week, but that was because he didn't want to be where he was. Now it was more a case of wanting to be where he was not. He hoped Mavis hadn't needed him while he'd been away. He had certainly needed her, and he planned to tell her so as soon as he got back.

'It can take you as far as the All Seasons. I will send a messenger pigeon to the Temple to let them know all is well.'

'Thanks,' said Ambrose.

'You'll have quite the tale to tell them all when you get back,' Orus said to his friend. 'They sent you out to find a hero and turns out they had one all along.'

Ambrose blushed in the lantern light and looked down at his feet. 'Me? I didn't really do all that much. I wouldn't have even made it out of the inn without someone looking after me.'

You're welcome.

'It's not like I did much of the heavy lifting.'

Tell me about it.

'Well, I know when I write it all up,' said Huggle, 'there'll be at least one hero in it.'

Thank you. At least someone was paying attention.

'Yes,' Huggle turned to the muscled warrior leaning over the sternward rail. 'Skar, I think you'll make it into my next book after all.'

Great. Even the baddy gets more credit than me. He did try to kill us, remember.

'Do you mean it?' Skar lit up as Thunder clumped back to the bed of straw laid out for him mid-ship. 'And my boys?'

'Every one of them. I guarantee it.'

'Wow. I can't wait to tell mum.'

Skar's maternal attachment picked out that niggle in Orus's brain.

'There is one thing,' he said looking up at the stars wheeling over the jagged mountain peaks, 'I've been meaning to ask on that front.'

'What's that?' asked Ambrose, following his gaze.

'If our egg was the last dragon, then how can it repopulate the species?'

'How do you mean?' Ambrose, it should be remembered, was from an order of monks whose membership was exclusively male.

'Well, in my experience, in order to get more of an animal, you need to start with at least two.'

Ambrose thought about this for a moment. The others kindly gave his adolescent brain time to fit the picture together.

'Oh. Oh! Right. I see. You mean… Yes.' The young monk may have survived a crash-landing in the Grimwood, broken into a king's kitchen and survived an encounter with Conrad Von Strauss but talking about 'that' with grown-ups was a bridge too far. 'The thing is that it is the last dragon. It just wasn't the last dragon egg. But you can't take two up here at once, or else they start fighting. We have a few more at the temple.'

'So what you're saying is?'

'Same time next year.'

'What about the magic field?'

As Orus said this, the sky to the north erupted with colour. Shimmering waves of gold, red, yellow, blue and green washed forward from the Fang Mountains. Their peaks stood as rocks in the storm as the reflected dragon fire surged across the night.

'He should be able to keep it ticking over until then.'

*

Far to the south, clasping a mug of hot tea, Grandmaster Argus Bach watched the celestial show from the top of the Dragon Temple. He had not seen the Aurora Draconis since he last delivered an egg to the Hatching Grounds, many, many years ago.

'You picked well.' The High Council's voice rustled like dried leaves in the breeze.

'Seems so. A good hero is hard to find these days. Best to stick to those you know. I'll have Brother Amphis send him a package of sugar lumps to say thank you.'

'And some of this,' the High Council reached slowly into his robes and retrieved a vial of lotion. 'For his back. Did you see the size of the one he was carrying with him? Much bigger than his last one.'

'Yes,' said Argus. 'Still, he is not one to complain.'

Their shuddering laughter kept them warm long into the night as they watched the dancing lights move across the sky.

CHAPTER FIFTY-SEVEN

Like many stories, it finished the same way as it started, only in reverse.

The Dragon Monks came to meet the returning heroes at the All Seasons Tavern. The place that brought Orus and Ambrose together would also be the place where they would go their separate ways. On one side of the bridge was the Worm-mound. On the other was the road back to Ditch. Underneath, not that anyone noticed, was a troll holding up two very hungry bandits.

The Grandmaster had been busy while Conrad's ship was making its way down river. First, he had sent a message to Old Grimmer telling him of Orus's success. He'd also sent word to Mavis, at Orus's request, to let her know that her husband had been slightly delayed but was now on his way back. Argus even sent Brother Amphis to Rivercrook to collect the Prince's carrot shipment.

The two friends said their farewells, each doing so on the condition that they visited each other regularly, then that was it. The adventure was over.

Skar left the party there too, but not before giving Orus his favourite sword as a gift.

Huggle decided to accompany Orus back to Ditch. He could catch a coach to the capital from there. Then he would finish the manuscript and have it published.

They slipped into town in the late evening, shadows moving in shadows. A light drizzle filled the gap between the mist and the charcoal clouds. The sound of Thunder's hooves mixed with the muffled sounds of a town turning in after another long, hard day. There was no fanfare, no trumpets and the only welcoming crowd was the one gathered outside the Crooked Tap, merrily shouting hellos and friendly obscenities at all that walked past.

The lack of a hero's welcome didn't bother Orus. Crowds were for Conrad and his lot. He didn't need it and he didn't expect it. He knew a job well done by the cracked skin on his hands and the ache in his back.

Right now, his back was aching up a treat.

And he wasn't the only one.

'It's alright, Thunder,' he said to the old donkey as they pulled up in front of Old Grimmer's hovel. 'I'll leave these here and take them the rest of the way in the morning.' Orus lifted the crate of Bolgovian Black Carrots from Thunder's back and set it down at the side of the street.

Oh thanks, for a minute there I thought I'd have to carry that thing all the way to the castle. I mean after those eight miles I'll bet the last two hundred yards will be a real struggle. I suppose that's it then too. No 'Well done Thunder, thanks for saving my life all those times'. Na, why would you? I'm just a donkey after all.

'Here,' Orus opened the crate and took out a large knobbly carrot. He held it out to Thunder. 'Not much of a reward, but we couldn't have done it without you. I hope this makes up for some of it.'

Thunder looked at Orus, then looked at the carrot. Just like the ones from his dreams, all long and pointy.

Really, for me…? I mean, it's a start I suppose.

The old donkey took the carrot in his teeth. He turned and trotted back to his bed. Safely out of view he dropped his head and wiped at his eye with his leg.

Old Grimmer appeared at his doorway. 'Made it back then, Orus?'

'Seems so.'

'All in one piece too. I knew you could do it.'

'Glad someone did.'

'And who's this?' asked Grimmer, the pupil of his better eye ducking under a roaming cataract to focus on Orus's companion.

'Grimmer, this is Huggle. He's a scribe and a bard. Huggle, this is Grimmer, a.k.a Felgrim the Blade. If you're looking for adventure stories, Grimmer is your man. I bet you could make some top notch sagas from the tales in that crinkly old brain.'

'That is a tempting offer. Perhaps when I have finished this,' Huggle held up the manuscript, 'I'll come back and you can tell me about some of your stories.'

'I'll be here,' replied Grimmer, both to Huggle and to any pale, hooded, calcium rich combine harvester precursors that might be considering paying him a visit.

From Grimmer's hovel, Orus led Huggle down Deep Street, along the back and forth twists of Straight Street, squeezed down Broad Street and entered Market Square from its fifth corner. The square was deserted, businesses of the day being closed up and businesses of the night not being the kind that need to waste money on advertising. The only signs of life were, on the left, the welcoming glow of the manure lamps flanking the entrance to the Drover's Rest and, on the right, the flickers of an economically conscious candle flame escaping between the curtains of a dressmaker's shop window.

'Well Huggle, I think this is you. They've got good beds in there, and drinkable ale. You can get a coach from here in the morning that will take you to the capital.'

'Thanks.' Huggle extended his hand. 'Thanks for everything. It's been nice to meet a real hero for once.'

'I don't know about that,' replied Orus, gripping his new friend palm to palm.

'Care for a drink?'

'Can't,' said Orus. The flickering candle drew his gaze across the square. 'I've got a beautiful maiden to rescue.'

'Ahh, yes, of course. Say no more,' said Huggle.

The door to the shop opened and the night brightened.

'Duty calls.'

Huggle watched Orus cross the rain-soaked square. The light from the Drover stretched the castle gardener's shadow tall and proud. That shadow swept the maiden up in powerful arms and they kissed, long and firm.

Orus held his wife close against him.

Now this, this is where I belong.

Orus turned back to Huggle and waved. Mavis wrapped her arms around his waist.

Huggle waved back. There was something strangely familiar about the image they cast on the high wall behind them. He was sure he had seen it somewh—

'Wait! Wait!' Huggle shouted.

Running forward, he slipped on the wet cobbles and only the fast reactions of his rediscovered romantics saved him from falling.

'It's you! It's really you! I can't believe I didn't see it.'

'Who?' asked Mavis, helping Huggle to his feet. 'What do you mean?'

'You,' he puffed, 'and you. You're the ones from the forest. You're the maiden and you, Orus, you're the hero that killed the wizard Garvock. This is great. Do you see? We can do a reissue. Restore you to your rightful place in heroing history. With this story and all this dragon business, you'll be the most famous hero in all of Drift. You'll be rich, you'll be loved. You'll have everything you've ever wanted.'

Orus looked at Mavis. He thought about Tag, and Grimmer and Thunder, and his little house with the sticking gate and the sloping foundations. He thought about the riches, the wealth, fancy parties with the Prince and his friends, the endless autographs.

'Garvock? Garvock? Sorry, Huggle. Never heard of him. Must be someone else. I'm just a gardener.'

'Not just,' said Mavis. 'Not just.'

*

That night Orus slept better than he had done in years. The next day he went to work and put in the hours like he always did.

Well, not exactly like he always did.

The shoulders weren't so hunched, the eyes weren't so tired and when he smiled at the end of it, with his back aching and grime under his fingernails, that smile filled up his whole body, head to foot, backbone to belly.

He came home that night with something in each hand.

In the right was a letter from Tag. He was coming to visit. He'd be there when Orus got finished tomorrow night.

In the left was the crate the Prince's carrots had come in. After dinner, and the dishes, he took the box into the hall, put Skar's sword inside along with the Guardian's dragon claw, closed the lid and pushed it into the empty space under the stairs.

Best to keep these things handy, just in case…

The End.

ACKNOWLEDGMENTS

Gigantic thanks to Rachel McHale for her invaluable advice and insight through many rounds of editing and proofing, and for her continued support which has given me the confidence to finally release HBD to the masses (however modest those masses turn out to be). Without you I never would have got here.

Thanks also to Rachel Lawston for her cover design, Claire Rushbrook for proofreading, and the team at Reedsy for helping me find them!

Much of the research on dragons and other mythical creatures featured in this book comes from Carol Rose's excellent 'Giants, Monsters & Dragons: an encyclopedia of folklore, legend and myth'. If you like those things (and why wouldn't you) I recommend picking up a copy and geeking out.

Finally, thank you to my girlfriend and best friend Jenny Kerr for keeping me sane, keeping me caffeinated, and letting me know when I get Too Turkish. You're allowed to read it now!

ABOUT THE AUTHOR

David P. Macpherson is an author, screenwriter and performance poet. He grew up in the wilds of the Highlands of Scotland and now lives in Edinburgh. In the past he has worked in an industrial grain dryer, an MP's constituency office, the House of Lords, the Police and a swimming pool, but not necessarily in that order. His favourite activities include scouring second hand bookshops, going to the cinema in the middle of the day, being licked in the face by puppies and saying hello to Jason Isaacs.

Find more of his writing at www.macpherzone.co.uk

You can also follow him on Twitter via @David_Mac13 and you can follow him in real life with a good set of binoculars.

Printed in Great Britain
by Amazon

13408626R00201